To Matt, Kate and the boys.

If it gets a terrible bore, it may come in handy as a paperweight or perhaps a DOORSTOP!

love Sean.

The Greenest Down

S F Hiscock

Published in 2016 by FeedARead.com Publishing

First Edition

A CIP catalogue record for this title is available from the British Library.

1. Today, Tomorrow, Yesterday

I am not a ghost. I am not a young man trapped in a concrete room being entranced by a ghost. I am merely the voice. The voice inside your head that relates the events, places and characters which come together from different times in the past and the present to form a story that may or may not have been. This is a story about a place in Somerset, a desolate coastal fort and ghosts. It is a story about life and death, love and fear, friendship and hatred. A story of people on the edge of life whilst hanging on to the edge of their sanity, stuck on a piece of land before it becomes the sea. It may ramble wildly and confuse easily, it will shock your senses and touch your emotions or simply excite and enthral, such as life. In the end, as was said, it's not only about life, but death as well, and how its fickle finger randomly chooses those who it wishes to consume and turns up when they least expect it.

But then, maybe I am the voice of a ghost. Or even the voices of many ghosts that have come together to haunt the living and tell a tale long since buried in secrets and lies. Whatever I am or whatever happens in this story, don't blame the voices in your head; blame the places where those voices came from. But to begin with, imagine the following scene and then think on, comrades.

Above the clouds the sky is clear. The daytime sun lights the ionosphere turning it bright blue and white until it reaches the outer layers of the stratosphere and becomes the black vacuum of space beyond. Between the edge of the cosmos above and the layer of cloud stretching off into the horizon below, the atmospheric void is bright and shining, full to the brim with illuminated openness and the calming influence of expansive clarity. The ceiling is the universe, the floor a carpet of floating cumulus, and in between is the freedom of nothingness.

As we gently move through this layer of heavenly repletion, almost hanging as if stilled by the silent eternity, we hit the top of the clouds and then suddenly we're falling, uncontrollably, faster and faster like rocks through the air, consumed in a suffocating grey mass of vaporising fog. And you tumble madly, blindly, unknowing of what is below, terrified and vulnerable. As the cloud thins you plummet towards the cold, grey world underneath with desperate eyes wide open. You claw unsuccessfully at the intangible blanket all around you whilst wishing for the floating freedom and Olympic brightness of the spatial world above. Before you hit the hard, dead ground, your spirit form majestically sweeps away from the impact and we glide without effort across the daunting landscape underneath, cold, grey and darkest green.

But now we're flying through the fog of time. A shadow cast under the clouds, flashing over the land like some fleeting non-descript misanthropic gist. A mistaken thrust of movement, seen yet unseen by only a few in the blink of an eye as you pass through the ages. And then…you see…

The young boy ran across the grassy hilltop laughing noisily to no one but himself at the simple game he was playing. Gusts of wind ruffled his thin blond hair and buffeted his small body causing him to wobble as he played and it seemed as though only his oversized red Wellington boots kept him upright on his bumbling feet. He was six years old, maybe a little older, but his movement still had the innocence and fragility that were the hallmarks of a toddler. Around his body a green snorkel parker coat kept the wind from biting his skin, whilst on his knees, two neatly sown patches sealed the holes over his play worn jeans. Grinning toothily, he chased another imaginary rabbit through the rough grass, stamping a foot occasionally as if trapping the invisible creature under his shiny boot. The boy didn't know about the healthiness of the fresh air he was breathing or care about the benefits of the exercise involved in his games. For him, it was the freedom of the space that was all around this place and the fact that wherever he ran, no matter how far, he could always see the sea. And he also liked the rabbits, real ones, all small and grey with rough, short fur, which would appear briefly when the boy was least expecting them, before they in turn caught sight of him and his bright red boots causing them to scurry back into their underground world.

"Shamus!" shouted a voice from behind that startled the child from his abandonment. The boy's father was calling across the hill hoping the wind didn't carry the words away into the unknown. He was waving an arm in a beckoning motion to catch his son's attention. "Shamus, come on! This way! Keep up or you'll end up in the sea!"

The boy stopped his chasing game and headed towards his father. When he reached him his dad looked down at the boy by his side. "Having fun son?" he said with a smile.

"Yes, but I haven't seen any rabbits yet," puffed Shamus.

His fathers' smile turned to a broad grin and he looked across to the horizon where a grey sky met a darker grey sea creating a vista of monotone layers full of the prospect of autumnal wetness. "I expect they'll be along soon, them rabbits always turn up in the end," he replied.

The man looked from the oncoming rain clouds back to his son and with a mild air of disappointment cast an eye out to sea once again to study the ominous grey clouds bubbling up in the distance. "Come on boy, we'd better head off, I think it's going to rain again," he warned, and they both began the long walk back to the car.

They often came to this place. They would always drive as it was a long way from home and they always wore their coats, even when the sun was out, because according to his mum, 'the wind is always blowing up on the Down and it'll chill you to the bone, even in the summer' which were wise words because mum was always right.

The road leading to this place was long and winding with a multitude of sudden twists and turns. As the coast got nearer, out of the window on his left side Shamus could see the brown sea peeking through the gaps in the hedgerows and trees. Sometimes the water would be up to the beach near the road and at other times it would be far away revealing a flat blanket of mud between the distant brawny water and the flotsam strewn sand. If he looked out the window on the other side, all he saw were fields of dark green grass scattered with cows or sheep, bordered with low cut brambly hedges and tangles of wild, stubby trees. Gradually, houses would begin to pepper the roadside, either lining the beach or obscuring the farmland. The houses were mainly bungalows and stone built cottages with sandy driveways and wind battered gardens. Occasionally, a dilapidated barn and a few farm sheds filled with hay and swarms of silent flies would precede a grander looking farmhouse set off from the side of the road. Soon, these buildings were slowly replaced by a selection of caravans and mobile homes as the coastal road which drifted through the ambling countryside reached an out of the way beach resort, only ever frequented by intrepid holidaymakers at the height of the summer season when the weather was at its kindest. There was a simply furnished holiday park with a sad, rundown funfair attached, complete with old style, death trap looking rides and an array of cheap amusements. For six months of the year, during autumn and winter, the whole place looked and felt like a deserted ghost town or the remnant of some apocalyptic event where all the people had simply disappeared into thin air.

At this point of the journey if Shamus looked straight ahead out of the car windscreen, the Down would loom up before him like a titanic wall of moss covered stone a thousand feet high. It made him want to climb to the top to see over the other side into the hidden world behind but at the same time warned him to stay away as if there was danger there, like the forbidden attraction of a building site or a disused quarry. It felt like the end of the earth and beyond it there was nothing, just an eternal fall towards the murky waters below.

'Don't go too near the edge, the wind will push you off,' his dad would say on savage days when the wind would blow strong. The howling gale could shake the car as if wanting to lift it up and carry it away like the house spinning through the tornado in The Wizard of Oz, which Shamus had seen one rainy afternoon and reminded him of being on the Down on very windy days. Although a little frightened by the power of the wind, the little boy could still feel exhilarated by the force of nature and he knew it would never really blow him away. Even so, there were no tall trees on the top of the hill because the regular winter storms would tear them down like pins in a bowling alley and the mighty wind seemed to shout at everything that didn't have strong enough roots, trying ruthlessly to tear it apart from the sacred land. It would buffet whatever stood in its way, for there was no shelter, no respite from its anger. People, cars, phone boxes, power lines, flagpoles, houses and the other additions of humanization didn't belong here because this was natures place and its isolation and independence meant it was natures duty to protect her domain. But even on fierce days in the vortex of winter, the boy and his father would come here and just sit in the car, admiring the force of the wind and the ferocity of the sky. They would gaze at the immensity of the landscape and the weather that poured over it as if they had been drawn by the danger and adrenaline that was created.

Generally, for the sake of safety and their mother's nerves, they would come to the Down on the still, grey days of autumn or the bright crisp days of spring when Shamus could run along the paths which lined the cliffs and chase the rabbits he longed to see. It was a steep climb using the worn access steps which led up from the gravel car park at the culmination of the dead end coastal road, but once there the view was breath-taking. Before you, the sea stretched its way to the South Wales coast on the horizon and in between, like stepping stones across a vast lake, two small islands sat, one flat and long, the other short and high, rising out of the water in a mysterious union. Behind you, along the coastline, there was a never ending stretch of beach which lined the lush fields of farmland below. It created a yellow border next to the patchwork of various shades of green which went as far as the eye could see. Alongside the beach, the tiny approach road snaked its way into the haze like a thin pencil line disappearing into the vast painted canvas of a landscape picture.

Towering above all this, on a place that felt like you were on top of the world, was a small boy's perfect playground, an endless space in which to run and jump and feel the freedom to explore. Shamus liked the cliffs and the sea which lapped around them. He liked playing in the bent over, stunted trees randomly growing on the slopes and he liked hiding in the piles of rocks from the tumbledown dry stone walls which meandered across the land. And of course he liked the rabbits, which darted in and out of the bushes and shrubs scattered around without order as though they were misplaced tufts of woolly green wire. Sometimes he saw more rabbits than he had ever seen anywhere in the whole world.

He had only ever been scared once when he was here. It wasn't the weather or the landscape or the wildlife. It hadn't been going too near the edge or falling on the loose stones along the pathways. It was something else. Something he'd never told his father about, or anyone else for that matter. Something he normally didn't think about and that only ever affected him if he accidentally stumbled across the place where it originally happened. For some reason, he subconsciously managed to avoid the area but every now and then, when chasing rabbits or wandering around aimlessly, he would find himself in the same spot.

When that happened, he would suddenly freeze, as if paralysed and unable to move whilst gazing hypnotically at a small grassy knoll a few yards ahead of him. Only then would he be brought back to the time the event actually happened and a vague but tangible memory of what might have occurred.

On that day it had been cold and grey and although it was not raining the air had an atmosphere of cloying dampness. Shamus couldn't remember when it had happened and at the time didn't know whether it was actually a ghost he had seen or just his fervent imagination, but more than anything else he had felt it, a sense of fear and loneliness which oozed over him like it did when he had awoken from a nightmare or seen something scary on the telly.

Whilst bumbling around as usual, on the grassy knoll in front of where the little boy was standing, Shamus saw a figure looking out to sea. The man was bathed in a hazy blue light against the grey softness of the sky and wore a uniform of some kind, his tunic all muddy and torn in places with splattering's of dark patches across the front and back. There was a smell in the air. Shamus didn't know what it was but he knew it was a bad smell, like the one that came out of the drains when they were blocked or when they went past dead animals left for too long on the side of the road. Then the figure slowly turned to the little boy and stared intently at him. His face was pale and drawn and although the man looked young his features were grey and ageing like an actor made up to look like an old man. The face looked ill. His mouth moved but the only sound Shamus could hear was the soft moaning of the wind which had suddenly begun to sweep and rush angrily past when moments before it had been silently still. The apparition stretched an arm out to the boy as if trying to reach for him but then sluggishly turned and pointed a long, bony finger to the end of the Down which led its way into the sea.

Shamus was frozen by a fear he was too young to understand. He could not speak or shout or cry but only stare open mouthed at the scene before him, trapped in a moment of time that seemed to be endless yet was actually only a few fleeting seconds.

Presently, the eerily illuminated figure stepped off the grassy mound and walked softly away in the direction of which he had been pointing and gradually disappeared into the swirling wind. Shamus was suddenly released from his hypnosis and he span round, frantically looking for his father, who was behind him, only a short distance away on the ridge of the hill staring in the opposite direction out across the farmland. His dad was oblivious to the spectacle his son had just witnessed. The small boy quickly ran towards him. He was cold and scared but did not cry. Confusion filled his small, worried mind and he desperately wanted to go home and surround himself with toys and games and things that made him happy. It was an instinctual need to get away from this place and the ghost he thought he had just seen. But as he got further from the knoll on which the apparition had appeared, the fear subsided, as if the sinister grip which held him there was slowly releasing the little boy and allowing him to escape both in mind and body. Warmth eased back into his tiny frame and his head filled with other simpler thoughts, like seeing rabbits and playing in the stubby trees. By the time he reached his dad he couldn't remember what had just happened and he looked behind to the grassy knoll in the distance and wondered if he had just been there at all. They were alone.

But that had been a while ago and Shamus had not seen the ghost again and to him it had just seemed like a strange dream he might have had or a scene from a book he had been read. It hadn't troubled him since as it rarely came to his thoughts, allowing the innocence of his young mind to guard him against the recurring possibilities of the unknown. Today, he certainly hadn't felt the sinister grip from that one small space around the grassy knoll which had held him on that particular day and now he was free to enjoy this private playground and simply hang out with his dad.

As his dad predicted a moment ago, the rain began to fall in sporadic, blobby droplets and the boy and his father pulled their hoods up over their heads as they trudged back towards the stone path leading to the car park. The next minute, the mottled grey clouds opened up and heavily dropped their full load upon the Down and its two visitors.

The man wondered why they had come on such a day like this, but he knew it was by no means the worst weather they had endured on their many visits. Watching the elements at work was exciting and taking in the landscapes was enjoyable but something else drew him to this place which he knew could be as miserably bleak as it was breathlessly stimulating. He believed there were other magnetic forces at work here. It was a feeling of excitement and tangible fear deep inside him that welled up with each step nearer the Down, and after a visit, this sensation would build again with every thought towards the next time he would come.

Perhaps it was the spirits that lived here. He knew they were not alone when they walked the cliffs. He too had seen the ghost of this place before, the same one that his son had seen and others as well. That's what brought him here, like a pilgrim to some secluded holy ritual, time and time again. It's what filled him with awe and wonder in a place that to everyone else was just a tourist attraction or somewhere to walk their dog. He knew secrets were contained in the earth and the rock of this place that stretched out into the sea. Secrets from a long forgotten history and left untold to anyone else but that still haunted the spirits who restlessly wandered in and out of the present.

As the father and son reached the car, the rain began falling so hard it bounced off the surfaces it fell upon creating billions of tiny exploding waterfalls all around. Their ears filled with the humming din caused by the white noise of rushing water and the rattling drum of raindrops on metal. The man quickly pulled out his keys and unlocked the car. They jumped into the front seats and slammed the doors shut to shelter themselves from the deluge.

"Rain, rain, go away, come again another day," the dad said as he wiped the wetness from their faces. He took the boy's coat off and laid it on the back seat and then did the same with his own before reaching into the glove box to pull out two bottles of lemonade and a bar of chocolate. He opened the drink for Shamus, broke off some chocolate and handed them to his son, whose face lit up with crazed pleasure at the sugary joy. "There you go boy, that'll help dry you up," his dad said smiling. "We'll hang on here till it stops."

The noise from outside was softened only slightly by the insulation of the car and they watched as the rain incessantly rebounded from the bonnet like wave after wave of watery, madly hopping fleas. Shamus looked out the window at the dark clouds rolling in from the sea. "I like the sound of the rain," he said innocently.

"So do I, son. I like it at night when I'm snuggled up in bed and it rattles on the window. It helps me fall asleep," his dad replied as he sat back in his seat and watched the rain trickle down the windows. The thought came to him that it rained here quite a lot, often when you least expected it, as if the place was doing whatever it could to keep visitors away. '*Perhaps the weather was crap to keep people from finding out its secret,*' he mused to himself. It hadn't worked on him though, and he remembered the countless times he'd been caught in a downpour whilst engaging with this place, trying to fulfil the strange desire that haunted him. He glanced at his son who was still looking out of the door window, trance like, at the weather enveloping itself around the seaward end of the Down. '*At least he doesn't know the truth,*' he thought. The man looked ahead at the hillside rising up to the heavens. The rain kept falling hard and fast, its hypnotic drumming reverberating around the inside of the car. The wind whipped up against the doors and threw sheets of fresh water over the roof. '*It had rained like this on that night I saw him,*' the father remembered, and the memory of the experience washed through his mind like the driving rain outside.

He didn't know the boy had seen the ghostly vision too, maybe not today, but he had seen it. If his father knew the boy had experienced the mysterious figure he would never have brought him to this place again. Because unlike his son's unremembered encounter with the spirit world, the man's experience had seared itself on his psyche for the rest of his life. He believed the encounter was personal to only him, as he had never heard the mention of ghosts in this place by anyone else, and once it had happened the event and its repercussions had become like a mental drug to his senses which he felt the urge to explore ever since. There had never been another moment like the one he had on that particular night. But although he felt the presence of something sinister during his other visits, without actually seeing anything other worldly; a feeling that was always outweighed by the excitement it would generate, there was still a nagging suspicion that maybe that night was just a crazy dream brought on by some off cider and a dose of bad weed. Perhaps he had never really met the figure on the Down after all.

Dream or not, it was nearly twenty years ago but the memory of that night was as vivid now as it was then and it was something he didn't want his son to have to go through as well.

At 21, Gordy knew there was a livelier social life to be had than the one he was having now. But over the last few weeks he'd grown sick of the same rubbish lager in the same rubbish pubs, watching the same people have the same fights and being led on by the same girls who just wanted him to buy them more drinks. It had just not seemed fulfilling enough. He always had a good laugh with his friends whenever they went out and there were always lots of pretty girls to look at. There was some fairly decent music to listen to now and again, and the odd interesting character to engage with, but in general he believed he was missing out on the mental stimulation he felt his life needed at the moment. Occasionally there was a night out in the city to break the monotony of this hometown social scene and they often included flashier places to go and perhaps the odd cheeky pill or two to liven up the experience. But the fact he had a crummy job stacking shelves in a crummy supermarket meant that he was always short on funds, which meant the fact of going out on the razz to somewhere other than his home town was pretty much out of the question most of the time. For the last two weekends, town had been pretty much out of the question. So even though he was on his own, because everyone else still preferred to ask the question to the town, and even though it had taken him ages to cycle all this way on his haggard old bike, being here on the Down was the best bet he'd found for a more enlightening night out, as far as Gordy was concerned anyway.

It was the middle of June and the sun was hot and bright, making the incoming tide of the estuary look almost Mediterranean blue in the early evening light. Gordy had hidden his bike amongst the bushes on the side of the track and he looked around one more time to check that no one had seen him and the bicycle was out of sight. He made a mental note of the layout of the foliage and nearby bushes so he could find it again on his return then looked across at the nearby car park. There were a few people sitting in cars or casually leaning against the sea wall watching the sun slowly fall through the sky but many of them were preparing to leave and those left looked old enough and had the relevant mannerisms to be the kind of visitors who wouldn't make the effort of climbing the Down and therefore possibly spoiling the solitude that Gordy was after.

He took a sneaky swig of the cider he had in his rucksack before zipping up the bag and putting it on his back. He then began the exhausting walk up the steps leading to the top of the hill and the best view of the area for miles around.

Gordy didn't know how many steps there were because every time he hit a particularly steep flight, he lost count. They zig zagged in courses of between ten to fifteen steps at a time, and halfway up, he had to stop to take a rest and catch his breath. He took the opportunity to look at the view across the flat landscape that stretched away into the hazy distance. On one side rolled the farmland and the tiny pocket of buildings that was the small holiday resort of Brean and on the other side was the serene, glass like surface of the incoming sea. The breeze was getting stronger already at this height and he breathed it in along with the striking view, which helped him overcome the sudden shortness of breath he felt. Excited about reaching the top he carried on, using the smooth tubular metal handrails cemented into the steps to help pull him upwards. His breathing became heavier as he climbed and he began to puff unhealthily but the image of the sights awaiting him at the top and the reward of a drink and a smoke spurred him on. Finally, he lunged up the last few steps and emerged, panting and moist with perspiration, on the wide open plateau of the Down that sumptuously reached out before him.

All around the peninsular, the beautifully calm sea filled the space as far as the coast of Wales on the horizon. Everything seemed tinged with the golden light of the approaching sunset and Gordy was filled with the awesome serenity of the surrounding world in which he lived. As he looked across to the town on the other side of the bay, he was overwhelmed with a gladness that he had come to this place instead of going there and he grinned happily as it dawned on him that this place, with its inspirational view of the summer sun setting over a glorious landscape, was the best that life could offer anyone, anywhere in the whole world.

The sky was turning orange as the golden orb arced towards the horizon. There wasn't much time till the sun set completely and then it would start getting dark, so Gordy headed towards the end of the Down which looked out to the sea where he knew the ultimate view at dusk could be had. There was no one else around. He bounded with long, generous strides heading for a grassy hillock just off the main path to a place he had discovered and sat upon the week before.

He was glad no one else was around. Sometimes people came here to catch the views or to take bracing early evening walks but today the place was barren of humanity. *'Lucky,'* he thought, but there was still a feeling in the back of his mind that there might be a few youths hanging around the disused fort or lying about on the rocks down by the sea. Perhaps there could be a few late night ramblers marching along who might give him an odd look. He decided that this was just his own paranoia and if anyone gave him an odd look he'd match it with a few of his own. Last week when he had come here Gordy hadn't seen a soul and whether or not there was anybody around he decided that it wasn't going to let it bother him. He would just settle down, drink some cider, smoke a joint and watch the sunset. If no one bothered him he wouldn't bother them, and that was the unwritten rule that most people who came to places like this adhered to. Besides, he was big enough to look after himself, sometimes.

There was a hot and pleasant breeze as he walked along the path, which was only apparent as a path because the grass was shorter and worn down on that strip compared to the longer, rougher grass all around it. The wind warmed Gordy's face as he looked to each side of him and he took in the changing hillsides that went from rocky, undulating cliffs to sweeping, ski-like but snowless, grass covered slopes. For half an hour he walked, stopping occasionally to take a breather and gulp down a mouthful or two of booze whilst looking out to sea or checking the slow descent of the sun. As he climbed up another ridge, which ran like the humps of a camel along the crest of the promontory, he realised he had almost reached his destination.

He stepped off the brow and the vista suddenly opened up before his eyes like an immense painting. There, straight in front, was the deep orange orb of the sun floating above the thin strip of coastline along the now purple coloured horizon. In the middle distance, resting silently on the vastness of the steely blue water, was the dark, shadowy hump of the island of Steep Holm and behind her, the much flatter, longer, sister island of Flat Holm. From where he stood, the grass sloped down gently towards the square, roofless buildings of a disused Victorian fort nestled on the rocks above the sea, thankfully free of drunken youths. Without looking away from the view, Gordy took off his bag, pulled out the bottle of cider and drank. The exertion he had just spent and the alcohol he downed made his head swim, not unpleasantly, and he diverted off the path to sit down on a grassy mound on the side of the slope. Looking to his left he noticed the flat roofed World War II gun emplacement, which consisted of two concrete bunkers, no more than ten feet square, built into the side of the rock facing out to sea. They were about twenty metres away and the thin path that led down to them was worn into the grass by the frequent daytime visitors and the sporadic pockets of kids who used the venue for recreational drug use and drinking, leaving behind graffiti and the unmistakable stench of piss. Tonight the gun emplacements were blissfully empty and Gordy relaxed a little more on the dry grass, safe in the knowledge he was up here alone.

From the rucksack pocket he pulled out his battered tobacco tin and opened the lid to reveal two ready rolled marijuana joints. The sweet smell of pungent weed immediately filled his nostrils and he tenderly took one out before replacing the lid and zipping the tin safely back into the rucksack. The two litre bottle of locally produced cider was already half gone but he took another long swig just to moisten his lips before lighting the spliff. He'd already decided not to drink all of the alcohol up here as he had rather sensibly realised he didn't want to be too wobbly for the long walk back in the dark once the sun had set, especially as he wasn't sure how strong this weed was going to be. *'I'll cross that bridge when I come to it,'* he thought, smiling to himself. He looked out to sea and once again came to the conclusion that it had been a good idea to come here rather than go into town. With a glorious sunset about to take place and a relaxing smoke to enjoy, it was the perfect getaway from the routine of going to the pub, getting drunk and ending up in a right state somewhere grotty. Being here was the mix of mental stimulation and easy sensationalism that Gordy was really looking for.

As the sun touched the edge of the world, he lit the joint and breathed deeply allowing the smooth smoke to fill his lungs and send a wave of pleasure and lightness flowing over his body. He smoked some more and admired the view.

Out to sea the sunset took on a streaky appearance. Thin strips of mauve and violet clouds, tinged with pink and red floated just above the horizon and overhead a light fluffy layer of orange candy floss like cumulus moved achingly slow towards the hot land. An inane grin spread across Gordy's face and as the initial buzz of electricity from his first puffs left his relaxed body the lids of his eyes began to droop. His head started to float softly on his neck with each draw on the smoke. The orange sunset intensified and the colours began to merge and pulse together all across the horizon. The glowing red sun edged closer to the Welsh coastline in the distance and the sea grew wider and more flattened as the light faded.

'*This is good stuff*', he thought to himself. His mouth felt dry and he took another drink. He toyed with the idea of walking down to the fort, but decided he didn't want to ruin the moment by falling in the sea and drowning and that he couldn't really be bothered anyway. He looked at the grass and rocks around him and they became blended and edged with softness. The land felt as fluffy as his dopey head did, and with the sun finally beginning to hide behind the ellipsis of the vast planet he was part of, Gordy led back in the dusky light and sensed his body melting into the surface of the hill. He was unsure whether it was the fatigue from the climb or the quality of the weed he had smoked but his body suddenly felt very tired. Without thinking about it, and with little control over it, his eyes started to flicker gently until they were nearly closed. '*I'll just shut my eyes for a bit and chill*', he thought, as the sky turned from red to purple and then an ever darkening blue. A sensual relaxation consumed him as the warm breeze stroked his face with her soft elemental hands. He could hear the sound of seagulls crying as they swooped in the sky and the gentle rustle of the wind as it danced through the grass. There was the rhythmic lap of the tide splashing against the rocks down below and a string of whispered words echoing from his dry mouth about 'having a look and seeing where the sun was.' But unplanned and without really knowing it and coupled with a graceful easiness and sense of inevitability, Gordy fell blissfully into an unwanted and heavy sleep.

It was the rain that woke him. Fat and heavy, it splashed over his face and soaked into the T-shirt underneath his open jacket. Opening his eyes in a startled panic, he lifted his head and felt the damp, clinging jeans on his legs and the raindrops exploding on his exposed eyeballs making them sting. All around was dark blueness like someone had thrown ink over everything. The sunset was gone. The view had disappeared. There were just blobs of shadows against chunks of darkness. He was cold, cold from the howling wind that whipped over him like sheets of fearsome breath, the soft warm hands from the summer breeze a distant memory, cold from the rain pouring down from the stormy heavens. It was deep, dark, night time.

What happened? What time is it? How long have I been out? Where did this rain come from? Questions raced through Gordy's panicked mind. '*Get up, get up'* he thought. *'You fell asleep, you stupid dick! You fell asleep and now it's pissing down. Get up!'*

He grabbed his bag and scrabbled upright. He was disorientated and clumsy. Blinded by the rain filled night, he couldn't work out which direction to turn to or where he wanted to go. Groggy and soaking wet he caught sight of the shadowy form of the gun emplacement a few yards away. *In there,* his scrambled brain resolved, *get undercover, shelter!* Even in the panic and confusion he instinctively managed to grab the bottle of cider led on the wet grass, as though it might come in handy for something, and began to scrabble along the path towards the concrete box as the wind and rain lashed him. Luckily, the path was the clearest outline to emerge in the blackness, as if it was somehow lit up to show the way to refuge. Even so, Gordy had to concentrate and focus his eyes to stop himself from slipping onto the rocks and ultimately ending up in the sea. "Why! Why! You dickhead!" he shouted to himself through the driving rain as he gripped one side of the wet grass to keep his balance. The dark entrance of the shelter loomed up as the building became outlined against the slightly lighter sea, making it an easier target to aim for. Above, the cold black clouds rolled through the night like herds of dark horses, bringing the rain which soaked his hair and ran down his back. The wind rushed around madly knocking him sideways, until finally, as if pushed by some forceful gust, he fell into the sanctuary of the gun emplacement.

Gordy threw the rucksack against the concrete side, shook the water from his head and slumped down on the damp gritty floor with his back against the inner wall. He breathed deeply to calm himself down and help gather his thoughts so he could get his bearings on the situation. It was night and he was stuck on the end of a lonely peninsular in the middle of a storm surrounded by dank gloomy concrete with a definite odour of urine and mould. This had not been part of the plan for the evening. The wind whistled through the open fronted stone box which looked out across the dark channel, the same way it had in the war fifty years ago, now like an unnecessary sentinel sadly waiting to be called on again if needed. The rain hammered on the concrete roof adding to the disconcerting noise swirling all around. His skin was cold and he shivered from his wet clothes but at least he was sheltered from the rain and out of the threatening wind and at least there were no dodgy drunks in here with him, unlike the pub.

His mind was still racing. He thought about how stupid it had been to fall asleep, how nice it had been before he had and how shitty it was now. He didn't want to be out here in the middle of the night, caught in a summer storm. *'So much for stimulation,'* he thought. "You've certainly got that now, dickhead", he chided to himself. *'A sneaky smoke, a quick drink and then watch the sunset before bumbling back home to bed, that was all it was going to be. How long had I been asleep? Had anyone come along thinking I was some drunken tramp crashed out on the Down?'* He smiled and closed his eyes thinking of the absurdity of it all. "Perhaps I should have gone into town after all," he said quietly.

Opening his eyes, his body suddenly froze, automatically tensing up like an animal caught in the sights of a predator. His eyes widened in fear as he focused on the corner of the room in front of him. To his left, on the wall he was leant against, was an opening; a doorway to another room behind the one he was in, a room he'd forgotten about in the escape from the storm. From the opening, a faint yellow light, as if from a fire, began to grow and dimly illuminate the corner of his part of the refuge. It hadn't been there a moment ago, only now after he'd just opened his eyes. Remembering the layout of the shelter from previous visits, he realised he'd neglected to check the second room, hadn't even thought about it. Now he realised there was someone else in it.

Gordy heard a shuffle and a low raspy cough before catching the smell of burning wood. Whoever was in there had lit a fire and in all the confusion he hadn't noticed it until now. He remained frozen in fear and tried to push his body up against the wall, trying to hide in the shadows, quiet and undiscovered, holding his breath.

"Don't be afraid, my friend. I know you're there," said a soft, creaking voice. It was almost inaudible against the noise of the wind and rain outside, but strangely Gordy could hear the words clearly. "I'm only sheltering from the storm too. Come in by the fire. I won't hurt you," it whispered hoarsely.

Gordy's eyes darted to the exit and he thought about running, but the rain was being thrown at the shelter like chucked gravel and he could see the wind battering the pathway. He tried to calm down and suppress the nervous tension rising all over his body. "Who are you? What are you doing here?" he squeaked with a dry sticky mouth.

"Just a visitor like yerself, shelterin' from the elements," the voice rasped. There was a pause and the only sound was the weather outside and the gentle crackle coming from the fire in the other room. "The fire's warm.

You must be wet mate," continued the voice which seemed to sound smoother as it spoke, "Come in and dry up, there's no need to be afraid."

Gordy steadied himself and listened intently, trying to work out if the man was alone. He felt the chill of his damp clothes, the coldness around his skin and the growing worry that ebbed through his body. Looking out of the viewing platform at the atrocious weather, he realised it wasn't going to get any better. He decided that now he had spoken it was too late to escape and that he was going to take the chance and engage with the other hidden occupant. Surely he was old enough to handle any situation no matter how freaky or fearful it might be and maybe the stranger would end up being the most interesting person he'd met in a long time. The voice did not sound like that of a man who was drunk, or drugged up. Indeed, there was a lucidity in its deliverance that took away some of the fear from the situation and an almost welcoming aspect that made the prospect of a warm fire ever more appealing. *'Don't run away, face up to the encounter, there's nothing he can do to hurt you,'* Gordy thought to himself as he slowly got up, grabbed his bag and walked into the other room.

The fire was in the middle of the floor. It seemed larger and fiercer than the impression it gave from the other side of the doorway but there was no smoke coming from the flames that rose briskly in bright, wavering branches. Opposite the opening in the far corner was sat the figure who owned the voice. Gordy tried to focus on him but couldn't make out his features as the person was partly obscured by the fire. Even though the flames burned brightly, the light was unable to penetrate the darkness of the corner he was in. Gordy could tell the man's face and hands were brown and dirty. His clothes were dark with a shabby appearance and Gordy noticed that the boots he wore were undone and falling apart at the soles. His knees were up in front of his chest and although he couldn't see his face properly because of the shadows they created, Gordy got the impression the man had a beard. His hair was long, matted and greasy and on his head he wore a hat like the ones bell boys used to wear in exclusive hotels from times long since passed.

"Alright friend, sit down. Make yerself at home," he said with a voice that crackled like the fire and he gave a nod to the wall opposite him. "You're a bit wet boy. Youse'll get dry soon enough with that fire a blazin'." Gordy looked round and sat down in the place the man had motioned towards.

"Thanks man. I'm sorry to butt in like this. I got caught in the downpour," he said nervously with an unsure smile.

"No need to be sorry, comrade. The weather can turn in a flash on the Down," the man said gently and Gordy noticed a kindly acknowledgement through the thick straggly beard. Though he still couldn't make out the features of his face Gordy guessed the man was in his late 40's or early 50's and was surely just a tramp hanging out on the Down for a while. He had a local accent with touches of a Devon twang but its quietness was smooth and soothing and although it rasped occasionally Gordy felt no threat from the figure and relaxed enough to begin enjoying the warmth of the fire. He was still a bit groggy from the booze and smoke and the shock of being woken up by the storm but his mind was starting to clear. "Nice fire, man. Thanks for letting me share it. I'll get out your way soon, once the rain stops," he said, leaning back against the wall whilst watching the gentle dance of the flames.

"No need to rush off boy. Tis nice to 'av some company. I thought I was in for another night on me own in this 'ere stone box. Don't get many visitors up 'ere. But wot brings ye up 'ere anyway, young 'un?" the figure asked in thick tones. Gordy snorted.

"I came up to watch the sunset," he began before pausing slightly. "Then I fell asleep. The rain woke me up," he added feebly.

"Ah, this place can do that to you, take my word for it. Take you by surprise it will. Jus when you think it's all nice and friendly it turns on you like a monster and bites you in the ass!" It was the tramps turn to snort disapprovingly. He stared mysteriously at his guest and then suddenly looked towards a square metal framed hole in the sea facing wall of the room which formed a small window. There was no glass, just a viewpoint outside to the sheeting rain and moaning wind. Gordy looked towards the window too and as he did so the fire seemed to die down noticeably and the room was filled with more nightly drawn shadows. Although the light had dimmed, the figure seemed to emerge from the blackness and leaned forward, crossing his legs, so allowing Gordy to see into a set of small piercing eyes that narrowly glared at him through the gloom. He noticed the thick metal buttons on the man's jacket and the frayed material around his strange hat. It looked a bit like a uniform of some kind and although the tunic was of a dark blue colour, the trousers were of a lighter grey and had dark patches on them which weren't the result of the increase in shadows, more like dirt or oil. The figure opened his mouth and showed a set of blackened, worn down teeth in a lined and haggard face. "Best stay 'ere boy," he growled a little menacingly. "The Down might chuck you in the sea or blow you on the rocks. She's angry. Letting the world know she can't be beat. Best let her calm down. Stay 'ere. Listen to her sing fur a while with me. Don't let her be the death of you."

Gordy shuffled nervously against the wall and stared at the man. He felt afraid again and thought about making a run for it but the old tramp was right, in the raging weather outside he might end up falling down a cliff and killing himself on the rocks or getting washed out to sea. *'Just ride it out,'* he thought. *'He's a bit weird, but don't let him freak you out. It's just a harmless old tramp.'* The outburst had helped clear Gordy's mind a little and he prepared himself in case he needed to make a quick getaway as a last resort. He noticed his clothes were less clingy and were beginning to dry. The other figure leaned back and suddenly the fire rose up again, the flames licking high into the air as if the gas had been turned up on a burner. Gordy thought maybe the stranger had added another log when he had leant forward and that it had only just caught but realised there weren't any spare logs in the room. The heat from the flames kept the young man sat down and warmed him further helping to ease the nerves of the situation. The other man retreated into the dark shadows once more and said in a much softer and friendlier tone, "I don't blame yer for comin' up to watch the sunset. I've seen many a beautiful sunset 'ere over the years."

Gordy sat up straighter before asking confidently, "So why are you here? Do you live on the Down or something?"

The figure almost smiled in the shifting light. "Sometimes I'm here, sometimes I'm there. If I want, I'm everywhere, friend. I move around see. Wherever I want to go, I go, free as a bird. But I always seem to end up back on the Down. Sometimes you can't get away from the world you're destined for," he replied cryptically. There was a quiet moment as the fire settled down again before the figure asked, "And what's your name then, young man?"

"People call me Gordy."

"Gordy! That's a funny name fur someone."

"I suppose so. My proper names Gordon, but it always sounds a bit official," the young man suggested.

"This place don't suit being official, lad. It's too rough!" the figure laughed sorely before it turned into a hacking cough and he spluttered into his hands as he covered his mouth.

Gusts of wind whistled through the window and the rain drummed a droning melody on the concrete cave. Gordy eased back a little and decided to make the most out of the strange situation he had found himself in and try to absorb the event in a more positive manner. It felt like parties he had been to where he didn't know anyone and not many people had turned up but he'd ended up talking to whoever was there with a sense of awkward wariness, usually under the influence of drink or drugs. There was only one other person at this party, but he felt the man opposite him was probably just a lonely traveller who appreciated the company and liked having someone to talk too. He thought that this encounter should be viewed as part of the stimulation that he wanted and had been one of the reasons for coming here in the first place. The bloke did have a wicked fire and was kind enough to have invited him in and take refuge from the storm. *'There's no need to be so edgy,'* he told himself. The man was sharing the only thing he had to offer and Gordy realised the most sociable thing to do was offer up the only thing he had to share. At the parties he sometimes ended up in, there was a rule he often resorted to when confronted with strange people in disjointed situations, 'when in doubt, get loaded!'

"Fancy a smoke, mate?" he asked cheerfully.

“A kindly gesture, young un, but I’ll pass, thank ye. You go ahead though, friend,” the figure answered with a sly smile and then wiped his hands on his coat.

“Cheers,” Gordy said, a little unsure now, even though he knew the smoke would calm him down whilst giving a welcome boost in pleasure. He was confident he wouldn’t let the weed bamboozle his body the way it had earlier. The atmosphere was different from then, more concentrated, and if anything it would take the edge off the scene whilst enhancing his senses. He reached across, took the tin out of his bag and lit the second joint. Taking a long drag, he breathed the smoke in deeply. This time he wouldn’t allow himself to get zapped by the smoke, instead he was just going to get warm and feel at ease with the stranger and the situation he was in. As the drug coursed up his back and tingled over his head, he looked around the damp, dark concrete walls and then at the conflagration in the middle of the room. The burning pyre cast silhouettes on the stone like a slow carousel of frolicking children. As he watched the parade move around, he glanced over at the figure hidden in the corner and noticed he was smiling. Gordy took another drag and offered it to the other man. “Sure you won’t change your mind,” he grinned.

“No thanks boy. Smokin’ never helped no one.” He shook his head slowly. “But I will try a glug of yer cider, if I may,” he said more jovially. “I haven’t tasted that in years. Jus’ for old time’s sake, you know.”

“I thought you homeless people drank cider all the time,” Gordon replied stupidly.

“I’m not homeless!” said the stranger sharply, as his smile disappeared. “This is my home and it always will be. If I told you how I ended up here it would make your toes curl young ‘un. And I haven’t had a drink for more years than you’ll ever believe boy. Maybe it’s about time I told someone the truth about this place, someone like you, eh.”

“The truth. What do you mean?” Gordy said continuing to grin like a simpleton and looking around sluggishly for the half full bottle of cider which was led on the floor by the doorway. He got up clumsily and grabbed the drink before wobbling around the fire and handing it to the man in the corner. The figure leant forward and took the cider with a grubby hand, looking intently at his guest as he did so. Close up, Gordy realised the man now looked younger than he first thought, maybe only in his early twenties, but it was a complexion that was gaunt and fevered like that of a poorly hospital patient. Even in the illumination of the fire he looked pale, almost blue in colour with dark rings around his tired, pleading eyes. His pallor was deathly and his long bony fingers were attached to a wrinkled and scabby hand. He suddenly looked vulnerable and afraid, like a fragile despondent who needed rescuing. Gordy shrank away from him and plopped back awkwardly to where he had been sitting. *‘The guy looks pretty ill,’* he thought, and suddenly a pang of pity swept over him. He took another puff from his smoke and watched as the tramp opened the bottle and drank in long, thirsty gulps. He kept drinking without taking a breath and drained the bottle of liquid until it was empty, then he wiped his mouth with his sleeve and casually rolled the plastic container into a corner before leaning back amongst the shadows. A faint smile spread beneath his brown, gingery whiskers. "Cheers boy, very kind," he hissed.

"No worries. I'd had enough anyway," Gordy said with a wobble of his head. He grinned oafishly and took another drag on his rapidly depleting joint before adding, "So how did you end up here?"

His head was swimming slightly but he felt reasonably relaxed and peaceful. The fire appeared to calm down again and this time it created an easy glow which softened the starkness of the building. The sound of the wind and rain outside grew softer and the room seemed more comfortable than before. The shadows continued to move around the walls like a ghostly parade of sinister elfish dancers and Gordy watched the pulsing embers of the fire as the stranger began to speak again.

"There are some places on this earth boy, where the elements of nature take over the landscape. They are the base on which the surroundings are built and on which life depends. Some places have the sun, others the wind and rain. All of them can push the living to their limit and make the decisions on what life can survive or die. Survival is luck, sheer determination and stubbornness. There's no protection for the great over the small. Even the might of man can be brought down by the smallest of cuts infected by the wrong disease in the easiest of places. But for all the variety of the world, my friend, there are some parts that are just cold, dark, wet and windblown."

Gordy nodded blankly, unable to think of anything to reply to the suddenly well-spoken tones of the lucid words. Instead he melted into the soft warmth of the fire. *'This is weird, he's gone all posh,'* he thought, glazing over as the figure looked with a solemn expression into the shadows cast across the roof. Suddenly, the man's eyes shot down to Gordon who was staring numbly at the hypnotic firelight in front of him. The tramp's glare was dark and menacing, boring into the young man as the surrounding face became a moving, mottled camouflage of shadows. His voice got louder and more determined, the accent was gone and the words were clearer and Gordon could feel the agitation rise through the stifled atmosphere of the room.

"Sometimes there is a cold that pervades the air and forms a secret layer over every surface as if a poison had been released. A coldness that invades every hidden corner and seeps its way into the slightest shrinking cranny until it infects and overtakes all before it, living or dead, like some terrible disease.

"Whether day or night there is a darkness that creeps across the landscape, fed by the cold and the shortness of the days as winter closes its icy grip around the world. A dark barely penetrated by light, regardless of its creation by the power of the heavenly sun or the flame of man's destructive fire. A darkness that blocks out hope and shrivels the hardest of resolves until everything before it succumbs to the enveloping stillness." The figure's hands moved around with the fleeting shadows on the walls as the volume of his words rose

"There is a boundless wind, powerful and unremitting. Wind that battles heavenly entities, that smashes what is built and hampers what can grow until it holds to ransom the world which lies before it. A wind so loud it deafens all who can hear its thunderous roar and defies any who try to control its power until they cower into submission.

"And finally there is always rain. A rain that soaks you to your heart until you feel you'll never be dry again. Hard rain that falls so immeasurably from a sky that never seems to break or recede. Rain that seeps into every surface of every object until everything it touches submits to a watery defilement!"

As the tramp raged he leant inwards and became animated, shaking a fist as he spoke, spitting the words out through the flames. When he moved the fire increased its ferocity and the raised flames heightened the angry, dancing shadows of the nightmarish carousel, making it move quickly around the walls and forming a kaleidoscopic battle between light and dark. This time a thin white smoke swirled from the flames and drifted around the room with the shadows. It had a sickly smell like burnt meat and lavender which made the atmosphere hazy and undefined, adding to the drowsy confusion that Gordon was experiencing. His head was spinning fast and he starting feeling queasy. He wanted to leave. His mouth dropped open and he could taste the smoke on his tongue, but he could not speak or make a sound. Trying to focus in the smoky mist he realised an inertia had overtaken his whole being. His muscles felt seized and stiff and his arms and legs became numb and frozen in stillness. All he became aware of was the putrid fumes in the air and the sound of the other man's ranting words, which he continued to spit forth, reverberating across the room.

"Even when faced with these surroundings, boy, some sort of life carries on its struggle with admirable bravery. Plants and animals survive with a determination even the elements struggle to defeat. They are the richest of wildlife that nature creates in landscapes unchanged over thousands of years. Some of them thrive in such places whilst others merely hang on for dear life hoping luck keeps them alive. Animals and birds, plants and rocks, men and beasts all call somewhere home. Even baron pieces of rock and mud bombarded by the elements are a home to someone, something, just trying to survive. There are many of these places around the world, boy, and one such place is here! It has a life! It has a name, boy! Brean Down on the bastard coast of the west of England!"

The figure moved as if he was going to stand up but remained crouched in the flickering shadows, only his voice rising to fill the room with its resonant bellow. "From millions of years ago to now it has a history of endless days and countless nights where nothing happens except nature and evolution taking its painful course, and nobody ever notices or even cares." He raised clenched fists up as if about to pound the dusty floor in frustration, but instead he unfurled his bony fingers and patted his chest as he continued his impassioned speech.

"Ignored and forgotten they are, and I should know, boy, if anyone knows, I should. But there was one night that shouldn't be forgotten, on a cold and wet February of long ago, boy, when man was part of that battle to survive. To survive not only the tempests that battered them and the landscape they clung too, but to survive from the monstrous ferocity men could unleash on each other. You would never believe such ferocity could exist, boy, but it did. Man left his mark on this place and his actions left his mark on me. And I'll leave my mark on you, boy, by God I will!"

Then, with those anger filled words, the rant stopped as quickly as it started and the figure leant back into the edges of the wall again. As he did so, the fire calmed down and resumed an easy, gentle flicker as the smoke slowly drifted away and the embers glowed more pleasantly as the atmosphere eased.

There was a pause allowing the disorientation inside Gordy's heavy head to slow down and, managing to overcome the creeping paralysis of his body enough, he sat up a little against the wall. He was still speechless as he tried to utter a word in reply but no sound came out of his mouth and his body felt like it was in a state of shock, finally seizing up into a blob of paralysed stillness. All he could do was stare trance like into the magical light emitted from the fireplace. Only the dark figure in the shadowy corner could speak, but this time it was with a soft, soothing tone again.

"Let me tell you a story about this place, young 'un," he began. "It starts off with the man who saved my life once. He was a brave man, braver than I'll ever be. He fought the demons in his head and the ones outside these walls and no one ever knew about it. His name was Elias, but towards the end of our lives I was able to call him Eli. I hope one day I'll meet him again in peace."

As the man spoke, the words drifted through the room and merged with the glowing embers of the fire to form pictures of people moving and talking in scenes created within the gentle flames. Mesmerized by the hypnotic visions in the flickering light and soothed by the gentle tones of the stranger's voice as it filled the room and echoed inside his head, Gordy fell into a transfixed stupor. He couldn't move a muscle. His body felt like it was heavy and filled with lead whilst his brain was engulfed by a series of intense virtual sights and sounds all generated by the fire. The real world fell timelessly away as he found himself seeing a dream of the place he was surrounded by, but in another age. And as it unfolded, the secrets of the Down were revealed with each word the figure said.

2. February 1884

It was a beast upon a beast. A union of monsters; one made of iron, the other made of rock. The Iron Beast heaved its hulking body along the gritty track carved into the rock monsters' mountainous hind, sending out groans of scraping metal and creaking wood as it moved. It had journeyed for many days before reaching this place and the cries from the twisted mass leapt forth as it hauled itself towards the nest in which it could lie down and finally sleep. Occasionally the beast would howl and whine or pierce the gloom with a fearsome screech, sending icy shivers down the spines of any cowering humans who could hear it. These ghostly noises were caught by the swirling wind and then cast away like a fine mist that drifted eerily across the bleak grassland. In the village on the far side of the hill, which hid like a frightened insect within a crevice of rock, the old wives continued to mend the fishing nets with aching and withered fingers. They chose not to look up at the hill and watch for the menacing but as yet unseen dragon-like creation which slowly, secretively slid his way up to the rocky lair above. They knew what was coming.

Its movement was heavy and laboured and it had taken many hours to travel a short distance. Tired and grouchy, sometimes the concentration required by the machinist monster to make the precarious journey floundered and the beast would slip dangerously out of control, skating towards the edge of safety on the stony road and heading instead for the treachery of the steep, bramble covered slopes of the hill. Only an almighty effort born from a determination not to destroy itself allowed the cumbersome creature to control the wayward movement and so carry on its painful and desperate journey to its final obscure destination.

Grey skies had followed the monstrosity from its birth in the fiery foundries of a faraway city. Those rain filled clouds had stayed overhead as it travelled along the iron road which flowed like a metal stream through the endless countryside, until they gathered and merged with other ominous clouds to form a darkened welcoming banner of grievous weather above the hilly form of that other beast which was made of rock and stone, so marking the Iron Beast's final resting place. At the end of a snaking track of mud and gravel it could stop, forever maybe, and wait for its own rusty end in peaceful stillness. And as the Iron Beast approached the end of its travels, his cries softened against the sharp winter wind and the groans which had hung in the damp morning air drifted unnoticed towards the cold metallic sea.

As if in recognition of its arrival and so calm the tempers of this beast, the sun began to mysteriously break through the heavy cover of ink smudged sky and shafts of warming light were sent down upon the heaving mass of dark metal, splintered wood and throbbing flesh spread across the ground below. God had finally taken pity on this unholy leviathan and the grey landscape on which it was to make its home was momentarily filled with a heavenly illumination.

But in the village the old women continued to mend their fishing nets with aching and withered hands. They glanced up only briefly towards the shafts of light which had been cast upon the hill above them, for they had seen the sun in this part of the world many times before. Each time, the endless grey skies had returned to block out the light and once again their world was shrouded in a suffocating blanket of thick airless cloud. But they did not mind. They sought solace from the elements around them in the church that stood above the village, halfway up the hill. And each time they found that solace. Tonight salvation would be found again as they knelt and prayed to whichever God they believed could offer them protection, and one day, with those prayers being answered, the Iron Beast would fall into the deep, dark sea, forever.

The Down rose out of the murky water of the Bristol Channel like a mountainous whale. It looked like a creature that was a thousand years old and had come to the surface one day many years ago to take a long awaited breath and whilst resting simply decided to stay where it was. Its shanks were a jagged line of craggy black rock and sharp grey stone, stained yellow and brown in places by the mark of the tide and the colonies of lichen that grew mould-like over them. Covering the rest of its aged body in a waterproof skin, was a patchwork of weather roughened grass and brown tangled brambles. It was as though land and sea had come together in a concerted effort to form the most durable and unmovable of structures, using the most sustainable and hardwearing parts it owned as building materials; a leviathan that broke the water like an ultimate statement of defiance and longevity by the powers of nature, but secretly within its own self, was waiting for a deluge of sea to come rushing up the estuary so she could dive down to swim away and finally escape from her monotonous landing. She seemed to be hoping, hidden in disguise with the landmass behind her, for something that would never happen.

It was a lonely place. One of the final chapters of the Mendip hills as they meandered their jagged, geographical story across the West of England before falling into the sea. It looked forlorn and unloved, disowned and abandoned by the commune of hills safely anchored on land behind her. The peninsular became the jilted lover whose only outcome for a broken heart was a soggy death. She had been dropped like a gargantuan rock on the edge of the shoreline, half in the water, half out, left to her own devices on the coastline of England. Approached from either land or sea she was domineering but in reality the highest point was less than a hundred yards from sea level. However, this change from hilly heath to jagged rocks was treacherous and the less sure footed visitors could be frightened by the sudden appearance of a cliff edge or a rocky crag, as if the Down was showing her anger towards careless trespassers at the solitude caused to her by the betrayal of those fellow elevations.

Foaming brown water from the Severn estuary lapped around the boulders and encrusted fissures of the shoreline adding to the sense of danger the place pervaded. The tides along the estuary rose and fell at an alarming rate, meaning at high tide the brown liquid would cover the rock around the sea level from the headland of the promontory to the beginning of the beach near the mainland, creating a maelstrom of whirlpools and currents in a vortex of volcanic rock and frothing river water. It was the jaws of an all-encompassing and rabid, fluid formed organism waiting for unfortunate victims at the end of a hideous fall from the heights above which resulted in a wet, crunching death at the rock strewn baseline below. Even at low tide there was no safety. The sea would slip away almost as far as the eye can see until it was just a thin line on the horizon, the water being replaced by a thick glutinous mud able to suck the flesh from bones and the very air from the congested atmosphere.

Her loneliness was cemented by the dislocation the promontory had to the rest of the mainland. She stuck out like a solitary finger pointing awkwardly out to sea, only connected to the coast by a sliver of permanent farmland a few hundred yards long. This sliver was further reduced by a border of sand banks and marshland which formed an inlet near the Down's landward side, allowing a stretch of water to split the coastline apart and weave its way gently inland for several miles, growing ever thinner until it disappeared into the ground before emerging again through the banks of some far off river.

On the other side of this mud banked inlet sat a small fishing village hidden behind a much smaller, geographically eroded hill. The village, known by the name of Uphill, was less than half a mile from the nearest point of the Down but the mud, sand and water between them formed a small, circular bay which meant, together with the inlet, the village and the rest of the northerly coastline were cut off from the segregated finger of rising land jutting out to sea. Although covered at high tide by seawater, at low tide the sand lay across this miniature bay, broken only by an outcrop of small jutting rocks called Black Rock which managed to rise above both sandy mud and water. To the foolish and unknowing the sand banks and Black Rock could have been a shortcut from the village to the Down but to the experienced it was a vitreous glue which could swallow you up to your waist with little time to be rescued before the incoming tide covered your head and drowned you ever so slowly.

The only road leading to Brean Down came from the other side of the village and had to take a detour several miles south along the mainland before curling through the farms and turning back up to follow the beach and arrive at the base of the hill. It was a journey that even by steam tractor could take half a day. On foot, instead of using the road, one could reach the Down from the village using a slipway which led to the beach. It was a short walk along the sand and one could then cross the inlet using a sodden and slime covered wooden footbridge built too long ago and in need of refurbishment. Even then you still had to traverse the sand and grassy marshland on the other side using a sketchy stone riven path before finally skirting the firmer wheat fields and grazing pastures that took you to the pathways leading up to the top of the Down.

The fastest way across the gap was at high tide using a boat that took you to a rocky cove called Fiddlers Point hidden at the easterly end of the peninsular which looked directly across the bay to the slipway near the village on the other side. But this required speed and skill with an oar to successfully navigate a way through the swirling currents and eddies, particularly around the sinister looking Black Rock. It was the tide that dictated the ease of accessibility to the Down by whoever wished to venture there. The tides, the terrain and enough time to negotiate both along with favourable weather was what one needed to get to the required destination, wherever it may be around the dismembered and inhospitable promontory.

The Bristol Channel split the nations of England and Wales, becoming the overwhelming factor that governed the coastal regions of both countries in this particular corner of the world. She could bring fear and destruction or tranquillity and awe inspiring beauty in equal measures to those who risked her use. Respect was due to the estuary as she was the authority that governed all along this coastline and the isolated cape of Brean Down.

But it was not the only authority which attempted to manifest itself within the fledgling growth of populations that inhabited the seaboard for miles around and in doing so, steadfastly battled against those mighty elements. At the end of a track which snaked its way across the top of this greenest of Downs before it finally fell away into the churning waters of the sea, lay a small and seemingly inconsequential fort.

Elias Harding sat on a grassy mound overlooking the small coastal fort below him and wondered what he was doing there. It was a damp, murk ridden late morning and he pulled the collars of his overcoat up around his ears to try and keep them warm. He was trying to work out if he actually liked this place or not, but realised that since his arrival two weeks ago to take charge of the fort it had rained for most of the time and therefore his view was probably biased towards the negative. He was sat on one of the highest parts of the Down and the fort lay at the foot of its soggy green slopes only a hundred yards or so away. It was far enough for Elias to disengage himself from its bleak reality. He had sat here before in search of a refuge from the difficulties he secretly endured and it offered a commanding view of the landscape in all directions, allowing his mind to wander and so divert it from the more distressing thoughts which sometimes unexpectedly invaded it. Several times the rolling green pastures with their hedgerow walls and edging of drainage channels leading inland, to the wide open vista of headland, sea and sky that stretched out towards the ocean, helped him escape from not only the monotony and discomfort of his present situation, but all the horrors and desperation experienced by him in the past. By sitting on top of the nature that surrounded him, with all its harshness, unpredictability and short-tempered beauty, he had the feeling he was in control of it, and therefore himself, if only momentarily, until the rain or the wind or the dark sent him scurrying back to the refuge of the fort, the refuge of the booze and sometimes the refuge of the laudanum bottle.

He looked out to sea towards the appropriately named island of Steep Holm and was suddenly surprised by the sight of an incandescent, bubbling ball of yellow flame flying elegantly upwards from the blob of dull green rock sat in the grey water. It was a distress flare used by the men of the artillery battery stationed on the island to get the attention of the other batteries on the mainland, either side of the channel. It was mainly for the attention of those on Brean Down as there was an underwater telegraph wire linking Steep Holm to Lavernock Point, the battery station on the Welsh side, thus allowing them an instant form of mutual contact. But financial constraints within the coastal defence budget meant no telegraph link had been set up with the fort on Brean Down. So the flare and semaphore system was the only means of speedy communication between the island and her closer English side and its use at any time, let alone right now, always sent a worrisome wave of uncertainty through Elias's body.

Now that worry swept through his body again, along with a realisation that he would have to go back to the fort and get his binoculars. Then, he would have to look for the signaller on Steep Holm whose job it was to frantically wave flags from a designated view point on the island, and via his binoculars, then work out what those flags were saying. This relay of messages between the two forts using the semaphore method was a system that often got in somewhat of a muddle, either through its disjointed nature, the weather at the time of contact or the lack of attention from Brean Down's inhabitants and sometimes, in appropriate conditions, this muddle resulted in the need of a boat having to be dispatched from the island to the Down. Eli began to feel nervous and wondered what the problem was.

The flare rose into the sky making a faint fizzing noise as it ascended. When it reached its peak the signal made a popping sound and a plume of bright sparks were showered against the dirty cotton sky. As he watched the flare fall gently towards the sea, the popping noise became something different and more sinister inside Eli's suddenly troubled mind. It morphed and resonated into the pop of a mortar shell as it was released from its weapon and the connected image flashed across his thoughts. Then his imagination changed the popping sound to that of a bullet, exiting the chest of a man stood next to him in a past experience of battle. In the back of his head he heard a scream and saw a man being hacked to death in a whirlwind of blunted, curved swords. He closed his eyes against the horrifying visions and began to rock in very small rhythmic movements, as if trying to steer the overcoming thoughts away through physical meditation. *'No! Don't think about this!'* He mentally barked to himself from inside his transcendence and began to murmur the words as he counted steadily.

"One, one hundred, two, one hundred, three, one hundred," he said as the numbers tumbled from his suddenly stressed brain. *'Beethoven!'* he thought through the numerals as they ticked over in his mind. *'Beautiful Beethoven, think of his piano concerto no.3! Remember the performance you saw, the full orchestra and the wild pianist with his insane hands and the pretty girl in the violin section with her soft brown hair falling in curls as she played so perfectly. The strings made you want to cry, remember, and you fell in love with the music and the girl, just for the night. Think about these things, not the horrors of a warrior's world.'* He kept counting as his mind struggled with the traumatic visions that the flare had suddenly brought on. "Ten, one hundred, eleven, one hundred" he said aloud.

He breathed deeply as the mind control began to work. The flare melted into the sea along with the shocking thoughts that had briefly invaded his inner peace. Elias closed his eyes tighter, then opened them again and blinked. He stopped rocking and shook the images from his head like dispersing dust into the wind and looked out over the rocks to the monotone sea. He couldn't tell where the mud ended and the water began as it was all the same shade of grey. *'Be glad of this place,'* he told himself. *'Be glad of the rain and the grey skies overhead. You escaped alive and this place is quiet and peaceful and the only thing you need to worry about is getting pissed on and blown about by the stinging wind. Be grateful you're here and not somewhere else staring death in the face.'* He quickly took a rolled cigarette from his metal case and lit it with a match in shaking hands. Rubbing his forehead, he felt the beads of nervous sweat which had gathered on his face and smeared it over his palms before wiping them on his trousers. It had started to drizzle lightly with rain but he didn't really notice.

To some degree Elias Harding could control the men that were under his command, as they were volunteers and all seemed to be glad to be here in some strange way, probably because it was more exciting than the usual drudgery of their everyday lives. He could control the routines of the fort because that was what he had been instructed to do and it was easily within the capabilities of his trained mind. But he couldn't control the weather and it was clear to him that wherever he was sent in the world under the auspices of his army career the weather seemed to be the underlining factor to dictate events. Occasionally, much like the weather, he couldn't control his thoughts either and his memories would take over, particularly in times of nervousness or unfounded worry. Memories brought on by the simplest of noises or the slightest of actions, like the snorting of a frisky horse or the bang of a slamming door, or even an innocuous comment from an innocent stranger. When it happened, instantly his mind would cast itself back like a coiled spring to a place far away from wherever he actually was. Somewhere that was hotter and bleaker. Somewhere years gone by, still seared on his memory like the skin of a spit roasted pig, crisp and scorched, just as his skin had been from the burning sun of a previously unknown world. The unrelenting heat of the day, the terrifying reality of death and the senseless destruction which exploded out of that place even now, four years later, tore into his unprepared mind and blocked his senses, outstripping all normal thought. *'Don't think about the past! Forward! Think forward!'* his head screamed when it happened. From somewhere deep inside would come this subconscious and rousing reply to the sudden malaise he would suffer. His mind shouted at him like a sergeant on a parade ground ordering his thoughts to change their direction as if they were new recruits learning to march. It was a way of dealing with memories that he had taught himself through trial and error. *'Snap out of it before it takes hold!'* he had instructed his psyche, time and again, whenever the panic attacks would occur. It needed practice to master his own mind, but he was getting used to it, most of the time.

The episodes had started shortly after his return from Afghanistan. There had been the odd nightmare during the conflict but he thought that was to be expected considering the traumas war presented. When it was over and he was sent home there was nothing to suggest he would be plagued by terrifying visions or extreme bouts of irritability and depression, poor sleep patterns and a tendency to get angry for no reason. Some of the old soldiers he spoke to simply said he might get the 'willies' every now and then, whatever they were, and the best remedy was to take a drink to steady himself and ignore it. Well the 'willies' came thick and fast once he got back and so did the drink. The army sent him on holiday several times and gave him easy postings at training camps and gun ranges which meant he was able to keep most of the nightmares hidden within the privacy of his own quarters. But there were plenty of times when an attack would hit and he would have to excuse himself quickly or merely disappear to go and sort himself out as best he could away from the view of other people. It was a lonely world and Elias found it difficult to cope with.

Ironically, it was being sent back to Afghanistan that helped him learn to deal with the psychotic reactions. The opium dens of Kabul took away some of the stresses he was experiencing but more than that was the solace he found at being back at the place where the traumas had taken place. He wasn't sure how or why but by confronting his demons in the world where they had come from he was able to handle them better. On his return to England the attacks became less common. When they did come, he faced them using his own mind control techniques which he learnt from the opium den servants, along with the odd drop of laudanum to calm the more affecting episodes and a steady intake of good, old fashioned booze.

He had seen war, experienced the violence and felt the immeasurable fear that it created. He had witnessed the terrible waste and destructive chaos it left behind. He had seen and felt it all before his thirtieth birthday and it was not an experience he had enjoyed. He knew some men did enjoy it, maybe even lived for it and Eli sometimes wondered if he had been afflicted with their desire, but deep within his soul he knew he couldn't be one of them and he was glad of that. He had endured the violence but not enjoyed it. *Had he?* Sometimes the anger boiled inside, fed by sadness and a sense of injustice at the despicable things that men can do and the results they caused. Occasionally it would rear up into thoughts of violence and an urge to destroy something. But Eli felt that was only natural under the circumstances and he would always be capable of controlling the part of his mind that generated these thoughts. *Wouldn't he? Deep down he was a good man, wasn't he?* War had certainly made him indecisive, he realised.

Elias forced a smile and looked at the fort again, his mind regaining its normal composure. The fortress lay perfectly still as if deserted by the men who lived there. There was no movement to soil its outlines, no sound which disturbed its peace. *'Maybe it's not such a bad place after all,'* he thought, before remembering his latest mental turn only a few seconds ago. He mumbled shakily in response to its possible trigger having been the place he had sat in. "Still, I'm not sitting on this bloody spot again," he muttered. He had forgotten all about the flare.

Out of the corner of his eye, Master Gunner Elias Harding saw a solitary figure riding a bicycle, approaching the fort along the only road on the Down. The Military road, as it was called, was a thin stretch of macadam surfacing which led from the main road, up the hill and along the northern face of the peninsular. Its original purpose was to enable the building and consequent servicing of the military outpost but was now only used by pedestrians, the odd horse and cart and a few bicycles, one of which belonged to the postman. The slowly moving figure looked tired and windswept as he cycled along and from his vantage point, Elias could tell it was Patrick Gill, the village postman riding his old, bone shaker, postal bike.

Eli stood up tossing the remains of his cigarette away as he did. He put his hands in the pockets of his tweed overcoat and started down the pathway which led from his viewpoint to the entrance of the fortress. He wanted to run so he could catch the postman before he reached the empty gatehouse but the muddy path worn into the grass was wet and slippery from the recent downpours and the thin drizzle that was now falling. He knew it would be easy to end up on his backside and he descended carefully.

"Patrick!" he called.

The postman peddled on, oblivious to the figure shouting down at him, concerned only with his slow progress to the destination ahead. Elias had met Patrick several times over the fortnight as he was the most frequent visitor from the outside world. Every three or four days he had turned up with the bills of sale for supplies or instructions from the War Office that needed administrating. The old man was friendly and Elias found him pleasant and distracting company.

"Patrick, up here!" Eli called louder this time.

The man on the bicycle turned his head and stopped his bike. As he waited, looking weary and a little confused at the figure coming down the hill, a damp smile slowly crept onto his exhausted face just as the young man reached him.

"I got your post, some of it urgent, supposedly. Special delivery from the town, this very morning," the postman panted lightly as he got off the rickety bike. Eli still had his hands in his pockets and was hunched up against the clinging damp air but greeted the old man with a warm grin. He glanced from the postman to his bicycle and noticed the bike looked as old as the weathered pensioner before him. He didn't know exactly, but Eli put the postman's age at the wrong side of sixty, although he could have been much older.

"Still on that old boneshaker, eh Patch," Elias replied affectionately. "It's about time they got you a new one."

"It's about time they got a new postman more like," Patch retorted sharply. "The blokes at the post office call this bike 'the old slag' cause she's bin ridden by everyone," he added more warmly with a raise of his eyebrows, "At least the hard rain held off until I got 'ere. The inside got a sweat on coming out this far and now the outsides getting wet too."

Eli looked at the old man apologetically, realising the isolation of this particular delivery. "The 'old slag' eh, nothing wrong with one of them, Patch old boy," he quipped. "Fancy a drink in the dry? I know I do." He nodded towards the guardroom a few feet away with a knowing smile. It wasn't just an idle offer; Elias was glad to see someone else to take his mind off the mental episode he'd just suffered. An outside visitor was a welcome distraction along with a stiff drink.

"Well I won't turn down the offer, seeing as it's such a bloody long way to come with the post, if you pardon me language," the postman drawled agreeably.

The officer had invited him in for a drink before. The old man knew the young soldier was fond of hard liquor and a couple of shots with a cup of tea had become a requisite for the delivery of the post, whoever met him at the gate. The two men grinned at each other again and the postman pushed his bike along as they headed towards a small bridge which spanned a deep, dry moat and led to the entrance of the defensive enclosure. The moat was roughly fifteen feet deep in places and as many wide and it ran across the front of the fortress creating a barrier which cut it off from the landmass approaching the main wall. The craterous trench went from one side of the rocks to the other severing the man made creations from the natural headland and added to the increasing isolation one felt as they entered the defensive battery.

"No one's about at the moment. Everyone's down on the main road bringing up the new weapon. I'm surprised you didn't see them on the way up," Harding said as they crossed the moat. The postman stopped in the middle of the bridge and looked over the wooden barriers to study the gap from one end to the other.

"I heard a commotion at the bottom of the hill. It looked like it was best left alone. The boys will have their work cut out getting that thing all the way here," he said showing a set of tobacco stained teeth.

"Oh they'll be alright; we're using old Lanes' steam tractor to do the donkey work. The lads are just giving it a push up the hill. Anyway it's about time they did some hard work, get them ready for when the French turn up," Eli replied. He smiled widely showing off a set of well-tended, youthful looking teeth.

"Not much chance of that then," mumbled Patrick, slyly.

The irony was not lost on Elias as he led the postman into the guardroom which was set into the main wall on the left of the gateway. Inside was a narrow space with a simple wooden table and an uncomfortable looking chair under a dust covered window that looked out onto the moat and the bridge. The young man stepped straight through the thin room into the kitchen next door. It was the same length as the guardroom but twice as wide and contained a similar type of table but much larger and with three, more welcoming looking chairs around it. In the opposite corner was a large wooden dresser filled with a selection of bowls and cups made of china and tin along with an assortment of plates, dishes and various cooking utensils. To the side of the entrance they had come through was a fireplace loaded up with gently burning coal and in a recess next to it stood a coal fired range with a large metal kettle sat on top. Along the length of the outside facing wall was a wide wooden worktop with a porcelain sink set into it underneath a large dirty window that looked out across the moat and the rising headland after it.

"Not much of a view for washing the dishes," noted the postman.

"I wouldn't know," replied Elias as he put the kettle on the hob. "I don't spend much time in here, although it does seem warmer than my side of the barracks."

"Ah, that be the privilege of the few, Mr Harding. Warmth comes to those who deserve it most, so the bible may say, and at this time of year it's difficult for even the righteous to find the solace of a warm fire. Maybe your men who bode here are the most righteous ones, don't you think sir," replied the old man with a wink.

"Maybe," Elias said, frowning a little at the poignancy of the statement. "Perhaps I was wicked in a past life," he added ruefully and then waved a finger at the chairs. "Have a seat. Take the weight off your feet. Talking of warmth, I'll go and get my bottle of winter warmer."

He left the room and the postman stood examining the contents of the kitchen and noticed the gently bubbling pot cooking on the range. Elias returned shortly after with what seemed to Patrick was a half empty bottle of rum. The old man pulled a chair out and sat down at the stained kitchen table. He took out a smooth looking wooden pipe and began to softly fill it with tobacco from a leather pouch using thick and wrinkly fingers. He looked across at the food simmering away on the hob and sniffed the aroma of boiling meat which drifted through the kitchen.

"Looks like dinners on already," he said as he finished filling his pipe. "It's awfully quiet and lonely feelin 'ere today. Feels like the gloom sent them all packing I dare say."

Eli searched the cupboards trying to find the necessary products to make a pot of tea. "I think the gloom will send me packing before it does them," he replied a little dismally. Realising he was still feeling edgy from the sudden turn he had on the hillside and that he must be sounding a bit tight, he decided to change tack with the next comment. "How long did it take you to get here? It's a bit of a trek I dare say."

Paddy struck a match and puffed away at his pipe sending thick clouds of sweet smelling smoke billowing into the gloom of the kitchen.

"Ah well, I cum along the paths from Fiddlers Point and crept up from the bay. It's a bit rugged along there and you got to push the bike along but it's quicker than following the road. At low tide we locals know the short cuts across the marshes without coming a cropper in the mud. No one else likes coming up here. They think it's too far. I don't mind though, keeps me out of mischief for the morning."

Eli brought the teapot over, took two crockery mugs and a spoon from the dresser and placed them all on the table. He glanced around the room looking for milk and sugar and saw them on the window sill.

"Fiddler's Point, that's at the other end of the Down, isn't it? I've stumbled out that way a couple of times, always looks a bit treacherous down there. I'll have to take a wonder that way and learn the paths. Maybe visit the village before long. How is village life anyway?" he said changing the subject again abruptly. "Is Miss Danvers well? I haven't seen her since I stayed at the Manor House when I first got here." He thought of the young landlady who had made a pleasant impression on him when he had stayed at the Manor cum guest house in the village before joining the fort. As he pictured her, he fetched the additions to the tea.

"She's fine Mr Harding. You should pay her and the father a visit. Get you off the Down for a while." The old man drew another puff from his smouldering pipe.

Elias took a seat at the table then quickly got up again, as if he'd forgotten something, and fetched two glasses from the dresser in the corner.

He placed them on the table then resumed his seat and carefully poured the tea through an unsavoury looking strainer. Then he took the bottle of rum and filled the two glasses with a healthy draught and immediately drank his down in one gulp before delicately refilling his empty glass. Patrick smiled at his host and respectfully did the same, following it with a sharp intake of breath. Elias, with the pride of a well-meaning servant, refilled Patrick's empty glass then lit a cigarette from his case and took a couple of long drags. Awkwardly, he added milk to both tea cups and politely offered the sugar to his visitor in a scene of distracted but strangely touching domesticity in such dour surroundings. Patch helped himself to a spoonful, then another and then another, before he stirred the contents into a swirling vortex of rogue tea leaves and milky brown, sugary liquid. Eli noticed the tea looked thoroughly stewed.

"Sorry about the tea. I'm not very good at domestic duties," he apologised while taking two quick puffs on his already strained cigarette.

"Looks like Channel water," the old man replied, taking the mug and gulping down a mouthful of the hot beverage. "As long as it's wet and warm, master. Wet and warm. That's all I'm worried about." He screwed up a rheumy, bloodshot filled eye at the young Officer. "If you don't mind me asking, are you alright Mr Harding? Only you seem in a state of concerned thoughtfulness."

Eli paused for a moment and looked at the aged postman sat in front of him. He studied the cracked lines of his elderly face and the close grey stubble on his sagging chin. His eyebrows were long and unruly with a determination to sprout out in all directions like strands of curly white wire. He wore a set of frothy, dust coloured sideboards and as he removed his hat it showed a head of bright white hair grazed short, yet offering the same multi directional desire as his eyebrows. He looked at Elias with sharp, enquiring eyes that belied the tired oldness his face presented. The younger man exhaled noisily and looked away to the dirty flag stone floor.

"Sorry Patch, old man. Don't mean to be miserable. It's just this place, you know. I suppose it gives one too much time to think and all that. What with the grey sky and never ending drizzle, you can get, well, a bit vexed," he said, taking another drag of his smoke. "One never seems to know where one may end up in this particular occupation." He sighed. "It's just the luck of the draw I suppose. Still, I know it's not that bad and I should count myself lucky. I've been in worse places." He looked the old man in the eye and tried to be more cheerful. "It's quiet enough really, which is a good thing in this game. And it is England after all. At least no one's trying to kill you, not here anyway." He smiled slightly, but it disappeared as he looked back at the floor. "We've spent so much time in other people's countries killing other people, it's nice to be in a place where the only danger is tripping over a goat and falling off a cliff," he added thoughtfully.

Paddy sat forward and rested one hand on his thigh and looked at the pipe in his other hand. He took a long puff and the embers glowed in the gloomy kitchen as the smoke filled the room with its hazy fog. His reply was inquisitive yet respectful in its tone.

"You bin in the wars have you master…" he paused a moment. "I'm sorry Mr Harding, you didn't tell me your first name, and I never asked you, I'm sorry to say, even though you bin good enough to make me a cup o' tea and to share your rum an' all that over these past two weeks," the old man rambled.

"Elias. My name's Elias, but you can call me Eli if you like Paddy, seeing as I made you a cup of tea an' all and shared my rum with you, numerous times. And yes I have been in the wars," he said directly, attempting a rum smile.

"Eli. Well I never. What a noble moniker that is, sir. That would be the Hebrew word for height if I'm not mistaken. It is true enough you are elevated to heavenly heights in a place such as Brean Down, Mr Harding, a hillside of peace and solitude, like you said." He took a puff from his pipe and remembered his original enquiry. "Where was your war, only it seems we've had so many recently that I've lost track?" Patrick asked attentively.

The tainted warrior looked through the old man's face to a place far beyond his aged presence and innocuously downed another shot of rum. He inhaled through gritted teeth and tensed his neck as the hot liquid burned his throat, causing a higher pitched rasping. "Afghanistan," he choked in reply, "Bloody place. That was my particular stab at war, Paddy, didn't really agree with me, if I'm honest."

The wise old man tried to focus in the ashen, smoke filled atmosphere and looked at the Officer thoughtfully as he leant back in his wooden chair. "I read it was a most unfortunate place to be, Elias. I am in admiration of your bravery. Too many young men are sent to these unnecessary places only to have an unnecessary death, I feel. I'm thankful you were not one of them." He paused respectfully as if thinking of the dead. "Elias is also a form of Elijah I do believe," he continued, "It means 'Jehovah is God', if I know my scriptures." He looked out of the window as if the gloomy outside light helped him remember the words.

"Elijah heard the still, small voice of God and preached against the wickedness of Ahab and Jezebel. And upon his death, was taken up to heaven in a chariot of fire," he said, as if reciting a sermon in church before adding more caringly, "There are enough wars in the world, and we are involved in most of them for one reason or another and I'm glad you were not taken to heaven in a chariot of fire, if you don't mind me saying, Sir."

The Officer of the fort broke himself off from his alcohol intake, surprised for a moment by the kind words from the postman, then raised his eyebrows and pursed his lips. He took a drink from his by now tepid tea and said mindfully, "Thank you Paddy, very kind of you to say so with such profound words. I should just be grateful to be somewhere quiet and safe, without anyone trying to kill. That's enough anyone can ask for in my profession, even if the weather here is bloody awful most of the time."

"Well, the weather's not always this bad and I don't think you'll get any trouble off our French brethren, Sir. I doubt there's much 'ere he would fancy havin' anyway. And besides with young men like your good self-standing guard over us, he wouldn't have a chance." Patrick the postman grinned with his cracked and lined face and showed his set of crooked tobacco stained teeth one more time. "You should pay Miss Danvers a visit again while you're stationed here. She asks after you, wonders if you're all right up here. You must have left an impression on her after you stayed. I'm sure this fort could cope without you for an evening," he added suggestively in a brighter tone.

The younger man thought for a moment. "Perhaps you're right, Patch. Maybe a bit of time off this rock will do me good." He watched the smoke from his cigarette swirl in circles up to the blanket of tobacco which hung like a grotty chandelier in the middle of the room. "I could always pop into the village later, see when she's free. Offer her the delights of a walk along the prom and an evening in Weston-On-Sea."

"There's many a delights in Weston-On-Sea, Mr Harding, particularly of an evening," replied Patrick with another wink. He drained the last remnants of stewed tea from his cup and then expertly threw back the glass of rum into his mouth.

"One for the road, Patch," asked Eli with a proper smile.

"Don't mind if I do."

And the two men, with a rejuvenated twinkle in their glassy eyes, drank another thick shot of rum from their sticky, scratched tumblers and with renewed energy, the old man tapped the spent tobacco from his pipe into the china ashtray and Eli stubbed out his withered fag. There wasn't much room left for their charred remnants and some old ash spilt onto the stained wooden surface of the table.

"I best be heading back Mr Harding," Pat said. "I've still got some post for the houses further down the coast. Which reminds me, I haven't given you your letters yet." He reached into the pocket on his blue Royal Mail tunic and pulled out a selection of wafer thin letters and a telegram envelope, which was addressed to the Officer in charge of the fort, and placed them all on the table.

"Thanks Paddy," said Elias. "I hope you've had enough of a rest. Sorry about the tea. Next time one of the men should be here, I'm sure they would make a better job of it than me." He looked out through the window. "It looks as though the rain's stopped too. Can't be bad, eh Patch." Both men stood up and Eli stood aside from the door to let the messenger out.

"I hope the weather's not too rough as you keep watch over our shores, Elias. It's much prettier here when the spring comes and that spirit enlivening season isn't too far off now," Paddy said as he stepped out into the gateway.

"I'm sure it isn't, my friend, and don't worry, we don't really do a lot of watching here. There's nothing to look out for really. We're snug as bugs in a rug most of the time. Like you said, the French wouldn't bother us now, it's not worth it. This place is a waste of time as far as invasions go." He shrugged and nodded in the direction of the sea. "The real enemy is thousands of miles away trying to keep us out. This place is just an expensive practice range, which is fine by me. Oh yes, speaking of practices, I nearly forgot," Eli suddenly remembered an arranged firing practice, "When you get back to civilisation just let the locals know there might be a bit of noise coming from here over the next couple of days. Once we set up this new gun we'll be doing a bit of practice with it, just to get her warmed up. I might give the lads a bit of practice on the rifles as well to spice up their day. They can get rusty in between deployments. Just so the locals know World War 1 hasn't started." He grinned.

"World War 1, blimey, I don't like the sound of that! No worries Mr Harding, I'll spread the word. Thanks again for the tea and the winter warmer, very kind sir," the old man said, tapping his nose with a stubby finger as he grabbed his bike and pushed it towards the bridge. When he reached the other side he put one foot on the pedal and gracefully swung the other leg over the saddle and began to gently cycle up the road.

"All the best, Sir," he called out.

"Call me Eli, next time..." Elias trailed off as the old man touched the front of his cap without looking behind him and swayed along the road in a steady rhythm upon 'the old slag'.

"Funny old bugger," Harding said as he watched the postman disappear up the road before heading back inside to the kitchen and flipping nonchalantly through the post on the table. His eyes fell on the officially marked telegram, severely stamped in red with the word 'urgent' across it. Suddenly his muddled brain remembered the flare from earlier and his mouth dropped. "Oh balls!" he swore as he quickly tore it open and read the message intently.

> 'TO OFFICER HARDING BREAN DOWN BATTERY. STOP. VESSEL INTERNED AT STEEP HOLM UNDER INVESTIGATION. STOP. CONTINUE WITH GUN EMPLACEMENT AND FIRING PRACTICE AS SCHEDULED. STOP. KEEP WATCH FOR WORD OF ANY DEVELOPMENTS. STOP. FROM CAPTAIN ACRES, STEEP HOLM BATTERY. STOP.'

He read it again just to make sure then quickly turned back towards his quarters, ran inside and fetched his binoculars. He lifted them off the hook just beside the doorway of his rooms and immediately bounded out onto the gravel towards the gun emplacements on the far side of the courtyard. He paid no attention to the seven-ton gun placed by itself on the edge of the battery and instead looked up to the sky. It was a light, fluffy, grey colour like a blanket of dusty mashed potato, but it held no drizzle now although the gravel courtyard and barricade stone walls were covered in a moist glaze. Eli skipped up the steps and stood on the roof of one of the magazine stores built into the rock of the Down and looked out to sea. He had a clear view of the channel before him and directly in front, roughly a mile and a half out, was the island of Steep Holm. It was short and fat, less than half a mile long and only a quarter wide but it sat in the middle of the Severn Estuary like a huge boulder waiting to trip up some fantastical giant. Elias looked through his binoculars and adjusted his eyes to the close up of the island. He slowly traced his way along the outline until the stone jetty on one side came into view. Moored on the small pier was a tiny yacht with its sails furled, gently bobbing on the grey swell. Eli estimated it was about twelve feet long, capable of handling reasonably rough weather and was the kind of boat that travelled up and down the channel every day either for leisure or business, be that fishing or delivering mail or small goods. Stood on the jetty near the boat were two men in coastal battery uniforms. One of them, as Eli expected with some degree of dread, was the signaller holding his flags, but he wasn't waving them anymore and they were dropped despairingly down at his side. He was being shouted at by the other man, who Eli recognised from the different uniform and peaked cap as Major Acres, the Commander of the Bristol Channel Coastal Defence Brigade. He ran the whole show in this section and was a man of such annoying and headache inducing qualities as to make him unfeasible as a member of functioning society, which was the way Acres seemed to like it. It was also the reason he made Steep Holm island the centre of command. It was his own little kingdom and he could rule it as he wished with only the rare sojourn to the mainland to spread his ghastly influence.

"Bloody Acres, what's he up to now," Eli mumbled to himself quietly. As he watched, the two men turned, looked and then pointed in his direction. He dropped the eye glasses down an inch with surprise, filling his view with still grey water, before suddenly a rowing boat with two seated rowers and another man who was stood up waving at Elias filled the binoculars' viewfinders. The boat was about halfway between the island and the end of the Down heading in his direction and he recognised the man waving as Lieutenant Pontefract, the young and unfortunate second in command at the Steep Holm Battery. Eli lowered the glasses and waved back slowly in reply.

"Oh Jesus, what does he want," he said through a false smile at the approaching boat. As he spoke, for some reason he looked up at the sky expecting the usual mass of grey overhead. Instead, his attention was grabbed by an unusual sight, one he hadn't seen since his deployment here. From beyond the muted leaden sky the clouds began to part gently and light crept warily into the undefined gloom. Gradually, beams of sunshine sliced their way through the atmosphere and hit the water. As they did, they were followed by more heavenly shafts of light which fell in a cascading domino effect onto the tiny rowing boat, the fort and the end of the Down. Looking around, Elias stood in awe as the bright sun lit up Brean Down into an enchanting slope of vivid green grass and brown glistening rock that cut into a clear strip of pale blue sea, which in turn was surrounded by a background of ever lightening folds of bright, creamy grey sky.

"Bloody Hell," Elias exclaimed. "The sun's coming out."

3. Paris

In a side room of the Palais du Luxembourg, home of the French Senate, Prime Minister Jules Ferry stood looking out of the window onto the ornate grounds below. The sun was shining and the enchanting gardens stretching into the distance had a brightness about them which made Jules wish he could go outside and take a walk. The sharply cut, lush green lawns lined with perfectly engineered walkways looked very appealing in the opaque sunlight of the late winter morning. *'Soon it will be spring. Flowers will bloom and new life will begin and everything will become joyful and less ...worrisome, perhaps?'* he thought. However, nothing was certain in today's world of political intrigue, and until then he had some less comfortable thinking which needed to be mulled over. As a result of the present complex deliberation unfolding randomly in his mind, his bald head began to shine in the sunlight, his brow furrowed which made his eyes narrow and his face took on a confused, goblin-like expression. He snorted noisily through his thin, Gallic nose and then turned away from the window.

Monsieur Ferry was waiting to meet someone who would undoubtedly add to his deliberation an increased amount of mental unfolding and the room in which he waited still had some of the decadence associated with a royal palace which also overtly added to the escalating unease he now felt. There was gold everywhere. The edging to the decorative wall features was gold coloured, the doors and windows were framed with gold layered leaf and all the furniture had gold painted detail on it. Above the granite mantled fireplace, a huge, spotlessly clean mirror hung in a frame of painted gold and, dominating the central ceiling space, an ornate three tiered, crystal chandelier hovered like a miniature cloud of gold flecked diamonds. The sunlight which bathed the room reflected off this mass of shiny material and created a flashbulb effect, which momentarily blinded the Prime Minister, causing him to blink as he looked around the room and its excesses. It all seemed distasteful to his Republican ideals and he squinted to shield himself from the opulent glare and wasteful indulgence.

Across the room from the window, in either corner, sat two bronze busts on white marble plinths portraying previous holders of the Presidency of France. They stood staring out with authoritative seriousness. One was of Napoleon whose face, Ferry thought, always had a look of arrogant disregard, while the other was of Marshal McMahon, the predecessor of the present holder of the title, President Jules Grevy. The Prime minister was glad Grevy wasn't in the room, either in person or in bronze form, as the subject of the meeting he was about to have would be best kept hidden from the President's attention. It could get people into a lot of trouble. *'Besides,'*

Ferry thought with amusement, '*when one is busy with a mistress or two, there's no need to be troubled with minor foreign policy issues which can be adequately dealt with by someone else.*' All three heads in the room, two made of metal and one organically human, stared into the centre of the golden space contemplatively, and together they resembled an alliance of disgruntled thinkers mulling over the answer to some unsolved and pleasure sapping puzzle. Jules closed one eye and focused on the two statues. "I wish you two weren't here, either," he said quietly.

The human thinker dropped his gaze from the unsettling, bronzed audience to the large, gold edged study table in front of the unlit fireplace. He focused on the open map which sat in the middle of the table and showed a detail of the South West of England centred near the English Channel and the northern coast of France. Around the map were scattered a selection of documents including officially headed papers and several hand drawn plans and scribbled notes, one of which resembled a detailed diagram of an artillery weapon.

"Crazy English, you're always in the way too. Always you," Ferry babbled, staring down in frustration at the gold embroidered Egyptian rug which the table stood on. Jules began rubbing his bald head before closing his eyes to concentrate. He gently stroked his energetic brown, slightly greying sideburns which shrewdly stopped before they covered his chin and instead grew outwards like weeds looking for new territory, resembling a mass of investigating tentacles. The stroking soothed his mind allowing him to think more clearly and as he stroked he opened his eyes to look up at the wall between the two bronze statues on the other side of the room. Hung there, covering most of the wall, was a large square canvas showing a colour coded map of the continent of Europe including Great Britain, Scandinavia and the coast of North Africa. Although it was grand in scale with fine detail, the oils were thick and blobby in certain places where it had been painted over so many times in the past and the edges looked frayed and worn from the regular re-framing. "How long before we have to change you again, I wonder," the Prime Minister mused aloud.

He looked over France's position on the map, its tone faded and uncertain within the different colours upon the canvas. The dangerous and corrupt world of Europe had become a disorganised multitude of neighbours with fragile alliances. Germany dominated the centre with its myriad of linked countries held together and governed by tenuous, overblown family relations. Constant restlessness among the Balkan nations caused upheaval of demographic proportions and the ever present shadow of Russia hung omnipresent over everyone, waiting to strike whenever the desire took them. Up in the corner looking towards France from across the sea was the arse end of Britain, waiting to shit on someone, a small island used as an almost untouchable base to control events around the world. Hanging in the dark end of the room the canvas felt like a sinister map of interwoven chaos. Each block of colour in cohesion with its partners but secretly, like a double faced psychedelic mirror, plotting against the other to achieve their own financial and sociological gains. There was no common wealth, no universal cause which could hold the factions together peacefully and beneficially. *'We French had it for a while. The revolution brought a common good and we tried to spread it around the world but humanity got in the way,'* pondered Jules in frustration.

Greed and ego became the powers behind the power and Jules Ferry was finally tired of it. He was tired of the fear, tired of the tricks and tired of the jealous stubbornness. It was a stressful job being a Prime Minister and the Minister of Foreign Affairs at the same time in a European Republic and he still had a lot to learn. He'd only been doing it for three months.

Ferry switched his attention from the large map on the wall to the smaller, apparently less demanding one sprawled across the table. Suddenly he looked up into the far corner of the room, an area out of reach from the sunlight which floated in through the window as if suspended on the dust. Straight across from him, dulled by the shadows, was an ornately decorated, gold rimmed chair with plush red velvet upholstery. For a second, he thought he saw a figure sat in it, and wondered if the man he was meeting had quietly entered the room and sat down. But as he looked, he realised the chair was vacant. The room went cold and an icy chill swept over him. Goose bumps formed on his skin and he felt the hairs on his arms rise and stand on end. It seemed like there was someone else in the room. He looked at the bronze bust of Napoleon which was opposite the chair and then to the darkened metal face of a menacing looking Marshal McMahon. Apart from the cold faces of these statues, the room was empty apart from him.

A sharp knock followed by the door opening brought Jules back from this disquieting reverie. In walked a stout middle aged man with a rim of shaved white hair around a balding head and a white bushy moustache upon his face. His name was Jean Baptiste Campenon and at the moment he was the Minister for War, until the next reshuffle came along, which was surely on its way. The unsmiling entrant closed the door behind him and stood in the middle of the room, almost but not quite, to military attention with his arms behind his back as if waiting to be acknowledged. He had been and still was a General in the army and today, although wearing a civilian suit of light grey tweed with matching tie, he exuded the air of a forceful military character. His face was serious and the tone of his voice had an unapologetic directness.

"I'm not late am I?" he said sternly.

"No, of course not," replied Ferry, trying to be pleasant.

"Are you alright Monsieur? You look a little disturbed," Campenon asked without any real concern.

Jules looked at him confusedly and began stroking his whiskers again. He ignored the cold feeling that still hugged his body and regained his composure enough before replying. “Yes I’m fine, thank you Jean, just a little chilled, that’s all,” he paused before setting the next question, “Have you any news?”

Campenon relaxed slightly, walked over to the table opposite his Prime Minister and looked him straight in the eyes. His manner was tense. “I’ve just received a telegram from England. It seems our agent has been caught and interned on a small fortified island in the Bristol Channel. I think things have taken a more serious turn and we may have to do something about it,” he said dourly. There was silence and the two men continued to look at each other.

“Yes Jean, yes we do,” Ferry replied with equal dourness. “But what? What is it we are going to do? It seems your man isn’t the master spy you thought he was. Getting caught has left us in an embarrassing situation and if the President finds out about this we’ll both end up chained to each other in the Bastille prison. I thought this mission had no danger of capture. If I’d known that I would never have allowed it. How did this happen?” he berated lightly.

Campenon remained defiant and kept a stony resonance about his expression before holding his head up and explaining clearly. “He was picked up by a routine patrol boat. It was unforeseeable. The English just got lucky. We still have a man in the vicinity monitoring the situation. He’s close at hand in case we need him.”

Jules Ferry looked at the map on the table and then back to Campenon with a sense of annoyance and anger beginning to rise through him, but before he could answer, the terse General continued, “Besides, according to our other agent, the English don’t know whether he’s a spy or not, as yet. His cover story of just being a tourist, boating in the area may see him through. His English is perfect and he’s an expert in these situations. With any luck the English might just let him go and be none the wiser.” He shuffled nervously on his small feet knowing the spy couldn’t possibly be so lucky.

The Prime Minister noticed the older man’s insincerity and looked at him gravely. “If they’ve arrested him they must have suspicions and if they find out who he really is they’ll interrogate him until he tells them everything he knows. We’ll have to do a lot of begging to get him back, or should I say, you’ll have to do a lot of begging, Jean. It was your idea to send him there and snoop on the English sea defences so it’ll be up to you to get him back without aggravating them too much. I don’t want the damn English having this over us, Campenon. As for the other man, I suggest you tell him to keep his head down. I don’t want him getting caught too.” Jules rubbed his chin. “I suppose if he does tell them about us spying on their defences, it doesn’t really matter, they won’t be that surprised. It’s the grovelling I’m not looking forward to and that’s why you can be the one doing the grovelling.”

Campenon curled his top lip preparing to remonstrate with Ferry but he held his temper and instead began to tweeze his bushy moustache before turning to one side and walking slowly over to the window to gather his thoughts.

"It may not be that simple Monsieur Ferry," he said calmly.

There was a pause and the room was filled with a spicy silence. The general kept looking out of the window as he continued to speak.

"Before he was caught I received a coded telegram from our man with regards to another mission I had given him before he left for England. Prior to this reconnaissance of the sea defences he was to go to London and make contact with a French collaborator working within the War Office of the English Government. That contact gave our agent the names of several English and German spies working here in France." He continued to tweeze. "I always had my suspicions that our Government structures have been infiltrated by our enemies but have never been able to prove it, until now. This collaborator contacted me personally with certain information which has since proved reliable. I have no reason to doubt him. He is a friend of our ambassador and a close aide to ministers within the War Office. His addiction to opium and one of our female operatives posing as a prostitute together with an obvious desire for wealth has brought him, and his knowledge, into our fold. With these foreign agents he's told us about apprehended and in our possession, it would give us a leading edge in any future negotiations with either England or Germany, indeed, it would give us an advantage over several other countries which is something you must admit could be of extreme value for all of us. Knowing the state of a country's defences is one thing, Prime Minister, but if the English find out our mutual friend knows about these spies working in France, they'll pull them out before we have a chance to arrest them and harvest their knowledge. Then we won't have any cards to play with at all, don't you think."

Campenon turned suddenly and looked Jules Ferry in the eyes. The General's face still had a look of determination in it, as did his fingers while they continued to rigorously tweeze his snowy lip hair. The Prime Minister's previously serious face had now been replaced by one of pain and shock.

"English and German spies working in France!" he said with an astonished air.

"In Paris, monsieur, perhaps even within this building," Campenon replied slyly. He had taken the admonishment expected but now it was time to turn the screw on the obviously beleaguered Jules Ferry. There was another plan he needed to pitch to the Prime Minister in order to make good the situation. They were working behind the scenes, making important decisions on behalf of the country without the knowledge of the President, because that was the only way to achieve anything in the presently chaotic administration. The General would rather not have to go through anyone, they only obstructed him, but Ferry was already involved and therefore he needed to have knowledge of what should happen. The old soldier was desperate for the names the informant held, if only for his own benefit, and his arrogance and steely reserve would get him those names, but he had to tread carefully. Campenon turned and strode gently towards the large map of Europe on the wall as if he were taking a stroll in the gardens outside. He looked to the red carpet lining the floor and then up to the map again, as if in deep thought, still fingering his moustache nonchalantly as he steadily began turning the screw a little deeper.

"The trouble with diplomacy, Prime Minister, is it takes too long," he perused as if discussing the subject with someone over a hand of cards. "The game has changed. There's more at stake. The risks may be greater but the rewards could be greater still and I think we should up the ante. In this day and age Monsieur Ferry, it's the secrets you have which can define the power you hold within the world's stage." He said this with an acute smugness at his own political acumen and he studied the map as he screwed further. "If we have these foreign agents in custody and have all the information they own in our possession, then we will be able to bargain at a much higher degree with the British and the Germans, as well as all their allies. Our diplomatic arbitration will be greatly increased. You could be making deals behind closed doors that will put you in a position of power that this country has not seen for many years. Of course, I'm sure there would be information beneficial to my office as well Prime Minister, but only in the interests of future peace, you understand." He turned briefly and flashed a foxy smile across the room before returning his attention to the map and continuing his screw. "We have to get him back, Jules," said Campenon passionately. "Get him back before he is interrogated. Before he is forced to tell of what he knows and get us in the shit!" There was a judged break for effect before he added more delicately, "We have to go and get him."

Jules Ferry's look went from pain and shock to wide eyed discomfort as if he'd just been electrocuted. "Get him. What do you mean go and get him?"

Campenon walked briskly back to the table in an animated manner, ready with his counter strike. "As part of our original invasion plans for Britain formulated many years ago, it was felt necessary to land a small group of men on the mainland to secure the forts which guard the Channel. By controlling the forts, any approaching ships would have been able to land on the important areas of the coast unhindered. We know the defences are often poorly guarded by volunteers, often massively undermanned because of the reduction in the military budget which our agent has already proven, and that well trained troops dispatched from small boats could probably take the forts in the Bristol Channel zone without even firing a shot. I suggest we use part of that plan to go there and kidnap our own spy back," he said enthusiastically.

The Prime Minister's eyes widened further as if the electric he was receiving from an invisible source had been turned up.

"You're mad," he said. "Stark, raving mad. First you come up with this plan to map the sea defences of Great Britain and now it's gone wrong you want to invade the place. You're insane Jean, insane!"

Campenon ignored the accusation. He had seen similar reactions from the Prime Minister before. The panic belied a weakness within Jules Ferry and over the many years Jean had worked with him, in the various councils and government departments of French politics, he had seen how it had affected his decisions. He knew the workings of the man's mind, what weaknesses could be exploited, what buttons could be pressed. Jean Campenon's eyes grew smaller like a predator stalking his prey and he started pressing the buttons whilst at the same time tightening the screw even further.

"It's not an invasion, Jules," he said determinedly. "It's nowhere near an invasion. We'll just be landing a few men on a very secluded island near a very secluded part of the mainland, under the cover of darkness. A few coastal volunteers will be under guard for a matter of minutes whilst we engage the release of one of our citizens, which in theory we have every right to do, and then all of our nationals will leave peacefully and be back in France before any of the population in England even realise. We won't even need to fire a shot. This has been practised by men who know what to do and are ready to do it. It could be done easily and without anyone getting hurt. When it succeeds we will have our agent back with his valuable information and if we do it now the English won't have time to interrogate him and turn this situation to their advantage which is something neither of us can afford, Monsieur Ferry." He looked at the Prime Minister with enthusiasm, eyes shining with adrenaline.

Jules Ferry slumped down in his chair and stared blankly at the map on the table in front of him. The electric had been turned off and he was in a resultant daze. He didn't know what to do or what to say and that was what Jean Campenon had been counting on, so the predator continued probing.

"Our man is being held on an island called Steep Holm." He landed a finger on the map on top of the island in question and left it there as he made his point. "That's where the first incursion, and the release of our prisoner, needs to be made. To make sure the authorities aren't alerted, we also have to land here." Campenon stabbed his finger an inch to the right, all the time studying his fallen prey slumped in the chair opposite. "Brean Down," he said in an awkward English accent. "We have to land there too. That's the part of the mainland we have to secure."

The Prime Minister kept staring blankly at the map and the finger on it without registering either. His arms were flopped over the sides of the chair and he brought one hand up to his mouth to nibble on a thumb like an overfed, tired baby before its bedtime and then whispered in a state of bewilderment, "That could start a war Jean."

Campenon brushed the comment aside with a flick of his wrist and he started pacing along the front of the gold rimmed table, back and forth. "No Jules. There will be no war because of this. I know the British. I have fought them in battle, dealt with them diplomatically over many years. Embarrassment will temper the English. They will not want anyone to know about what has happened regarding either the incursion on their borders or the fact that we will have their agents in our custody. They know that common knowledge of their involvement with the Germans against us on our own soil will cause an angry storm in the corridors of Europe. The Russians, the Balkans, the Arab nations will all be justly concerned with an alliance between Britain and Germany and make future negotiations over colonies and trade very difficult for both countries. Any infiltration by our forces on their land will be brushed over with the kind of bargaining power we will have on our side. They would pay a hefty price to keep this whole episode out of the realms of the rest of the world, the economic and military consequences would be too costly. I believe they have enough trouble keeping their empire in order around the world and therefore it will be the British who will do the grovelling, not us. As I said before, monsieur, the rewards far outweigh the dangers."

Jean finished speaking, stopped pacing up and down and put his arms behind his back, again sticking out his chin triumphantly whilst waiting for the next attempt to dissuade his confidence in the plan of action so he could heroically rebuff it.

Jules Ferry looked his fellow politician in the bushy moustache. He took his thumb from his mouth and scratched his own enormous whiskers. He rubbed his face to try and smooth away the fog of indecision. Campenon had made it sound so easy and without consequences, but deep down he knew there were always consequences, that nothing ever ran smoothly or without difficulty. This was the kind of foreign diplomatic mess he was tired of, the shady back door politics that seemed to be the only way decisions could be made and futures forged. He also knew that in a twisted way Campenon was right. Sometimes the consequences were worth it when compared to the profits that could be made. As a Foreign Minister as well as the Prime Minister he knew the kind of knowledge at stake in this situation would be invaluable to the country. In today's cut throat world of foreign policy, it wasn't how tough you were on the battlefield or how many guns you owned, it was all about how much you knew of your opponents and their weaknesses. Knowledge was the power behind a country and this episode was all about knowledge, as the old soldier had so rightly pointed out.

Jules glanced across at the busts of Napoleon and Marshall McMahon, whose silent faces looked over the intrigue being played out before them. They would have liked to have been involved themselves in a situation like this. *'You wouldn't have grovelled to the Brits, not if there was a prize that could be garnered from being brave,'* Jules Ferry thought.

"What if it goes wrong," Ferry said quietly, weakly attempting to counter the General's argument. Jean Campenon looked him in the eyes with opposing narrowness.

"It won't go wrong," he said confidently, "I have the ideal man for the job. His name is Colonel Castille. He has a specially trained group of Legionnaires under his command who are perfectly suited for a mission of this delicacy. They are based in Cherbourg, have a steamship at their disposal and could be in the area within a day. Our agent could be back in France in just over 48 hours. If anything goes wrong and anyone is captured or killed, which I don't believe will happen, we'll just cut them all loose. Everybody involved. We just say we have no knowledge of their actions, that they are independent of France and without status, merely a group of renegades, Revolutionaries on their own crusade and that the man they have in custody is their leader. We apologize on their behalf and offer recompense, perhaps a beneficial trade agreement with one of our colonies or something of the like, all the while informing the British about our knowledge of a spy network between themselves and Germany. They are as slippery as any of our adversaries and won't want this situation to blow up in their faces." He shrugged his shoulders uncaringly. "I don't think whatever would happen if it did go wrong, would outweigh the prize if it went right," he added.

It felt like a knockout punch by Campenon and the old soldier smiled inside at the fight surely being blown out of the supposedly weak Prime Minister. "This is all just a game to you, isn't it Jean," the knocked down minister replied despondently.

"War is a game Prime Minister. A game where you have to take your chances whilst at the same time be cunning with your losses. I think we have to take our chances in this particular game, sir." Campenon pouted slightly and raised his wispy eyebrows in a final, facial, victory dance.

Ferry looked around the room. It didn't seem so grand anymore. Shadows and darkness had crept into the corners like mould in damp air and the previously sparkling décor took on a dull and hampered sheen. The sun had gone behind the clouds again. It felt like a prison to a trapped and cornered prey that the jaded Jules Ferry had suddenly become. He got up slowly and walked with measured steps towards the huge map on the wall. There was a resigned look on his face and he could feel Campenon watching him as he moved, looking for the final death throes, the disabling indecision, waiting for the moment to strike the cowed creature and make his kill. Jules didn't like Jean. He didn't like his arrogance, his overbearing demeanour, his twisted old soldier view on the world. He didn't like the distrust and inequality of twisted corruption that fuelled the old boner's skewed decision making. He didn't like the feeling the old dog had been turning the screws on him, the Prime Minister of France, pressing his buttons to get him into this dingy corner. And he didn't like the tone of the slimy words that he heard come from behind his back, like the final flick of a spine stabbing knife, subtly administered from a man who thought he had got the better of him.

"If we are going to do this, Prime Minister, we have to do it now. Time is of the essence," oiled the old war pig.

Jules stared at the map on the wall. The brightly coloured countries and borders glared at him with their intricate calligraphy and detailed place names pointing out the dynamics of the countries and the gulf between the societies within them. People had to take charge in situations like this, control the wayward direction that mistake after ill thought out mistake created. The Kings and Queens, Presidents and dictators of countries were what formulated this chaos. It was up to other men, the sensible ones behind the scenes to take a straighter path and resume some sort of order. He was the Prime Minister and he still had the power. The tin pot Generals of the world could still be stopped before it was too late. Smiling to himself and imagining the shock that his final decision would cause, he thought carefully as he rebuilt his confidence, *'No old man, not this time. We won't play your game the way you want to play it'.* He turned and looked at Campenon. The old man's gun metal grey suit matched the steely glare from his timeless pinhole eyes.

"I'm sorry Jean. I won't allow this," the Prime Minister said smartly. "The risks are too great. I will not be held responsible for an international incident that could drag us into an unnecessary conflict. Whatever information this man has he must be left to whatever fate befalls him. There is a chance he may use his guile and end up being released, in which case we will benefit. If not, I will negotiate terms to secure his release and if that fails he will end up in an English prison and we will all have to take our chances and move on to the next game, as you put it. Either way your plan must be shelved immediately, never to be spoken of again so long as I am in office. You are Minister for War, Jean, but there is no war, and until one comes along I suggest you keep yourself out of the way for fear of creating one out of nothing." His voice was raised slightly as he finished speaking portraying his renewed determination.

The general was suitably shocked. "But Minister," he blustered, "you are making a grave mistake. We must take this opportunity. I cannot allow your instability to leave us at a disadvantage."

Ferry's frustrations overflowed into vitriolic anger. "No monsieur!" he shouted crossly, pointing an accusing finger at the General, "It is you who have made the mistake. I am in charge and you will not dictate your crazed foreign policy ideologies to me!" he walked up to Campenon and stood face to face with him. "I assure you, if you insist on this course of action, I will enact the statutes of the senate and have you barred, not only from office but from your military position as well. Do not try to hood wink me, not now, not ever again, monsieur!" he snarled with fierce vigour.

Jean Campenon turned down the corners of his mouth and breathed in noisily through his nose. His bouncy moustache quivered on his lip and he looked as though his head was going to explode from rage but instead he straightened his jacket, smoothed out his trousers and stood to attention.

"As you wish Monsieur Ferry," he barked. "But rest assured the President will be informed about your abandonment of France to the insidious forces of our enemies!"

Campenon pushed his shoulders back still further as if pushing away the insidious forces at work on his paranoia. He felt the coldness of the room suddenly and nodded angrily to the fireplace.

"You should light a fire in here if you insist on leaving the window open and allowing your senses to escape," he whipped snappily. With this final insult he marched to the door, opened it and left the room, slamming it behind him as he did with such force the golden wall and its ornaments rattled along with the golden furniture.

Jules Ferry walked to the table and took a final look at the map laid over it, his chest rising and falling heavily, breathing hard to calm himself down after his own unusual outburst. Inside there was relief at releasing the tension on the man who had created it. He didn't care what happened now, the point had been made. He looked at the island of Steep Holm sat in the middle of the channel and then glanced across at the peninsular Campenon had pointed to earlier.

"Steep Hom, Step Home, Steep Holm?" he repeated awkwardly in English. "Brean Down? What kind of places are these?" he murmured and thought for a moment. "No place to start a war, Monsieur Campenon," he decided.

He looked around the room and this time felt truly alone. Insecurity had crept into his being. He wondered if he had done the right thing, if he had sacrificed the freedom of a fellow Frenchman and threw away the chance of uncovering a dangerous network of spies that put his nation on the back foot. A wave of isolation and vulnerability swept over him causing his nerves to tingle and the overwhelming grandiose statement of the room imbued a sense of foreboding that made his skin crawl. He noticed the vacant chair in the corner and shivered involuntarily remembering the cold feeling he'd sensed from thinking someone else was in the room when there hadn't been. He thought maybe it was just because he was cold and he walked over to the window to close it but looked briefly out across the gardens instead to let their beauty fill his mind with pleasant thoughts again. When he looked at the glass and around the frame he realised the window wasn't even open.

"Stupid old man," he whispered wearily.

Jean Campenon marched forcefully down the corridor away from the gold room with his mouth hair bristling angrily as he stared ahead with an aggressive expression of fortitude. The confrontation he just had with Ferry ticked over in his mind like a mechanically revolving carousel. '*Idiotic bureaucrats will never get us anywhere in the world,'* he decided. *'That moron will find out. He won't divert me from what I know is right and stop me from instigating the actions that I know need to be done,'* he thought to himself angrily.

Emerging through the shadows from within the recesses of the various rooms lining the corridor, a small, wiry, creature of a man with a twitching, rodent like face silently glided up alongside the striding Minister for War. He fell into brisk step alongside the taller, stouter man with graceful timing and the hardened soles of their well-made shoes echoed a sharp rhythmic beat through the empty walkway.

"Jacque," the soldier said to the wiry one as they walked together. "I want you to send a coded telegram to Colonel Castille in Cherbourg. Tell him to enact the plan as discussed immediately. He has 48 hours. Tell him to use whatever force is necessary but don't, I repeat don't, kill anyone."

Elusive Jacque nodded but made no sound and the two men began to descend the stairs to the next floor of the Palais du Luxembourg. As they did so the staccato tapping of their footsteps drifted airily away down the corridor until there was nothing but a deathly silence and a stillness broken only by the sweeping disappearance of a fleeting, non-descript shadow.

Joel the messenger boy stood at the counter of the Cherbourg harbour telegraph office picking his finger nails and hopping from one foot to another. Some might have said he had a nervous disposition due to his constant fidgeting and incessant movement, but it was probably just a case of general disposition in his nervous and fidgeted life. This was because being a messenger boy wasn't his only job at the harbour, although it was always a welcome relief from the other jobs he had, such as cleaning up or being the gofer to whoever frequented the dockyard and required someone to gofer this or gofer that on their behalf. His income relied on tips and the random generosity of sailors, merchants and bureaucrats who would employ him at any given moment. This was probably a good reason for his disposed nature but as he stood at the counter in his ill-fitting shorts and beaten up shoes, jiggling his skinny legs and looking around nervously, there was also an air of excitement in the boy's present character given away by the flash of an erratic smile or the sparkle of a saucer shaped eye. He knew that this particular message would service him with a very good tip indeed, for he had already been promised such by the receiver.

However, the telegraph operator, who wasn't getting any tips from anyone, was being so diligent in the performance of his duties that it felt like time had stood still for the boy at the counter. The small ferret looking man who was the operator, with a pair of cheap wiry glasses on his face and wearing an over boiled shirt on his scrawny torso, sat behind his desk and was double checking what he had written against the inscription on the machine. When he had checked, and checked again that it was correct, he slowly put the message in an envelope and in agonisingly slow handwriting wrote the name of the recipient on the back, a Monsieur Baliol. After what seemed like an age, he finally reached across and handed the envelope to the fidgety child. Without making a sound, Joel snatched the message from the operator's hand with the reactions of a coiled snake, shot out the door, down the outside steps and then through the courtyard towards the harbour area. He ran as only ten-year-old boys do, with precision and agility, darting around obstacles and through alleyways like a cornered rat looking for an exit. Emerging onto the dockside, as all good rats did, Joel encountered the assortment of boats and small ships that clung to the sea wall, tightly crammed together and jostling for space in the still, oil slicked waters of the harbour. All around was the industry of a bustling dockyard. Dozens of busy men, wearing cotton jerseys, frayed woollen jumpers and stained leather aprons were moving and sorting the imports and exports that lined the quayside. Some carried crates balanced expertly on their shoulders, whilst others pushed sack trucks piled awkwardly high with boxes or sacks filled with all manner of goods and consumables. In every direction, heaps of fish, cloth, fruit, china, vegetables, pots, chickens, furniture, bricks, sand and whatever other products were involved in the dealings of the sea, were unceremoniously piled. Joel weaved in and out of the working chaos and ignored the shouts and cajoles of the busy men as he went past, heading straight for the quieter part of the dock at the far end of the harbour. As he turned a corner into a bright open area, the business all around him suddenly stopped, as if he'd been magically placed in a totally different dockyard, and in response to this sudden relief, Joel slowed his eager run to a jogging pace. He headed to a medium sized boat sat at the end of a causeway all on its own. The boat was around eighty feet long and had two masts pointing up from the deck at equal distance from the bow and stern. In the middle was a compact one storey boathouse with a long black funnel coming from the flat roof. Written in small elegant lettering on the bow was her name, 'Marin Corinne' and underneath that, written in even smaller lettering, was a second moniker, 'Le Petit Poisson'. It made Joel giggle a little every time he saw the name of the ship moored on her own in a secluded part of the dock.

The small fish wasn't that small but she didn't look like the kind of vessel that wanted to go on too many ocean going voyages anymore. Bigger than most fishing boats, yet smaller than other steam cruisers, it looked a bit old and battered and too soft hearted for rough seas. Although ill equipped for such journeys, she was relatively fast and friendly to her crew and ideally suited for short regular trips across small stretches of water, such as the English Channel. For most of her life she had mainly visited the ports of southern England, Ireland and Scandinavia with the odd trip to the Mediterranean and was happy sticking to those frequently used trading routes. The small boathouse belied the fact that she had a rather cavernous hold for such an innocuous little ship.

As Joel approached, he noticed a group of fifteen to twenty men on the deck, some of whom were sat on two, long, upturned rowing boats near the front of the ship. The men watched him as he got to the edge of the quay and some smiled and waved in a welcoming manner, so Joel, feeling encouraged, called out in an excited voice, “Monsieur Baliol, Monsieur Baliol, I have a telegram for Monsieur Baliol!”

The man nearest him turned around and looked at Joel with a reassuring grin then coolly threw his thumb behind his head a couple of times. “Come aboard boy, he’s at the back, at the back of the boat, come aboard,” he motioned pleasantly.

As Joel went to scamper up the gangplank, a large, gruff man in a thick navy blue sea coat and a well-worn canvas cap stood in his way.

“No boy!” he grunted, “You’re not allowed on board. I’ll give him the message, give it here,” and he abruptly held out a hard worked hand, ready to take the message.

Joel was a little scared of the sallow looking man but the thought of a decent tip subdued his fears and he held his ground. “Pardon sir,” he said confidently, “But I must give it personally to Mr Baliol because those were his instructions to me.”

The sailor’s face turned menacing but before the stand-off could escalate, another man walked towards the gangplank from the rear of the boat. He was tall and muscular, wearing a cream roll neck woollen jumper and a smooth, welcoming grin on his weathered face. Joel wondered where the man got his tan from at this time of year and imagined that he and his crew had just returned from an adventure in a far off, sun soaked land. Sitting comfortably in one corner of the man’s grin was a heroic looking but actually rather unsightly stub of a well sucked, fat cigar.

“It’s all right Captain,” the smooth man said coolly, “We’ve been expecting this.”

The gruff Captain cautiously moved aside, out of the way of the man who walked down to stand in front of Joel on the platform. The young boy got the impression the Captain wasn’t in command of this ship and admired the bounty of the tanned man’s stature and the forceful nature of his charm. Most adults used Joel to carry out menial tasks for little or no reward, but the man now stood before him had shown the boy a tender respectfulness that he liked. Without saying a word through his own over awed smile Joel handed the man his telegram. Baliol took it, while all the time looking at the boy with shining eyes and a flashing grin. He opened the telegram and read it without fully removing it from the envelope. “Good work friend,” he flashed. “I believe I owe you something, don’t I.”

In a smooth motion, full of cool abandon and expertise, he flicked a one-franc coin from his trouser pocket into the air. Joel caught the coin with equally practised expertise and gazed at the fortune without properly acknowledging what the man said next.

"Remember, if anyone asks about this boat, you haven't seen us, o.k. We don't want anyone knowing our business, eh. There'll be more of that when we get back, o.k. Now off you go and don't spend it on booze, understand."

The man winked at the boy and showed more teeth and damp cigar. Joel gave him a thankful gaze. "Of course Monsieur, merci, merci!" he blurted, before turning around and running away towards the harbour side like the rat who had escaped with the cake.

Baliol walked up the gangplank back to the ship and stood in front of the Captain with an overpowering manner. His cigar, which didn't seem alight, smouldered in his mouth mysteriously and his friendly grin had disappeared.

"Well Captain, it's time we made our move. Let's see how fast this small fish can go, eh," he commanded.

The Captain didn't say anything, just nodded, and the swarthy younger man walked away towards the back of the boat.

"Mr Baliol," the Captain called after him with a certain reproach. "Where are we going?" he asked.

The tall man turned round slowly and grinned again, but this time the expression had an underlying threat of menace.

"The Bristol Channel, Captain. Head for the Bristol Channel." He waited a second and there was only the sound of the waves slapping against the side of the boat. "I'll tell you when to stop," he smouldered, as if the cigar had suddenly ignited and decided to speak for him. The Captain nodded disparagingly.

Colonel Castille stepped thoughtfully to the stern of the ship where he joined two men who were lazily sitting in cotton backed deck chairs. One was a small, stout man with dark skin, short cropped hair and wearing a heavy dark blue jumper. He had a squashed pit-bull dog-like face and from the corner of his thick lips hung a thin china pipe which released a slow trail of light smoke. The other man was much taller and athletic looking, with a tidy, well-tended chin beard without an accompanying moustache. It gave him a studious, even artistic look and in one hand was a baguette smeared with aromatic cheese which only added to the misleading appearance of a sensitive artisan. In his other hand, appropriately, was a small glass of red wine. His shoeless, stocking covered feet rested on top of a long wooden crate and similar crates were led on the deck at the far side of the ship behind the two seated men. These boxes were being used as benches by a handful of other brawny looking males wearing leather coats and thick jumpers, smoking hand rolled cigarettes whilst chatting casually. A few of them glanced at the Colonel with expectant looks.

"Baliol. What kind of a name is Baliol?" enquired the pit-bull with a thick North African French accent.

"One I had to think of in a hurry," replied Castille. He picked up his glass of wine which had been resting on a nearby crate and took a healthy swig. Then he looked out to sea and squinted in the mid-morning sun before speaking as if addressing the metal hulk of the ship rather than any one person in particular. "We're not going back to Egypt yet, I'm afraid. We've been given the go ahead for that little soiree we thought we'd never need to go on. Something's come up and it's time to make our move. We're leaving right away," he said gently.

As if on cue the smokestack on the boathouse coughed into noisy action and soot filled smoke billowed from its opening. Behind Castille, two deck hands pulled in mooring ropes and wound them around metal bolsters. He fleetingly watched them do their work before he turned back to the pit-bull.

"Let the men enjoy the sun while it lasts and then tell them to get some sleep. Tomorrow night might be a long one depending on how this fiasco pans out. I'll brief them on the plan when we're nearer the destination. The less they know the better, until the last minute. Then it'll be too late to change their minds." He ordered this like he was conspiring with the dark dog man, whilst smiling at the men in question who were still sat on the makeshift benches, out of earshot.

There was a minor pause and the pit-bull raised his eyebrows to nobody but said nothing whilst taking a puff from his china pipe. The artisan swallowed a mouthful of cheesy bread and gulped down the last of his wine before examining the empty glass.

"No Egyptian belly dancers, eh, shame," sighed the chin beard. "I better have a couple more of these then, to help me sleep. I never really liked going to England, it always gave me indigestion. Too many English people," he said laconically.

Suddenly the ship's propellers spluttered into action and turned the calm waters around the boat into a frothing green mess as the vessel gently eased itself from the causeway. The sun was still shining through a break in the clouds as the 'Small Fish' smoothly pop, popped its way out of the harbour, through French waters and headed unnoticed into the English Channel.

Later on that day, Joel bought a quart of rum with the payment he received and after a joyous half hour, spent the rest of the night in a bank of nettles sleeping in a pool of his own vomit. The next day, he didn't do any gofer work on account of the raging headache he had and the itchy rash plastered all over his body, but did wonder, in moments when his headache receded slightly, where the friendly man and his mysterious boat had travelled to this time and what adventures they would have when they got there. He decided to ask them all about it when they got back.

4. The Hill

All across the English Channel,
Cold and choppy, as if chaotic rows of underwater pistons were battering the oily, foam flecked surface,
All across the sea, where the land is never far away,
But always beyond your reach,
As you carve a furrow through the creamy, bitter waters so endlessly,
From the mid-morning sun, into the suffocating cloud,
Waiting high and low, blind to the distance, lying all around,
On to another land and a far off hill,
Where strange men are led, tired and exhausted, scattered on the ground,
One man stands alone, looking out upon a second sea,
His hands on his hips, his boot on a rock,
Shirt undone with the sleeves rolled up,
Close cropped hair joins a whiskery whip
That curls round his face across a pair of charmed lips,
The man who should be king!
But he only made Sergeant,
His name was Eves,
Zanzibar Eves!

Zanzibar, what kind of a name is Zanzibar for a man? No one knew if it was his real name, and if it was, no one knew the real reason why he got it. If asked, and he was in a jovial mood, Zanzibar Eves would sometimes tell the enquirer that it was because he had been born there. Otherwise, in less jovial mood, he would tell them to 'mind your own damn business!'

But there was a rumour, circulated by certain men of arms around the mess halls and barrack rooms which the sergeant had frequented during his career, that he hadn't been born in Zanzibar at all, and that in fact he had come from Birmingham. Because of his reputation and stature no one ever confronted him face to face with this alternative theory, so Eves continued the possible truth of his origins with wild stories about his supposed life.

He would tell of his father, who had been a soldier in the British Army. After a deployment in the said country of Zanzibar his father had fallen in love and married a local woman of mixed race who according to local legend had been found wondering the African grasslands under the apparent protection of a herd of wild elephants. She was supposedly a fortune teller who could read the runes of the future from pebbles gathered at riverbeds, and after a tempestuous period of mind altering rune reading and naked engagement, the unusual couple had found themselves with child.

The family then travelled the world together in the caravan of the British army and visited all the corners of her Empire. As a result, Zanzibar the unexpected child had grown up with not so much a love of, but more a habit of, the British army and as a result, conflict in general. It was a habit that continued from the death of his father during the Sikh Wars in the Punjab, and shortly afterwards blossomed following the disappearance of his mother with a mystic healer tribesman, also from the Punjab, which then led to his own joining of the army at the not so tender age of fifteen. The habit of warfare was then honed daily by constant conflict and onwards to this present day until his instinctual knowledge of the workings of war had seen him fight in the Crimean, at Balaklava and Inkerman, through the various Indian mutinies which followed, and beyond, more recently to the Zulu conflict in South Africa.

So it was no surprise that within this child of the army there developed an all-round hardened nature with a cool and reasoned head even in times of extreme stress. It was these skills that had kept him alive during the many battles he'd been involved in and the men he had led into and subsequently out of these engagements realised and respected this. To superior officers he was known as 'a good egg' and could be relied upon, when most of the time superior officers couldn't, to bring soldiers through the fiercest of fire fights with the fewest of casualties. To the men he led, the Sergeant had a worldly wisdom they could not really understand and had never seen before, which only strengthened the rumours of his natural supremacy and supposed mythological upbringing. For those who followed him in times of war and peace he had given off an aura of invincibility and experienced immortality, and in his presence, other men seemed to bow to his wiser judgement and calm superiority.

It helped that he was a big man of course, not fat or overly muscular, just of good stock like the finest bull responsible for fathering a herd of the healthiest cows. He had a strong face covered in gingery whiskers containing eyes that twinkled, animal like, with a wary yet trusting constancy. His head sat on top of a sturdy neck which was above a back that was wide and dependable. His arms were thick and brawny and on the end were large hands that looked as though one of them could gather you up safely in its hold whilst the other knocked down stone walls or devilish guardians that lay at the root of some inescapable finality, so aiding your own, grateful rescue. It was for all these reasons and more that no one really mentioned, at least not face to face, the possibility of his coming from Birmingham.

Regardless of his true origins, after nearly forty years, Zanzibar Eves had grown tired of the habit of war. He was tired of killing people, tired of watching people be killed and tired of waiting to be killed by other people. After returning from South Africa he'd taken the job of a training role within the army and after managing to avoid a stint in the latest Afghan 'carve up' he was frowned upon by his superiors and seconded to the Royal Artillery to help train volunteers in the Coastal Defence brigade. That was why now, in the twilight of his formidable career, he found himself on top of Brean Down, rolling up the sleeves of his shirt and watching the sun break through a previously monotone grey, English winter sky.

"Good gravy sergeant! Look at that!" exclaimed Gosfor, a man of little means led amongst the group of exhausted Coastal Brigade men also led on top of the Down, many of whom had even lesser means than George Gosfor.

"That is called the sun, Gosfor," replied Eves casually as he looked out across the Bristol channel. "We haven't seen it around here for a while, have we?"

It felt like it had been raining for weeks. Although the winter had been mild, it had also been very wet. The land was flooded in many parts of the region. Heavy storms from the Atlantic Ocean had slaughtered the South West coast like a violent atmospheric army at the head of an invading hoard of precipitous cumuli. These tempests had nailed their banners to the coastline and remained, stuck like a plague of pulsating, moisture filled leeches feeding off the landscape, until their united hunger was sated and they moved on to another part of the world to wreak their meteorological havoc. But still it didn't stop. Dark grey skies filled with rolling clouds of unremitting rain followed the storms and the wind blew them on, one after another, across the coast with a scything coldness that kept all living creatures undercover and hidden. The wind seemed to blow on and on endlessly, and brought with it fresh blankets of soaking rain and yet more crushing storms that battered coastlines with monstrous rogue waves and hurtling high tides. Gales roared. The ground was sodden. Streams became torrents through the woods and fields as the rivers overflowed across the county, bursting their saturated banks. All the while, the sea ached under the weight of its own immensity.

Thankfully it had eased considerably in recent days. The driving rain was replaced by the regular atmosphere of windblown drizzle and sharp wintry cold. Glimpses of the sun had been non-existent. So this latest occurrence, as the men of the coastal brigade caught their breath, had a mesmerizing, other worldly sensation about it which bathed the men in a glorious light, renewing their energies and warming their damp bones. On many of the burdened, weather seared faces, a smile had been cracked open like ice splitting upon the surface of a frozen pond.

However, it had still been cold and damp in the mornings, so the men had earlier wrapped themselves in coats for their outing to meet the fort's newly arrived, seven-inch calibre, seven ton Armstrong gun. But now, the emergence of the sun and the result of their previous exertions meant some of the men had removed hats, scarves and gloves whilst also unbuttoning their thickly woven, dark blue cloth tunics. A few had even taken their coats off altogether, just as the Sergeant had done, and were now led in their dirty grey work shirts on the damp grass which aided their cooling down process and helped overcome the trauma of their exhaustion.

"Bless us! I nearly messed meself," spluttered a man called Smales, who was by far the oldest member of the troop. He was also famous for having the loudest sneeze within the detachment and was often responsible for frightening the life out of many of the fortress's incumbents with his shocking nasal outburst's and the accompanying 'ATTCHOO!'

"ATTCHOO!" The old man suddenly sneezed as violently as if he'd just been stabbed, while he gasped for breath in the cold, damp air.

"Bless you!" Gosfor laughed and then animatedly gobbed a thick ball of spit into the grass.

In the middle of the scattered humans led on the stone covered track, stood a steam tractor, panting noisily as if also trying to regain its breath. It was a Garrett 4cd moveable traction engine of the type used on many farms as a substitute for the use of horses to pull medium sized loads and work mechanical field ploughs. But this one, compared to others on the circuit, had obviously seen better days. It was rusting on most parts of the bodywork, which when mixed with its original dull red paintwork created the appearance of the craft being completely covered in brown mud. It also made a lot of uncomfortable noise as if the moving parts on its motor could detach themselves from the structure at any moment and torpedo themselves into passers' by. After pushing its latest load up a fairly steep hill, the machine looked slightly 'over done' and sweated drips of hot water onto the stones of the track while intermittently squirting jets of scolding steam from its tired engine parts. Connected to the tractor was an open backed wooden cart with four metal rimmed wheels, on which lay the thick barrel of an artillery gun. Around the long, bottle shaped iron cylinder of the barrel was an assortment of crates and boxes in various shapes and sizes which contained a selection of fixings and necessary parts relevant to the weapon's final construction.

To the side of the cart, on the grass verge, stood two shire horses exhaling hot breath through their nostrils, as if they too were powered by steam, and were now releasing their excess of vapour as they settled down after the effort of the hill climb. With their long heads drooped down catching their breath, they would occasionally rip up tufts of grass with such easy vigour it seemed as though the limestone rock underneath would come away with the edible covering. Then, the laboured animals would munch on the fodder rhythmically like sailors standing on the dockside of a harbour chewing a ball of tobacco whilst waiting for their next job.

"That were a bit of a bugger, won it Sarge," offered a well set man with a Somersetshire accent. He was sat on the verge near the chewy horses and looked uncomfortably sweaty around his fat face. "Don't fancy doin' that again," he added and then puffed out his reddened cheeks as if to add visual effect to the statement.

"We got one more to go yet, Lumpy. So lap it up you young 'uns, its gonna turn to shit again," replied the King as he looked across to the horizon, where at the end of a slowly disappearing patch of clear white sky, a bright gleaming line of sun drenched, phosphorescent cloud sat on top of a newly darkened mass of vapour rolling ominously towards them like a wave of wet gloom.

"No rest for the wicked," Eves said ineffectually to the bank of cloud.

"We must of bin very wicked then, Sarge," said the puffy man called Lumpy.

Carting the gun up the hill had been hard work for the men, the horses and the tractor, and had been the most difficult part of the gun's journey so far. The weapon, its carriage and all the various hardware which came with it had been brought by train from the Armstrong gun foundry at Woolwich to the main station of Weston-on-Sea, its final rail destination closest to the fort, which although only across the bay was still eight or nine miles away by the indirect coastal road. Armed guards had accompanied the gun on its train journey and once it had been loaded onto the two wooden carts in a siding at the station, three men from the fort accepted the responsibility of security and continued to monitor the iron beast during its travel on the elongated road section towards the fort. The steam tractor pulled one cart containing the heaviest part of the gun; its barrel, and a large section of its mounting, while the two shire horses had pulled a second cart loaded with the rest of the gun carriage and the other hardware. It had taken all morning and over three tanks of steam engine water to complete the journey along the winding, bendy roads that meandered quietly through the countryside towards the edge of the Down. The convoy had been solitary on most of the lonely road, apart from one brief interruption by a local farmer moving a herd of sheep into different fields. Nothing was said during the hold up, just a respectful nod from the farmer to one of the soldiers and vice versa, and a growly, acknowledging grunt from the farmer who owned and drove the contracted tractor.

When they finally arrived at the beginning of the long stretch of straight road which followed the line of the beach and led to the foot of the hillside, the travellers could see Sergeant Eves and the rest of the brigade waiting for them at the bottom of a track. This track worked its way steeply up the side of the Down until, at the top, it became the military road which led to the fort. The journey up that track, which from far off looked innocuous enough, now looked decidedly dodgy once seen close up.

So, the men of the troop had decided, in the interests of safety, to do the journey up the slope in two trips. The first cart weighed more than seven tons and the steepness of the ascent would put the small tractor at its working limit. On the advice of the tractor owner it was calculated that if the two shire horses were used to pull the cart, then the tractor could go behind and push the load upwards, taking the strain off the animals whilst at the same time working as a form of emergency brake. With the use of added human strength and a series of holding ropes it was roundly believed by all involved that the engine, horse and manpower would achieve enough energy to get the heavy carts successfully moved without any serious drama.

The steam tractor belonged to Herbert Lanes, who owned and worked the farmland closest to Brean Down which also incorporated the fields that edged the lower slopes of the hill. His ownership of the traction engine alone meant he was one of the most modern and up to date of the farmers who worked in the area, but his appearance and demeanour failed to show this hidden aptitude for forward thinking. He was tall and wide with a hard face and spoke in a thick West Country tone which at times could be as tart as the local cheese. On his head he wore a brown, corduroy engine drivers cap with a short peak. The hat seemed permanently attached to his body along with the thin dirty green scarf around his thick neck and the leather gators which sat above the tough, muddied boots which also seemed to be externally welded to his large feet.

He was usually surly and quiet, but sometimes prone to the occasional outburst of excited regional dialect, including terms such as 'Go on my lovely!' or 'Get on up there you bloody basturd!' which generally came forth when dealing with stubborn animals and humans or if he was having difficulty with a particularly problematic job which needed completing, like fixing engines or tying ropes.

Still, his behaviour and mannerisms belied the fact that his farm was neat and well managed in what were often difficult conditions and this resulted in a highly productive return which was the reason he owned a tractor in the first place. The farmhouse and yard were simple and plain looking but they had a sturdy attractiveness about them that gave the place a gentle, old world-like, countrified idyll. Its position at the foot of the Down, along with the sometime presence of Lanes' surprisingly young and attractive wife, meant the farm was a welcome and comforting sight in the dark seclusion of the area.

It was her appearance, adorned with the teasingly inappropriate smile she wore, that was now cheering the men up as they waited for the steam tractor and wagon train to pump its way, foot by laborious foot, along the long winded, country road.

"She's a beauty, in't she," commented a lanky young man called Pickles. The farmer's wife was smiling alluringly, as if prompted by the attention of the others, as she pumped water into a bucket from a standpipe in the yard a few dozen or so yards away from the group of volunteers behind her. She didn't get out much, apart from the yard and farm fields, so the sight of the fort volunteers waiting near the gate brought out her flirtatious countenance.

"Don't let the farmer catch you lookin'," said another man with a knowledgeable tone. "He'll cut you up for dinner!"

"I'd like to cut 'er up fer dinner," replied Pickles with a twisted grin. There were a few sordid grunts of agreement from some of the other men and they all continued to watch the enchanting female sideshow.

"Pack it in, you lot!" snapped Sergeant Eves. "Show some respect for the lady of the land. She's a thing of beauty that deserves more than your filthy lechery. 'Ere comes her husband now, so watch your tongues you shits, and just be grateful he's letting us use his tractor to get this ball bag cannon back 'ome!"

They all looked up the road toward the approaching wagon train which was shrouded in a cloud of smoke and steam billowing from the leading engine and added to the drift of faint sea mist coming in from the sea. The noise of the rumbling machine got louder as it neared and the rattling and spitting gave off the impression it was about to blow up as a result of its long journey. It felt like an agonisingly long time before it reached the waiting party at the bottom of the hill. When it eventually arrived, the noise continued unabated whilst the engine came to a sharp, juddering halt as steam bellowed from its working parts and smoke blobbed out of the thin, charred chimney stack poking out from on top of the clunking engine case. Lanes stood up in the driver's seat and nodded to the sergeant, "Mornin' Eves. Bin waitin' long av 'e!" he called out with an amused scowl.

"Not too long, Mr Lanes," replied Eves coolly, before adding with a cheeky smile and a well-aimed wink towards the farmhouse, "We've been admiring the view whilst waiting."

Lanes flashed a look across to his wife who was still absently cavorting in the yard with her bucket. He stared back at Eves menacingly and growled under his breath in a moody manner, "You bloody basturds."

Eves ignored the comment, walked past the farmer and then looked into the cart behind. He turned his attention to the three men sat in the second horse drawn cart.

"No problems lads, everything present and correct is it?" he asked the leader of the men who was sat on the end of the bench: a young, stringy, officious looking volunteer in glasses called Barnes.

"Yes Sarge, all done and dusted, took a while getting back here though, as you could see," the young man said in a well-spoken but soft sounding voice.

"No rush lad, no rush," replied Eves as he continued to peruse the contents of the wagons.

Lanes stepped down from the steam tractor and stared at Eves with a face which reminded the Sergeant of pictures he had once seen showing the rock statues on Easter Island made famous by Captain Cook, all stony brows and hard forehead.

"I'll move the Garrett out'o the way. I got a refill 'er water tank an' get some more coal. She'll need a rest before we make a start on that hill. Youse'll av' to wait a bit longer Eves. You could get yer clowns to 'itch up the horses to this wagon whilst yer waitin'," said the rocky statuesque face.

"No rush Mr Lanes, we got all day. Sure your traction engine will manage this wagon up that hill? We could unload some of it and take it up in more trips, if it makes it easier on your steam machine?" Eves said nodding to the clanking jalopy next to them.

Lanes tensed his granite mono brow. "This Garrett will do al'rite Mr Eves, don't you worry yerself. Just make sure your clowns help out at the same time an' don't get 'emselves in the way," he replied moodily and started unhitching the machine from the cart. Without further comment, once he was done he climbed aboard the tractor and opened the steam valves whilst at the same time releasing the brake lever. The contraption moved off noisily, hissing and popping its way towards the farmyard pump and his delicious looking, innocently playful wife.

Eves turned to his men still sat on the second wagon looking aimless. "Get those horses hitched up to this wagon!" he ordered before turning to the other troopers, who were still dumbly stood around by the gate. "You lot! Get those ropes tied on to this cart! Get a couple on the chassis and one on the axle!" he shouted and the men straight away stopped gawping at the steam tractor slowly moving away and instead started clumsily fiddling around with ropes whilst trying to look busy.

Farmer Lanes parked the tractor by the standpipe in his yard and left it to idle gently with a steady fizz and dangerous bubbling sound. He turned sharply to his wife, who had stopped filling her bucket and now stood looking at her husband nervously.

"Bin makin' a spectacle of yerself in front of the soldier boys 'av we," he said venomously as his wife switched her eyes to the ground like a told off child and then quickly picked up the half-filled bucket.

"I jus' come out fer some water, I didn't know those idiots were stood 'ere," she said defensively.

"Ah well, why don't you go back inside an' get me sumthin' to eat an' a bottle of cider to drink instead of dancin' around 'ere like the farmyard fairy. I'm starvin' 'ungry after all that travellin'."

He watched her walk away obediently towards the house, her pretty hips swaying softly as she walked, fresh mud splattered around the bottom of her skirt and along the visible hem of her petticoat. He was immediately struck with a pang of guilt at being so snappy with her. It wasn't her fault she was such a fine looking girl with a shapely figure. Her pretty features were few and far between in these parts and he knew he was lucky to have her. But he also knew his jealousy was hard to control whenever other men noticed that attractiveness. It was lonely out here and if other people were around she had the tendency to be charming and a little flirtatious to achieve some attention, but Lanes was confident she would never be enamoured by the approaches of another man. He had never been violent towards his wife but he kept her in check with the sense of fear and threat of retribution that his moodiness seemed to portray. For her part, she respected this side of his personality and in some ways was attracted to his manly over protectiveness. He was far from being an ugly man, just a bit fierce looking and sometimes, in his less moody moments, Herbert Lanes could be engaging and funny in an unchallenging kind of way. She knew in this area of the country she could have done a lot worse.

But the soldiers of the fort always wound Lanes up when it came to them invading his farmland, especially if they looked at his wife. He didn't like the fort on the end of the Down and was one of the many in the local population, and for that matter across the country, who felt the coastal sea defences were a waste of time and an unnecessary drain on money and valuable resources. The threat of invasion had disappeared decades ago and the presence of these men and their weapons were an unwelcome distraction to the working land and the routine of his farm. If it wasn't for the fact they paid him so well for the use of his tractor, carts and horses when they needed them, Herbert Lanes wouldn't have anything to do with the folly fort and the clowns who manned it.

Across the yard, the fourteen men of the Coastal Defence Brigade were busy hitching the horses and tying ropes to the first of the wooden carts which was pull the heaviest of the loads up the hill to the plateau of the Down. The ropes would be used to help steady and brake the momentum of the wagon should the horses and the steam tractor lose grip and slip on the wet, stony track of the slope. There were also large wooden chocks, carried by the men and specially made for the purpose, which could be thrown behind the wheels should the wagon begin to roll backwards.

Eves started talking to the scholarly looking young man he had spoken to earlier. Robert Barnes was the volunteer used by Master Gunner Harding and the Sergeant to do anything that required the slightest ounce of intelligence, as the rest of the Brigade was sadly lacking the skills to do anything in the realm of administrative or officious tasks. He was a smart young man in his early twenties who worked in his father's accountancy business, but became a part time Coastal Defence volunteer so he could get out of the stuffiness of office life occasionally and indulge in a change of scenery. Shooting large artillery weapons and generally playing at soldiers without the threat of actually being killed was a welcome distraction from the day to day tedium of accountancy apprenticeship. As they spoke, Eves was looking at the manifest of the weapon parts and the contents of the accompanying paperwork.

"I ticked everything off, Mr Eves. Took a while, but it's all there," said Barnes.

"Good work lad. I would have gone along, but I couldn't bring myself to deal with Lanes all this time. His moods would have brought me down, methinks. Besides, someone had to keep an eye on this rabble," replied Eves as he gestured towards the motley crew fussing around the wooden carts. "As soon as he gets back with that jalopy, we'll get this circus show on the road. I want to get it all up that hill before the sky starts tipping down again."

He turned to the horses and soothingly stroked their soft necks. "Ready for this next bit, boys? Let's see if we can't get you something to eat first, eh," he whispered. The whisper turned to a sudden bark aimed at one of the men fussing around, "Pickles lad! Seein' as you like the look of Mr Lanes' wife so much, why don't you get these horses some water and a bag of oats to give 'em some energy before we climb that there, bastard hill."

Pickles jumped round. "Yes Mr Eves, be my pleasure," he chirped and grabbed a bucket and the empty nosebag from the back of the wagon before scampering lankily towards the farmhouse. When Pickles reached the standpipe, Lanes was still filling the tractors' water tank

"Alrite, Sir? Sergeant Eves wondered if we could get the 'orses some fodder, theys is lookin' a bit tired, like," he said in his droopy local twang.

The farmer stood upright, stared over the lanky soldier towards Eves in the distance and grunted offensively. Then he fixed the younger man with steady eyes, whilst bellowing loudly towards the farmhouse, "Alma! Alma! Where's that cider!"

As if in response to the call, his wife came out holding a bottle of cider and carrying a plate with a thickly made sandwich of cheese and bread placed unceremoniously on it. She put the two items on the step of the tractor, still chugging away but now with a smoother resonance, and looked at the two men shyly. Lanes caught her with a steely glare and said grouchily, "Fill this nosebag fer the 'orses and the young 'un 'ere will feed 'em. Quick now, mind!"

She flashed a crafted smile at her husband and swept away towards one of the barns, nosebag in hand. "And get me a bucket of coal while you're at it!" her husband shouted as she moved off.

"I'll give er a hand if you like Mr Lanes," Pickles piped up bravely.

The farmer shot him down with a nasty, threat filled look and growled like the grinding of a broken machine. "You stay ere, boy! She'll be alrite. I won't hav' the likes of you stumblin' round the farm, breakin' everythin'."

Pickles tried to smile but instead withered backwards as Lanes reached behind and grabbed the bottle of cider before taking a long, thirsty gulp, all the while still staring menacingly at the lanky youth before him. He then released Pickles from the intimidating stare long enough to sit down on the step of the steam tractor and take a bite from the giant sandwich, before beginning to chew mechanically on the mouthful of stiff bread and hard cheese. The stranded Pickles shuffled his gaze around the farmyard awkwardly but couldn't help noticing that Lanes continued to look at him with dark, squinting eyes and that in between the farmer's bites, a sinister smile was beginning to manifest itself on the edges of his large, cheese filled mouth. The atmosphere was comically tense and in an attempt to soften the edges, Pickles said stupidly, "Nice day fer it, Mr Lanes," even though it blatantly wasn't.

Through a full facial orifice of damp bread and spitting particles of cheese chunks across the yard, Lanes replied sarcastically, "Not really, is it boy?"

Pickles made a face as if someone had stood on his toe and resumed his nervous shuffling whilst looking pleadingly to the barn door in a desperate hope that Mrs Lanes would appear and ease the situation. Her husband continued to glare at the lanky young man, his mastication gradually easing, and he swallowed enough of his mouthful of food to present an adequate amount of menace in his tone, before saying quite deliberately with just a hint of a snarl, "You not bin lookin at my wife along wiv all your mates, 'av 'ou boy?"

Pickles nearly shit himself. Suddenly, the nonchalant comment from earlier regarding the boy being eaten by the farmer came alarmingly into his head. He fearfully looked at Lanes who had begun chewing again on another mouthful of sandwich and Pickles imagined it was one of his own lanky limbs being scoffed by the giant farmer. An image of his head on a plate with an apple in his mouth like a stuffed roast pig upon a banquet table came to his mind and it was all he could do to stop himself laughing nervously. "I wouldn't dare do that Mr Lanes, you'd 'av me fer breakfast," he blurted out uncontrollably.

Lanes grinned wider, "Not enough meat on you, sunshine! I'd choke on all them there bones!" he said cleverly through sandwich smeared teeth.

"Too right, Mr Lanes! You'd be pickin' my bones out of yer teeth fer a week!" Pickles squeaked.

Thankfully, or unthankfully, Pickles wasn't quite sure which, the farmer's wife emerged from the barn with a full nosebag in one hand and a bucket of coal in the other and wobbled sexily towards the two men. The younger man made a conscious effort not to look at the approaching woman and instead glanced over the farmhouse in front of him, as if looking for a facet of architectural interest to point out to the dowdy owner. Alma Lanes handed the nosebag to Pickles and he momentarily caught her eye. She smiled politely but without any flirtatious aspect and then added quickly in the manner of a stern school teacher, "Make sure you share that bag between the two of 'em, we don't won't one of 'em gettin' wind when goin' up that bloody hill."

The young man focused desperately on the nosebag and he tried to nod a thank you in her direction before turning hastily around to make a quick exit. He was stopped dead by the threatening voice of farmer Lanes. "Hang on, young 'un. Havant you forgotten somethin?" he growled.

Pickles turned round slowly and looked at the farmer who was washing down the last of his sandwich with the rest of the cider while his eyes teasingly bore into the tall, young man. The big farmer then motioned with the empty bottle of cider to the still unfilled bucket Pickles had originally brought with him. "What about their drink? They'll be thirsty," he added disquietingly.

"Oh ah, forgot about that," Pickles shakily replied, looking at the bucket underneath the tap of the standpipe as if it was a thing of great desire and the only object left in the world that could get him out of there. Pickles raised his spare hand and slowly worked the pump arm. The water splashed out in large globules inside the empty vessel and there was a tinny splattering sound with each push of the handle. His nerves and the overloaded tension of the edgy atmosphere made Stanley feel like he was going to explode and he lost the ability to control his actions. Without realising what he was doing and with no thought as to why, Pickles looked drunkenly to Lanes on one side of him before turning his head slowly around to look at the man's wife on the other. A stupid lunatic grin slid across his face at the absurdity of the predicament. Alma looked almost apologetically at Pickles in return and they both smiled sadly at resignation of what they knew was undoubtedly about to happen next. Either as an act of defiance or just because he couldn't help it, he took a momentary glance at Alma's breasts, which although well covered by a thick woollen jumper and outer coat, were large and shapely enough to allow a sensuous outline through her clothes.

It was then the mood changed from one of farce to one of certain, unavoidable aggro-filled chaos. Herbert Lanes' fragile grip on the tenuous control of his anger slipped and the air crackled with electricity as he stood up and grabbed Pickles by the front of his undone tunic. The big man pulled the lanky youngster away from the standpipe and brought the boy's shocked face up to his own, breathing over him with a mouth gas of cheese bits and cider. His mono brow had dropped and it cast a dark shadow across his rocky expression. Pickles let the nosebag fall to the ground, spilling its overfilled contents onto the mud.

"Hang on Mr Lanes," he squealed helplessly. "That's a bit strong init, I was only sayin' thank you!"

"Youse is starin' at my wife in an unmannerly way, you bloody nobskin," grunted the big farmer angrily, raising an arm and preparing to strike in a release of pent up aggression.

"Steady on Mr Lanes, settle down now. I don't think the boy meant any harm."

The voice was a forceful but reassuring one that came unexpectedly from beyond the two men by the tractor. It was Eves. He had come over to try and hurry the farmer along and had arrived in the nick of time for the unfortunate Pickles, who had gone limp under the grip of his attacker, who in turn, gave Eves a look of stifled anger and frustration before dropping his gangly victim into the wet ground.

"The boy should keep his eyes in his head, instead of drippin' em all over my missus," he said snarling. The air crackled like a testy firework unexpectedly exploding at a bonfire party, then immediately defused like a shower of sparkles disappearing into the night sky. Lanes and Eves stared at one another. They were totally different characters and although they didn't like each other, there was a mutual respect between them arising from the appreciation of the skills and standing they had both achieved in their respective fields of expertise. There was also the unspoken understanding that undoubtedly occurred between all men of size and strength. They were both big men and any fight would be a messy one.

"Get yerself and that fodder back to the horses and look sharp about it," Eves ordered Pickles whilst keeping one eye on Lanes. The straggly young man scrabbled up, grabbed the nosebag and half full bucket of water and stumbled away to the rest of the Brigade. There was the faint sound of derisory laughter as he skidded his way through the mud and across the yard. Eves looked plainly at Lanes and his wife before nodding to the woman respectively.

"I apologise on behalf of the lad for any misunderstanding," he said.

"That's quite alrite Mr Eves, no harm done," she replied quietly, returning the nod. Eves turned to her husband who was still sneering angrily under his darkened brow.

"Let's try to get this done, shall we Mr Lanes. Then we can all get back to what we're supposed to be doing. Don't you agree? The horses and wagons are ready. We're just waiting on your engine, sir. The quicker we get this done, the better, eh. I'm sure you got more important things you need to be doing." The calm but commanding tones seemed to slightly soften the hot head and fiery temper of Herbert Lanes.

"Ay," he grunted in reply after an airy, thought filled pause. "I'll get some more coal," he said, turning sourly away. Lanes took hold of his wife gently by the arm and walked her with measured steps back towards the house whilst grinding his teeth and muttering angrily under his cider imbued breath about how one day he'd 'like to kick that fort off the end of the Down with all those bloody basturds in it!'

The stony, mud splattered road was gradual at first and the horses that pulled, and the steam tractor that pushed at the heavy carriage found the going easy enough to begin with. Half the men of the troop plodded behind in a straggling guard of honour, two holding the wooden chocks and absently taking in the countryside, whilst a few others watched jumpily as stones kicked out from the rims of the revolving wheels. The remainder of the men walked with the horses, pulling on their reins to coach them on, or trudging a few yards ahead holding the gathered up ropes, ready to lash them around the short trunks of the stumpy trees that lined the slope, hoping the gnarly growths would hold the weight if required in time of need. Eves paced to one side, next to the hill, supervising the whole scene with his silent and reverential power.

Twenty yards on, the track began to rise much more steeply and the waist high brambles and thorny bushes on either side seemed to darken, enveloping the slope in a shadowy green tunnel. The rise was unnoticeable when looking up the ascent from the bottom, but actually walking the track meant it soon became physically apparent.

The horses began to tire within seconds and the wagon they pulled obviously slowed. The steaming tractor behind took the strain and pushed against a slowly disintegrating hay bale which was hung from the back of the cart to act as a buffer between it and the front of the tractor. The machine showed no signs of viewable effort, apart from its usual cacophony, which allowed the wagon to continue on its upward journey without serious drama. But inevitably, the carriage with its heavy load did begin to slow to a snail's pace.

"Get on up there, you bugger!" shouted Lanes as he opened up the steam valve a little more to boost the pressure. It made the tractor push hard against the reinforced wooden back of the wagon making it lurch forward markedly as the horses took up the sudden slack. Eves looked worried by the immediate forward roll of momentum. "Stay alert there men! Keep an eye on those wheels!" he bellowed.

They were barely a third of the way up when the wagon shot forward again, this time by several feet, sending loose stones skidding from underneath the thin knobbly tyres of the tractor, causing its grip to give way and the wheels to excitedly spin out of control. The horses spat as they heaved, suddenly burdened by the increase in weight as the engine behind them came to a stop, their strain showing in the hot breath which squirted from their flared nostrils like dragon's fire on scolded water. The tractor steamed erratically, its wheels span crazily, and slowly, the Iron Beast ahead began to roll back.

"Stand fast!" shouted Eves. "Stand fast! All hands!" he demanded.

Panic bolted through the whole troop and the men at the back of the train jumped forward pushing the cart at the corners, either side of the hay bale, some with outstretched arms, other's using their backs and shoulders. Eves instinctively grabbed the thick spokes of one of the front wheels and held it with all his might, trying to stop it from turning. The men pulled on the horses and the cluster of straining wagon handlers helped to halt the creaking beast before any momentum could send the cart careering back down the track.

"Get a grip on, you bloody basturd!" Lanes shouted gravelly as he worked the steam valves trying to get the traction to find some purchase on the greasy stones. Then, as if answering his profanity, the wheels caught on the slope and the tractor tumbled forward hitting the back of the carriage and its straw bumper with a woody crack, pushing it onwards and heaving the Iron Beast into movement once again. The men at the back jumped to one side to avoid being crushed and slipped into the mud.

"You bugger, you!" screeched Lanes, half laughing, half growling as he maniacally worked the steam engine from his raised position like the demented Captain of some ridiculously small, unseaworthy, boat-like contraption. The horses were able to ease back, as this time all the men used their strength to slowly roll the cart up the steep roadway and so help the tractor to force the heavy load onward; a human back up to the scraping rattle of the overheating push from the taught traction engine. With each step the slope steepened, with each breath the human engine seemed to tire, increasing the burden on the steam engine and the horses; with each squirt the tractor seemed to suddenly struggle. But every few yards the precious oxygen and spurts of energy required were gathered in the disjointed mix of animal and man-made machine. Tunics were loosened and hats were used to soften the chaffing of flesh on hot wood and sharp metal. The men looked set to burst and the horses would have dropped to their knees without the steadying human hands that held them. The monster whined as it ached upwards. Onwards it crawled, painfully slow like an injured animal, every inch quivering and breathing heavily so it could equip itself with the necessary energy. Farmer Lanes whooped with a previously unknown animation as he rode the creature on.

Before them a dim light emerged through the tunnel of hedgerow and the road gave way to open sky. They were nearly at the top. The thought of water to wet their dry mouths pushed them on. Fresh air in their tired, aching lungs stimulated their final actions. They were only yards from the top of the hill, when suddenly, the tractor hit a patch of soaking grass and mud and began wildly skidding backwards.

Without the pushing power at the rear, a gap opened up between the cart and the engine which had started sliding helplessly back down the angled road. The horses, unable to take the sudden weight, immediately let go of the strain and staggered shockingly to one side with the carriage lurching violently behind them. Sergeant Eves shouted out, "The chocks! The chocks! Hold it! Hold it, all of you!"

It was the speed and strength of one man that saved the caravan of wagon, horses and desperate humans from sliding across the track and tipping over the side of the hill to the inevitable carnage of atrocious physical injury and possible death. Gunner Grayard Evans was a tall, athletic man of maybe thirty or more (his age was something he hadn't really kept a proper count of) with a rugged face and a hardened nature, like that of a matured and well-crafted tree. He was watchful and contemplative and wasn't a man who enjoyed taking control, preferring to leave that to other people. But when, as so often happens in life, those people couldn't be relied upon, he would feel inclined to take the responsibility upon himself and control the situation as quickly as could be achieved with the least amount of fuss. He was an unassuming creature and although prepared to take the shit with the wind, in the end, he just wanted to be left alone and lead a quiet, unburdened life.

Grayard had seen the threat of what could, and was about to happen and had already picked out the nearest thickest tree in preparation long before the tractor had started to skid. When it did and the horses had been let down, and while his Sergeant struggled to control the lolling sideways momentum, he had bounded to the relevant nearby tree he thought would take the weight, secured the rope he held around its minimal trunk twice and held on, using his feet to push against the tree and try to steady the slipping cart without busting the thin staff of nobbled wood. Luckily, it took the strain long enough for the two chock men to wedge the wooden blocks behind the rear of the wheels and halt the cart. This allowed the lurch of the carriage to falter and after swaying for a few agonizing moments, it miraculously held firm.

"Quickly, get the other ropes tied off up ahead!" shouted Zanzibar as he held the front wheels with wide bulging arms. All the men closed their eyes and gritted their teeth as they held on. The two other rope men ran to the crest of the hill like panicked mice and tied the two remaining ropes to whatever anchors they could find, which ended up being two short and crooked, but well rooted entanglements of gorse bushes. Over the creak of tensed bindings and the groans of straining men, the clunking, whistling sound of the steam engine could be heard as Lanes struggled to work the brake of his machine. He had halted the skid, but there was a look of panic in his rock hewed, distorted face as he tried once again to inch the tractor forward.

"Bloody, bloody basturd!" he screamed. The manic cursing mixed with the whistle of the steam engine seemed inconsolable as the wheels finally found a groove within the sloughy track and the whole contraption shot sharply forward, quickly making up the space between it and the cart. The engine clattered into the wooden back, just missing the remnant of hay bale which had now slipped in the commotion and the collision nearly resulted in crushing the skinny body of Stanley Pickles as he unwittingly pushed against the back of the wagon.

"Get on up there, you basturds!" Lanes hooted. "Watch out you stringy bugger!" he whooped as the whole train jerked up the slope. Eves put his huge shoulder to the wooden monster and shoved. "Push men! Push!" he called to his gathered throng.

The horses were pulled and the ropes slackened off. The men in one mighty movement pushed against the wall of wood they were wedged into and slowly the obtuse creature began to heave itself to the top of the stony road. The ropes groaned, metal scraped, men shouted as the agony of exhaustion set their heads ready to burst. Hearts pounded in chests, hands and faces wept, cut raw against wood and hemp. Pickles began to cry with exhaustion and emotion.

Finally, the undergrowth opened up onto the top of the hill. First the men pulling the loosened ropes reached the level, stumbling forward as the slope faded. Then the horses staggered over the top and their straining gave way to a sudden burst of speed as they reached the flat and the incline no longer impeded the animal's movement. They trotted coolly to the left as the track became the Military road and turned to face the sea along the summit of the hill. The Iron Beast lurched after them and rolled easily over the final rise taking the immediate corner in the road as it did so. The men behind suddenly had no wall to lean on and with comical timing fell to the ground in a human mass of sweaty hotness. The tractor rolled on afterwards, missing the men by luck and a matter of inches, until it too finally spluttered to a halt just past the stationary wagon and horses.

Eves stood at the side of the road, bent over with his hands on his knees, breathing heavily, his round, blue artilleryman's hat all askew. Around him the mass of crumpled men untangled themselves from each other and crawled to the edges of the road. They spat as they desperately gulped in air to refill their burning lungs, each one sapped of energy, choked with a lack of air and moisture. Pickles and another man vomited over the brambles, bringing up their breakfast in glorious globules of spit, bile and half-digested porridge.

Lanes, still stood atop his raging tractor, looked behind him and grinned annoyingly at Eves who was now stood upright drawing in long, deep breaths through his curly moustache. "I think we'll make that second cart a bit lighter, don't you agree Mr Eves!" Lanes called out. He laughed crazily, in tune with the bubbling rattle of his pissing little steam engine, as the rest of the men coughed and choked their way over the damp grass at the top of the Down.

On the end of the peninsular, oblivious to his men's exertions, Harding watched as the little rowing boat nodded its way towards the rocks near where he was standing. The craft was being carefully controlled, but with an added degree of necessary hastiness, by two concerned looking oarsmen. Sat between them was the eager but slightly frightened looking figure of Lieutenant Pontefract. The stretch of water between the island and the Down was relatively small, but was still considered a hairy journey by the Coastal Brigade volunteers when done in small row boats. This was even on calm days and especially only a couple of hours after high tide when the sea was rapidly receding. Thankfully the weather wasn't too shit today but Elias wondered what was so urgent that Major Acres had sent a boat over, as it was rarely required except in the most extreme of emergencies. But whatever the reason, he was just glad it hadn't actually been Acres on the boat, looking to spread his misery on somewhere other than his own precious Island.

Oliver Pontefract was a young officer of only twenty-four years old. Brought up by a well off, middle class family in Gloucestershire, he hadn't been the sharpest knife in the family picnic basket. Even after a public school education, he had shown little aptitude for the worlds of finance and medicine that had been the usual avenue for other members of his family. As a consequence, Oliver had scratched a way through the Artillery Officer training school in Aldershot, paid for by his accountant father, who was anxious to see his youngest son in some sort of career that made the boy less of a drain on his own well-ordered financial responsibilities whilst also getting the lad out of his ever thinning curly grey hair. Oliver showed enough endurance to gain his commission as an Artillery Officer but his senior commanders felt it would be best to keep him away from any action abroad, in case he was injured, or even worse got killed whilst managing to injure or kill any number of his own men at the same time. They thought that his talents would be better utilised somewhere peaceful and mostly unpopulated. So in an attempt to try and roughen up the overly smooth edges of his soft temperament, he was made the second in command on the Island of Steep Holm, under the brutal stewardship of Major Erasmus Acres.

Oliver was a friendly and well-meaning sort, but prone to bouts of confused indecision mixed with large doses of clumsiness, which made one wonder how he had managed to secure a commission, although even in this modern age of Army careers money still did the talking. But Elias Harding found his colleague's oafish nature charming and funny and felt anyone stuck on an island controlled by a psychotic delusionary obsessive like Acres had the right to be shown a great deal of respect.

As the boat nosed its way next to the rocks, Pontefract was caught by one of these sudden doses of ill thought out clumsiness and he stupidly stood up in the jostling swell of the receding estuary tide, saying in a loud and jovial voice in an attempt at a seafaring joke, "Ahoy there shipmate, permission to come aboard!" This caused the boat to wobble precariously and the two oarsmen had to quickly grab the rocks available on either side and prod the water in between cautiously with the oars to steady the little row boat. One of the rower's retorted angrily to Pontefract in a clipped Southern country accent, "Hang on sir! Let us steady her before ye go standin' up, otherwise we'll all end up swimming in the soup!"

Pontefract was caught off balance by the swaying of the boat and was suddenly unceremoniously tipped forward towards the rocks. He managed to grab hold of them and stop himself falling into the soup, before gingerly stepping up onto the flattest looking ones and cautiously using them as stepping stones towards the firmer mainland where Elias was stood waiting to greet him. As the clumsy young man clambered along the rocky headland Eli thought the Lieutenant resembled a frail old lady on her hands and knees trying to crawl up steep stairs on the way to the bog.

As Pontefract made his way across the rocks, the oarsman in the front of the boat worriedly looked around at the clashing waters of the tide and said with a tone of annoyance, "Better make this quick Mr Pontefract, we gotta get goin before the tide turns too far an' we get's sucked out to sea on the way back. We only got a couple of minutes, mind."

"Don't worry, this won't take long," came the still jovial reply as Pontefract finally stood up on the grass with a pale and slightly queasy looking complexion. Eli went to meet him and the two officers shook hands while Pontefract took a moment to regain his composure.

"I say Harding, that's a rum trip across there, it's enough to make one bloff up their breakfast," he said with his plummy public school accent.

"Bit nasty isn't it Ponty, even when it's calm. Still, what's the old man got you doing it for anyway," asked Elias, smiling with disguised concern.

"The old man's hopping mad over there. We've been trying to get your attention for the last hour. Poor Symonds has been waving those flags like his arms on fire. Acres sent me over to see what was going on. He's too tight to use any more flares."

Harding apologised, "Yes, sorry about that, I sent all the men to collect this new gun, I think they're having trouble getting it up the hill. Anyway, I was doing paperwork when I noticed the flare," he lied, "then the postman turned up and I forgot all about it. Do you mind keeping it to ourselves Ponty, only I don't want the old man finding out? He'll give me a right earful."

"Don't worry old boy, I'll keep him off your back. Besides he's got plenty to keep him occupied. Did you get the telegram he sent this morning?"

"Yes. I've just read it. They brought it up from the village as soon as they got it. What's he doing pulling in innocent boaters?" Eli asked with a quizzical expression.

"Old Acres wanted a firing practice, so he went out with the steamer to clear the area and bumped into this poor blighter on his yacht. For some reason Acres got all suspicious, said this chap had maps with all the battery positions marked on them. I don't think there's much in that but Acres got all over excited and searched his boat and ended up finding a pistol. He interned him until further investigations were made." Ponty raised his eyebrows and leaned in closer to Harding, speaking as if relaying a secret to a fellow conspirator. "He reckons the pistol he found was the same as the Frenchie's use," he whispered.

"Bloody Hell," Eli whispered back with a hint of sarcasm.

"This chap sounds more English than you and me old boy. He ended up losing his rag with Acres, called him a lunatic!" Pontefract laughed freely. "It was a right show; I can tell you. Anyway it all got grumpy and old Acres ended up in a right two and eight and now he's called in some chaps from the Ministry of War."

"Ministry of War, that's a bit strong!" Eli exclaimed with a gasp. "What the hell for? Sounds like a right to do. I think Acres has spent too long on that bloody island. I reckon his paranoid delusions have got the better of him."

"Too right Hardy, my old boner, I don't know what it's all about but those Ministry blokes won't be here until tomorrow or even later and now Acres has locked this poor blighter up in the confinement cell."

Both men gave each other looks of open mouthed puzzlement and Hardy shook his head. "I feel sorry for you Ponty. I bet he's got his head up his ass now, making everyone's life hell."

"I'm glad he sent me over here to be honest," said Pontefract whimsically, "even if the journey made me a bit green around the gills! He told me to tell you what was going on and to let you know that you should continue with the firing checks on the new weapon when it's ready. We're not bothering with our practice, not until this is all sorted out at least."

"Well, it'll be a couple of days till we're ready for that. Hopefully by then everything will be back to normal. Whatever normal is," Harding smiled.

Ponty raised his shoulders and threw his head back towards Steep Holm, "Nothing's ever normal on that island, Hardy old boy."

"Time to head back now, Mr Pontefract!" shouted the lead oarsman tartly from inside his little boat. The swirling tide around the rocks of the promontory had become more agitated in the past few minutes as the mass of water in the estuary was being viciously sucked back towards the open ocean. Where the currants of the receding waters met as they passed around the headland, the surface had become bubbly with fluid confusion and areas of sinister, whirling undertow had quickly developed in the chaos. The air was thick with the smell of the sea and dead fish. "Right on shipmates," Ponty called out.

The young officer turned to Harding and they shook hands warmly, giving each other friendly, but saddened smiles. "Oh well, Hardy old boy, I better crack on. Don't want my first sea command to sink on her maiden voyage. Enjoy your gun practice, and remember, don't fire both of them at once or you'll run out of ammunition," he said half-jokingly. "I'll tell the old man you've got this end covered. Just keep your eyes peeled for any messages. All the best, old boy," said the young Officer, smiling broadly.

"So long Ponty. Thanks for coming over."

Harding smiled as he watched Pontefract hesitantly cross the rocks and step back into the rowing boat before sitting down carefully as the two rowers pushed themselves and the precarious vessel away from the foaming rocks. The oar strokes were smooth and deep and the little wooden craft picked up speed quickly as it crossed the churning maelstrom back towards the island. Elias watched the boat and its occupants grow smaller and gave a final wave to Pontefract who was grinning inanely back at him whilst being unashamedly and severely snapped at by the lead oarsman. Eli wondered who was in charge of whom, and with a smile he turned round to make his way up the grassy rocks which led onto the parapets of mostly empty gun emplacements and the temporary seclusion of the empty fortress.

He didn't notice the man sitting near the summit of the Down overlooking the fort and the open air meeting that had just been convened. The man was partially hidden behind a bank of gorse bushes and ferns and was in such a position that he would only be noticeable from close range. As Elias walked across the parade ground the seated man raised his binoculars like a creeping voyeur eyeing up knickers on a washing line and looked out towards the little boat bobbing through the waves aiming desperately for its island of destination on the increasingly turbulent waters. Using a short stubby pencil, the man wrote a few lines down on the pages of a small leather bound notebook, then raised the binoculars again to his beady eyes and surveyed the horizon. This time he absorbed the entire vista of open water, from the coastline of South Wales directly opposite his position, to the far off edges of Devon forming the corridor which led to the start of the Irish Sea and the Atlantic beyond.

The figure wore a thick green, heavy cotton coat and loose black trousers tucked into woollen socks wrapped in sturdy leather walking boots. On his head he wore a checked, fur lined Canadian style trackers cap with the flaps let down around his ears like the lobes of a specialist breed of tartan dog. He put the binoculars down and lit a cigarette thoughtfully, but then suddenly looked around, startled by the misplaced thought that someone was approaching his secreted viewpoint. Then he visibly settled, after reassuring his alert senses that he was indeed alone and safe to enjoy the smoke and solitude. He wrote some more words in the notebook, looked out upon the seaside vista and then stood up with his cigarette in his mouth to brush down his damp trousers. After taking one last look out to the open sea, he turned around and headed back across the Down towards the mainland. He was unnoticed, unseen and irrelevant. Someone who could be just another walker, a tourist or an academic of nature wondering to themselves at the amazing beauty along this coastline that was the South West corner of Somersetshire, England.

By the time the second cart of artillery parts had been dragged up the hill, thankfully without the dramas of the first, the brief episode of sunlight observed earlier had now been consumed by the dark band of cloud which followed it and it had now started to piss down, just as Sergeant Eves had predicted. It wasn't raining really hard, just long and steady, with a regularity that ensured a consummate wetness to whatever was underneath. Tunics had been put back on by the men of the Brigade and buttoned up to the neck to try and keep out the soaking rain. Hats had also been replaced and pulled forwards on heads to try and shield their faces from the cold droplets. They trudged alongside the freewheeling carts with a degree of resignation that only came from walking in penetrating rain. The men coughed soundly and spat expertly as they walked, still recovering from the exertions their untrained bodies had endured. Lanes sat with a petulant smirk on his face at the head of the caravan, his own hissing steam machine spitting expertly as it clunked along. Above his head there was a strip of oilskin material, propped up on broom handles, which formed a crude but effective waterproof covering over the small tractor and, apart from his damp forearms and slightly wet boots, he was relatively dry. His mood had been improved by the smugness that came from the knowledge that he had won a small victory in the never ending competition he privately held with the soldiers and their unified battle with the elements; they were getting wet and he wasn't. He ignored the sight of Sergeant Eves striding confidently next to him. Although he was coated and head covered and just as soaked as the others, his immense stature was erect and determined in a small gesture of defiance against both the weather and the obdurate farmer.

Upon reaching the fort Elias was waiting for them, sheltering from the incessant rain under the roof of the main entrance gate. As the bedraggled group reached the bridge, Sergeant Eves stood to one side, ordering the men to wait with him outside the boundary walls until the wagons had crossed the moat and entered the courtyard. There was a crunching sound as the wheels of the tractor and cart ran over the gravel surface of the open ground, closely followed by the clip clop of horse hooves. Only then did the men of the brigade follow mournfully behind, tired and drenched, resembling a band of weary warriors returning home from a murderous defeat in some traumatic battle.

"I'm sick of this bloody weather," one of them said as they huddled together under cover of the entrance way roof, smelling of wet dog and mould. Harding walked over to Eves.

"Everything go alright, Mr Eves?"

"It was a bit wobbly coming up the hill, Sir. We nearly lost one of them. But we managed it in the end. Mr Lanes was his usual moody presence. Nearly took apart Pickles for looking at his wife, no harm done in the end though."

“I’ll offer him a drink and see if I can get rid of him. We’ll unload the wagons when this bloody rain stops,” Harding replied with an air of resignation.

He walked across the courtyard through the teaming rain to Lanes, who was still closing valves on his tractor whilst sat in the dry under his makeshift awning. Elias tried to lean in as much as he could under the protection of the covering.

“Much appreciated for your help today Mr Lanes,” he began pleasantly, trying to talk over the drumming of the rain drops. “Can I offer you a drink before you head back, my men will un-hitch the wagons,” he thought a little constructing the words wisely, “and if it’s convenient, you can come and get them tomorrow, save you hanging about. It might take a while to unload them in this weather.” He smiled up at the farmer.

Lanes eyed the young man suspiciously, but seemed tempted by the offer of a tot of booze without making any actual reply apart from a derisory grunt.

“Follow me to the office and I’ll sort out the rest of your payment at the same time,” Harding added with more enticement, resulting in a sultry nod from the farmer. With the tractor steaming gently on the gravel, the two men headed across the courtyard to the officer’s quarters.

There was a large, dark blue wooden door at the end of the building near where the men were now stood undercover of the gateway. Opposite this door was a gun emplacement, formed from a six-foot square of concrete with a semi-circle of iron rail embedded into one half. Sat upon this rail were the wheels of a traversing wooden platform onto which was mounted the carriage holding a 7 ton, 7-inch calibre, Armstrong Rifled Muzzle Loading cannon, partly covered in a green tarpaulin to protect it from the rain. Out of the seven gun emplacements built into the fort, this one was the only one that had a gun on it. The rest were, so far, empty. To one side of the covered weapon, a high stone wall was part of an enclosed structure built into the boundary formations that contained the structure of an underground magazine room. This main wall then fell away to a smaller three-foot stone wall which was part of the parapet over which the gun sat, ready and waiting. A steep grass slope on the other side of the wall led down to the rocks below and in front of all of it was an unobstructed view of the estuary and the island of Steep Holm, little more than two miles away.

Harding stopped before the door and called back to Eves, “Get the men to detach the wagons and push them to one side, Mr Lanes will be leaving in a minute once I’ve thanked him for his hard work.” Eves nodded through the cascading raindrops and in return Eli opened the unlocked door of his quarters allowing the two men to enter the building.

The officer’s quarters consisted of four rooms. These were enclosed together in a rectangular shape, along with an adjoining space which was connected to the outside wall of the seaward end of the building. Two of the rooms were Elias's bedroom and sitting room, while one was a makeshift office and the other a disused kitchen. The adjoining space was separate to the living area and extended out slightly from the edge of the foundations of the building creating an overhang, which looked down upon a small and precarious landing platform built into the rocks next to the sea. It was here that supplies and light loads could be brought to the base by boat during high tide or if there was a blockage on the landside approach. A hatchway in the floor of the elevated room allowed access to the landing strip below and a rope on a pulley hung from the ceiling of the room, which was dropped down through the hatch so the loads could be pulled up. On the outside wall of the quarters near the fortress parapet a second heavy duty rope and pulley allowed more awkward and oversized loads to be hauled in and an already rusting metal ladder led down the outer walls to the exposed part of the landing bay and surrounding rocks below. The whole system hadn't been used for years, as any supplies the fort needed could be brought in from the road. But when the fort had started to be built, most of the materials had been brought to the headland by boat and landed on a large jetty built into the side of the Down about halfway along. The jetty had been constructed when an ambitious plan for the promontory had first been established and put into action even before the plans for a fort had been made. Some had thought the Down could be used as a landing station for tourist trips by steamboats and yachts, making the headland a destination for holiday makers. But since its original construction, the ill-fated jetty had subsequently been battered by the weather and shortly afterwards was washed away in a series of fierce storms. Subsequently the rest of the fort's construction, which itself had taken over fifteen years, was facilitated by road from the mainland. The plans for the headland as a tourist attraction reached by boat were also put on hold until finally being forgotten, much like the original jetty. The only remnant was this thin slice of concrete underneath the outer walls of the fortress accessible by nothing bigger than a lifeboat.

Elias led farmer Lanes through the wooden door into his simply furnished living room and headed straight across to the door opposite. They then crossed a thin corridor into the makeshift office situated in the corner of the building next to the entrance of the fort.

"Have a seat Mr Lanes," Eli motioned to an empty chair waiting forlornly on one side of a bare topped, wobbly looking old desk. The room was dark and unloved with a layer of dust floating eternally in the stale atmosphere. The only light came from a dirty window which looked out back across the Down. Apart from a cabinet opposite the desk, there was no other furniture in the depressing and claustrophobic room. It felt like the rest of the fort, neglected and unnecessary.

Elias opened a drawer underneath the desk and took out a bottle of rum, different from the one he had drunk earlier with postman Pat, as this one was nearly full. Appropriately there were two glasses in the drawer, one with a layer of the obligatory dust around it and one that looked as if it had been used recently. Eli wiped out the dust from the older one using the sleeve of his coat before putting it in front of Lanes and filling it to the brim with the darkened liquid. He did the same to his own and returned the bottle to the drawer.

Lanes looked at the glass doubtfully from beneath his singular brow and then studied the room.

"So this is the officer's quarters is it. Not too dark and dismal for you, is it Mr Hardin?" Lanes asked unimpressed.

"Oh, it's not so bad Bert. You don't mind if I call you Bert do you?" Eli took a swig from his rum. "Nice and quiet here really, except when there's a storm." He got up and went to the wooden cabinet and unlocked it, revealing on the base shelf a small iron safe. He knelt down and began silently fiddling with a bunch of keys.

"You weren't put off by the story of the previous couple then Mr Harding," said Lanes mischievously whilst Harding continued to examine the keys.

"No not really Bert, I pay no attention to idle gossip and ghost stories," he replied nonchalantly.

"Well, that night certainly put the willies up the previous ociffer and his wife. They were only 'ere a week and then they done a runner. Sumthin' scared 'um, I tell you." He paused before adding, "I take it you 'aven't seen anythin' sinister or ghostly since ye bin 'ere."

"No. I don't really know much about it to be honest with you, ah that's the one," and he excitedly pulled out the relevant key and slid it into the lock.

"Very sinister it was, Mr Hardin, very sinister," continued Lanes undeterred and he took a gulp from his dusty glass of rum. Harding pulled out a five pound note from the safe along with a small notebook and closed the door, closely watched by the farmer. Standing up from the cabinet, he went back to his seat whilst asking, "Really, so what was it you heard. Fill me in on all the gory details," deciding to play along with the farmer's games. He drained his own glass and refilled it from the bottle in the drawer and topped up Lanes' at the same time for good measure.

"Well they come a knockin' at me door on the night it all happened they did. Very distressed they were. Seems they had only just moved in that week, jus' the two of 'em it was. They were waitin' fer the rest of the soldier boys to turn up."

"They must have had a change of deployment. Sometimes you're on your own waiting for the new crews to turn up," suggested Eli starting to show an interest.

"Is that so? Well, anyway, very distressed she was, and the ociffer was agitated too by the looks of 'im. I thought I'd 'av to fetch the doctor but they jus' hopped in their 'orse an' cart and set off up the road. Lucky they 'ad an 'orse an' cart, otherwise they'd a bin' a walkin' back." He took another slug of rum. "It was a windy and rainy night see, black as pitch. Could 'ardly see yer hand in front of yer face. Apparently, she woke fer no reason at all. She said she just got up an' walked out that there door we just come in through."

Lanes looked round and pointed a finger towards the exit. There was a slight pause as he turned back to face Eli who watched with intrigue at the farmer's movements as the stony faced man spoke. "Lookin' across the courtyard, she saw a figure in the shadows, someone in a uniform like one of them soldier boys out there. She said she couldn't see what 'e looked like, jus' his outline an' that 'e had a gun in his hand. He was pointing it down in one of them gunpowder rooms. She called out, thinking it was someone trespassing." His brow had lifted a little in the excitement of his storytelling and he leaned over the desk towards the listener waiting for a reaction from him.

"Is that right," replied Harding non-conformingly, a little taken aback by Lanes' over interest, so much so he started to write in the notebook so he didn't have to look at the farmer directly.

"Yes. She was a wailin' and a sobbin' in my kitchen so badly I had to sit 'er down an' give 'er a glass o' cider to calm 'er nerves. She'd frightened the life out of my poor wife and the 'usband looked most worried too. Anyways, she was a sayin' she was tryin' to call out when she saw this figure, but 'er mouth was too dry and she couldn't make a sound because of the terror she felt. Then she said the figure turned around and looked at her. That is to say, if you can be looked at by a man with no face!"

Harding looked up from the receipt book and began to stare at Lanes again. He felt a tingle in his shoulders. "What do you mean," he said carefully.

"All he had was a bloody black hole where his face should'av bin'. No eyes or nose or mouth, jus' an empty bloody hole lookin' back at 'er. That's when she let out her scream and fainted." Lanes leant forward still further with a wild look in his piggy eyes and took another gulp of rum, finishing off his glass.

Harding had stopped writing his receipt by now and was just staring at Lanes with grisly interest. "Go on, what happened then," he said, a little too eagerly.

"Well er husband said he heard the scream, came a running and saw her lyin in the doorway getting soaked by the rain with the wind howlin' like a banshee through the courtyard. There was no one else around, 'e said. When she woke she was in a right state, had to leave right away, they couldn't stay another minute. There was nothing he could do to calm her down, although I reckon he might 'av tried a bit 'arder," Lanes flashed a cunning smile, "probably should've given 'er a swipe or two to try an' snap 'er out of it."

"Very noble of you," said Eli witheringly, Lanes' grotty comment snapping him out of his own fixation.

"Still, that didn't work either, so he packed 'er up in the pony an' trap and headed down to me. Middle 'o the night it was, two, three o'clock in the mornin'. He said they were gonna head into the town, said the fort was empty and he'd sort out a replacement as soon as he could. Never saw neither of 'em again." He blinked his black piglet eyes and licked the conversational foam from his rubbery lips. "So, what d'ya make o' that then, Mr Hardin!"

"Well..." Elias tried to think of something to say. "Perhaps the loneliness got to her. It's not everyone's cup of tea up here," he said, before hesitating a little while he evaluated the story. "Maybe it made her see things that weren't really there. This place is full of shadows, especially at night. Stuck here on your own, it can play tricks on the mind."

Lanes seemed to retract into his black, moody manner and his brow fell back into place casting a shadow over his eyes in the dust of the heavy and airless room.

"Maybe, who's to know either way? I wonder what happened to 'em in the end," the farmer mumbled.

"I don't know. I haven't heard anything of them since." Eli replied slightly agitated. "Someone told me a rumour of the story before I got here, I didn't pay much heed to it, just idle gossip in the canteen."

"Oh well, best keep it that way."

"Yes I dare say, Mr Lanes, although I'll keep my eyes peeled for any faceless ghosts that might come out on a stormy night." Harding looked down at the notepad, tired of the farmer's attempts at being mysterious but still a little unnerved by the story. He preferred the farmer the way he was normally, just plain moody. "You wouldn't mind signing the receipt for the payment would you Mr Lanes then you can have the rest of your money and be on your way."

Lanes picked up the pencil and scrawled in slow joined up childlike handwriting the simple moniker of 'Lanes' across the bottom of the page. Harding ripped out one of the carbon copies and handed it along with the money into Lanes' thick calloused fingers, then he stood up and returned the pad and empty glasses to their dusty homes and locked everything away as if the room had never been used or would ever be used again. He held out a hand to the farmer.

"Well thanks very much for the ghost stories, Mr Lanes, and much appreciated for your hard work today. Come back any time tomorrow for your carts, they'll be unloaded by then."

Lanes stood up awkwardly and shook hands badly, unsure of the etiquette of manners a simple goodbye required. The young officer led him through the building out to the open courtyard. It was still raining but less hard. As they walked, Lanes looked around, taking in the empty gun batteries.

"You only got two guns 'ere now then Mr Harding, includin' that new one. I suppose you'll be in need of my services again, before long," he grumbled.

Eli answered him, a sense of irritation rising in his attitude. "Not for a while. Cut backs in the War Office. Two guns will be all we'll see here for a while. I'm sure it'll be enough; I believe the French have got better things to do than try to invade England."

"Wouldn't be much point, nothing worth having' on this desolate bit o'rock," said the farmer blackly.

Moodiness restored, he walked up to his steam tractor, which was still chugging defiantly away in the middle of the courtyard. The two shire horses were tethered to the back of the machine and the carts had been removed next to one of the far walls. He got into the driving seat, released the brake and made a large noisy turn in the courtyard with the horses following obediently behind. Under the roof of the entrance the brigade stood to one side as the machine passed between the buildings heading towards the bridge. Lanes glared at the men as he went by and some of them smiled at him in return whilst a couple saluted sarcastically as he passed. Steaming across the bridge with the rain drumming on his makeshift oilskin roof, Pickles piped up from the back of the throng, "Thanks again, Bertie. All the best. Say 'ello to yer missus from me!"

A couple of the men laughed, but luckily the remark was drowned out by the racket of the steaming engine and the heavy drum of the steady, soaking rain.

Eves and Harding stood in the downpour on the gravel of the parade ground by the officer's quarters. The master gunner's dark hair was stuck to his head and there was a look of disgruntlement on his face as he squinted against the raindrops. He glanced towards the two carts on the other side of the open courtyard space.

"Did the surly fellow have much to say, Sir?" asked Eves.

"Not really." Eli thought for a moment then added, "These locals are an odd bunch, nothing but ghost stories and gossip. I could do without those."

Eves nodded and handed the young Officer the paperwork from the gun delivery which received a rueful look from the fort commander. He stuffed the wet papers into his coat pocket.

"Get the men inside and dried off. Tell them to get a feed and have a cup of tea. There's no point doing anything until this bloody rain stops." He paused and looked skyward into the downpour before adding, "If it ever does? I've got some paperwork to do. Oh, by the way, keep an eye out for flares from Steep Holm, Acres has interned a boat for some stupid reason and there might be a message from them at some point. Don't ask me what's going on. It's just the old man getting confused as far as I can make out. Give me a shout if anything turns up."

Eves acknowledged the request and felt the exasperation from the young Officer as Harding turned sadly around and entered the officer's quarters through the heavy wooden door, closing it gently behind him. The Sergeant thought the young man seemed a little depressed but put it down to the rain and then ran off to get everyone inside.

Elias walked into the sitting room taking off his wet grey overcoat and hung it up on the back of the door. He went to the fireplace, which although lit, only contained a few sad embers and smoking ashes left from the first lighting earlier on that morning. Kneeling down, he placed a handful of kindling sticks and a couple of thin weedy looking logs from the small stack on the hearth over the dying embers and then blew into the pile with sharp bursts, breathing life into the fading hot ash. The dry kindling caught immediately and small flames erupted around the wood sending strands of wispy smoke into the up draught of the chimney. Standing upright he glanced around the bleak room. There was an upholstered but heavily threadbare armchair opposite the fireplace and in one corner a long, equally threadbare cushioned foot rest. Underneath a barred window stood a heavily varnished, round wooden table on which were sat an empty, dust caked fruit bowl and an empty, brown glassed ornamental vase. Opposite, near the door to the corridor, a small writing bureau leant against a wall fronted by a thin creaky chair and opposite this, in another corner stood a cheap looking pine cabinet and dresser, decorated with a sparse selection of books including a well-worn volume of 'Great Expectations'.

Stood among the books as if waiting to be picked up and perused like some important work of non-fiction was a framed photograph portraying a disciplined, authoritative middle aged man with a voluminous set of sideboards and a very stiff collar around his neck. It went well with the stiff looking expression the subject offered.

"Lanes is right," Eli said to himself sadly as he looked around. "It is a bit dismal in here."

He headed towards the cabinet and reached into the lower cupboard. He removed an unopened bottle of gin and studied it, unsure if christening the virgin bottle was a good idea. Looking across to the window, he acknowledged the pattering of the rain upon the glass and the overcast sky outside, thought about the depressing room and the equally dismal weather for a few seconds, then shrugged and took a glass from the top of the cupboard before pouring out another drink under the disapproving glare from the image in the photo frame.

"Just a couple, while it's raining," he said to the faded photograph. "Better not get too pissed before lunch, eh father."

Sipping from his full glass, Eli sat down in the worn armchair opposite the now rising fire and relaxed in front of the growing flames that cheerfully licked their way around the outside of the logs. He thought about the story Lanes had told him in the office. Eli had known about the previous Officer leaving after only a week following his wife's psychotic episode, thanks to a quick mention from the Commanding Officer at his previous deployment, but the local farmer had filled in many of the missing details to the previously obscure story. He sensed the dark and dingy corners of the room he was in, which was lit only by the grey sky outside and the beginnings of the small fire and he realised they were prevalent in the whole fort; from the eerie, darkened crevices of the ramparts and walls to the moving, shadowy corners of the haunting rooms within. Lanes' account of the incident had shaken him up but he didn't know why. He reassured himself that the loneliness the lady would surely have felt out here, surrounded by the bleak atmosphere and fleeting shadows would have been enough to fry anyone's fragile mental state. Perhaps without the company of other people in this secluded fortress, maybe even his own unpredictable psyche would fall foul of phantasms conjured out of the looming darkness by a desperate and isolated imagination.

Eli rolled the glass of gin around his fingers and laughed slightly. "Bloody place this is," he muttered. "I've got enough ghosts to deal with as it is, thank you Mr Herbert Lanes, without any more from you," and he finished off his glass of gin in one blast whilst letting his head fall back into the soft embracing weave of the worn headrest. He then closed his eyes and thought of nothing but the soft and enchanting adagio's that floated through the sensuous music of Ludwig van Beethoven.

5. Loaded

Gordy was completely paralysed. His eyes seemed dead as they blankly stared upon the images being played out in the slow burn of the flames that pulsed before him. Indeed, to an onlooker the young man had the appearance of someone who had expired during mid-sentence from an instantaneous, pain free death. Only the figure in the corner was lucid and alive. He waved his hands energetically and pointed fingers towards the fire, gesturing like a magician performing an illusory magic trick. As each character in the story was presented, so the storyteller's face morphed and changed shape to create the haunting image of that person, one moment laughing when the dialect was funny, then twisting suddenly to anger or terrified panic when the atmosphere mutated. The phantom silhouettes still danced around the room and were emanating from his shadowy form one after another like black misshapen birds flying from the branches of a dead and withered tree. All the while, the figure continued to recount the tale now being ominously performed within the flames of the mystical fire.

Gordy wanted to escape from the sinister show but was trapped inside his inert body. He felt the overwhelming instinct to run but knew he was caught in a strange disabling web spun like a spider by the mysterious hands of the speaking figure. Gordy felt the need to piss. Unable to control his bodily functions and as if the figure initiated it with a cruel smile from his changeling face, Gordy urinated calmly into the soft material of his underpants. He couldn't control the anguish racing across his mind or stop the demented smile creeping across his otherwise frozen face as the warm liquid soaked into his trousers and formed an ever increasing damp patch which quickly went icy cold.

Throughout this, sometimes in slow motion, sometimes speeded up, the visions continued to be played out in the wavering incandescence of the fire. *'The fire, that weird fire,'* Gordy thought as he harnessed small tokens of independent thought from the fog of entrancement that kept creeping over him. Maybe the figure had put something in it, something bendy, a suspect tincture that made its victims drowsy before paralysing them and causing their mind to hallucinate wildly. He knew it wasn't the weed he smoked, no weed was this powerful. What the blazes was happening to him?

Then the figure spoke about another fire, not the weird one entrancing Gordy, but a different one, a friendly, positive fire from a forgotten past that emitted light and warmth to a previously dark and damp barrack room. Around this fire sat men, drying themselves and absorbing the pleasurable embrace of the flames whilst talking about the events of their day and the simple realities of their lives. It was a nice fire, around which normal things were happening relative to the needs of everyday life. A far cry from the situation Gordy had now found himself in.

The barrack room was the largest building within the fort and at over sixty feet long it could hold twenty to thirty men in comparative comfort or forty to fifty at an uncomfortable, overcrowded squeeze. One length of the rectangular, stone construction formed part of the outer wall, making up the land side defences of the whole enclosure and it looked over the dry moat which segregated the fortress from the main headland of the Down. Four windows looked out towards the grassy slope and over the deep gully immediately underneath and these windows were interspersed with open slits, a foot long and only a couple of inches wide, presently blocked with wood to keep out the wind. When opened, these slits allowed the occupants to fire upon any attackers coming at them from the mainland.
An internal door allowed entry from the kitchen, which was adjacent, and at the opposite end of the room another door led to a short corridor which allowed access to the NCO's room on one side and a washroom and toilet on the other. At the end of this corridor, a strong metal exit door led to a small area of the courtyard in which a separate, simply roofed but otherwise open latrine was tucked away. At either end of the main barrack room wall facing the sea, thick, metal plated, wooden doors exited directly onto the main expanse of open parade ground outside.

The gravel covered parade ground was bordered by the fort's seven, strategically placed gun emplacements. It was noticeable that out of the seven concrete bases set at various angles to the outer wall, each with a view towards the sea, only one of those emplacements actually contained a weapon.

Inside the barrack hall, the whitewashed plaster walls gave the space a clinical, hospitalised feel and the heavy metal doors, although keeping out the strong winds that blew straight off the sea, helped instil a sense of entrapment and inescapability. Depending on how many men were manning the fortress at any one time, a relevant number of thin looking, wiry beds lined the edges of the walls and down the centre of the room there ran a single line of slim wooden tables accompanied on either side by even thinner looking smooth wooden benches. The papery white walls actually seemed grey due to the overall gloom, like they were paying homage to the sea outside, and the clean factor was further scarred by blobs of damp that were blotted around the corners, creating scattered areas of bruised and flaking, discoloured plaster. The room had hardly any decoration except for a large map near the kitchen door showing the southern and south west coast of Britain. It had the large towns and cities along the coastline written in bold lettering but the main cartography of the map plotted each of the coastal batteries in the Bristol Channel and around the coastal areas at Portsmouth and Dover. These positions on the map were symbolised by a simple cannon motif enclosed in a band of rope. The words of the heading along the top of the picture proudly announced 'The Coastal Forts of Southern England' in pointlessly frilly and over grandiose lettering. Written in pencil by the motif on Brean Down, someone had scribbled the profound statement of 'The Hole in the Ass!' No one had positively owned up to the defacement, but as no one had also either cared to remove the words, the scrawl had become an allowed epitaph in which the volunteers described their general feelings at being stationed there. Along the same wall, a large generic print of Queen Victoria sternly watched over the unmade beds which stuck out from the wall and the piles of discarded clothing that adorned them. She, with due respect from the occupiers, had remained without graffito.

Only fourteen men shared the barrack room for this present deployment, so while half the room contained beds on either side, the section near the kitchen was able to accommodate the benches and tables width ways in front of the fireplace, as if they were school tables laid out before a worthy teacher. The fireplace on the bedded side of the room was now strung with a makeshift drying line, heavily laden with the wet dog smelling, steaming coats and trousers of the brigade, that earlier in the day had been soaked with rain during the collection of the fort's new gun.

Sat around the tables in front of a raging fire, drying their damp feet, wearing warm vests and long johns of brushed cotton or the fresh grey shirts with loose white trousers that made up their general fatigues, the men of the brigade talked in easy voices. They laughed intermittently at jocular comments or tried to speak over one another on mutually acceptable subjects. The speech came in gushes of local dialect, fast and long, interspersed with short, clipped replies that were rarely serious and often funny. Empty plates with half full mugs of lukewarm tea adorned the tables and the air smelt of damp mould and boiled cabbage mingled with the heavy claw of soot smoke and cheap tobacco. The light from the fires cast a friendly and comforting glow through the cold, grey smog of the wintery afternoon. This end of the room was a relaxed, warmth fuelled oasis of joyous comfort in an otherwise draughty corner of a wet and windblown world.

The men were scattered around the fire like grey pebbles on a white washed beach taking up positions of heat in whatever areas were available. Some sat on the long benches pulled at angles towards the fire whilst others took up single wooden chairs, sprawling lazily against tables or leaning forwards to engage in the myriad of conversation.

A large portly fellow with a twist of curly brown hair and a squashy face, who had earlier commented on the hard work of getting the gun carriages up the hill, leant back against one table and thrust his feet towards the fireplace.

"It's times like these you should be glad his place isn't full up. Fifty sods in this room and you wouldn't get near the fire," he said to no one in particular whilst wriggling his puffy toes. His name was Lumpy Bolter and the nickname was ideally suited as it described his round physique but was also a play on his real name of Lawrence. He had been a volunteer for five years, all of them spent on Brean Down at various times of the year, and it accompanied his day to day job as a watchman at the nearby docks of Bristol. It was a sedentary occupation which only exacerbated his growing weight problem and although he gave off an air of a man ready for action and worthy deeds, in reality he indulged in very little of either. Many on duty thought he only volunteered for the free food.

"More food as well with less people," added Stanley Pickles, rubbing his tummy and grinning inanely. Another man sat in the corner rolling a droopy fag, pitched in to the banter quickly.

"Yeah, with fifty blokes sharing the gruel, you'd soon lose some weight, Lumpy," he said, smiling widely at the portly man and winking at Pickles.

"Don't be so sure. I'd get me a couple of them there goats wonderin' around the cliffs and have me a plate of mutton chops every night," Lumpy replied with a grin.

"You wouldn't be able to catch 'em! They're quick as hares when they want to be," said the man sat next to Lumpy, smoking a long pipe and watching the fire contentedly. He was much older than most of the others, perhaps in his fifties, and had the appearance of a man who had worked hard all his life in a variety of manual roles, resulting in a toughened, over cooked and aged look. In contrast to the dough fleshed Lumpy, his hard, wiry body was covered with leathery skin over which a series of thick veins bulged when he exerted effort. The rest of the brigade called him Mule, after the hardworking donkeys used to pull tourist carriages up the beach in the nearby town of Weston.

The man who mentioned Lumpy's weight problem struck a match and lit his rolled fag whilst eyeing the leathery Mule. "He'd just send you out to catch 'em, Mule. I expect you'd make a better fist of it," he said loosely, blowing smoke across the orange firelight. His name was James Burden and he was a labourer on building sites, becoming a volunteer to supplement his income during periods of little work. The shilling a day for time deployed would be saved and spent after each posting on booze and the pleasure of various women. Women whom he would stay with, possibly under the promise of a securer future until the next labouring job could be found, which would then result in a discreet disappearance of the wayward cad and his false promises.

On a bench, along the wall under the defaced coastal map, sat two scrawny youths in their late teens. They were brothers with the family name of Pearce and their childlike faces displayed a selection of reddened whiteheads, while their closely shorn, badly cropped brown hair was the only solution to a recent bout of nits. Growing bored with the direction of conversation, the oldest brother, whose name was Richard, sat forward and guffawed, thus changing the subject awkwardly as only the impractical social skills of the young can do.

"Ay, wot about old Lanes giving dirty Pickles a fist of it earlier, then. I bet you nearly messed yerself, aye Stan," he sniggered, through a cheesy grin of large, crooked, brown stained teeth. Stanley Pickles looked at the brothers disdainfully and replied with an affronted seriousness. "It was a good job Eves turned up when he did I can tell you, or else I might have given that blockhead a whack." This statement brought howls of laughter from everyone in the room and Pickles put his head down with embarrassment to sip bashfully from his cold, stewed tea.

"Don't you worry, Stanley boy. Farmer Lanes is stuck on this bit of rock every day of his life, that's why he's so grumpy. He's bound to take it out on someone every now an' then. At least we can all leave after a week or two," said Mule kindly with his luxurious West Country accent.

"Yes," agreed a soft toned young man with long, thin hair and a thoughtful face, who had been writing on a piece of paper at one of the long tables. "I think I'd go mad, stuck out here forever," he said wistfully.

At this point the younger of the two brothers, Daniel, who earlier had been accompanying Pickles with a bout of vomiting after the struggles of the hill, leant forward and added his effort at philosophical study.

"Yea, and when this ere gun is made, we'll be able to take pot shots at Lanes' pissing steam machine," he said.

"Old Lanes can shove his tractor up his ass, for what I care," Pickles replied testily.

"Still, imagine be'in stuck out 'ere day after day, nite after blimin nite, only seein' the sun every free munfs or so, and getting soaked all the bloody time. It'll be enuff to make any sod grumpy," Gosfor added, with his heavy London drawl, which was a notable difference in speech tone from the others whose more regular countrified accents made up the majority of conversational sound. The men nodded silently, aware of the moist, cold gloom that coloured everybody's personality at some point and seemed to be prevalent everywhere upon the Down apart from here, now, by the glowing fire of the barrack room.

"It wouldn't be so bad, as long as you didn't have to spend all the time with you lot," boomed a smooth voice from within the dim light at the other end of the barracks. Eves strode down between the beds wearing a fetching all in one baby suit of grey flannel underwear and a pair of checked, lounge slippers. He padded softly along the floor with a curved wooden pipe hanging from his whiskery face and had left the solitary bunk of his own small room at the back of the barracks to join the men and share in the warmth of their companionship.

He sat down on the end of one of the benches in front of the fire and the other occupants moved along courteously to make room. They absorbed him into their gathering as if he was one of their own, which he was; because like all the best leaders of men, Zanzibar Eves knew when a group of men needed leading and when those same men could lead themselves; allowing this motley crew to develop a sense of unity with him and each other. He relit his pipe and watched the fire as it sleepily danced and jumped around the coal lumps, casting its tempered lightshow warmly around the group.

"Would you like to shove Mr Lanes' tractor up his ass, Mr Eves?" asked Lumpy thoughtfully, continuing Pickles' earlier suggestion.

"I think that would be a messy job, Boulter. I'll leave it to someone else. I'm sure that someone will come along one day and not take too kindly to Mr Lanes' moribund manner," replied the diplomatic Sergeant.

Sitting behind them, the writer of letters with long greasy hair had paused from penning a letter to his wife, and continued his theory of happiness for all mankind. "Still you can't blame him for being moody all the time, what with the wea…"

"Oh don't kep on, Scribbler," interjected Mule with irritation. "Youse is always bangin'on about the weather. Let it go boy. It's nice and quiet up ere, better than that constant hum-drum you gets in the town. Foods alright, an' we don't get put upon too much, not like we do by the bosses at work, or the wife, or the young'uns." There were nods of agreement from some of the men, ones also 'put upon' by wives and children and bosses.

"I think old Scribbler likes bein put upon by 'is wife, that's why e's always writin' to 'er," young Daniel Pearce supposed.

"What are you writing to the good lady about this time, Aldous? I would have thought you'd be runnin' out of things to talk about. I wager you've penned the wife a letter every day since we got here," enquired Lumpy.

The scribbler looked at Lumpy with distrust. "Not that it's any of your business Mr Boulter but I tend to write about the events and effects of the day, like what we did, where we went, what the weather was like and so forth," he said in a slightly educated sounding, local accent.

"Blimy! She'll be asleep before she gets half way through," butted in Gosfor rudely and he chortled like a squirrel.

"That's if the milkman can pull his cock out of 'er long enough so she can read it," quipped Jimmy Burden with a sly smile. The rest of the room broke into cackling laughter, apart from the scribbler, who looked around contemptuously.

Just then a shaven headed man with a round, heavy stomach adorned with a white apron which was stained with food, walked in from the kitchen carrying a wooden tray stacked with glass tumblers and a large tin jug full of dark rum. The man looked startled when he caught sight of Eves sat with the rest of the men.

"Oh Mr Eves, I didn't know you was 'ere. I thought we could all 'av a tot o' rum, to keep out the cold like," he said squeamishly as he put the tray on the table. There was a quiet feeling in the room that Eves might not be too impressed with the brigade drinking so early; it was alright at the end of the day, but there was probably still work to be done once it had dried out enough. They'd only just had lunch, even if it was a late one.

"Don't worry Mr England, I think we all deserve a tot after the soaking we got this mornin'," Eves said, showing his continued affinity with the men, and the room visibly relaxed as a result.

Mr Arnold England, the round bellied cook, who although not a proper chef was a very capable cook and made the regular rations of potatoes, hard winter vegetables and cheap cuts of meat into reasonably appetising varieties of different mixtures, poured out the booze into generous measures and the tumblers were passed among the men, including the teenage brothers. There was a pause as they drank silently, the young ones sipping the hot sour liquid, others draining the glass in one go and licking their lips, savouring every drop. The cook sat down on a spare end of bench next to Eves and fully poured a glass of rum into his stubbly mouth, letting out a raspy, satisfying exhale when he'd finished. "Phew. That helps perk up another hard day on the frontline," he said, smiling widely.

"Pushin that cart up the 'ill was the most excitement you've 'ad round 'ere, fatty, apart from peelin' potatoes," chirped Pickles.

"That's all the excitement I need, thanks lad," replied the cook, unmoved, before turning to Eves directly. "Any chance of another, Sarge, it was a long mornin's wait in the cold for that steam tractor."

Eves thought for a moment and felt the warmth of the fire and the heat from the rum caress his insides. "Go on then cookie, seeing as yer fried eggs was so good."

The jug was passed around and the men sat silently smiling, pleasurably induced by the alcohol, until Jimmy Burden broke the hazy peace.

"What about you Mr Eves? It must be boring up here for you to. All of us lot lead lives of drudgery and dreary toil, none of us can deny that, so this is the only bit'o' action we'll ever see in our lives and none of it's real. However, you've bin fightin' all over the world for most of your life. You must miss the excitement of a real war."

Eves kept watching the fire. "Sometimes you have your fill of real war, Burden," he said gently in his indefinable tones. "This empire was built on seeking out conflict in all parts of the world. She found fighting for men who wished it wherever she dared to tread and there was nowhere she dared not go. Some men could seek the fighting with her, while others just happened to be there when it came round. I suppose it was a bit of both for me. But it's been the same in all times of war and battle; that those men who've seen it most are the ones that are used when it comes round again. Isn't that right, Mr England?"

"Too true, Mr Eves, too true," confirmed the cook. "Fightin' and eatin' always went together when I was a youngster and it's gone on ever since. I've ad enuff of the fightin' so I'll stick to the eatin' for now. I think this is the best place to keep as far away from any fightin' as is possible in this day and age."

Eves nodded. "With that I do concur, Mr England, with that I do concur. As with you, I am most grateful for an easy life in these twilight years. A bit of peace and quiet is all I want now, Mr Burden."

The cook raised his glass to the crackling fire. "Here's to peace and quiet," he toasted and took a healthy swig of the dark liquid.

"Wot about Mr Harding, Sergeant?" inquired Gosfor. "He's only young and he's been to war, wouldn't he like to be in the thick of it again."

Eves looked across at the Londoner and then said calmly, "I believe Mr Harding thinks the same as us and would be glad if he never saw or heard a gun fired for any reason, as long as he lived."

Some of the men looked at each other knowingly. "He'll get a shock when that gun's all set up an' we start 'avin a go at it, hey sarge," Burden suggested roughly. He paused for a moment and then thumbed his nose. "Is that why he seems a bit…you know, troubled sometimes," he asked, pushing at the boundaries between inquiry and intrusion.

Eves threw a meaningful glance at the pensive looking cook sat beside him before replying judiciously.

"Well, war is war, Mr Burden. It is a terrible thing. That is surely known by everyone here, but sometimes it can be more terrible than anything you could imagine in your wildest nightmares. I've been in wars where we spent weeks shooting at rocks and shadows and chasing locals through bushes but never saw anyone killed or even hurt. Other times there can be the fiercest battles that put the most heinous death and murder before your eyes for hours on end and all, no matter how hardy they may seem, are affected by it. Violence so brutal, Mr Burden, you never forget it."

The cook beside Mr Eves nodded slowly and looked to the floor as did some of the others. The room had lost the jocular atmosphere of before and a solemn glow of peacefulness floated delicately outwards from the firelight.

"Did Mr Harding see such violence then, sergeant?" asked Pickles sombrely.

Eves looked at the young man with twinkling eyes. "That he did, lad. That he did. For all the blood and guts I've seen in my time, he seen it as bad as it gets." There was an abated silence that Eves decided for better or worse to fill. "I presume you all remember our time in the province of Afghanistan, not long finished. Or should I say finished for the time being," he said, looking round the room, before continuing. "Well, there was a battle near a place called Maiwand which you would have read about in the papers."

"The massacre at Maiwand," interjected Lumpy with a whisper. "Long live the 66th," he added, tipping his glass slightly.

"That's right Mr Boulter, the massacre at Maiwand. Well, Mr Harding was there, and it's something he and all those who were with him will never forget for as long as they live," said Eves in the manner of a wise old man giving evidence to a court of the young and inexperienced.

"Never 'eard of it," said young Daniel with inappropriate enthusiasm.

Eves threw the spotty youth a stern look.

"Well maybe I should enlighten you then, Mr Pearce, and maybe you'll understand why our Master Gunner seems, how did you put it Mr Burden.... troubled."

And everyone listened intently as Eves poured himself another glass of rum, filled his pipe with another dose of tobacco and began recounting the less than glorious battle of Maiwand and Mr Harding's part in it.

*

"Bloody hell, it's hot," Gunner Williams said to anyone who could hear him as he again wiped the sweat from his constantly sweaty face with a moist handkerchief. "Why are we just sat 'ere like fish in a barrel, waitin' to be caught an' gutted by the fuzzies? It's madness I tell you. We all gotta get back to that village or we'll be surrounded an' then we'll all be goners!" he added, his voice rising with agitation as he spoke.

Harding heard the panicky comment from where he was stood but said nothing in reply. Williams' statement had summed up the situation they were in ideally, and Eli felt there was nothing he could say in return to counteract the man's concern. He looked behind him to the village called Mundabad that Williams had referred to. It was only fifteen hundred yards away and was comprised of a handful of rough stone buildings and mud walled gardens, the occupants of which had fled days ago. It didn't look like much of a sanctuary but compared to the open position they were in at the moment, it seemed like a lifesaving refuge.

The men of Harding's artillery squad stood as close as possible to the nine pounder, the rifled, muzzle loading cannon they were manning, looking nervous and subdued in the chaos gradually erupting around them. Suddenly they ducked in practiced automatic unison, as another shell from the Afghan guns exploded only a few dozen yards away. Luckily it landed in an area free of men, equipment or horses and merely threw up a cloud of sand, dust and rock in a shower of loose debris that scattered over the heads of the jittery gun crew and the surrounding area.

"Good job these fuzzy wuzzies are lousy shots," sparkled one of the crew as he slowly raised his head with a nervous laugh, squinting his eyes under the khaki coloured, cloth wrapped pith helmet he wore. The men closed their tired eyes and dry, parched mouths to keep out the dusty, acrid tasting smoke which hung in the air momentarily after the explosion before it slowly began to clear. They tried to relax their hunched backs and tight necks, but the worried, frightened expressions which were etched around their faces, like the crumpled surface of a poorly painted portrait, remained; as did the unremitting tension. The next one might have their name on it, the way several of the other shells had had other unfortunate men's names on them and the results of those could be seen in the confusion that surrounded them. Dead and injured were being sent to the rear on stretchers or makeshift ambulances formed from supply carts and gun trolleys. Maimed, untreatably tortured horses were being shot by hard faced soldiers whilst supplies of ammunition and equipment was desperately salvaged from the twisted carnage of bomb craters by frightened, civilian clothed baggage handlers. The pungent fumes that filled the air rounded off a scene of degradation and slow destruction that had now been going on for an hour.

All around them in a strange curving line of humanity that stretched across an area of open ground, in front of a ravine which skirted the village, stood seventeen hundred men of the British and Indian army. They were waiting in the open facing a wailing horde of twenty-five thousand Afghan army regulars, tribesmen and religious fanatics known as ghazi's who had joined the rising tide of insurgency against the status quo within their country. The British contingent and their allies now stuck out in the open had been surprised to find themselves confronted by the size of this army before them due to a lack of decent reconnaissance and overall planning on their part, coupled with a general underestimation of the situation as a whole by their far off superiors. This gathering mass of Afghan forces was the army of Ayub Khan, grand leader of the uprising, and had been on its way to Kandahar in an attempt to lay siege to the town and help begin the deposition of the Amir of Afghanistan, a British protégé, presently holed up in the capital city of Kabul and protected by the main spearhead of the British Expedition Force who had originally been sent out to secure these lawless lands in favour of the Empire. With success in Kandahar, the insurgency believed it would be in a better position to replace the Amir with Ayub Khan and a selection of his most loyal supporters; so removing the British and their interest in the region altogether.

But on the way, not far from the town of Maiwand, in the Province of Helmand, Ayub Khan's army bumped into this thin khaki line of opposition, sent out from the Generals in Kandahar a few days earlier to intercept and disband the revolt. Brigadier George Burrows and his force of two and a half thousand men, which included the 66th regiment of foot and E Battery of the Royal Horse Artillery, of which Elias Harding and his crew were part, as well as two regiments of Indian infantry and cavalry, were this thin line sent to stand in the Khan's way.

Elias now realised that along with the other five guns in his battery and another six smoothbore guns sectioned along the line, this was what he, his troop and the rest of the force were trying to do; stand in the way of twenty-five thousand Afghan infantry, cavalry and over thirty opposing cannons.

"Bloody hell," he whispered to himself repeatedly.

To say he was scared was an understatement. He had been in Afghanistan for six months and seen sporadic skirmishes on several occasions but spent most of the time firing pot shots at groups of Afghan locals during minor insurgencies. He knew this engagement today was going to be completely different. This was going to be his first real battle and he suddenly realised, as if it had never quite occurred to him before, that he might die, probably in a quite horrific and most painful way.

Earlier on, when the defensive line had formed in front of what seemed like a few groups of enemy horsemen beneath some high hills, no one had felt much fear or vulnerability. But as the morning wore on and the enemy cavalry moved around like a gently swirling pool of viscous liquid, behind those horsemen, far away on the hills, dark masses formed which at first looked like belts of trees. Then, as they moved forward through the haze, it gradually became clear they were actually thousands and thousands of men. When it was realised how many soldiers they were facing, murmuring and paralysing fear had swept through everyone in the lines, but as skirmishes had already taken place in the forward line by over excited British units, before the full realisation of their predicament was appreciated, the opposing sides were now inevitably engaged and thus the course of action irrecoverably put into motion. The British and Indian army obediently followed the order to stand to and stayed out in the open ready to face the attack with only the cavalry and supply train under cover in the relative safety of the village behind.

The scorching heat bore down on the men from the early start of the morning. By nine 'o'clock it was 120 degrees with no shade to take cover under. As the force took its positions beneath the hot sun, the ground which had been softened by the cool of the night became hard baked again and the compacted sand lightly burned the touch of bare skin whilst an unquenchable thirst raked in the thousands of dry, scratchy throats waiting fearfully in the open.

At eleven 'o'clock the bombardment began and both sides fired upon each other with artillery as if they were boxers in a ring, throwing punches and trading blows to test one another's resolve. It was probing at first and made little impact on the opposed gatherings but then the barrage quickly achieved a sustained repetition that caused steadily deprecating casualties on both sides, particularly amongst the Indian infantry exposed in the open on the far left of the British line. Harding's team, like those stationed around them, had fired all their rounds during this preliminary bombardment and the repetitive workload had taken their minds off the immediate surroundings. But it was while they were waiting to be re-supplied that the realisation of the situation they were in finally dawned on them.

Elias surveyed the British lines before him. Men and horses were led around dead or wounded, some missing whole limbs from exploding rounds or torn apart by direct hits of dissecting shrapnel. The injured were being carted away by panic stricken drivers of horse drawn carts and groups of Indian reinforcements ran around blindly in the dust trying to fill in the holes along the line caused by the hale of arcing enemy missiles. An enveloping swirl of smoke hung in the air, shouts and cries came from all directions regularly cut out by the staccato BOOM from their own firing guns and the high pitched whistle followed by the ear splitting crack of a returned incoming shell.

He looked at his watch. It was just after twelve. Through the mesh of madness in all directions he thought he saw the horizon move.

Suddenly, magically emerging towards him from the sand and smoke, there thundered a small baggage cart drawn by two highly agitated and sand caked brown horses with fear fuelled, yellow eyes and twitching muscles. It pulled up sharply behind the gun in a shuddering wall of shocked beast and rattling wood.

"Thank God!" Harding shouted to the driver, "We ran out of bloody ammo ages ago!"

The driver was a young Indian soldier and looked as wide eyed and yellow with dust as the horses.

"It's happening Sir!" he screeched. "They're attacking our left! They are coming. There are too many!"

Harding's gun crew were already frantically unloading shell boxes and gunpowder from the wagon and piling them by the cannon.

"Only ten boxes per gun, Sir. That is the orders!" the driver called out between anxious looks towards the left flank, almost grinning with panic driven hysteria.

"What? That's not enough!" Harding shouted back. Fear heaped upon unsurmountable fear now cracked in his voice. At three rounds per box that meant they only had thirty rounds which would soon run out with a rapid rate of fire. Another enemy shell whistled over and fell dangerously close, causing an eruption of grainy smoke and shuddering noise. It landed amongst a group of infantry soldiers just in front of the gun position. Cries of pain filled the air with the impact and through the ensuing fog Harding saw men fall away like toppled wooden poles, broken and destroyed by the revolting orbit of the explosion. When he looked round again to remonstrate with the Indian driver, the ammunition cart was already haphazardly galloping away to the next gun position.

"They're attacking, Mr Harding! Over there!" called Gunner Williams as he pointed with his finger towards the left flank of the Indian lines only a hundred yards away. Eli realized the horizon moving had been the Afghans launching their attack.

A terrible noise erupted from inside the earth as the guns along the line opened up violently, underscored by the heart stopping primal scream from thousands of human throats as the first wave of Afghan cavalry clashed into the Indian infantry. It was like an earthquake shaking the landscape with a terrifying power and the air shuddered with the unstoppable force of war.

Harding felt he was floating in a twisted, uncontrollable nightmare. The horrific sound blocked out his ears causing a muted buzzing in his head and there was a sensation the blood had drained away from his body making him feel light and feathery. He was numb with shock and he stared inanely ahead with his mouth open like an entranced child. In his eyes all he could see was a silently moving mouth in a contorted angry face of a man a few feet away. It turned out to be the mouth of his section Officer, Lieutenant Osbourne, shouting at him angrily through the chaos.

"Harding! They're coming Harding! Sort it out man! Turn to the left, over the top. Support the left flank. Now man! Harding! Now! Or I'll bloody kill you myself!"

Eli remained blank.

Then Osbourne was nearby and he had hit him, a hard smack across the face with the back of his hand, the knuckles rattling on Eli's cheekbones. Eli shook his head, his mouth still gaping open but the numbness in his face replaced by a stinging fizz. He shook his head and the din of battle filled his ears again along with the snarling orders from his commanding Officer.

"Harding! You Bastard! Don't fail me now. Fire over the top, support the left flank, now! Or I'll tie you to one of our guns and blow you to fucking pieces!"

Eli nodded stupidly and responded automatically, his mind resorting to training and indoctrination, jolted into action by Osbourne's violent reprimand. Gunner Williams and the rest of the crew were already turning the cannon, loading it with a Palliser shell (the small torpedo like round used as ammunition) and were priming the breech with gunpowder whilst Harding worked out the angle required to land the projectile over the heads of his own side into the attacking groups of enemy horsemen.

"Raise twenty degrees!" Eli shouted.

The tumult continued before them as the crew changed the angle of projection on the nine pounder gun.

"Ready. Fire!"

The firer pulled his lanyard connected to the firing pin as the crew stepped almost casually aside from the weapon. There was a shuddering crack and smoke poured from the muzzle of the gun as the recoil from the explosion sent the carriage rolling backwards. Everyone watched for the pall of smoke. The shell landed in a seething mass of the white and beige robes of Afghan horsemen, pressing against the backs of their own front ranks which were engaged with the line of khaki clad Indian foot soldiers that were desperately thrusting and gouging at the onslaught with bayonets and long pikes.

"Keep firing!" ordered Osbourne as he swung athletically onto his twirling horse and galloped away toward the next gun position.

Harding and his men set to the repetitive action of cleaning the barrel, loading the shells, priming the mechanism and firing the cannon in a rush of adrenaline fuelled activity. Occasionally they moved the carriage left or right to spread the field of fire but all the while kept up the well trained professional system of artillery warfare they had been schooled in. They hid the fear and nervous panic coursing through their bodies with practised organisation and a focus on support for the front line, all underpinned by a desperate need for their own survival. The gun cracked again and again and the flank they were supporting seemed to shudder with each shell that exploded between the opposing cavalry and supporting foot soldiers. Other guns had joined the barrage to form a line of airborne death that fell upon the landscape to form a bouncing, ear splitting sound married to a terrible and shattering image of violence.

Elias tried to shallow but there was no moisture left in his mouth. He flicked his dry tongue over the sweat that ran down his face and felt the tingle of the drips that poured across his tensile body. He saw men in the skirmish lines fall backwards, sliced and carved open by swords and lances or holding other ghastly wounds from small arms fire and torrid explosions. Horses stamped and raked the casualty strewn ground with crushing hooves whilst spikes and bayonets gouged at the riders sending them into the ghastly melee of pain and unceremonious death underneath. The sand soaked red in places with blood and guts but the fragile line of defenders held against the beastly attacking surge.

Time stood still. It felt like days had passed but it had only been minutes. The carnage pulled reality into a distorted state. There were different bubbles of chaos within a range of hellish separate worlds that seemed to be involved in this one great storm of savagery. As the left flank was engorged by a tangle of anarchy, the other parts of the British line seemed to wait in suspended animation for the same things to happen to them. Explosions rocked the ground around the obsessed gun crews as they worked and the enemy guns relentlessly continued to fire into the rest of the ranks along the British lines. More soldiers ran through the smoke heading into the fearful fray to support the end of the line being attacked.

Williams was plunging a sponge rod down the muzzle of the cannon, trying to clean the dust and gunpowder residue from inside the barrel when he stopped and looked out across the open ground to a ravine in the opposite direction from the battle line being engaged behind him.

"Look Sir, over there!" he said, gawping.

Harding couldn't really hear the comment through the noise but understood the shape of the words coming from his gunner's mouth and looked in the direction the man was gazing at. Eli screwed his eyes into focus over the heads of another group of infantry waiting in two lines, one crouched and one stood, fifty yards or so to the side of where their gun was pointing. Two hundred yards further away across no man's land, badly hiding in a range of dry water beds and ravines, he could just see the heads and banners of the leaders of another orgy of Afghan warriors. The leaders were sat on horses just visible above the top of the ravine and all around them, obvious now because of the sheer numbers they contained, were an obscene mass of rifle and spear wielding foot soldiers who had gathered stealthily under cover of the dried beds while the other battle had been going on. Eli flashed a look over the men of the British lines and saw the soldiers of the 66th foot regiment with their Martini Henri rifles aimed en masse at the ravine and the new front of the next attack.

The two men stopped what they were doing and looked at each other, suddenly aware of the sinister new danger to their already fragile existence. There was no time to fire the cannon again into the battle already going on, not even enough time to fully acknowledge the sense of foreboding that was beginning to flood over them. From behind the hidden hordes of enemy they heard the irregular BOOM of Afghan artillery batteries and saw a huge cloud of smoke rise from behind the ravine and a curtain of sand float from the ground as if a huge blanket was being shaken at them. A second later, a shower of ordnance clattered into the defensive line of men awaiting the attack from the dried river beds and their supporting gun positions behind them creating a jolting, brain splitting domino effect of shattering explosions.

Hundreds of heads ducked while others threw themselves to the ground like the workings of a crazed human machine set off by the bombs that rained down among them. Whole bodies along with bits of men and animals mixed with rock and metal, wood, clothes and rifles, flew through the air as mushrooms of brown smoke rose upwards in blobs of flowering destruction. Harding threw himself behind the wheel of his gun carriage, covering his helmeted head with his arms and tightly closing his eyes as a vicious wind pulled at his cowering body. When he opened them again after the shockwaves had passed a few seconds later, he caught stunted glimpses of men running forward, then falling down like shot rabbits, hit by shrapnel or gunshot and others sprawled along the ground trying to crawl out from beneath the falling clouds of debris. He closed his eyes again and when they reopened all he saw was the sky filled by the blinding light of one massive sun.

Then Gunner Williams was shaking him, shouting in his face maniacally.

"We've got to fire, Mr Harding, straight ahead, they're coming on the other side now!"

Harding could see the desperate soldier pointing to the ravine. He lifted his head, heard the whistle of bullets streaming through the air above and felt the carriage being turned by his team. Still crouching low, Harding moved to the side and saw the enemy charging towards them in a heart stopping, seemingly overwhelming attack on the lines of riflemen waiting yards away.

"Right wheel, lower fifteen degrees!" he shouted, fear breaking his strained voice.

The crew had already shifted the carriage around and hastily loaded and primed the gun in a fluid series of panicked movements. "Loaded and primed," they directed to the Master Gunner. Eli stood up straighter and took one last look around as if time had stood still for a second. The defensive lines were ready, holes in parts of the ranks where men had fallen due to the barrage but otherwise complete, rifles raised at the oncoming blanket of Afghan warriors. Behind him more men on horses moved around in confused disorder and to one side he noticed the commander of the Artillery battery, Major Blackwood, lying on the floor being treated by medics. There was now the familiar crack of his fellow nine pounders being fired and Harding looked ahead concerning himself wholly with the new front of battle that was about to be engaged, and the stopped clock of terror suddenly started again.

"Fire!" he screamed.

The recoil sent the death machine rolling back but Harding stood still, looking for the explosion up ahead, focused on altering the trajectory if the shot missed the charging Afghans.

"Reload!"

The ball of smoke billowed up from within the wave of attackers like the petals of a rose opening.

"Fire!" bellowed Eli again. The firer pulled his lanyard releasing the pin which ignited the gunpowder. The gun spat forth and another grey and black rose opened her petals within the mass of approaching warriors. The plumes of deadly growths flowered across the battlefield from the other guns and as they did so the robed hordes of dedicated ghazi's and village tribesmen bore themselves down upon the thin khaki line. As Harding and the rest of the artillery fired, so did the infantry rifles. Volley shot after volley shot mowed down the screaming enemy as they tried to cross the open ground from the ravine but sadistically, like a slowly overflowing vessel of thick, human formed oil, more followed in their wake. With unbelievable discipline, the sustained, well drilled impact of two lines of continuous rifle fire kept back the invaders with each determined drive. The battle raged like a boiling pot of molten metal over a spitting, angry fire, relentlessly pursued under a scorching white hot sky.

Harding was in a trance. Training had taken over his bodily actions and worked the necessary areas of his brain but his mind had ceased to acknowledge the gravity of the death inducing madness he was participating in. The noise had turned into a constant drone that hummed around his head, dulling the senses which earlier had been buzzing uncontrollably, and the minutes passed once more as if in slow motion. The turmoil happening before his eyes found a terrible regularity that enveloped him and all the other soldiers within his section in a cushion of unreality. With each death that occurred, a living soul would take the dead man's place within the line, so no man was ever truly alone in the slaughter or felt the full lustre of vulnerability within the desecration of life as it unfurled itself. Their solidarity kept them part of the war machine they were now inescapably involved in. There was nowhere else for them to go, no other place they could be. The whole line of British and Indian fighters had morphed with each wave of attack, growing at times with reinforcements from another part, bending and turning with others as surges came and went and sections of men died. The fight was like a living, breathing organism fuelled by human lives fed from all sides of the battlefield, growing and dying with each moment as it sucked in its helpless victims.

Elias saw teams of horses moving guns to and fro but kept firing his own weapon on the masses of men who charged time after time. He didn't notice the left flank weakening from the original first attack, or the smoothbore guns being calmly trotted out of that action like a troop of horse guards on a Sunday parade. They were being withdrawn in an attempt at being replenished in the village which was now also under attack and being defended by the reserved rifles of the Indian cavalry. He didn't notice one of his gunners get shot in the neck and lie down quietly as if he was going to sleep, holding the wound pointlessly with sand covered hands and reciting the Lord's prayer through the bubbles of blood on his lips and in his throat.

He didn't notice the horses being gathered behind the guns or the Captain taking control of the battery as the injured Major was taken away to the rear where a redoubt was now being organised in the village. And he didn't fully wake up from the terrible trance he was in until he saw Gunner Williams' shocked face mouthing at him once again through the madness. "They've given way, they've broken us. They're coming!"

Elias turned to the left where the flank had finally been broken by another surge from the hugely greater numbers of the enemy, and saw the infantry line roll up like a scattered wave of khaki coloured animals running from some deadly predator. Through them he saw Afghan chiefs trotting triumphantly across the dead and dying, leading their yelling and wailing army, carrying their tribal banners of blue, yellow and deepest red. They were heading for the guns that Harding and his fellow crews were manning, eager to cement their victory with the spoils of war.

On his horse, sword drawn, Captain John R Slade, who had taken command of the battery once his superior officer had been taken from the field, calmly gave the order for a section of the cannons still pointing in the direction of the breakthrough to load rounds of case shot. These were shells containing dozens of small lead balls which when fired would spray a deadly barrage of burning metal spheres upon an approaching force putting a deathly halt to those at the front and many behind. He waved his sabre to the other crew's, including Eli's, and said loudly but without panic, "Limber up!" It was the order to retreat.

Harding heard him and shouted at the crew as they immediately scrambled to hook the guns onto the draught horses twisting and turning in fear behind them. Aware of the oncoming danger, he grabbed a rifle from the ground and feverishly pulled a bayonet from his webbing belt before slipping it over the end of the barrel with shaking hands. Then he opened the breech and pushed a cartridge from his belt pouch inside the rifle trying to swallow down any saliva for his thick, parched throat. The distinctive bursting sound of case shot being fired came from somewhere in front and he noticed the advancing tribesmen fall as the horrid wave of metal balls ploughed into the front runners. Harding took the opportunity to look in the other direction and registered the lines of the 66th and their supporting Indian infantry still holding off the onslaught being aimed at them with their regimented volleys of rifle fire.

Suddenly he looked ahead again and saw the frightening sight of the guns nearest the left flank horde being overrun as the horses and men who had desperately been trying to hook the guns away were caught in a whirlwind of close quarter fighting. The gunners fought with hand spikes and long knives cutting the horses legs and lashing out at the opposing men as they moved through the scene, Afghans falling on them two or three at a time screaming and yelling like crazed witches. Indian and British soldiers on horses galloped towards the stricken guns to help those crews being attacked and out of the indistinguishable din, one piece of artillery was pulled away as the attackers were momentarily forced back.

Harding dropped to one knee, picked an Afghan out of the melee and fired. He saw the man's head jerk to one side and his halted figure fall awkwardly over the already prone bodies underneath him. It was the first man he had ever seen killed by his own hand even though the cannon he had worked undoubtedly killed many more before this one, but it was a milestone his mind did not properly register under the harrowing circumstances. Instead, all Harding could feel was the breath pounding in his chest and the fuel of fear pumping around his body controlling the necessary actions he took. Glancing left and right, he caught sight of Williams crouched behind some ammo boxes firing dementedly at the attackers. For a strange second Eli had the bizarre thought that neither of them would be able to find their jackets in all this mess.

Eli reloaded, fired, reloaded and fired again, dropping Afghans like they were falling apples from an over ripe tree. He saw a sergeant whose name he didn't know miraculously running back to the scrum and picking up a wounded driver before placing him gently on a carriage as it was being pulled away, then regaining his horse, mount the beast and gallop headlong into a throng of crazed ghazi's, swaying his sabre to and fro, opening heads up with hideous wounds and lacerating limbs of the manic faced foes before spinning his terrified animal around and retreating. Harding looked across at Williams whose eyes had become wild with fear and adrenaline, a twisted unnatural grin manifesting itself on his face as he shot, reloaded and shot again and again into the enemy throng. There were more clouds of dust as another gun was pulled away by the draught horses. He saw the dead body of Lieutenant Osbourne being mercilessly hacked to pieces by three or four robed men.

"Retreat!" shouted Captain Slade from somewhere to the side. "Retreat to the village!"

Harding grabbed at Williams' shirt whilst he was stood up firing madly and fumbling for each round in his rapidly emptying ammo pouch.

"Williams, come on, we've got to go!" screamed Eli, and he pulled the gunner away as the rest of the units fell back in the direction of the tiny village that had become the only refuge. On all sides men were moving backwards, firing at the oncoming enemy then reloading as they moved again surrounded by the dust and smoke that hung in the air, ears filled with the scream of agonised comrades as they were overcome. Swords flashed in the afternoon sun as the oncoming enemy enveloped the slowest of the retreating soldiers.

One Afghan tribesman wearing a grey turban, long beige robes and waving a short curved sword ran from behind the dust cloud screeching wildly at Williams. The gunner parried the swooping blow with his empty rifle which threw the assailant to one side, then club like, he began to bludgeon the attacker across the head with his weapon, smiting him to the ground.

Another screamer came at Harding but he dropped to one knee and fired into the stomach of the running man who crumpled to the sand at Eli's feet. Then another, this one with a long spear, who came rushing at him stealthily which made Harding need to twist his body to one side to avoid the rusty point aimed at his abdomen. Awkwardly but somehow on target Eli thrust the spike of his bayonet fully into the Afghan's side, snapping ribs as it slid inside the man's body, piercing the vital organs and causing the poor beggar to let out a wretched groan as he fell to the ground. The man stretched out in pain whilst trying to hold the wound as if covering the hole would repair the internal damage.

Meanwhile Gunner Williams swung his rifle like a cricket bat at all sides as the surrounding dust was filled with screaming enemy banshees that came insanely running at anyone in a khaki uniform. His hair was plastered with sweat and his trousers were streaked with fan shaped sprays of other men's dark red blood, the woollen putties above his boots unravelling as he moved to and fro. Harding had fallen to the floor but managed to reload his rifle and shoot a man in the chest before the attacker could bear down on him with a musket style rifle onto which a long, serrated knife had been crudely tied with twine. A horse clattered by in a state of panic and nearly ran over him, but through luck rather than judgement, Eli speedily rolled to one side and scrabbled up. As he did so, he immediately realised that he had lost his rifle. He looked across to Williams who was fighting hand to hand with someone, snarling like a dog trying to bite the nose off his terrified opponent before head butting him remorselessly several times as if he was a bar room brawler in a late night fight, until finally the attacker fell away into a lifeless rag doll; his face all smashed and bloody from the heady onslaught.

Harding felt his adrenaline replaced by the debilitating swoon of hysterical panic as he glanced in other directions and saw several comrades fall under the blows of swords and spears. It felt like the enemy were all around him about to destroy his life as they swarmed in for the kill but instead it was an Indian infantryman that came stumbling towards him in a daze, his head gashed terribly, his eyes half closed in confusion. As he wandered past the soldier's chest was suddenly popped open by the force of a bullet and Harding was covered in a shower of blood. He wiped the spots of gore from his eyes and looking down, remembered, as if he had just woken up from a crazed, frightened dream that his pistol was still sitting in its unopened holster. He shakily opened the clasp, took out the hand gun and automatically raised it to the nearest opponent. Pulling the trigger with a jolt, the gun almost popped apart and the recoil felt unusually delicate as if it hadn't worked properly but the approaching man Eli aimed for went down in a heap. He aimed again, POP, and another target fell. Then shockingly, an Afghan flew out of nowhere so close to him that Eli had no time to aim and fire, a short sword held above his attacker's turbaned head ready to fall and strike. Instinctively Harding grabbed the sword arm as the warrior fell on him making both men hit the ground with a jarring thud, the enemy's angry sand covered face only inches from his own, growling and shouting in Arabic like a hideous gargoyle, trying to bring down the blade onto his opponent's head. Luckily Eli held on to his pistol after the fall and was able to bring it up to the face of the attacker while holding his sword arm with all the panic fuelled strength he could muster. When the barrel was near the man's cheek it fired, as if by itself, and threw the swordsman's head and the rest of his body to one side, his flailing body immediately becoming silent and still. Harding rolled over and saw into the open eyes of his victim, then catching sight of the awful injury that the gun had caused, he let out a wail of horror like a child hurt in a playground accident. He desperately pushed the dead man away with the gun still shaking in his nerve wracked hand and looked around in dread waiting to be surely consumed by more and more attackers. *'This is it'*, he thought. *'This is how it ends'*. This would be how his unplanned and unfulfilled life would finally be finished, in this crucible of brutality. This would be the last place he ever saw; the last sky he would ever see in a world that he thought he would surely see so much more of. He had not loved yet, not shared the intimacy of experiences or lived truly happily with other people. Now it was going to end. And the end would come so unbearably painfully.

But for some reason, and for the rest of his life he would never be able to understand why, no more attackers came in those simple few seconds of respite from the battle raging around him and Eli was able to crouch on one knee breathing deeply to regain a small fragment of composure in the surrounding madness. *'Keep going,'* his brain whispered through the white noise, *'Keep going, stay alive'*, came a rousing inner call, *'Whatever happens, stay alive!'* He focused on this mantra of survival and ultimate escape from the butchery before his eyes and allowed his natural reflexes to take over his tired body; guiding him to either hopeful salvation or a mistaken and inevitable damnation.

Williams was on all fours by this time, trying to scrabble away from a tribesman holding a spear who was prodding at the gunner as if he were a mouse trying to escape from a broom wielding housewife. Harding eyed the spearman down the sight of his pistol and POP! The man's face fell into a hole of red and pink and Williams laughed madly, his own face covered in spit and blood.

Suddenly explosions erupted among the oncoming killers throwing them in the air like tossed branches of a felled tree or causing them to dive to the ground and end their searching attacks. Harding grabbed Williams by the braces and they stumbled through the dust and putrid fumes which were being fanned by plumes of more grey roses exploding behind them within the crowds of suspended enemy, bunches of roses delivered by the covering fire from the saved guns and the rear guard which was forming in the village of Mundabad only two hundred yards away.

It felt like time stood still once more as they crossed that final two hundred yards, pulling and pushing each other as they traversed their way through the bullets that whizzed overhead and the stray explosions falling across their precarious pathway. Other comrades were around them too, helping each other as some fell, caught in the crossfire or winged by the edges of an eruption. Stragglers were consumed by the line of marauding warriors that made it through the barrage sent from the village. Handfuls of retreaters were hit directly, killing them as they attempted the desperate journey, victims of the necessary blanket of weaponry needed to keep the main force of Afghans at bay and allow the survivors some chance of escape.

Finally, after yard upon yard of devastating open ground, the two men fell into the confines of the walls within the relative safety of the village, helping hands of fellow comrades pulling them under cover to where Captain Slade had formed a defensive line of the remaining artillery and infantry, supporting the retreat of the remnants of the broken units that trickled away from the main swamp of the battlefield and the baying forward line of Afghans that danced their way around the leftovers like buzzards on a desiccated carcass. The regrouped remnants were also sending in fire to try and help the men of the 66th who were miraculously holding off the rest of the Afghan army from a defensive position in the dried out ravines some distance from the village.

In the village it was chaos. Wounded men were being loaded onto carts pulled by camels and mules or whatever horses could be spared and sent away. Weapons and ammunition were distributed to the stragglers being put together to form the rear-guard entrusted with the job of protecting a full retreat of whatever could be salvaged of the main force and their long trek back to the fortress at Kandahar.

An Indian soldier came up to Eli and handed him a canteen of dusty water which he drank from thirstily before handing it on to a dazed Williams, whose look of distemper had now been replaced with one of exhausted bewilderment.

"Did you see the horses, sir? Did you see them? Kicking and plunging in agony, they were! In agony!" the gunner babbled. "Slaughtered we were, man and beast. I told you we would be, I blasted told you!"

"My God, it's not over yet," replied Eli closing his eyes to the tumult happening around him. He was shaking uncontrollably, covered in filth and the blood of others.

Along the walls of the village survivors sat in various states of shock. The sun streamed down on the red and brown faces as it had been all day long and the heat and horror of what they had experienced emanated from the shattered warriors like an all-consuming toxic gas. Men groaned and coughed under the weight of the heavy air still defiled with dust and drifting sand carried on the floating clouds of bitter smoke tinged with the stench of vaporised gunpowder. On the other side of the village Harding noticed hundreds of exhausted looking men and horses trying to form a line of cavalry, and realised this disjointed gathering were going to attempt a charge to try and aid the remaining right flank of the original defensive line still engaged in vicious battle along the shelter of the ravine nearly a mile away.

"Bloody hell, there's going to be a cavalry charge," Eli said, his dried out words loaded with hopelessness.

The line of doddery horsemen, Indian and British, fatigued by the sun, the barrage and the earlier defence of the village, suddenly jolted forward without being set up properly and the thundering sound of hooves grew louder and louder as they picked up speed heading towards the mass of men in the ravine now being harassed constantly by the throes of the enemy. Some men stood up to watch while others gazed from behind the walls as the distended wave of cavalry fell upon a horde of ghazi's attacking the infantry in the ravine, a place which was also being swelled by the arrival of loose pockets of soldiers fleeing from the earlier routs.

The horsemen, their beast's eyes bulging with shock and terror as they galloped, hacked and trampled over the first of the Afghans but by sheer weight of enemy numbers the cavalry were driven off to one side; dozens being lost to gunfire exploding from the masses of insurgent's infantry coming around to encircle the remains of the British and Indian forces in the ravines. The cavalry charge immediately faltered and was spent almost as quickly as it began as the depleted horsemen with no energy or confidence left to regroup and charge again peeled away and cantered or trotted tiredly back to the village, utterly routed. Harding saw a dishevelled looking Captain whose name he couldn't remember, blood and gore splattered across the haunches of his horse, riding dejectedly towards the other officers who were trying to issue panicked orders to overcooked and beaten soldiers, "It's no good, there's too many of them," Harding heard the Captain say and realised it was something he himself had already been told that day.

For the next half hour Elias Harding and the only other survivor of his gun crew, Williams, watched over the top of a roughly built, village wall as the army of Ayub Khan now focused entirely on the rest of the British ranks trapped on the battlefield. They watched as Indian infantrymen arrived from other parts of the broken line, drawn to the ravine by the hope of joining together with the hardened English regiment and the possibility of fighting their way out. The 66th was swelled uncontrollably by the intake until they broke out from what little cover there was in the dried river beds and were forced into the open. Minute by minute, dozens of men were cut down by the slowly surrounding tribesmen and horsemen of the Khan's army.

Too far away and too few in number to offer any support, the rear guard could only watch helplessly as the surrounded regiment hopelessly battled on, Slade's leftover artillery guns merely adding extra minutes to their ensuing destruction. Some in the village couldn't bring themselves to watch as the men in the open fought back to back and managed a retreat to the next small outcrop of stone buildings known as the village of Khig. But they knew there was no respite for the embattled soldiers there. They could hear the screams, the gunfire, the clash of battle as the surviving members of the 66th Foot were brought down one by one from 200 to 100, from 50 to 25. One by one the regiment was disintegrated, dismantled, man by fighting man, strangled in the ever tightening noose of a deadly, unbreakable human rope made from thousands and thousands of fanatic warriors baying for blood and freedom, until only eleven British soldiers and the regimental dog were left.

Holed up in a walled garden, almost out of ammunition, protecting the regimental colours between them, pride, bravery and the astounding acceptance of the reality that lay in a hopeless but glorifying death, made those final eleven make their triumphant last stand.

With his binoculars, tears streaming down his sand caked, destitute face because of the unforgiving scene unfolding in front of him, Harding saw through the viewfinders, a magnified image of sheer undeniable bravery and courage, born from the soul of unshakable men who knew they were going to die and chose to accept it. Completely surrounded by the baying hordes, the remaining eleven survivors, without a thought of surrender, valiantly charged out of the final comfort which was their circle of comrades and attacked the masses encroaching upon them with all the challenge and belief of a victorious force. Killing many of the enemy as they drove outward, they were finally cut down by the surrounding Afghans until they were all dead and their valour and sacrifice would forever be cemented in the history of the British army and its many futile conflicts.

The end was over relatively quickly. But on the faces of the ultimately conquering Afghans as they surveyed the aftershock of the demise, there was a look of awe and respect at seeing such heroism and honour.

Harding slowly lowered his binoculars and wiped the tears from his dust smeared face with a trembling hand. He wanted to cheer or shout out loudly to show his admiration for the freshly dead, but his body and mind was racked with almost inconsolable grief. He felt the overwhelming misery of defeat and death. Underneath the cracking like sound of the artillery that still vainly fired away behind and amidst the furore of the crazed events happening all around him, he was sure he heard a dog barking.

For the next two hours Elias hid behind a dry stone wall in the village of Mundabad taking pot shots at the pulsating formations of celebrating Afghan warriors that gathered on the outskirts of the battlefield. He had a Martini Henry rifle and a pouch of ammunition which was regularly refilled by a constantly smiling, dust smattered Indian infantryman, whose job it was to go along the ranks supplying the defenders with a copious amount of bullets. To all intents and purposes Eli was now an infantryman himself, his artillery weapon being manned by other surviving members of different gun crews, part of the rear guard which had formed in the village and along another nearby ravine which ran next to the outskirts of the abandoned dwellings.

Around him were crouched a random selection of shaken and twisted survivors including engineers and sappers, drivers, baggage handlers, scouts and what was left of the British and Indian infantry, who had gradually filtered their way from the scene of chaotic battle out on the open ground into the apparent safety of the re-inhabited village.

The annihilation of the 66th Regiment had in many ways saved the rest of the force. It had sated much of the blood lust of the Afghans who had been impressed by the bravery of the doomed regiment and the final hopeless charge from its handful of leftover men. Impressed to such a degree that they were now showing respectful wariness to the surviving army in the village. Also, the remaining twenty thousand men of Ayub Khan's army, instead of expending more men trying to destroy the remnants of the British forces, halted their onslaught and regrouped to make camp before the onset of evening, which would make fighting difficult and also allow them to revel in the glories of the day's victory.

Khan tried early attempts at attacking the men in the village but had been held back by disciplined volley fire from the embedded survivors and a constant barrage of fire from the saved artillery and smoothbore cannon. Now it was too late in the day to engage in a full scale attack. However, there was still a large group of tribesmen and white robed, veiled ghazis on the edge of the battlefield moving like a stalking band of pale dogs, skulking around an injured prey, waiting for the opportunity to strike and make a final kill. They danced and shrilled in the heavy afternoon heat.

The sun filled the sky and baked the hard ground, cooking the sand and dust causing superheated particles to irritate the skin. It was like being inside a furnace. Mouths were torturously dry, lips cracked sore from the evaporating heat and there was no respite from the unrelenting, late afternoon yellow orb above. Water was running low. What was left was dirty with grit and dust.

The seriously wounded, of which there were many, had been loaded onto carts, mules, camels and on the backs of strong, willing men. Accompanied by the walking wounded, this straggling train of miserable animals began the long walk back to Kandahar, followed in dribs and drabs by small groups of armed men hoping to protect the vulnerable wagons as they made their painful march. As the afternoon wore on into early evening, the throngs of Afghans lost interest in the survivors left in the village and instead turned their attention to the wasted lives strewn across the landscape and began to scavenge among the debris of the battle site. It was covered with dead humans, torn and broken, smashed and cut. Guns, uniforms and personal possessions were stripped from them by the enemy and worn as trophies. Weapons and destroyed machines littered the ground along with exploded, fly covered corpses of dead horses and countless men; next to the hundreds of mortally injured who were still alive in the kill zone beneath the burning sun.

Gradually the guns in the village fell silent as they were hauled cautiously away for the slow, tired grind back to base. As evening enveloped the village, like a collapsing bag, small bands of riflemen dissipated off from behind the dry walls and defensive ravine to join the long line of refugees. Harding, Williams and a large group of men led by a few determined Officers stayed behind to offer a line of defence should the enemy follow. Eli tried to sleep and fell into a disturbed, broken stupor during the night with the words of Captain Slade, spoken just as he was leaving the village to control the retreat, echoing in his head.

"Try to keep them back if they make a move to follow us, men. I know the circumstances are trying, but you might be the only hope of some of us getting back alive," the overly calm Officer had suggested. *'The circumstances are trying,'* repeated Eli monotonously as the events of the day soaked into his shattered brain until fatigue finally overcame him and he blacked out for a few hours deep into the turgid night.

Hours before the sun came up and roused the enemy from their more peaceful, victorious sleep, Harding was woken by the others within his group and they all crept from the abandoned village and headed towards Kandahar over fifteen miles away.

So the pockets of bloodied life struggled through a cold, sleepless dark until a new dawn broke across the sky and another landscape emerged, still tested by the burning heat of the sun, suffocating airs of choking dust and the threat of atrocious death. It was not over yet. The pockets were harangued by groups of local tribesmen and bandits sent from the main force still camped at the battlefield in order to pick off the soldiers as they retreated. Harding and the other men took up positions in the rocks above the distributed injured and distressed survivors and helped to ward off the harassing horsemen, laying down covering fire and offering themselves as decoys to the marauders. Gunshots could be heard further along the trail where locals had out flanked the end of the line and attacked the forward survivors but most of the gangs of following insurgents had trailed the rear-guard through the village after sunrise.

And so for miles Harding and the others ran, turned, hid and shot back at the attackers losing some of their beleaguered force as they did so. There was no rest, no peace and there was no water or food.

Sometimes they worked a gap between them and their chasers allowing the group to walk for a while, but constantly they looked around them waiting for the shriek from approaching riders or the crack of a rifle shot. In a state of heightened stress and terrified alertness they would come across the bodies of injured who were left after dying on the long trek through lack of medical attention and water. The animal on which they had been draped, be it horse, mule or camel, would be led beside them also dead from exhaustion or injury. Sometimes they were solitary figures led by the side of the rough road or members of dissipated groups scattered randomly along the outskirts, the carts on which they travelled left abandoned, unable to be pulled away quickly enough from a swooping attack by their hunters. The faces of the dead were contorted in the final throes of pain or agape with the dazed confusion of death.

Again, there was the crack of a rifle shot, the piercing whizz of the bullet as it flew menacingly close a split second later. Now only a handful, the group of men in which Harding and Williams clung too, ran to the nearest selection of rocks and returned fire, unable to see the attackers, tout with fear whilst wondering if the whole of the Afghan army could emerge from the craggy hillsides and totally consume them. But deluding themselves that they may present enough of a defence to keep whoever was out there at bay, they waited in hidden readiness and sacrificial abandonment. They watched silently, on edge.

From behind the rocks a straggly haired, white and grey mongrel dog came running towards the crouching soldiers. It weaved in and out of the boulders panting steadily as it darted along, it's pink tongue lolling in its dry mouth. The dog didn't bark or jump up at the men when it reached them.

"Bloody hell boy! You frightened the life out of us," breathed Williams as he knelt down and furiously fussed the animal which still looked around twitchily, seemingly unaffected by the attention he was receiving. "It's Bobbie, the 66th's dog. He got away, the lucky sod!" gasped another one of the men.

The gathering looked at each other in amazement and then nervously turned towards the rocks where Bobbie had emerged. Everyone expected a group of ghazis to appear from behind the pathway giving chase to the mascot. But no one came. The mongrel looked at the soldiers with tired and panic stricken eyes. It was almost a look of pity on its face that said, *'You humans, you're no good, all you do is kill each other, I'm off,'* before swinging its head fitfully from side to side to shake free from the stroking hands of William's and then Bobbie the dog bounded off down the stony slope in the direction of Kandahar.

"Blimy, he didn't hang around," said one of the men watching the dog disappear.

"I don't blame him," said Harding eyeing the opening between the rocks further up the hill behind them. "Let's get the hell out of this bloody shithole."

Without hesitation, the small band of men warily crept away from the hiding place and followed in the direction of Bobbie, all the while keeping a steady eye on the rocks above them.

After what seemed like hours without any contact from Afghans, they continued the retreat, step after exhausted step and mile after sunburnt mile until they caught up with a large group of survivors who had reached a lifesaving watering hole. It was covered in dust, filled with dirt and the brown water was only enough to just about keep the survivors alive let alone sate the unquenchable thirst of the dishevelled, disparate band of tormented soldiers.

But it was enough, enough to keep them alive and to allow them to carry on the torturous journey until finally after miles upon miles of fear, pain and sun bleached misery, one by bedraggled one, the survivors from the battle of Maiwand fell into the gates of Kandahar and the security and relief that came from unbelievable salvation.

*

When Eves had finished telling the story, he looked around the faces of the men he was with. All of them were utterly transfixed at the account he had just given in his own inimitable way. Some were staring into the fire thoughtfully whilst others gazed at the tables they were sat behind or stared directly at the storyteller, aghast at the realities of warfare that had been portrayed but at the same time secretly riveted by the excitement of it. Eves hadn't been there but he knew what it must have been like, for he had seen and experienced similar battles in his long army career.

"Not even half the men who left Kandahar on that ill-fated expedition got back alive, and many of them died of their wounds afterwards." The old soldier puffed on his wooden pipe. "As for the 66th they were wiped out apart from the dog and a handful of men who got away before they were surrounded. They earned a medal for that, lads," he said roundly.

"My God," whispered the scribbler. "When you read about it in the papers you can't imagine what it's really like."

"Never like it says it is in the papers," said Eves. "It isn't a bad thing if you never see it in your lifetime. Be glad you never do," he added ruefully and the men of the room nodded quietly as the big Sergeant stood up in a measured way with an unexpectedly woeful look on his face as he remembered his own battles, scenes of devastation and the loss of many close friends. He softly left the room, just as he had arrived, padding away in his old man's slippers, as the men stared reflectively into the calming flames of the fire and thought to themselves about the horrors of war. Outside, the damp afternoon slowly wore on.

Then, with the same regularity that had infused its falling and the equal steadiness that had determined its endurance, the rain gradually stopped. Although the sky was still a canvas of grey, its shade was the merest hint of a degree or two lighter than before and the darker clouds which had held the rain rolled slowly away inland. The eternal sun still shone above the ceiling of cloudiness overhead but its light could not penetrate the thickness, or even lever a crack in the heavy atmospheric blanket so releasing a chink of light through the leaden, February covering. It was still cold and everything felt icy wet to the touch.

But it had already stopped raining in one man's sleeping mind. In fact, the rain never played a part in the visions that filled the dreams sourced from the experience of this tormented soul. If only it had been raining there, in both the real and the remembered worlds, and the nightmare bright sky had been filled with grey clouds of cooling water instead of the shocking white light of the overpowering, blinding sun.

There he is again.

That face, that man.

Out of the same shocking white light comes the snarling, lunatic face of a frantic comrade, crazed by the desperate fight for survival, veins flowing with the hot blood of mad slaughter and an all-consuming desire to live. A sword in his hand hacks mercilessly at a screaming, agonised face and body of a doomed man, trying to crawl away from under the horrific blows, his arms and back cut and slashed, until thankfully a final fatal stroke cuts his head open and releases the victim from his atrocious endurance.

There's the noise again.

Tap, tap, tap. Tap, tap, tap.

A tinny clanking sound made from the connection of a bayonet onto a sword. Two opponents dancing the duel of death, a stand-off in which both men are afraid to make the first move in case dropping their guard allows the other a chance to strike one fatal blow. So they probe gently with each other as they circle in a ritualistic meeting of tinkling metal and taught nerves, both knowing they are inextricably trapped within a fight to the death.

Rat, tat, tat, the blows get louder.

Rat, tat, tat, the fear is stronger.

Rat, tat, tat...

Elias woke up with a sudden start, confused for a second by the tapping sound which had echoed through his head from the visions that filled his sleeping mind and the same sound that now seemed to be floating eerily around the reality of his stuffy front room. He blinked repetitively, sat forward, tensing his neck to relieve the aches he felt from falling asleep in the undersized chair and rubbed his eyes with his fingers as if to pop them out of their sockets. His body and head were clammy from a thin film of sweat which had oozed from the pores of his skin. The room felt deathly cold.

He looked around dopily, still unsure of what was happening then looked across at the window and saw Eves tapping his knuckles on the grimy glass. Tap, tap, tap came the sound. "Mr Harding, Mr Harding Sir! Its stopped raining," the sergeant called.

Eli stood up stiffly and tottered to the door. As he opened it he was temporarily blinded by the grey light outside attempting to stream into the cavy room.

"Eves, everything alright?" he asked quivering. "I must have fallen asleep."

Zanzibar approached the door and said calmly, "Yes Sir, everything's alright. It's stopped raining now. We're unloading the wagons. Wondered if you wanted to start putting the gun in place, the men are all fed and watered and eager to get going and I thought it would be good to give them something to do, stop 'em getting pissed."

"Yes, yes of course, Eves. Good man. I'll um.... Just get my coat and be along in a tick," Eli replied waveringly. Eves smiled, nodded and then walked off towards the other side of the courtyard. Closing the door Elias wobbled backwards like a drunkard at the bar and then leant against the wall, still shaken by the disorientation caused by the visions in his sleep and the suddenness of his waking. The fire in the room had burned down low. The clock on the mantelpiece ticked loudly. His head felt groggy from the gin and rum consumed earlier and he wiped the foam from the corners of his mouth with his fingers and rubbed his short hair with a clammy, shaking hand. He shivered, suddenly feeling cold. He thought he saw a shadow move through the door into the darkened hallway.

"Who's there?" he said, suddenly frightened. "Who's that? Cook, is that you?"

It occurred to him that someone else was in the quarters, moving down the hallway. Eli walked gingerly to the open door and slowly poked his head out into the hall. He could see across into the office and down to the end room above the landing bay and the open doors of his bedroom and the disused kitchen, but there was no movement. It was silent and still. He walked down the corridor, confused and doddery, listening for a sound of someone. Standing at the entrance to both rooms he looked round the bedroom and saw no one, then glanced over the kitchen space with its dust covered worktop and cold, extinct stove. It was empty and the only sound came from the wind mournfully whistling down the chimney and through the cracks around the hatchway door in the adjacent storeroom.

Even Beethoven had done a runner in his mind. It was still full of the ghosts from his dream, the same dream that visited him regularly in his unconscious hours and even sometimes during his waking ones. The fear wasn't of the shadows in the gloomy rooms he lived in now but of the past and the events connected to its violent extremes. *'Get yourself together man!'* he told himself. *'There's nothing in here, it's all back there in history. Shake it off, get outside, move on!'*

He rocked back into the sitting room and thought about having another drink to calm him down, perhaps even a shot of laudanum to settle his frayed mind, but decided against both. *'Maybe later,'* he thought, *'after I've sorted this bloody gun out!'* The cold prickled his skin and he looked to the coat stand in the far corner by the outside door. He had an array of coats gathered over the years from shops and boutiques visited during his limited travels, suitable for all types of weathers and occasions. He liked the warmth and sense of protection a good coat could offer and his favourites were the thick winter ones. It was a fascination which had only really started since Maiwand.

He had a beautifully made sheepskin lined coat from Afghanistan, bought at a market in Kandahar shortly after the battle, and a hand sown greatcoat made in a basement tailors on the side streets of Moscow which he had bought on a trip to Egypt. Having a decent coat must have been a subconscious reaction to his battle stress but he never knowingly made the connection. His grey tweed overcoat bought in London was still damp, so he grabbed a dark blue, woollen Dockers jacket bought several years ago from a Swedish fisherman trapped in Dover who needed money after being left ashore due to an argument with his captain. Putting it on, Eli remembered the fisherman's angled Scandinavian accent through his tight ginger beard and the suitcase of seafaring accoutrements he had for sale to fund his return ticket. Buttoning it up fully and pulling the collar around his neck and ears, he looked back towards the hallway as if expecting to see something emerge in the shadowy recesses. "Bloody ghosts," he said, as he opened the door and stepped out onto the wet gravel.

Using a small, moveable hand operated crane with a geared pulley system, the men of the fort were able to unload the heaviest gun parts from the wagon with relative ease. The rest was unloaded by hand and placed around one of the many empty gun emplacements. Harding had ordered one of the brothers to stand on the parapet and keep watch in case Major Acres sent another message. This was also a good way to keep the brothers split up so as to avoid irritating anyone, which they inevitably did when they were together. Two other men had the task of storing the gunpowder and Palliser shells inside the magazine room and cook had been sent to the kitchen to prepare dinner.

Everyone else was able to help with the creation of the weapon and although most of them would probably stand around watching helplessly, Eli thought he would try to involve everyone at some stage in the construction process and give them experience in the fineries of putting together a piece of fortified battery, traverse platform mounted, artillery hardware. Everything was still wet from the earlier rain and there was a chill, damp feeling in the air which meant the crew all wore their navy blue winter jackets with brass buttons and some even had woollen gloves on to take away the chill from their cold hands.

Acres had decided it was best to place the gun next to the only other weapon of the battery at the front of the fort so both weapons could be used to offer a concentrated range of covering fire across the large expanse of water between Steep Holm and the Down. There were supposed to be seven guns at Brean Down but it had only ever been fully gunned once, shortly after the fort was built nearly twenty years ago. This was in an effort to show the politicians its majestic superiority over the estuary. It was a public relations exercise by Lord Palmerston, the instigator of the Coastal Defence system and his administrators of the project, to present the fort fully operational and allay any fears from the public over the waste of money and resources the construction of these forts may have been. Gradually over time, when the public lost interest and it was deemed Brean Down wasn't as strategically important as her counterparts, the weapons had been removed from this particular fort, one by one, and taken to equip other forts as they were completed along the Severn Estuary and the South Coast of Britain.

However, with this new arrival at Brean, two guns was still the most number of armaments the fort had had since the opening of the place. In the intervening years it was previously decided that the volunteers would only ever need one gun to practice on and in the end the battery would only ever really be used for practice. There had even been times when there were no guns on Brean Down at all, leaving Steep Holm as the only defence in the middle of the channel, although the public were never aware of this. But even with two guns about to be in place, Elias Harding new deep down that the fort wouldn't actually offer an adequate defence of the estuary in its present situation and if the French did ever decide to invade, this would surely be the ideal place for them to try. Not that they ever would, everyone was confident that the powers of Northern Europe had enough on their global plates without bothering in a cross channel carve up. Still, Eli was happy in the knowledge that, regardless of the fact the French would never invade Britain, the possible defence of her coast wasn't really his problem and its military inadequacies were down to someone else.

The only real issue for now was that Eli had forgotten how to put the thing together. It had been a long time since his artillery and engineering training at Woolwich and all the guns he had previously used on a regular basis were smaller and had been mounted on horse drawn carriages. This weapon was bigger and bulkier due to the nature of its purpose and had to be mounted on a traversable platform which was altogether a more intricate and time consuming job. He had studied the plans and drawings on the build of the gun and had fathomed out the basic requirements of the structure but some of the detailed workings of the platform and inner mechanisms were still a bit hazy. It was going to be a case of trial and error, or 'suck it and see' as a prostitute in Exeter had once told him. His memory had become less acute since his days in Afghanistan and, on his return, reasoned thought had sometimes become befuddled.

When everything had been unloaded, everybody stood around looking at the array of parts and sections led on the ground with confused looks on their faces. Eli raised his eyebrows and pouted. "Right, let's see if we can't work out how to put this pile of junk together then," he said confidently.

So for the rest of the afternoon, the men of the fort toiled over the creation of their new gun, swearing fruitfully whilst generally getting in each other's way. They argued over who had the most superior knowledge in the fields of engineering and mechanics, which in reality turned out to be no one in particular, while others just stood around intermittently, with hands on their hips shaking their heads saying things like 'that's not the way to do it' and 'ere, give it to me, I'll try.'

Eves took control during the easy parts of the assembly but would often sit to one side merely smoking his pipe content to leave the practical technicalities of the build to the rest of the group. Harding would delay the whole process for what seemed like hours by poring over the plans one more time, trying to work out the finer principles of some intricate working.

Halfway through the fiasco he decided to venture into the magazine room, housed on one side of the new gun's emplacement, to check on the progress of the two men he had tasked with storing the ammo and tidying the ordnance. The door to this room was level with the courtyard but immediately opened onto a flight of stone steps which went underground to a short, tight corridor leading to the main magazine room set into the bowels of the headland. The room had been carved into the limestone rock which formed the perfect protection for the highly explosive materials stored inside.

The space was dark and foreboding, lit only by a series of dull flickering lamps enclosed inside the wall behind specially built, glass fronted partitions to avoid the lamps being dropped or knocked over and so reducing the risk of a fire and any subsequent explosion. Wooden walking boards lined the floor and soft material covered the lower parts of the walls to eliminate sparks should any metal objects be dropped. The men working inside wore calico overalls with wooden buttons and special canvas slippers so that no bare metal fastenings or buckles could strike rough surfaces. There were three magazine rooms built into the Down to service a fully operational battery but only one of them ever had any ammunition in it during the forts existence. The one being used at the moment was on the seaward side opposite the Officer's quarters next to the only other gunned emplacement.

Elias called out to the men inside the claustrophobic cave and Gosfor padded out of the blackness up the corridor from the cold, damp, dark underground room.

"How's it going, Gosfor? How much have we got altogether now?" Eli asked. Gosfor turned down the corners of his mouth and raised thin eyebrows beneath his rounded cap. "Well, we got sixty shells and 500lbs of gunpowder. That won't last long if we get attacked by the frogs," he smirked, before throwing a wide, knowing grin at the Master Gunner.

"It may not be enough to turn Frenchie away, but it's enough to blow this place up if needs be," Eli said and returned the grin to the creamy, calico clad George Gosfor. "Anyway, tidy up, get it locked down, extinguish those lights, then get yourselves back and tell cook to put a brew on for everyone."

"Right o, Sir," Gosfor nodded and disappeared back down the corridor into the darkness. Harding turned around and whilst pretending to take in a view of the surrounding walls, let out a long, airy shot of flatulence down the small stairs into the confined space. "And get a load of that," he said smirking as he closed the heavy wooden door shutting off the subterranean bunker from the outside world and trapping the noxious release inside. He walked back to where the men were fussing over the emplacement arguing about what to do next and he looked at the platform carriage that had been more or less completed and gave it a quick test by moving the wheels along the circular rails already built into the concrete base.

"Well that looks alright," he exhaled. "Let's see if we can't get this barrel on, then," he said still smiling as they all started fussing around again.

It took another hour for the barrel to be lifted up using the pulley, placed on the carriage and semi fixed to a reasonable state of security, at which point Eli decided the men had peaked in today's knowledge of artillery engineering and with the light beginning to fade he ordered the lads to cover up the half-finished weapon, tidy away the rest of the parts, collect the tools and then retire to the barracks to get cleaned up for dinner.

When the volunteers had filtered back to the main building Harding turned to Eves and said easily, "Well that didn't go too badly, seeing as I can't remember bugger all about putting these blasted things together." Eves nodded back in agreement.

"Yes. I'm afraid it's not my area of expertise either, Mr Harding," he said with an educated airiness through his whiskery moustache.

"Well I've forgotten more than I can remember to be honest sergeant. Still it's not rocket science, is it?"

Eves looked at him blankly, his bushy eyebrows joining forces in confusion. "Rocket science, what's that then?"

"I don't know really," Harding replied, suddenly unsure himself. "Read it in the paper somewhere, sometime ago, must be some kind of new-fangled thing. Anyway, we're nearly there, we can finish it off tomorrow and give it a test firing," he said vaguely whilst shrugging.

"That's what they're all waiting for. It's hard enough to keep 'em from bickerin' with one another in the meantime though."

"Yes, although it's not as bad as I thought it would be, they all pull together when they need to."

Eves made a noise as if to agree without being fully convinced of it and Harding looked out across the parapet and noticed Boulter stood on top doing his stint of watch, looking fat and tired.

"We'll keep the watch going all night, Eves," he said. "I doubt they'll send a message but we better be on the lookout just in case. Hopefully Acres has got enough on his plate torturing prisoners without worrying us as well. Besides, it'll give the lads a taste of what life is like in a proper working fortress."

They turned towards the barracks, the courtyard empty, quickly darkening under the early evening fade of light. "Right, I'm starving Eves, I haven't eaten all day. Let's go and see what delights Mr England has made for dinner," said Eli enthusiastically.

"Boiled veg and stringy meat if I'm not mistaken," replied the Sergeant as they stepped towards the cosiness of the kitchen.

They were greeted by a pleasant smell and the sight of cook adding the finishing touches to dinner. It was indeed a selection of boiled vegetables in a thin stock with added lumps of fatty but not too gristly meat which formed an aromatic and not unpleasant but still greasy looking stew.

“Oh ‘ello gents, welcome home. I think there’s still tea in the pot in the dinin’ room,” said the cook as he rolled balls of dough with his puffy, floured hands which he was about to drop into the stew to form dumplings.

The leaders of the troop entered the barrack hall which was a scene of shuffling business with men moving benches into positions ready for dinner. Others were stoking up fires and collecting coal or wood for the evening and a few were tidying up their bunk areas, hanging up coats and hats preparing for another night in front of the fires. A small group were sat on a bench nearest the door to the kitchen and the new entrants went across and joined them, sitting down on a spare section of the bench.

The scribbler and Burden, who had been the most useful during the creation of the carriage were sat rolling cigarettes and drinking stewed tea at the table. Harding poured himself and the sergeant a cupful each from the massive teapot in the middle of the table using a small meshed tea strainer to filter out the soggy looking leaves. It was still warm but looked very brown, like a dark oxtail soup. Eli lit a cigarette and the atmosphere felt informal and easy.

“Good work today lads, getting that carriage up and running. I thought we all worked well, seeing as nobody had much of a clue about how to put it together, me included,” offered the Master gunner casually as he blew out a lungful of smoke.

“Well we got there in the end after a few squabbles Mr Harding,” said Burden. “Still, the proof o’ the pudding will be when we fire it tomorrow and it all falls apart,” he added, drawing on his own fag long and slow. Harding winced, remembering his time in Woolwich when a similar weapon exploded on firing, killing one of the crew and badly injuring several others.

“I’ve seen that happen before. It’s not nice. We’ll cross that bridge if we come to it,” he said still wincing, this time because of the bitter taste of stewed tea. “I take it none of you have put one up before,” he asked throatily, his mouth stripped of moisture by the thick drink.

The scribbler sighed. “No Sir. This place has been hardly manned at all over the last year or so. Our time between deployments has got longer and longer. I wouldn’t be surprised if any of us can remember how to fire the bloody thing, let alone build it.”

“Yes it seems Brean Down is always the last place to be thought of by the Brigade administration, sort of gets left to its own devices,” Eli suggested.

Eves lit his pipe and looked down the table through the swirl of white smoke. “I think Steep Holm is the place that gets all the attention. I suppose when resources are scarce, it can only go to the most important part of the line,” he said.

“Bit cheeky if you ask me,” replied one of the Pearce brothers sitting down at the bench.

"Well maybe this new gun will be the start of better things to come. Hopefully they'll add a few more before too long and this place will be fully manned and get the recognition it deserves. You'll be sick of firing RML's in the end," Harding offered.

"Well I fer one can't wait to start firin' sumthin'. It's gettin' a bit borin' up ere," suggested the other brother, Richard Dicky Pearce, as he took a seat next to his sibling.

"Coming up here must help to get you all away from the chaos of the town or the boredom in the village," Elias asked trying to be hopeful.

"It makes a change I suppose," replied the scribbler sadly. "But I don't think any of us would want to be here permanently, that would be somewhat trying, no matter what they say, it's nice to get rotated with the other gun crews over the year. Sometimes they only leave two or three men here at a time, just to keep an eye on the place."

"What about you Mr Hardin," said Burden inquisitively, almost interrupting the droning lament from the scribbler, "How come you got lumbered with this 'ere postin' all of a sudden."

Elias leant back a little and smoked. "I think after the last Master Gunner decided it wasn't really for him they were a bit stuck getting somebody up here. I was polishing brass in Aldershot when I got the call to come to the Down for six months. I wasn't doing a lot else so it was nice to have something constructive to do. It might be a bit lonely when you lot go but the other crews will turn up after and they'll need practice so I don't mind being here, it will keep me busy. It might not be too bad when the summer eventually comes."

"That feels a long way off yet, Sir," snorted Burden. There was a quiet pause as the other men in the room stopped their business and settled down in their own spaces either at tables or led out on bunks waiting for the dinner to be served. The silence was broken by another forgetful youth.

"You must have fired a few guns in yer time, Master," piped up Pickles squeezing his lanky frame behind a table like he was made of stretchy rubber.

Harding took a long suck on his cigarette. He could sense the direction of conversation was turning towards him and his past, something he didn't feel comfortable with. "Just a few, Pickles," he said vacuously.

"We 'eard you was in Afghanistan. Must 'av made you very proud," added Daniel Pearce thoughtlessly, looking for an insight into the sergeant's tale from earlier in the day. Harding swilled the thick brown tea around his mug contemplating how to tackle the question adequately without seeming affected by it.

"Yes," he smiled. "I did what was asked of me at the time, no more. Sometimes that is all anyone has the right to ask. Just as we are doing what is asked of us in this place, during this time now. I don't believe there's much pride in killing, Mr Pearce, and there's no pride in warfare no matter who the victor is. As they sometimes say, 'pride comes before a fall.' It was a bit hairy over there with the locals for a while but it wasn't too bad in the end. I spent a lot of time in India watching Elephants afterwards."

"Elephants," gasped Pickles wondrously. "I've never seen a real elephant. Mighty beasts they are Sir."

"Yes. Mighty beasts," said Eli, glad his simple diversion had hooked the simpleton away from asking more difficult questions.

"We could have done with one of them getting that gun up the hill," chipped in Grayard Evans who was quietly sat smoking in the corner of the room. Light laughter broke out in the barracks releasing the anxiety Eli was beginning to feel and he took the opportunity to make a quick exit. Besides, he needed a drink, a decent one.

"Well elephants aren't much good at firing guns I've found, so we had all better give it a go tomorrow. I've got some reports to write; I've been neglecting it the last few days so I'll leave you to your dinner lads. I hope it tastes as good as it smells."

"Don't we all, Sir," said Burden drily.

Eli rubbed his cigarette into the ashtray, got up and headed into the kitchen, relieved not to face any more questions. "Give us a shout when that stews done, I'll pop over and get some," he told Mr England on the way through. The cook looked at him whilst smiling pleasantly. "Course, Sir. Won't be long now," he replied.

"Good man," said Harding behind him as he walked out into the darkness towards his quarters.

He headed straight for the drinks cabinet without lighting any lamps and poured himself a large gin. He tipped the glass to the photograph of his father as he had done earlier in the day.

"Cheers Pater. Here's to another evening of fine wine and exquisite dining accompanied by intelligent conversation," he said, draining the glass in one and immediately refilling it. Surrounded by the inky blackness of early evening and the prospect of trying to light a dead fire, he had the feeling it was going to be another long, lonely night and tried to wonder what tomorrow would bring instead.

Gideon Harding was a deeply religious man. He was brought up in a Presbyterian household and schooled in the fine arts of spiritual atonement before becoming the owner of a cloth mill in the sheep swathed hills of West Wales. There he married the gentle natured Eleanor Jones who managed to temper the repressed early Victorian piety that the sometimes generous but often distant father tried to influence upon their only son. Family life was usually straight laced due to father's demanding rigidity but Elias and his mother had an understanding respect for the patriarch and his deep beliefs. There were moments of love which sometimes broke free from Mr Harding's trapped emotions allowing his son to believe his father was a good man inside, just a little jaded by the endless biblical teachings of his youth. However, the veil of conformity would always return to his steadfast attitudes and so ensure a lasting image upon his son of a man whose collar was just a bit too tight, all of the time. Meanwhile Eli's mother supplied the tenderness and loving care that every child needs and helped breath an easy going nature into the determined little boy.

Gideon never drank a drop of alcohol throughout his life and was an outspoken critic on the use of strong drink by the working class masses. So he was not impressed when his only son was caught drinking beer in the dormitories of his boarding school and was even less impressed when that grown up son decided to become an Officer in the Royal Artillery. But he still paid for the commission and still tried to exert his own stoic religious beliefs on his singular offspring while Eleanor was just extremely proud of the son she dearly loved.

Gideon Harding died of a long established lung condition shortly after finding out his son had been demoted to a Master Gunner when the nine-inch calibre cannon he was in command of exploded during a firing practice session, killing one of the crew and seriously injuring several others. There was no fault on the part of Elias, the explosion being caused by faulty casting in the foundry; but it was felt someone should be punished for the accident such were the attitudes of the time.

Still, such were the attitudes of the time, that if Gideon Harding had been alive he also wouldn't have been overly sympathetic when his son returned from a foreign war with a traumatic stress disorder. The devout Christian would have tried to cure it with a bout of religious scriptures and a heavy dose of emotional repression. He certainly wouldn't be impressed that his only son now spent most of his time getting tight on strong liquor and illicit tinctures of opium based alcohol.

6. The Dolphin.

"My name is Edwin Ralph, Mr Acres. I am a businessman and I live in Worcestershire. I've told you that several times and it says so on my identification papers. Deep down I think you know that's true but you're too embarrassed to admit it because you also know you've made a ridiculous mistake, and frankly, Sir, I am getting tired of this."

Up until now the confident looking, well-dressed man sat on a chipped and scratchy chair behind a grubby wooden table had been, under the circumstances, rather polite about all of this. But it was obvious he had reached the zenith of his politeness and was now showing a degree of simmering anger and annoyance at what was happening to him. Acres stood in the corner of the room looking at the man sat behind the table. He was sucking his teeth and wriggling his piggy toes within the shiny boots he wore to try and alleviate the aching soles of his feet. The smallest sensation was creeping up on him that maybe this guy was right.

However, the Major's stubbornness in situations he believed were of great importance was virtually unsurpassable. Indecision in a case like this had to be put to the back of his mind, especially since all the wheels of officialdom had already been set in motion due to his previous arrogance and self-belief. Acres still wasn't sure if the investigators from London were coming because they knew the man behind the table could be a genuine suspect or whether they were merely following up the lead in response to Acres' overexcited accusation. He thought it was an accusation that might be followed up because the authorities had an obligation to, once they'd been informed of such things, and that in the end they could find the man bona fide and totally innocent.

The Major knew it would be unwise to show any weakness appearing in his argument and decided he shouldn't actually tell the prisoner about the men from the War office coming. Not yet. Something in his mind told him to keep it in reserve, to use it as a bargaining tool when the need arose. So, he decided to stay quiet for the moment and instead continued to suck his teeth and simply stare at the man behind the table, probably in an attempt to wind up the subject in question and perhaps reveal a flaw in the man's counter argument.

For his part, Edwin Ralph was wondering how to play his next move. He had been sat in this room for nearly six hours and knew that there was only so long a man in his position would be able to play it cool. The victim of a genuine case of mistaken identity would start kicking off about now, if not earlier, but Ralph also knew that he had to build himself up gradually to represent that particular characterisation of grievance as competently as he could and so achieve the right amount of gravitas for the situation. He was trying to gauge how quickly he should raise the temperature of this persona because he didn't want to blow all his best moves too early on. There was still a chance that playing it cool could cause Major Acres to cave in and suddenly reach a conclusion that he had made a rather silly mistake and release Edwin Ralph from his unnecessary incarceration. But the man under scrutiny was also wise to the fact that this clown who had fortuitously apprehended him, although probably not realising the full extent of his lucky move, was still capable of seeing it through merely because of his sheer arrogance and annoyingly stubborn personality. Understanding this trait in his opponent's demeanour was the reason why a small degree of nervousness was also beginning to creep into the man sat behind the table.

It hadn't been so bad earlier on in the day. After being fingered on his yacht by the bungling Major and then dumped in this room, the situation had seemed uncomfortable, but with a bit of fine acting, perfectly surmountable. The Major had played a few old interrogation tricks; coming in and out of the room without speaking, leaving him to stew for periods, pretending to be nice, pretending to be shitty, asking the same old questions, but he felt he had dealt with them all remarkably well. After a couple of hours, he was still confident of being released before too long without having to change his act of a cool, easy going, obviously wealthy, educated Englishman with an interest in nature and an obsessive slant towards ornithology. There was paper work and false records in official departments both in London and Worcester to back up his story and if necessary there was even a network of fellow conspirators in the most unexpected places to offer actual personal confirmation of his identity.

The man playing the part of Edwin Ralph was actually called Cyrano Shrott. He was a French spy extraordinaire who had swum the seas of international intrigue like a slippery clandestine dolphin throughout his exciting adulthood and in the course of his career had been caught in positions of discomfort like this one many times before. In Egypt and Africa, he had spent several days locked up in various sweaty jails yet overcame the insinuations of spying without ever being found guilty and properly imprisoned. He had escaped from various difficult situations through guile and quick thinking and faced more dangerous foes than the likes of Major Acres on his travels but always came away unscathed, remaining confident in the success of his mission. But for some reason getting stuck in England always seemed terribly annoying to him because it was fraught with more bureaucratic dangers and document based official stumbling blocks rather than life threatening peril.

'Why did English fortresses seem so much more miserable compared to forts anywhere else in the world, always so wet and cold,' Shrott wondered to himself as he sat in the room during another bout of purposely disrupting solitude. Cold, dark, wet and windy, this room contained all these

traits but they were tempered by the good fortune it was an internal room, bordered on three sides by other internal spaces, meaning only one wall faced the outside forces of nature. The cold was slightly combated by a feeble fire set into one side of the room, a fire that had only been topped up once during his stay and did little to alleviate the dark which was only negated by the grey light from outside which crept in surreptitiously through the barred window. The wet was replaced by a filmy dampness that seemed to linger across the walls like perspiration and attach itself invisibly to the mouldy atmosphere, whilst the effect of the exterior wind was thankfully kept to a minimum by the thick stone walls, which reduced it to a cool breeze delivered in the form of numerous draughts that blew gently through the joints of the window frame and the corners of the bare walls.

It wasn't exactly a prison cell, although the bars on the window didn't help and the locked door confirmed the captive nature of the occupant, but after a few hours stuck on this island, most of them spent in this suffocating room, the downcast feel of the enclosure and sense of imprisonment was seeping into the normally upbeat attitude of the man behind the table. He heard shuffling sounds and the dull thud of boots as they paced up and down the outside corridor, making him think of over enthusiastic prison guards in places like Germany or Turkey, and the man wondered what the next move in this clumsy operation would be by the ludicrously fluky but still incompetent Major Acres.

The alleged incompetent Major Acres was the man wearing those boots that were pacing up and down the hallway, waiting for the usual under enthusiastic guard to come and stand outside the door so he could enter the room and resume his questioning of the suspect. He had allowed the guard to disappear momentarily to relieve himself and Acres thought the few minutes of being alone would help him to formulate the right thoughts for the next period of questioning and decide on what he was going to say to the man he had interned. A man whom he still believed was a French spy or, failing that, at least some other equally untrustworthy individual. It was a belief he was completely adamant of when he first came across the sailing boat and its solitary sailor, but a belief that was now suffering from disillusionment instigated by the Major's own complicated mentality.

In fact, from the moment he'd created this event and onward over the last six hours, Acres' schizophrenic mind had begun to argue with itself about the doubts that his convoluted psychology secretly harboured in not only this occurrence but just about everything else he did. Unknown to others, in his mind, his daily life felt like a constantly unwinnable game of speeded up, oily hinged, brain tennis; with decisions being batted over an invisible net by unreliable, squeaking, indecisive mental robots. It was this battle of wills and incessant white noise, along with his desperate need to hide his discomfort that made Erasmus Acres the kind of person he was and so produced the difficult and unpredictable creature of annoying habits that ruled the secluded domain he had been left in charge of.

During his childhood and early adolescence, Erasmus had suffered at the hands of strict, cane wielding teachers and vicious classroom bullies whilst at boarding school, and when at home, strict cane wielding and constantly irritable parents. Over the years, this shit filled existence dislocated and scarred the young boy's fragile mind and resulted in a twisted, untrusting view of the world and the people in it by the time he reached adulthood. But it also gave him a stubborn streak and a mental resilience which served him well working in the back offices and administration sections of the army once he'd left the confines of his abusive school and home life. He wasn't cut out for the world of action and real warfare that Queen Victoria's army was famous for but his eye for detail and a creepy love of bureaucracy got him the paper chasing jobs that were always required to keep the wheels of Empire turning back home. After fiddling the figures for casualties during an uprising in India, which helped keep it out of the papers and so saved the bacon of a Brigadier in the process, Acres was amazingly promoted to a 2nd Lieutenant as a reward for his paperwork and in this position his arrogance and frosty manner found new heights. His efficiency helped him rise through the ranks over the years until at the age of 48 he was made a Major and given the unenviable post of commanding the Coastal Batteries of the Severn estuary. It was a job he managed with admirable skill and anal finesse, often with limited resources, and got him the reputation of being a right pain in the ass to the men he commanded, but at the same time allowed the rest of the administration to forget about this little grey, mud splattered corner of the Empire; which was just the way the administration liked it.

Erasmus Acres still had a twisted view of the world and regarded the people inhabiting it as wholly unreliable, a belief he didn't bother to conceal from those around him. But at the same time his cane filled life as a child had also permanently screwed his mind up, leaving him on the edge of mild schizophrenia and indecisive mental imbalance at all times. This was something he worked hard to keep secret from everybody and in general he was remarkably successful at it. His stubbornness and unshakable self-belief helped keep him afloat and maintain a semblance of control in not only his own thinking but also everyone else's.

So when he started the present process with Mr Edwin Ralph, full of buoyant confidence that he had come across some sort of conspiracy, the Major had made the decision to share the burden of possibilities that his fortitude had thrown up by getting in touch with the War office, more for reassurance under the cover of official duty if anything else. The first stunted conversation by telegram (Steep Holm had the luxury of a direct underwater telegraph line to the Welsh side of the Channel and therefore onto the rest of the English mainland that the telegraph system served) had taken a couple of hours and when it was clear they would send down two men to question the suspect, his confidence grew to the point of orgasmic over indulgence in the belief that he had made an expert, intuitive command decision. However, over the last three hours during his own interrogation of the prisoner, who had shown no weaknesses or allowed any cracks to appear in his story, the natural see saw of Acres' brain had created waves of uncertainty that were splashing around his mental imbalance. He remembered part of a conversation he had with Lieutenant Pontefract on the ramparts of the battery shortly after the first session of questioning.

"I don't trust him. He claims to be a naturalist but I'm not convinced," Acres snapped.

"A naturalist, there seems to be a lot of them around at the moment. I suppose they're all welcome as long as they don't start taking their clothes off!" exclaimed Pontefract, looking shocked and spitting out a guffaw.

"That's a naturist, Lieutenant," said Acres drily.

"Exactly, might be alright on the beaches of Spain but it won't go down too well here in Somerset! It'll put people off their battered fish."

After explaining the position more clearly and asking the young second in command to contact Master Harding on Brean Down, Acres remembered the softly spoken, parting words of the young Officer.

"I hope your right about this, Mr Acres," Pontefract had said bravely.

"When I want your opinion, Pontefract, I'll ask for it. Until then do as your told," was the Major's tart reply.

'Was he right?' It was a thought that had played on his mind ever since. No one else knew about the insecurities that plagued the Commanders everyday life, if they did he knew his command of the island and the other coastal forts would fall apart pretty quickly.

The guard came skidding around the corner, scampered up to the side of the doorway and stood untidily at ease, a large, visible patch of unshaken urine apparent on the crutch of his grey trousers. Acres stopped pacing and glared at the guard with his beady, bird like eyes.

"Next time you can piss yourself son!" he said sharply, not noticing that the young guard virtually had. The major took off his hat and smoothed down his dark, oleaginous hair, leaving streaks of damp sebum on his shirt sleeves as he did so. He was unusually extra greasy today, sweating with excitement and nerves that released a mixture of oils into his normal perspiration. He had a face like a sparrow and was smaller than most men, so had to look up at everyone he dealt with which only exacerbated his irrational nature. Flaring his nostrils and replacing his hat, Acres walked into the room to begin the next session of questioning.

"What are you doing sailing around the Bristol Channel then, Mr Ralph?"

"As I've already old you Mr Acres..."

"Major."

"Major Acres. I am a bird watcher, studying the birds on this wildlife rich estuary."

"And what has marking down the gun positions on channel forts got to do with bird watching?"

"Because Major Acres, I am trying to find out if where there are more guns there are fewer birds or whether, where there are fewer guns there may be more birds. The Bristol Channel has an amazing array of sea birds and I want to know if you and your forts hinder them or not."

"And what about owning a French make of pistol then, Mr Ralph? What does owning a French army issue pistol have to do with watching birds?"

"Well, like any sensible sea farer I carry a weapon to protect myself from brigands or thieves at work on these or any waters I might sail on. The only reason it's French is because they happened to be the cheapest ones on sale from the particular gun salesmen I bought it from."

"Oh well, is that right? We'll have to check up on that then, won't we Mr Ralph. Until then we'll all have to wait here,"

"Wait! I've been waiting here for six hours Acres and I've just about had enough of it!"

"Oh have you indeed. Well I'm afraid you'll just have to keep waiting Mr Edwin Ralph, until the gentlemen from London get here and then it will be up to them to prove who you may or may not be."

There was a pause.

"What gentlemen from London?"

"Investigators Mr Ralph."

"What investigators?"

"From the War Office, Mr Ralph."

"The War Office?"

"Yes Mr Ralph. You'll have to prove to them the true nature of your identity."

"Prove! The only thing they'll prove is that you've made the biggest mistake of your twisted lunatic existence and when they prove I am who I say I am; they'll make sure that you're never put in charge of anything ever again. I'll make sure of it!"

"Well, we'll just have to see about that then, won't we Mr Ralph."

"You really are an annoying little man aren't you, Acres."

"Little! I'm not little! I am a Major in the Royal Artillery and it is my job to keep this channel safe. Part of that job is keeping an eye out for people suspiciously floating around in boats, of which you, Mr Ralph, are one, and until your story is verified I will continue to be officious in the duty of my job!"

"Officious! Overly officious I should say. Deluded and downright paranoid I should say and I'm going to make sure everybody knows about it!"

"And when you're put in jail for being a French spy I will make sure everybody knows about it too, and when they do they will also know it was me, in the performance of my officious duty, who achieved that!"

"Oh, so it's all for your own personal glory."

"The safety of Britain and my Bristol Channel."

"Ha! My god, you really are quite mad, completely deluded."

"Well for your information Mr Ralph, it wasn't my idea to bring those two gentlemen from London to question you. I could have dealt with this quite easily by myself, thank you. No, that was their idea. I was ordered to hold you here until those two men arrived. So whoever in London knows about this is obviously interested in you Mr Ralph and frankly, it will be up to them to deal with you."

There was another, even longer pause.

Major Erasmus Acres gave his teeth one last suck, turned his greasy body round and walked out of the door, locking it noisily as he did so. A wave of newfound worry swept over Cyrano Shrott's mind as soon as the Major was gone. Perhaps the War Office in London was aware of the spy network in Britain and therefore knew not only about him but the importance of the information he held. Shrott suddenly became very concerned about the predicament he was in but was careful not to show it in the fake persona he was presenting in case someone was watching him from a secret spy hole somewhere within the walls. He tried to act cool.

Then he thought about the possibility of ending up in a cold, damp, dark, windy English cell for the rest of his life and the idea for the necessity of escape entered his mind. For the first time in this unfortunate fiasco he began to think about how the hell he was going to get out of here.

As he did so, a gust of wind rattled through the glass of the barred window behind him and blew a shadow from the dying embers of the fireplace which flashed across the damp stone wall and disappeared into the grey light outside. Shrott shivered as the chill brushed the hairs on the back of his neck.

"Bloody wind," he grumbled worriedly.

The man walked through the rear door of the guesthouse, closing it behind him to the rain that was falling steadily outside. He was tall and wet, and shook his athletic frame casually over the straw matt like a big, well-toned dog. Taking off his deer stalker hat, he flicked the raindrops away and then hung it up, along with his binoculars and the wet coat he had been wearing onto a free standing, ornately carved wooden coat stand. Miss

Victoria Danvers, the lady of the guest house, appeared at the doorway which led to the kitchen and smiled pleasantly at the man.

"Hello Mr Stone. You must be soaking. It's turned awfully wet again. I thought I saw the sun earlier but perhaps I imagined it," she paused for a second as if thinking of what to say next. "Would you like a cup of tea? The kettles just boiled," was all she could think of.

The handsome faced man smoothed his floppy hair back and bent down to begin untying his boot laces without looking at her. "No Miss Danvers, you didn't imagine it. The sun was out earlier and made everything appear quite pleasant but it didn't last long and started raining on my way back. Hazard of the occupation, I suppose. It was still very enjoyable though." He took off his boots and put them tidily to one side and then turned his head towards her and added with a slightly forced smile, "Yes, a cup of tea would be very kind, thank you."

The glass panelled conservatory he was stood in was really just a utility outbuilding connected to the main house and it felt cold and exposed with the rain dripping down the panes. They both walked into the kitchen which was warm and well-lit with natural light from the large windows looking onto the conservatory and the side of the house. Mr Stone sat at the sturdy wooden table in the middle of the room and turned his chair towards the stove behind in order to dry himself a little. His well-made outdoor coat had kept off most of the rain but his trousers and socks were damp. Victoria put the kettle on and they politely smiled at each other again.

"How was the Down today? Did you see many birds?" she asked.

"Yes, most productive. I believe I saw a Purple Sandpiper, but I may have been a bit far away for a definitive sighting. However, I definitely saw a Curlew and a Bar Tailed Godwit along the beach, which was quite exciting," he replied smiling more broadly this time. She couldn't tell if he was being sarcastic or not.

"I'm afraid I wouldn't know what any of those look like, Mr Stone. The only birds I recognise are Seagulls because there are so many of them. They do make an awful racket sometimes," she mentioned absently, as she prepared the tea. He didn't say anything for a moment, just looked at her intently, smiling in an unsure almost forced kind of way which showed some of his tidy, overly white teeth. She didn't notice him watching her as she hovered between the stove and cupboards.

"Seagulls are very beautiful birds Miss Danvers, very hardy, superior survivalists." The smile drained away as quickly as it was pulled but he continued to watch her as she moved. "They have the ideal attributes enabling them to dominate the coastline. It's something you have to admire in a species really. They're very powerful creatures," he added artfully but with the merest sense of hostility.

"Yes, I suppose they are, I never thought of it that way," she replied, drawing away from the debate and submitting to the passionate response from the bird watcher and his superior knowledge. She caught him looking at her intensely and to avoid awkward eye contact, switched her viewpoint out of the window instead. "However I must say I find the job of cleaning their constant droppings from the conservatory windows rather depressing and time consuming," she added airily.

Victoria arranged the tea set on the table along with a plate containing a large cake. "Would you like a piece of walnut cake, Mr Stone?" she asked without catching his eye.

"For a lady of the Manor, Miss Danvers, you have the air of a domestic goddess," he said alluringly, pulling another smile.

"I'm afraid the days of Manor Houses and Ladies are long gone. I wouldn't be taking in paying guests if the luxury of such status were available to me. Most of our land has been sold over the years Mr Stone as I'm sure I must have mentioned before. The only land we still own borders the sand dunes and has been described as…well," she hesitated as she sliced the cake, thinking of the right word, "unsellable, according to our accountants. Now our only income comes from two house rents in the village and any paying guests we can attract. As you can see, Mr Stone, you've been our only guest in the last two weeks," the young lady said, with a hint of rebuke in her voice as she finished cutting a piece of cake and slipped it on to one of the plates.

She sat down opposite him and poured the tea from a hand painted, fine china tea pot into a pair of matching cups. She noticed he was smiling at her again, his eyes exposing a sly twinkle in their off putting blue fix which she found discomforting. Victoria began to wish she hadn't offered to make the man a cup of tea at all, let alone a slice of cake.

Rufus Stone had been at the guest house for four days and she hadn't really seen that much of him apart from in the evenings after he returned from his bird watching and nature trailing. Then the pair, along with Miss Danvers' father, would sit down for an evening meal together, which was part of the bed and board lodgings that the Manor House now offered. The trio would then indulge in mutually non-intrusive, respectful conversation until bedtime loomed. They had always found Mr Stone polite and friendly enough with a well-educated and courteous manner but Victoria was still not sure what his true personality beheld. She assumed he was singularly interested in his ornithological studies and nature mapping, which was the premise for his visit to the area but she often got the feeling the young student had a wider experience of society and knew more about the ways in which the shadier side of the world worked than he actually let on. He was well versed in his knowledge of birds and the eco systems of nature, however she sometimes got the impression he might be viewing her with the same interest as he had for his feathered subjects and she didn't feel comfortable with the thought of being seen like some sort of bird, waiting to be examined in an unflattering, voyeuristic way.

She hoped she wasn't leading Stone on or giving him the wrong impression by offering too much polite conversation, cups of weak tea and slices of walnut cake.

"So will you be requiring dinner tonight Mr Stone or are you off out again studying the nocturnal habits of our bat population," she asked, referring to his late arrival at last night's dinner due to being engaged in the apparent study of bats. He ate his walnut cake carefully and dropped his gaze to the teapot, swallowing his smile along with the nuts.

"Ah…yes, Miss Danvers, I will be at dinner tonight although I'm afraid I plan to go out afterwards, if that's not too rude, only it seems the later you are for bats the better."

She automatically smiled at him then quickly soured, remembering his possible misinterpretations of her naturally kind manner. "Of course Mr Stone, the study of nature must keep you out at all hours, I suppose."

He narrowed his eyes at her, souring a little himself in response. "Yes it does. I hope I'm not disturbing you or your father with my comings and goings."

She sipped her tea. "No, we haven't noticed at all really, you've been very respectful towards us. You are obviously free to come and go as you please. Unlike other lodging houses we do not burden our guests with a restrictive curfew which is why you have a back door key. We are all adults here Mr Stone, I'm sure we can trust you, as you can us."

"Of course Miss Danvers, but please let me know if my studies cause you any concern at all, I wouldn't want to forsake that trust in any way," he said simpering like a creepy child. "The information I need regarding the wildlife of the estuary is nearly complete, after a couple more days I'm sure I won't be causing you any more nuisance."

"Really Mr Stone, that's a shame," she replied trying to show concern. "It's been very interesting having a naturalist in the house. I hope I haven't offended you in any way with my interest in your routines. When do you think you'll be leaving?"

The corners of his mouth turned up into a sort of disaffected smile and he widened his sticky blue eyes. "I think the day after tomorrow. Everything will be complete by then. I'll be heading back to Edinburgh and the university so I can start my thesis." He shifted in his chair and stretched the smile over his nice teeth.

She didn't want to force any falser concern or give him the impression she wanted him to stay any longer, so Victoria noisily gathered up some empty plates and crockery which had been left on the table from breakfast.

"Well it's been very nice having you stay with us and I hope your thesis is well received," she said without looking at him. Getting up she put the tea things on the side and then patted her dress down lightly. "Well I really must make a start on dinner, then," she said a little awkwardly then turned towards the sink and began preparing a selection of vegetables.

Rufus Stone watched her working as he slowly finished off his cake and drank the last of his still hot tea. She didn't look round again and there was a stilted silence for a few moments until he finally said, "Of course madam, I'll get out of your way and head up to my room, I've some notes to work on." Then he got up and walked towards the doorway leading to the hall. He went to walk out but then stopped suddenly and looked at the young lady stood on the other side of the kitchen. His eyes became hawk like again and he said smoothly, "Thank you for the tea and cake. It's been very nice staying here Miss Victoria Danvers. You've been a most approachable landlady. It would be nice to come again when I return to follow up my thesis. You are a most welcome distraction in my educational work." He stood gazing at her for a second as if she was a Purple Sandpiper.

She turned and looked at him, feeling more like a seabird getting eyed up than ever before but still managed to smile pleasantly. She felt a little ashamed now of her terse behaviour a moment ago. "Of course Mr Stone, it would be lovely to have you stay again," she lied.

He nodded thoughtfully and walked out into the large mahogany clad hallway and quietly climbed the heavily varnished stairs to his room halfway along the landing. When he entered, he noticed the bed had been made and a fresh towel hung over the rail by the wash basin. He reached up to a small leather suitcase on top of the wardrobe, took it down, opened it and checked underneath the clothes inside to make sure his gun hadn't moved. Replacing the suitcase, he went to the writing table in the corner and took out the small notebook from his waistcoat pocket and read the notes he had made earlier on during his observations on the Down. He looked out of the window onto the leaf strewn garden of the Manor House, with its straggly looking bare twigged bushes amongst the unkempt evergreen hedges which curved underneath the leafless winter trees and wondered, rather absently, if he'd have to kill anyone before he left this place.

Later, in a darkening room on the other end of the Down, Eli thought to himself.

'I can't do this again! I can't sit in this room, on my own, getting drunk in the dark again. It's not helping me! I've been doing it for two weeks now and it's not working, it's not helping me. I thought I could handle it, this place, the isolation, the monotony. I thought it would do me good. Maybe it did at the start. Maybe it helped me cope for a while, but not now. It's starting to put me on edge, the cold, the wet, the dark, the endless sound of the wind. I can't hear the music anymore. I could always hear the music no matter what happened but now it's faded, gone quiet, apart from the wind. I thought it would be good to get away from society for a while, sort myself out, get free. But maybe I need the input from society, to....to connect.

There's a room across that walkway with other people inside. Perhaps I should join them, talk to them, converse with them. But every time I do, all they talk about is war and guns and shooting things. I can't handle it! All it does is set me thinking again and I'm finding it difficult to shake it off. This gloom, this darkened room, even with the lamps on I can't see a bloody thing. The only warm place is by the fire, the shadows move and the darkness creeps up all around you like the fingers of an enclosing hand. I'm starting to get the willies! Sending me bonkers it is. If I'm not careful I'll end up like that other master's wife, getting my head screwed down by the ghosts in the dark.

Am I going mad? Perhaps it's the booze. Bloody booze, perhaps I should take some laudanum instead. Helps me sleep, but then all I do is dream. I never know if the dreams will be good or bad. If they're good they're really good. If they're bad they're really bad, I just don't know. I can't take any now, not while I'm on the edge like this. I'll go potty. I don't want to go back in there and talk to the men. They should be friends, comrades, but all they talk about is guns and shooting things. If only they knew. Maybe Patrick was right, maybe I need to get away for a while, just for the night, for a few hours. Get out, walk around the streets, feel a bit of civilisation around me. Perhaps I should see Victoria. She could play me the violin. I could try and play the piano again, hear some music. She's very beautiful and lovely. She's the kind of woman I could fall in love with if my head wasn't so caved in. But she wouldn't want to see me. I wouldn't make a lot of sense to her tonight anyway.

God I need another drink! No, no not here. Don't get drunk in this chair again. It's no good. It will do me no good. Go for a walk. Yes, go for a walk, get out, go for a walk on the Down or go to the village. See Victoria, just to say hello. I could ask her to a concert. We said we'd like to go to a concert together. There must be one in this God awful town. Just pop in and say hello and try not to be too strung out. Or maybe I could just go to the pub, drink with some strangers. That'll be better than just sitting here getting drunk in the dark. I can't do that again, can I? Christ alive man! Do something other than this!'

Elias stood up, walked over to the bureau, feeling his way to it in the dark like a blind man, lit the oil lamp and waited, blinking as his eyes got used to the dull orange glow the lamp produced. He fingered through some papers in the recess and pulled out a thin local newspaper that had been delivered along with the post only three or four days ago. He checked the date on the front page, 10th February 1884, only last week, and rifled through the pages towards the back where the adverts, announcements and obituaries were contained. Looking down the columns he saw an advert for a forthcoming concert at the Winter Gardens Pavilion in Weston-On-Sea. It was at the end of the month and involved an afternoon performance by a local chamber orchestra playing a programme of works by Brahms and Mozart. Eli became excited and looked up from the paper, his mind racing with an agitated expectancy.

'Bloody hell, that's a stroke of luck. Maybe it's fate. I could ask Miss Danvers if she wants to go. The orchestra might be a bit shonky but I'm sure they'd be competent enough. I could take her for dinner afterwards, make an evening of it. It's worth a stab. What have I got to lose, it's either that or sit in this shithole all day. I'm going to do it! I've got to do it. Bloody hell I've got to try, I could go round tonight, see if she's interested. Get me out of this damn fort for the night anyway. Stuff it! If she's not in, I'll go to the pub for a pint or three. At least I won't get too tight that way. By Jove, that's what I'll do!'

He left the paper on the table with the advert facing upwards to remind him about getting the tickets and then went to the bedroom, washed his face, changed his shirt and added a dash of French cologne to his stubbly chin. He examined his pale and lined face in the mirror, pulling his tired looking eyes down to try and brighten them a little. He was looking older and more worn, as if the life force was draining away bit by bit, so he rubbed his short cropped hair with his hand and tried to push the blood back around his face to give him a rush of colour. Next to the cologne he eyed the small bottle of laudanum that had been left out after his last dose a few nights ago. He picked it up and put it in the drawer, "Sorry pal, I won't be needing you tonight," he said confidently before going to the living room to put on his navy pea coat and a pair of light leather gloves. He picked up his empty plate from the table, extinguished the lamp in the hall and walked across to the kitchen. Cook was washing dishes at the sink as was usual at this time of night and Eli added his plate to the pile.

"Thanks for that Mr England. The stew was delicious and those dumplings were a real eye opener," Eli said with forced joyfulness.

"Well thank you Sir, it's not often my old dumplings get called eye openers."

Eli breezed into the barrack room where everyone was sat around in front of the fire. They were smoking and chatting quietly in the fullness of after dinner digestion. They all looked at him with faces of wary surprise as he came in, Mr Eves included.

"Alright lads, don't panic. Stay where you are," Harding said smiling. "Mr Eves, I'm popping out, going for a walk along the Down to get some air. I might even go to the village, check on the telegram office, so don't worry if I'm not back anytime soon."

Mr Eves arched his eyebrows. "You sure Sir, bit dark out there, wouldn't want you trippin' up or anythin'," he said questioningly.

"Don't worry old man, I'll take a lamp just in case," Eli replied. He rubbed his chin thoughtfully before adding, "Can you sort out the guard shift to keep an eye on the island. It'll give the men some practice on watch routines. I shouldn't be too late."

"No problem Mr Harding, I'll sort that out before they all get too comfortable. It'll be good for them to remember they're in the army, ay lads."

There were a few groans from some of the men. Eves batted them away with some diplomacy. "Don't worry lads, no need to get in a pickle. You'll all get some sleep. We'll share it out fair."

Eli looked around them all, the young, the old, the fit, the fat, the good, the bad and the dishevelled. "Well done lads. There'll be extra grog in it for you tomorrow night."

The mood was raised in the room, along with a few discerning eyebrows and confused looks, as Elias turned and strode out picking a lamp up from the guardroom as he made his way towards the bridge and the road that led across the Down.

It was cold and crisp on the military road. The night sky was miraculously clear and held a host of twinkling stars and a bright, smiling, wintry moon. Eli could make out the constellations he recognised. Orion's belt and Ursa Major, along with her tinier sibling the Seven Sisters which pinpointed their way across the sky like old friends who sat in the same chairs at some overhead celestial lounge bar. The moon and clear sky lit up the road and surrounding area with a thin milky light which meant Elias didn't need the lamp for the moment. Instead he smoked, blowing thick jets of exhalation into the crisp air like a human train, gently gliding along the tarmac track of the road.

The tide was in and he could hear the dark sea lap against the rocky shoreline whilst the moonlight reflected off its gently pulsating waves. It was inspiring and Eli felt good, glowing with a renewed belief in life stimulated by his burst of enthusiastic optimism. He ate up the yards of road quietly, watching as the lights from the town shimmered in clusters thrown across the bottom of the night sky. Occasionally he looked back at the fort melting into the blackness, only the cosy light from the barrack room windows showing the world its position on the land as it was slowly consumed by the moonlit rippled water. It could have been a lamp from some boat floating on the sea for anyone else knew.

The wind was soft, but Elias still pulled the collars of his coat up around his neck when he reached the uppermost heights of the Down as he headed towards the pathways which led to Fiddlers Point and the other end of the peninsular near the route to the village. The beauty of the night and the warmth generated by his resurgent optimism made him definitely want to see Miss Danvers, just to say hello and ask if she was interested in going to the concert with him. He wanted to absorb her beauty and the warmth of another person. There was also a renewed interest in the village and a desire to see what it would look like bathed in the aura of night. It might take a couple of hours to get there on foot, as the Manor House was at the other end of the village but anything was better than spending another night in that gloomy fortress.

The road became a track and the track became a worn down stony path before eventually turning into the thin strip of short, rough grass which led across the spine of the Down. Although he'd been walking for nearly an hour Eli realised he hadn't noticed the time pass. Before he knew it, he was stepping through the rocks which now bordered the pathway leading into the crevice of Fiddlers Point and he could look down onto the moon flecked bay and the inlet that curved away towards the mainland which held the first few lights of the village houses, a few yards up from the beach.

The moon had lit his way up until now but he decided to light the lamp so it would help him find his way down the craggy rock face track that led to the marshland bordering the bay and the wooden walkway across the inlet.

As the rambler climbed down the rocky slope, he was glad the weather was good otherwise the journey down might have seemed more treacherous and unnecessarily difficult than it actually was. It was steep but the frequent use by locals looking for a short cut had carved out a series of tiered, soil faced steps which could be used to aid the descent down the rock face. He wondered how Postman Pat could drag his bike up and down this route compared to the easier but long winded flatness of the main road; coming to the conclusion that the old man had done it so many times that the craggy postman was able to fly up and down like some sort of old mountain goat, bike and all. Raising the lamp to one side Eli saw a sheer drop down to a pebbled cove falling away to the water's edge. In the middle of the sea filled bay, sticking out of the muddy water, stood the jagged outcrop known as Black Rock. The moon glinted off the sharp edges of stone like they were shards of inky black glass embedded into the seabed.

Harding part slid, part tumbled and then part fell down the helter skelter pathway slicing through the cliff face. Somehow he managed to hold the lantern throughout the descent, which cast a sandpapery yellow orb along the darkened route. Not always sure if he was on the right path or just recklessly rock climbing in the dark Eli simply followed his nose, the force of gravity and the disc of glowing lamplight. He was filled with a boundless energy and elation, the likes of which he hadn't experienced for ages, infused by the awakening cold and the enthralling landscape filled with a shoreline cast in the universal spell of night. He was even laughing when he hit the bottom of the pathway that fell through the rocky fissures such was his enjoyment at being out in the open and utterly free of the far off fortress.

Walking along the track which skirted the bay Elias kept looking out across to the lights of the village and the town further away in the distance.

The expanse of water lapped at the mud by the side of the track causing it to shimmer in the moonlight. On the other side of the path the reeds and the tall grasses growing out of the marshland, before it turned into Farmer Lanes' fields, rustled in the sea fed breeze. Looking behind him Eli saw the Down rising up like the torso of a huge black sleeping dog, its head trailing away towards the sea. In the enveloping pitch the only light source came from a single sheltered window at Lanes' farmhouse.

He turned back towards the light spots of society and crossed the wooden bridge spanning the inlet. Holding the lamplight in front, he gingerly stepped over, careful to avoid slipping off into the oily black water. Once across, after a small stretch of hardened sand leading through a border of marsh, he felt the beginning of the softer beach sand under his feet and saw up ahead the concrete slipway leading to the village.

The road through the village from the beach was still and quiet. The left side was lined with a terrace of small, two storey fishermen's cottages and on the other side stood a waist high stone wall behind which a fascia of brambles and leafy bushes hid the slope of a small hill. It was part of a collection of hillocks that connected Brean Down to her betraying partners on the mainland, which made up the rest of the Mendip Hills further inland.

Hands tucked into pockets, back hunched against the cold, Eli noticed the homely warmth that radiated softly around the dim, glassy light floating from behind the thinly curtained windows of the houses, but there was no movement to substantiate the cosy effect, no other signs of life. It was as if the houses were empty and all the people had vanished, leaving the village to the shadows of night with only the lamps left alight to ward away the spirits. In eddies created by the wind, sand swirled across the cobblestones in the road and the smell of the sea blew strongly through the air. He passed the tiny post office on the corner end of the terrace and saw the telegraph room next door with the overhead line following the road, hanging loosely on the poles and swaying in the wind before gradually disappearing into the darkness towards town. It was all closed, silent and unmoving. Another road led down into some grass covered sand dunes stretching away into the blackness and on the other side of this junction, opposite the post office, stood the village pub. It too was silent and free of movement apart from the squeaking sign, swinging gently in the winter breeze. There was no picture adorning it, just the name in flaky, bold lettering, 'The Dolphin.' The ground floor had the same glassy, dulled glow coming from the netted windows as the houses had done. Eli couldn't make out the sound of drunken voices or the murmur of whispered gossip and he wondered if the pub was even open. Deciding not to find out yet, he stepped away and continued walking up the main road towards the far end of the village and the Manor House on the outskirts.

The houses continued alongside the road, interspersed with a few simple looking shop fronts; a butcher, a greengrocer and the obligatory village fishmonger, whilst on the opposite edge the bramble, tree lined slant of the hill opened out into a grassy slope with a gate built into the ongoing wall. Elias' eyes followed a stony path leading up from the gate along the side of the hill through a sparse collection of gravestones until it stopped at a modest, moonlit church, built near the brow of the rise which overlooked the village and the coastline. Elias felt the church's ominous religious overtones and sensed it was not a place for refuge or solace but a destination for the unforgiving administration of Godly penance. He carried on walking.

The village ended at a tree lined juncture with the main road leading one way towards the town of Weston and in the other direction inland, roughly following the coastline where at some point it connected with the approach road leading to the Down. Eli headed the other way towards the town, and was soon swallowed up by the darkness of the surrounding woods. But after a hundred yards, the trees suddenly stopped and became a stone plinth which posted the side of a gateway that led along the drive and associated gardens of Uphill Manor. It was here that Eli Harding stopped and looked up towards the house.

The Manor wasn't huge, like the stately type set in hundreds of acres of rolling countryside lived in by aristocrats and industry millionaires. It was much smaller and respectful, more a guardian of the village type of building, presenting class and distinction without the overbearing or dominating insistence of similar level homes. It had clearly seen better days during its history, the aura of Manor like resonance being replaced by a more unkempt and money saving decorum. But it was still obviously cared for even without the workforce required to uphold it and in the dark the place emitted a presence of honourable stoicism.

There were four sets of windows on the ground floor, two either side of the front door, all of them alight with the outlined, gauzy fields of oil lamps behind netted curtains. Elias remembered that the window closest to him was the dining room, and realised that Miss Danvers, her father and whoever would be staying with them would all probably be having dinner about now. As he stood rooted to the road near the gateway, his mind wondered back to his own time as a guest and the two evenings he spent with the Danvers' during his brief stay in the house; whilst he waited for the arrival of Major Acres to present him with the keys and show him around the, as was then, empty fort.

Had she really liked him or was it his imagination running away with itself? He knew her eye lingered on him when she thought he wasn't looking, just as his eye had lingered on her when he hadn't thought she was paying attention. Did her smile betray an attraction more than just polite engagement? He certainly felt as much, but as with everything else in his own uncertain world, he couldn't be sure. Maybe she was just being nice to him because he was a soldier and a paying guest. Perhaps she was like this with everybody?

But no, there was more to it than that. He had felt it, especially during that final evening, after dinner. Their nervousness around each other had gone, replaced with a relaxed enjoyment in each other's company built upon their mutual affection for music and the inspirational benefits of artistic endeavour. They had talked about London and the culture it bestowed upon the rest of the country, the galleries they had visited containing the works of art that inspired them and the orchestral music that they had seen performed and so enthralled them.

Her smile, her enthusiasm, her delicate energy had infected him and he was enticed by her. So much so, that she even persuaded him to play the piano again. Tentatively, at her insistence, he had fingered the keys and made music after four years of being unable to play, often because his hands shook uncontrollably whenever he toyed with the idea of even approaching a keyboard (shakes and insecurity that had only manifested itself since his time in Afghanistan). But that night she had brought it out of him, even if it was just a simple and undemanding accompaniment as she played the violin. It had only been an intermediate violin practice piece by Shuman, but the sound of music had broken him free from his angst and had shown him the joyous abandonment that both he and she received from connecting with a fellow musician, even if he was a rather rusty and unpractised one. Elias had never been so glad of his father's insistence at learning the piano during his adolescence than he had been during that night with Victoria.

He had felt it with her, the connection, but in the end maybe she hadn't felt the same with him. Nothing had been said to cement the flowering of a permanent relationship, even after the comment her father had given Elias during a moment alone before the household had retired for the night. The old man had looked at his guest through happy shining eyes and with a flush of fatherly joy said, "Thank you Mr Harding, my daughter has not had such an enjoyable evening in these few years since her mother died. You should visit again and wash the house with the joyful sound of music."

Elias had left to attend the fort the next day and the couple had not seen each other again since. He festered in his gloomy cave chair while she, in the twisted whisperings of his mind, had probably forgotten about him. The thought engorged his brain that maybe his piano playing had been rubbish after all.

Harding looked at the dining room window, listening to the wind rush through the trees, and felt the zap of indecision warp across his being. *'They would be eating; he would be disturbing them. They wouldn't be expecting anyone; he might annoy them. Maybe this wasn't the best time to make an appearance,'* his mind parped. He began to feel wiry, the earlier optimism draining out of his body like used bath water. Looking at his watch he formulated the excuse that it had gone way past 9'o'clock and therefore it was too late.

“Bloody hell,” he swore under his breath, full of his own insecure disappointment. “I’ll try tomorrow,” he reasoned to himself. “Sod it, I’m going for a drink,” was his final, defeatist judgement.

He walked fast along the road, away from the house, away from his indecision and away from the fear of rejection. The next thing he knew, he was outside the door of ‘The Dolphin’, her sign swinging its creaking song in the cold whip of an ever stiffening late night breeze.

Elias Harding always found walking into a pub a lot easier than trying to walk out of one. He’d been in loads over the years, some of them nice and welcoming, making you want to stay in them forever, and others that were just horrid little boozers that gave you the shits. ‘The Dolphin’ was one of those pubs that was just a bit croaky and the kind of place that you only went into because you really wanted a drink, or ten.

Walking inside, Eli finally heard the gentle hum of bar room murmuring that was absent from outside, however the volume was still pretty low as there were only a handful of people in the pub and the sound was immediately silenced as the newcomer allowed the door to close behind him with an interrupting bang. The patrons watched as he hesitated a moment whilst looking around the room taking in the occupants and studying the layout before striding confidently over to the bar straight in front of him. He stood at the counter looking into the barman who was staring back at him through blood shot eyes whilst rubbing an enlarged, purple, cider blown nose between his thumb and forefinger. The barman nodded an acknowledgement to the newcomer.

Eli took his gloves off and said to the publican in an experienced tone, “Evenin’ landlord. How’s the ale today?”

“Off,” was the landlord’s sharp, nosey reply. “All we got is cider or whisky.”

Eli looked at the men sat around the edges of the room still staring at him as though he were an alien intruder come to invade their space, which in a way he was, and the young man took the diplomatic step of nodding to them respectfully.

“I better have a whisky to start with then,” he said, locking the barman with a distinguished gaze and noticing the man had a thin, stupid looking moustache under his beetroot coloured honker. The barman took a tumbler from the shelf above his head and a bottle of plain looking whisky from behind the counter and filled the glass. Eli downed it in one to show the patrons he wasn’t some green horn out to make a spectacle of himself with his first drink. “And again barman, please,” he beckoned to the empty glass. The landlord filled it for a second time and smiled under his bulbous nose.

“That’ll be half a shillin,” he said, nodding to the glass.

The murmur broke out again amongst the people in the pub and they returned to their drinking. Eli pushed some coins across the bar and took his glass in hand before heading towards an empty table in the corner of the room and then slid along one of the benches by the wall. He undid his coat and took out his cigarettes, lighting one whilst drawing in a lungful of smoke and then washed it down with a mouthful of booze. He took a good look around the pub.

'The Dolphin' wasn't large, just a ground floor room with an unfussy three sided bar jutting out into the centre. There was a large fireplace set into the back wall near Harding's table, fuelled by one massive slow burning log, the ashy embers lazily trying to digest the huge piece of wood whilst sending tired wisps of white smoke up the spacious chimney. An oil painting hung above the fireplace depicted the scene of a three mast sailing ship caught in a ferocious storm, the frothing waves sending it towards certain death onto an outcrop of darkly painted forbidding rocks. It was an impressive and evocative image. Elias liked the picture but wondered if it was a good idea to have such a constant reminder in the dangers of seafaring to the poor fishermen who undoubtedly frequented this establishment.

On a table near his end of the room two young men were drinking cider. They were talking and laughing with alcohol induced abandon. The men's thick winter coats were undone and their faces shone with wobbly inhibition, supplying a dash of pub like atmosphere to the stoic bar. They seemed unconcerned with Eli or the wider world, innocent of any burden it may possess while they enjoyed these few hours of simple pleasure.

Further along the wall he was sat against, Eli noticed something nailed to the yellowing plaster. He leant forward and craned his neck round to get a better look and realised it was a long, thick, wooden handled harpoon. It was about six feet from the shaft end to the point of the spear and what at first looked like rust on the blade, upon closer focus, turned out to be a strip of dried blood, obviously encrusted on from either the last whale it penetrated or, as Eli imagined from the ambience of the regulars, the last stranger to walk in and buy a drink. He laughed a little to himself and as he did his gaze fell onto an old woman sat at a table just underneath the harpoon near the opposite corner of the pub. She was wrapped in a thick wad of woollen shawls, nodding her head between the giant dart on the wall and Eli with a pair of creased but shining, drunken eyes which poked out from the top of her overwrapped covering. Next to her was an even older man, also heavily layered, asleep with folded arms as if he'd just dropped off halfway through his pint.

Across from the elderly couple, the barman was leant on the bar talking to two men who had come over from a table near the front door. They had left two other men seated at the table but all four took it in turns to look over to where Eli was sat in between gulps from their glasses of cloudy drink. They all wore thick seafaring coats and one of the men at the table wore a fisherman's cap which hid his features whilst the other had thick wavy hair long enough to surround his large, hardened face. One of the two men at the bar also had a fishing cap on and the other had short cropped hair with sturdy, thickly cut sideboards which led down across his cheeks. They both looked over towards Eli as they conversed with the barman, toying with their drinks and whispering from corners of mouths whilst diverting their eyes when Eli caught them watching him through the flickering, smoky haze.

The whole room was poorly lit with two oil lamps behind the bar and a few candled lanterns hanging from the wooden beams. It was almost as gloomy as his lounge and Eli contemplated leaving the pub to its creaky social scene. He'd been in worse places, bars full of threatening, thuggish drinkers or dangerous underworld types but this place was just odd. It was too quiet. Apart from the two younger drinkers and the old man, Eli could see everyone else was looking at him in turns, but not in a threatening way, just warily as if they were concerned with his presence in their world. They probably knew he was from the fort and were nervous of someone official snooping around their inner sanctum and they probably didn't get many strangers in here anyway so he realised he was bound to attract attention. But still, the young drinkers, who were talking more loudly as they downed their glug, were oblivious to the outside world and its effect, while everyone else gave the impression of being plagued by it, as if guilty of knowing something they didn't want revealed to a stranger. They watched as if waiting for the something they hid behind to reveal itself to the wider world and so relieve them of their secrecy.

Eli decided to accept the attention, let the locals get on with their disquiet and hang the pub out for a bit longer. He didn't want to head back to the fort yet, even if it did seem a bit friendlier than 'The Dolphin', so he leant back against the wood panelled wall, smiled to the old woman still nodding at him from underneath the sinister harpoon and downed his cheap whisky, savouring the malty tickle that came from the thin, watered down drink and quietly carried on smoking his cigarettes.

Then, from a door at the back of the room that Eli hadn't noticed before, a figure shuffled in who brought a little ray of sunshine into both the gloomy aura of the pub and Eli's attempt at the diversion offered by a night out from the fort. It was the postman, Patrick Gill, hunched against the night as he entered, with a dark grey overcoat on and gloved hands that he rubbed together furiously as if trying to start a fire.

Patrick saw the young soldier as soon he walked in and a smile broke across his craggy face. He nodded and said a greeting to the landlord and the men at the bar before walking straight over to Eli's table.

"Mr Harding," he said through the collars of his thick coat. "Nice to see you out and about, although I must say you're the last person I expected to see in 'ere tonight. I owes you a drink I think Master, but unless the landlords smugglin' rum now, it'll be whisky or cider I'm afraid, an' the cider's not sumthin' to be enjoyed lightly, or so I'm told."

“Whisky’s just fine thanks, Pat, and I hope you’ll join me for a while, only everyone else seems to be giving me a wide berth.”

“Ah, they be harmless enough, jus’ not used to havin’ strangers around, that’s all.”

The postman went to the bar and ordered the drinks, speaking quietly to the barman and the two men next to him as he did so. The close nit sideboards and his sea cap companion nodded in unison as the old man spoke and the barman poured the drinks. Patrick returned with, contrary to his earlier comment, a glass of cider and the whisky and then took a seat opposite Eli in front of the still struggling fire. He stretched back in the chair and undid his great coat before fishing around inside a voluminous internal pocket to find his pipe and tobacco.

“So you took my advice then Mr Harding, and got yerself away from that there fort fer an’ evenin’,” Pat said as he filled the pipe.

Eli rubbed out his cigarette into a small metal bowl on the table. “So I did, Patch old man. Thought the change of scene would do me some good, like you suggested this morning.”

“And has it?” Patch asked as he struck a match and lit the pipe.

“I think so. I was going to see Miss Danvers at the Manor House but thought it might be a little late, so ventured in here instead. I was settling down to a night of being stared at when you came in. I’m glad you did, now it’ll make the walk back home seem worth it,” Eli said while offering a friendly smile to the old man.

“How was the walk down? Did you follow the road or come across from Fiddlers Point, only you said you never bin down that way before?” the old man enquired.

“I more or less fell down from Fiddlers Point. It was a bit steep through the rocks in some places but the moonlight helped. The climb home might be a bit more of a challenge methinks, especially after a few of these,” he tipped his glass, winked and took a swig before adding, “that reminds me, how the blazes do you get your bike up there?”

“Ah well Mr Harding, a word to the wise,” Pat said blowing smoke into the air. “Before ye get about twenty yards from the top of the rocks, if you look to yer right, there’s a skinny little path that leads the way down to the bottom in a more, shall we say, sedate an’ leisurely manner than fallin’ down those rocks. If on the way back you walk on along the track by old Lanes’ field, you’ll see the other end of the path. The rise up is much more gradual, Sir, a lot easier on the back, especially if yer as old as me.” Patch winked back from beneath his white fuzzy cropped hair as if relaying a secret route to a fellow smuggler or treasure seeking pirate.

“I’m glad you turned up tonight, Pat. I might have come a cropper on those rocks in the middle of the night.”

“You wouldn’t be the first to have done so, Mr Harding,” Patrick replied wisely, rubbing his stubbly chin. “Will you be calling on Miss

Danvers again soon?" he asked, changing the subject subtly whilst casually blowing pillows of pipe smoke into the candlelit air.

"Yes," said Eli remembering his enthusiasm from earlier. "I'm going to invite her to a concert in the town." He looked down and played with his fingers as if suddenly flushed with embarrassment, then added, "I don't know if she'll want to come along, but it's worth a try. I don't want to end up going with Eves or the likes of Pickles if she doesn't, unless of course you fancy an afternoon of chamber music Patrick."

"People may talk, Mr Harding, but I am partial to a bit of fiddle music." He chuckled and drank some more cider. "However, I think Miss Danvers will be welcoming enough to an invitation for a visit somewhere other than the village shop. I believe she finds village life, you know, frustrating. She's too young an' beautiful to be stuck in a place like this all 'er life. You should run away wiv 'er before she ends up marryin' some boiled dry, whip crackin' Lord'o'the Manor."

"Steady on Mr P, I haven't even asked her out yet. Anyway she might not even like a dunderhead like me," Eli answered coyly.

"She'll like you young Sir, I'm sure of that. She's mentioned your name several times when I've been round wiv the post and the young lady has enquired after yer health and welfare on more than one occasion."

"Really," said Eli with added zest. He was about to inquire further but stopped himself, bursting his own bubble of interest with the well-used pin of insecurity which he often pulled out to protect himself from the disillusionment of false hope. "We'll see," he added, before moving the subject in another direction. "Anyway, it can't be that onerous living in the village. I'm sure it's quite nice once you get to know everyone. What's so bad about it?"

Patrick fixed him with a serious look, eyes narrowing through the smoke. "Can't you feel it, Sir?" he said quietly.

Eli frowned a little at the old man. "What do you mean?" he asked.

The old man took a puff from his pipe and leant into the table, resting his elbows on the top whilst looming through the cloud of smoke he'd created. "Is everyone still looking at you, Mr Harding?" he said softly, taking his glass between his stubby thumb and fingers.

Eli turned the level of his frown up and surreptitiously glanced to the men at the bar. They were both looking at him, this time with a subtle hint of menace. The barman was leant back on the shelf behind the bar drying an already dry glass with a bar towel whilst also staring at the soldier, a curled lip underneath his sinister nose and moustache. This time they didn't drop their eyes from his. Instead Eli looked over at the woman near the corner. She was also looking straight at him but now her head had stopped nodding and her eyes weren't shining anymore. The old man next to her was now awake, catching Eli's glance with his old dark eyes which somehow hauntingly stood out in the creeping shadows of the pub's dark corner.

The soldier was suddenly spooked. In desperation for some relief from the sets of warning eyes directed at him and the intense surroundings they had created, he cast his look towards the two young men on the other side of the room hoping they weren't part of what felt like a demonic bar room conspiracy and he thankfully saw they were still innocently soaked in their cider fuelled reverie. He breathed a visible sigh of relief as he saw one of the men break the now obvious silence within the pub with a raucous laugh, his associate shaking on his stool holding his stomach, caught in the joyous cramp brought on by a fit of the giggles. Both were still honest, oblivious to the world around them in their own halo of soporific cider intoxication.

"Them boys aren't from the village," said Patrick darkly.

Eli looked him in the eye and saw the old man was still deadly serious. "Well I'll have what they're having, then," he replied trying to smile. He looked back towards the men by the bar and watched as they diverted their gaze and walked back to their table by the door and began talking with the other men still sat there.

"What's up with this place, Patch? Why's everyone wrapped so tightly," he asked, taking a cigarette from his box and lighting it. He was finding it difficult to temper a rising annoyance at how the regulars were behaving towards him and the reasons behind their frankly bendy and unnecessary social manners.

Patch sipped his cider as he spoke. "It's a small village Mr Harding. It ain't far from the town but it's far enough to get left alone. It's always been like that. Those men are just simple fishermen. It's what the village was built on, fishin'. Life is hard, work is hard, and their minds are hard." The old man's eyes looked sad. "The outside world frightens them. They don't know how to live in it or what else they could do if they weren't here. The town creeps up on 'em, waitin' to swamp their world in the ways of modern livin'. The train brings more people. The people build more houses and use more machines an' all the time the world these villagers live in gets threatened with extinction. I suppose they is all just scared." Patrick nodded thoughtfully and poked some more tobacco into his pipe and sparked it up. "They see you as the outside world, Mr Harding. Your fort on the end of their Down is part of that modern world and is a danger to them. That's why they look at you, Sir. You bring the outside world in, bring it closer. To them the fort is war, modern war, like you have seen Mr Harding. You bring the war, the trains bring the people, the people bring the town and the town will bring their end, and they don't know how to stop it."

Eli looked away from the postman into the dying fire. He felt thirsty, his whisky was gone. "Why are they so worried about the modern world? It might stop their lives being so hard and miserable. Give them something else to do other than fish." He paused and licked his lips. "Fancy another cider, old boy?"

“Very kind Mr Harding,” Patch said thankfully.

Elias got up. “And my name’s Eli, Patch. Call me Eli,” he said as he headed towards the bar. His annoyance had risen and when he reached the barman he glared him down. “Cider, two of ‘em!” he snapped.

The purple nosed landlord rocked forward rudely. “You sure about that young ‘un? Strong stuff our cider,” he smirked.

Eli re-smirked at the misshapen nose above the ill-judged moustache. “As long as it’s stronger than your whisky, I don’t really care,” he pointedly replied. The barman looked a bit shifty all of a sudden, turned behind to the wooden kegs led on their sides in timber stillage’s and started distractedly pouring the cider. Eli darted a fierce look at the table of men by the door and held them with it. “What the hell are you lot looking at,” he snarled, his lip curling as his brow dropped, turning his face into an angry pinch of fizzing menace. He was tired of being stared at.

Three of the men looked away, backing down from the reproach by Eli but the man with the sideboards kept glaring, his face beginning to contort in anger. He looked to be in his mid-forties with a well built, thick frame and was obviously the leader of the pack. Eli had already measured the man up in preparation but still didn’t know how he would tackle him if the situation got fruity, however he was sick of the evil eye and decided the best way to combat it was to get confrontational and see how it panned out. After all, it wouldn’t be the first bar room scrap he’d ever had.

The thick man went to stand up but as he did, one of his hat wearing friends held his arm and muttered something Eli couldn’t hear. The sideburns stopped and slowly relaxed back onto his stool, his body receding from the threat of action due to the unknown words, but his face still quivered in simmering contempt. The barman turned round with the drinks, unaware of the burst of angry engagement. Elias took one of the glasses of cider and began to drink, still keeping eye contact with the leader of the table as he gulped. The cider was thick and cloudy and looked like urine with a powerful smell of mouldy apples and wet, rotting leaves. It tasted like squeezed fermenting fruit thrown over freshly cut hedgerows and was truly amazing. Eli drank the whole glass in one go. As he finished, his head wobbled nicely like the swaying branches of an apple orchard in the push of a warm summer breeze.

“Doesn’t hit you till you get outside,” snorted the sideburns.

Eli looked him down again. “Nor do I,” he said malevolently in reply, and the thick set man curled his lip and turned away. His surliness reminded Eli of farmer Lanes and he wondered if they were related. Eli swung around to the purple nose behind the bar and said with a smile on his face as he raised his empty glass, “I’ll have another one of these if you please.”

Once refilled Elias went back to his table, put the drinks down and slid into his seat. It was getting colder and he pulled his coat around himself a bit more. The two young, town boys went to the bar and ordered more cider, and the men in the corner were again chatting quietly within their huddled group, only the man Eli had confronted looking over his shoulder at him once or twice. Even the old couple added a gentle murmur to the low humming ambience of the pub.

"You've fallen for the cider I see, Mr Harding," said Patrick, eyeing the drinks.

"Too right Mr P. I wanted to see what all the fuss was about. Good stuff, tastes bloody gorgeous."

"Ay, it only hits you when you go outside," the old man warned.

"Yes, so I hear," Eli confirmed, smiling. He nodded to the table by the front door. "So are those chap's fishermen," he asked.

"Yes they are. The one you crossed is called Morris." Eli thought the postman hadn't noticed his altercation with the big man but realised the wily old coot was too smart not to have. Patch rattled on. "Most of the men in the village are fishermen. They work the boats near the slipway on the beach. They don't go far, only along the estuary to catch whatever fish they can, mackerel, cod, dogfish, crabs, anything. They say the fish are getting fewer these days. That's why they worry so much."

Eli had another fag to warm up. "Perhaps they should think about a new line of work," he said.

"It's a bit late for most of 'em I think Mr Harding. Fishin's all they know, husbands fishin' is all the wives know. If they didn't fish they might as well die," Patrick said as he gulped his cider, eyes beginning to shine with alcohol.

"Fishing might be the death of them anyway," Eli replied, signalling the painting over the nearly extinguished fire. "It's a dangerous occupation."

"So it is, young Sir. They may not be sailing in ships as big as the one in that there painting, but the estuary is a tricky bit'o'water. A few from the village have not come back," the old man stopped speaking, drank a little and drew on his pipe before continuing. "Only two years ago now, four souls were lost at sea. One of 'em was Morris's brother. That's why he's so fierce in his ways. They say he fishes every day to keep the soul of his brother company." He looked away into the fireplace.

Eli was hit by a feeling of remorse, momentarily angry at his impetuous behaviour and loss of control at the bar. "What happened?" he asked.

Patrick gazed up at the painting as if the image was priming his memory. "They went out on one of the highest tides of the year. They were excited cause they thought it would bring in more fish. It weren't stormy at first but the wind was howling strong and the squalls of rain seemed to throw 'emselves up out of nowhere. Others came back early but a few waited out there fer as long as they could cause they grabbed so many fish, includin' Morris's brother. A storm blew down the channel and the weather suddenly turned worse. The rain came down like stair rods and the waves whipped up big 'an frothy. Then some of the boats got caught as the tide turned. They capsized fightin' against the current and the changin' winds. The others tried to help but were forced back by the high sea. Some of them smashed their boats up on the rocks along the Down. Four men were missin' by the end. The next day a body was washed up on the rocks by Fiddlers Point and two more were found in the mud on the flats. Morris's brother was never seen again. He must have been swept out to sea." There was a contemplative silence and Eli's eyes were drawn to the painting. "It's worse when no body is found, the dead need layin' to rest," Pat added solemnly. The two men looked down at the dying embers of the half scorched log. The fire was nearly dead. They finished their cider. Patrick wiped the corners of his craggy mouth. "They say you can see the spirits of the dead men wonderin' the Down and the mud flats at low tide. Morris believes his brother's soul is on the end of Brean Down looking for his way back home. That's why he hates the fort so much. He reckons it's in the way of his brother's spirit finding peace. Everyone in the village seems to believe in ghosts."

"Bloody hell, poor buggers," whispered Eli beginning to understand how they felt.

"One fer the road, Mr Harding," Pat suddenly chirped.

"Aye, go on then."

Another trip to the bar and another round of drinks followed. The two hat wearing men from the table by the entrance left, leaving Morris and the young long hair to scowl and mumble to each other in the corner. The two drunken lads called time on themselves and wobbled comically out of the back door chuckling as they went. The hum was replaced by a few chinks of glasses being washed and tables cleared. The candle lantern above Eli's table went out increasing the gloom and marking a sense of closure to the evening. Postman Pat prodded the fire with a poker, trying to push one last flurry of ignition into the beaten log. The pair of old crones had fallen asleep again.

"So do you believe in ghosts then, Patch," asked Eli, the previous conversation still on his mind.

"No, I mean I don't think so, but who's to know either way really. I'm not from the village. I married a woman who lived here many years ago but she died from the fever and I just stayed on. I go to the town every day so I'm not scared of the modern world, not like the people in the village who were born and raised here. They've all been trapped by their belief. I think their grief turned to superstition which then became mistrust." He left the fire alone and looked towards the front door with a nod of the head that pinpointed beyond the door to the hill outside. Eli noticed the fire suddenly burst into action again, small flames licking the underside of the log causing a hissing sound.

“Everyone here goes to the church,” Pat continued still looking towards the door, “They pray for salvation, for their souls to be saved, for their old world to be preserved in the afterlife.” He turned his eyes from the door and smiled a little, knocking the spent tobacco from his pipe and re-filling it with fresh. “Just suspicious mumbo jumbo if you ask me. The village men say Jesus was a fisherman, just like them and he’ll save them from the stormy seas and the dangers of the new world. Religion gone too far I say. My wife went to church but I never did, I don’t believe in it the way they do here. Everyone still talks to me of a kind but not in the same way as the other villagers talk to one another. I’ve always been a bit of an outcast but I’m too old to leave now, and besides, my wife’s buried in the churchyard. I loved her very much. Maybe I stay to keep her company.” He stared into the remnants of his cloudy cider as if looking for his own salvation. Eli warmly touched his arm.

“It’s alright Patrick, I’m glad you’re still here. You’ve been the sanest thing I’ve known since I got to the fort. You’re a good egg, old man,” Elias said compassionately. He drained the last of his beverage which made his head sway and his eyes water slightly. “Come on postie, let’s call it a night and get ourselves home.”

The postman nodded, forcing a more honest smile as he stood. “Aye,” he said. “No need to make ourselves morose, it does one no good to be too thoughtful about such things. Besides, any more of this an’ we’ll end up in the gutter,” he added with a cheerful note motioning to the empty glasses. They did up their coats and headed for the bar. The barman gave them a nod as they walked past, showing a slither of respect towards the old man and his friend which Eli returned, more in sympathy for the landlord’s bulbous purple beak than anything else. Morris and the long hair were now also stood at the bar and as Eli reached them Morris threateningly stepped forward, almost barring the soldier’s way. His face was still creased with scorn and his sideburns bristled with excitement like the hairs on the back of an agitated dog. Eli stopped.

“You should watch yer tongue when you come in ‘ere, young ‘un,” Morris spat.

“Is that right,” Elias replied calmly.

Patrick stepped in. “Now now Morris, there’s no need to carry this on, is there,” he said with a wise countenance.

Eli glanced at the old man with admiration then studied his thick set opponent remembering the story Patrick had told him. He decided it might be best to show some understanding to the man’s traumas. “Maybe if you’d been the point of attention for the manner of looks I’ve been receiving all night, Sir, you would have had your patience tested, as I have. None the less, my over reaction was uncalled for and I apologise for my earlier comment and any unnecessary misunderstanding that lies between us.” He accented the final phrase hoping to placate the charged sideboards stood before him. The cider was deadening his reactions. He didn't fancy a fight now and he also didn't want Patrick to get involved, but inside, he prepared himself for action, watching for the possibility of a fist fuelled, village boozer, toe to toe.

"Come on Morris, it's a bit late for all this now. The young man said he was sorry," the landlord finally piped up in an almost pleading tone, trying to avoid a bar room brawl and the possibility of pricey breakages.

Morris flashed the bar owner a reproachful look but realised there wasn't the necessary support for a late night scrap. The long hair had stayed back from the fray and the soldier before him had already shown a more than capable conduct. He eased back slowly to the bar and stepped away from the cause. Eli pursed his lips, nodded a final show of deference before reaching for the door handle and opening it. A cold blast of air entered the room and Morris let forth an open ended farewell comment.

"We 'aven't 'eard them gun's yet, soldier boy. Paddy says you was gonna be lettin' 'em off sometime," he said with a hint of snipe.

Eli turned his head to Morris, biting back his irritation. "Yes, Paddy was right. You might hear some firing practice tomorrow," he said flatly.

Morris screwed a glowering look at Eli. "I pray them guns blow 'emselves up and 'fall into the sea, takin' you lot wiv 'em," he said darkly.

"Who knows Mr Morris, perhaps they will one day. Till then, you'll just have to put up with us. Goodnight all and god bless."

With that, Eli and the old man stepped out of the doorway to 'The Dolphin' and walked into the cold, night air of the lonely seaside village.

Eli left Patrick at the gate to his fisherman's cottage which sat nestled in the terrace halfway down the road towards the beach. The curtains to the houses were still drawn and a few had lost their hazy glow. There was no sign of life along the street. They shook hands warmly and waved each other goodbye, both men suffering from a medium level of inebriation after the heady cider, Eli a bit more than the old man due to the extra whisky he'd drunk. As warned, the Moorish rotten apple juice had indeed hit the friends as they got outside into the fresh air and brought about a slight wobble in the gait of the men as they walked. After saying goodbye, Eli managed to find the lantern he'd hidden earlier behind the wall and lit it, somehow crossing the bridge over the inlet with enough sure footedness not to slip into the muddy rivulet. He walked along the track, scuffing the odd step as he did so and found the pathway Pat had told him about in the pub. It was a straight path rising steadily up through the bushes and brambles growing steadfastly over the slope. He was glad he could go this way as he realised his whisky and cider head would never have got him up the rock face pass. He imagined that if he had gone that way having to give up early on in the attempt and find a cave within the pebbly cove to spend the night in, probably freezing to death as a consequence and ending up as another sad casualty from a poorly judged night on the sauce.

As it was, he now found himself gustily bouncing along the top of the Down, his lantern illuminating the way through the darkness with its gauzy field of light. The clear skies had clouded over and the wind was whipping across the grass in blasts of icy sheets. He was glad he had his gloves on, that his coat was warm, and it wasn't raining.

Although the water was still lapping around the rocky shore of the peninsular it was starting to recede, replacing the previous calm flatness with swirly, frothing rhythms of thin grey tide. Further ahead, the land had shadowy patches in places where the gorsy masses of bush inhabited the slopes, falling away to the blackened rocks of the seething water line underneath. Where the tide had backed out, the darker shade of mud and sand was being revealed like the huge mattress of some rancid, God sized bed after having the slithering all enveloping covers being pulled away in the middle of the night.

Then, just as he reached the beginning of the road at the end of the grassy pathway which led across the undulating heights, the wind noticeably picked up even more than before, pushing Eli's lantern from side to side and forcing his still drunken body to slew across the path. He shielded his face from the cutting zephyrs with a bicep. The temperature dropped just as measurably and he narrowed his eyes to protect them from the freshness. But out of the corner of his vision, only a few feet away, he saw a distinctive shadow move from one trembling clump of indefinable undergrowth to disappear behind another, still darker and larger mass of bushes. Eli tried to focus on the movement through the changing fields of murky shading and ignore the effect of the sudden change in elements that were now bombarding him.

"Hello! Is someone there!" he tried to shout above the sound of the wind, which only seemed to absorb any other sound and blow more shadows around the landscape. "Hello! Who goes there! Is somebody out there!" he called again.

Eli went to walk towards where he felt the movement had been, but the wind and disorientation of night confused his mental compass. He wasn't sure where he was looking now, even doubted if he'd seen anything at all, but his brain was telling him something was out there, he could feel it. He held the lantern outstretched and stumbled towards the bushes lining the slopes leading down the hill in the direction of Lanes' farm. The ball of windblown light from the lantern only covered a foot or two of space around its oily burning wick making it impossible to see clearly further ahead. Apart from the swaying foliage and the wind, nothing else moved.

"Bloody goats!" Eli shouted to the rustling bushes. Then he felt something definite across his back, like a hand brushing swiftly along his coat, and he turned around in a panic, expecting to come face to face with whoever was out there. "What the hell!" he called out as he turned. There was nothing there, just the vista of the coastal bay awash with darkness and the twinkling lights of the town in the distance. He made out the road a few feet away. *'It must have been the wind'* he thought, as the trickles of fear and alarm ran through his body.

"Bloody cider," he whispered under his breath as he headed for the road and the last stretch of his journey back to the fort. He looked around furtively as he walked, picking up his pace with each step, a feeling of malignity forcing a turn of haste in his desire to get home. He was sure he'd seen someone, something in the darkness, but told himself it was just an animal or a startled bird. He walked faster still, almost jogging. The thought entered his mind that maybe it was Morris come to frighten him on his way home or even worse the ghost of Morris's brother searching for the way back from his watery tomb. By the time Elias saw the lights shining out from the entrance of the fort, now safely within reach, he was virtually running, the childhood fear of being chased down a dark hallway by malevolent spirits returning to his grown up, cider soaked mind.

As he got back to the walls of the fortress and crossed the bridge, a wave of relief washed over the alarmed Officer. The fort felt safe, a place of refuge from the vagaries of the night and the isolation of the hill. A shadow loomed out of the guard room doorway as he entered the open main gate.

"Alright Master Harding," Lumpy Boulter cheeped, his fat head emerging from the shadows. Eli jumped back, startled at first then relieved to see a friendly face.

"Bloody hell Boulter, you gave me a fright, again."

"Sorry Sir. How was yer night out? Yer back late. You must 'av bin down 'The Dolphin'," Lumpy said chirpily, a grin spreading across his face.

"Yes. I did end up in there for a couple. Why, what time is it?" Eli had lost track of time.

"Nearly 1'o'clock Mr Hardin'. Must 'av bin a good night out?"

"Not really, if I'm honest, more enlightening, if anything. What are you doing up anyway?" Eli asked dazedly, still shaken from the walk back.

Boulter looked podgy and confused. "Don't you remember, Sir? Guard duty. You told us to get some practice in. One of them Pearce boys is watchin' the sea view and I'm gaurdin' the gate'ouse. Keepin 'an eye out fer the frogs," he said continuing to grin, his swollen eyes red with fatigue.

"Frogs, it's not the frogs you need to worry about around here," Eli said looking behind him up the road into the darkness.

"What?" said lumpy even more confused.

"Oh, never mind," replied Eli. "Well, have a lie in tomorrow morning. It's been a long night. I'm going to bed. Here take this," he said and handed Lumpy the lantern.

"Right oh, Sir. Night, night then," Boulter replied taking the lamp and blowing out the weak flame while wondering what it was that seemed to be troubling the Master as he watched him disappear through the door into his quarters.

Once inside Eli headed for the living room and lit a table lamp. The fire was out and the room was cold. He kept his coat on and poured out a stiff gin. The creepy journey back from Uphill and the fright on the Down had sobered his mind, suddenly waking him up. He kept thinking about the story Patrick had told him regarding the dead sailors and their ghosts wandering the Down, and he asked himself again if he'd really seen anything on the way back or whether it was just his imagination. Then the idea formed that maybe the apparition seen by the frightened wife of his predecessor at the fort was something to do with Morris's brother. Maybe the ghost she saw was him. There was still the tingling sensation around the back of his neck that he felt when the demons chased him down the landing when he was small. He drank some more booze and felt fuzzy again before reasoning in his mind that he was tired and all this spirit talk was just over imaginative madness on his part. He topped up his glass and headed to bed.

Elias tried to sleep, but was plagued by the shadows of the night creeping through his rooms. He reached into the drawer by the bed and pulled out the laudanum. He took a healthy swig straight from the bottle and within a few moments it brought on a gentle delirium and the relief of approaching unconsciousness. Curled into a foetal ball, fully clothed with only his coat undone, he finally fell into a deep, fitful slumber.

In the vivid, opium tinged dreams that haunted his sleep that night, eyes stared at him from murky corners in a fetid labyrinth of obscure, dingy rooms connected by pitch black corridors and foul feeling hallways. Those malicious eyes would turn into the twisted blood filled faces of screaming men, women and children running and being chased by floating blades of curved swords swung by invisible riders upon demonic horses with bulging, yellowed eyes. These horses were covered in hateful lacerations that were being fed upon by evil wasp like flies. The flies would then gather into sinister, malign formations that turned into the deformed and misshapen bodies of Morris and his brother along with other naked fishermen caught upon the rocks around the Down like a netted shoal of broken and disjointed human starfish. As he slept, tossing and turning, his visions morphed onto a storm hewn scene on top of the promontory and the awful corpses crawled from the rocks and became outlines of shadowy black figures that moved towards him, wanting to devour his being and entrap his soul in an abhorrent, eternal, Faustian darkness.

Eli kicked out in his nightmares, throwing his body in contorted, involuntary animation. The oil lamp by his bed hissed through the night, his mind buzzed with the intimidation of his subconscious hallucinations and, as he dreamt, he called out incoherently for the shadows of the night to stop.

Outside, Daniel Pearce heard the calls made by Master Harding in the officer's disturbed sleep. Pearce was sat on the parapet keeping watch, his back against the grassy roof of the magazine bunker, the edge of the gun emplacement walls offering a semblance of shelter from the wind. He was cold and felt tired and wondered what the point of being on watch was as nothing could possibly happen on a night like this. He had lost interest in this particular part of playing soldiers and just felt like falling asleep. He paid no attention to the ramblings of the tortured Master inside the officer's quarters. Lots of people called out in their sleep he decided, including his bastard brother, who sometimes used to wake him up in the night when they were children. Instead, the on guard, young Pearce boy was too busy staring hypnotically out to sea at a distant point of light shining in the middle of the blackened horizon. It had been there during his whole shift and hadn't moved. *'It must be a ship out in the channel,'* reflected the dozy lookout, imagining what it must be like to live on a boat floating on a vast expanse of water with the whole world before you waiting to be explored.

'I wonder where he's heading,' he thought dreamily.

The Iron Beast slept in its nest out of the wind, behind the shelter of stones, covered in dingy rags of cloth and oil. In the fetid corner it lay, half finished within its waterproof cocoon, like a heavy metal insect waiting to metamorphose into the mighty Iron butterfly it would soon become. Waiting patiently, watching peacefully and preparing quietly for its new awakening. To be born again, to make its name known for the reason it was made in the fiery pits of creation. The journey is almost over.

In the lightless church on the side of the hill, two men prey for the end of a new world with a dream of the old world in their hearts. An old world free from the shadow of the beast and the desperate fear that it brings, an old world where souls can be saved and the dead find rest. Two men are preying upon the land, the Iron Beast soon to prey upon men.

'Who's that?' Yet a different man hides within the shadows of another sleeping beast. This beast, a leviathan of rocky flesh with folds of thorny skin, ageless and unmoving, into which this unknown spectre secretes itself like a parasite burrowing into the unfeeling monster, waiting and watching for the new day to come, like the Iron Beast before him who rests within its stone and mortar citadel.

'Wait,' breathes the stone beast into the wind, 'Wait. Then hear my roar and the death it soon shall bring.'

Tomorrow, when the change is made, perhaps the final change for some, for then it will be the time to live or a time to die. Till then the beast sleeps. They all sleep.

7. The Day.

The sun had gone in and all the men had gone in too. The Captain of the ship and his nightshift crew were still awake during this late hour, keeping a watchful eye on the pinholes of light emitted from the landmass in the distance, steering clear of the darkened hulks, wishing to be unseen and invisible. Strips of shaded black were all around, near and far, skulking in the cloak of night like the waiting forms of sinister predators. Only the churning sea showed up in the consuming dark like torn ribbons of creamy white cotton around the dipping haunches of the aged, chugging boat as she moved through the water. They were nearing another land, close to another destination, within touching distance of a foreign soil. But after following the tide down the estuary at the start of the night and then hugging the coast of this new land for a while, they then turned around and preceded the surge of water out again. Now they had been ordered to circle, dead slow, in a stretch of sea at the widest part of the channel and await their final instructions. For what or for why they came and went, the crew did not know. That was for the other men to know. As they approached and retreated from the dark land, a nervousness flicked around their senses like the spumes of brown sea that were thrown upon the bow of the ship as the small fish carved her dizzy furrow. For what of for why they were nervous, the crew did not know. That was for the other men to know.

Those men, who had earlier cheerfully adorned the outside deck of the 'Small Fish', had by now poured themselves into the vessel of her steel hull and escaped the chilly grasp of outside which arose from the creeping fall of pitch darkness. The once roomy hold was now brimming with the stinking testosterone of tingling, expectant males. No female attributes decorated this space, either material or organic, although such fleshy decoration would surely have been appreciated by the occupiers and warmed their manly, frigid souls on this cold night. There was no softening of the hardened atmosphere with the gentle whiff of a seductive perfume or the sublime beauty that comes from the presence of a woman's figure, no matter what size or shape that figure may be. Instead, it was the heady concentration of tightened manliness, born from the purest form of that human gender and sculpted over countless generations, which filled the metallic surroundings. Sixty pairs of intense eyes stared expectantly through the dimly lit shadows, squinted but alert, acclimatized to the gloom. The only sound came from the constant buzz emanating from the frayed burn of low quality oil which meandered tiredly throughout the moody lighting system.

To an onlooker it would have been exciting and impressive, almost erotic to be in the attendance of such a group of honed and crafted males.

They wore the faces of men who had marched in the Egyptian desert under a burning sun, clawed their way up a rock face in the dust of Morocco, hacked their way through the tearing undergrowth of a jungle in the Congo and had their bodies immersed in the icy waters of an Alpine lake. The resulting physique was flailed with ruggedness and enduring stamina, those faces handsome in their own distinctive and commanding way but also seemingly full of preparation for death, gained from the experience of their own and each other's pain and torture.

"I expect some of you are wondering what we're doing on this boat, in the middle of the English Channel," Castille said in a testy manner. "Well don't wonder, just do, because this one should be easy!" he added with more vigour.

"Nothing's ever easy if you've got anything to do with it," boomed a cave deep voice from the back of the darkness. The men laughed in recognition that this statement held more truth in it than the opening one made by the Colonel.

"Yes, yes, very good," smiled the Colonel, relaxing a little and raising his hand as if to instigate control again as the men settled once more into reverential silence. He looked around the room, fixing the shaded profiles of his soldiers in the nightclub like, dusky illumination of the ship's hold.

"To be honest, I didn't think many of you would want to be part of this particular job, I'm not even sure I do really. But whatever we feel about the circumstances or the outcomes, it's still just another job and we're the ones who've been told to do it. And in the end, we don't question the reasons why we're told to do things, we never have and we never will, even when we know the things we've done have been wrong. Because if we did, they just wouldn't get done and sometimes.....well, things need to be done."

"Get on with it, Colonel. You're waffling and it's making my shit stink," replied the dog faced man who had earlier lounged in one of the deck chairs, momentarily taking the china pipe out of his mouth so he could speak his mind.

"Don't tell us we're invading England again," said another man near the front of the group. "I'm not invading that shithole at this time of year."

There was more laughter. Castille glanced at the artisan type man stood beside him and folded his arms, biting his lip at the same time, aware of the irony in the man's comment. The artisan stared at the floor with a serious face, his flippant manner from earlier in the day noticeably absent. The ship lurched softly as it made another wide turn.

"Spit it out, Sir. They're all dying to know what the hell we're doing here," suggested the dog face, smirking. His name was Arturo Ben Arfa, Benno for short, and his position as the second in command of the legionnaires meant he could say it as he saw it and Castille respected that. He had opted for the army instead of prison at the tender age of sixteen after being caught stealing the watches and wallets of unsuspecting gentlemen on the streets of Marseille nearly twenty years ago. With a previously unknown talent for killing people given an output, Benno had shown guile and a rare combative sense that saw him picked for the formation of an elite fighting unit alongside Castille within the French Foreign Legion. They had been through the grinder together since the initiation of this specialist outfit and had saved each other's lives numerous times over the years. The Colonel trusted him more than any other man.

"Alright Benno, alright," countered Castille, taking the hint from his friend and comrade whilst gearing up for the forthcoming explanation with a narrowing of his steely eyes. "We are invading England," he said, and felt the following silence, noticing some of the mouths of his men drop open, before adding quickly, "But not for long. There's an island in the Bristol Channel called Steep Holm, some of you probably saw it on our way down, and one of our agents is incarcerated there. We have to get him back." He looked at his watch. "And seeing as it's three in the morning, we'll be getting him back some time later on tonight." Castille stopped and waited for the barrage of opposition to be spat at him from the tightly packed gathering.

"Bullshit," was the only audible reply from the cavernous voice at the back of the hold that had spoken a moment ago. The other men flashed suspicious looks at one another and a few murmured amongst themselves in the darker recesses. A tall man from the front nodded to the Colonel, "How the hell are we going to do that without getting caught. I don't want to end up in a British prison for the sake of some spy," he offered smartly.

"Relax, Rene. We're not going to get caught. Remember, we trained for this on Sardinia years ago. The island and the peninsular we have to deal with will fall under the same plan; we go in, get what we want, and get out." The Colonel opened up his hands in a gesture reflecting the simplicity of the idea. The men weren't convinced.

"But when we practiced that scenario, it only succeeded if we killed everybody," said a hard faced man with a thick scar across his neck. Everyone looked at him and then switched their eyes to the Colonel, nodding shortly and silently as they did so. Castille heaved a sigh, pulled out a smoke and lit it. The artisan rubbed his tidy beard and looked up at the low, buzzing ceiling.

"I know," Castille said quietly in acknowledgement. "And obviously this time," he hesitated, taking a short drag before finishing the sentence, "this time, we can't kill anybody. That would start a war and we're not allowed to do that." He tried to smile in jest but just got the feeling he sounded stupid. The men began to murmur and shuffle around adding to the sway of the boat. Some of them lit cigarettes and pipes and began to smoke as well.

"Well I suppose if we don't kill anyone we might not get hung," said the artisan drily.

"But they'll sure as hell try to kill us!" burst a voice from the crowd. "Why should we risk our lives and the possibility of a crappy war for the sake of some guy we know nothing about? He got caught, let him hang," claimed the man, supported by several agreeing mutters from his comrades.

Castille tried to calm the men. "Look I understand how you feel. Like I said, I don't want to do this anymore than you do, but I've been ordered to attempt this mission and I think we can do it without killing anyone and without getting caught. If I could do this and not get you involved, I would. But in all honesty I can't do it alone. I need your help. We've been through a lot of tough missions over these past few years, missions which no one else could do, missions only we could have pulled off. And yes, most of those jobs meant killing people to get them done, often lots of people, which we never questioned before, but sometimes we did it without having to kill anyone," there was a tone of pleading in his voice now, "and this is just like those times. Imagine pulling this off. Landing on the coast of Britain and releasing one of our citizens and not a shot fired, that would be truly outstanding." Castille looked around the room. "It would make us the true Gods of war," he said emotionally. The Colonel raised a fist in front of his face like a boxer and pursed his lips, catching the eyes of his men as he did so. Then he coolly dropped his fag butt and rubbed it out on the steel floor with the toe of his boot.

The bull dog wrinkled up his face and slow clapped a few times. "Very good, monsieur, very good speech," he said condescendingly. "Now we're all in line for the Republican medal, why don't you tell us how sixty men are going to take over two coastal forts and a hundred British artillerymen and not get shafted," he added, raising his eyebrows on the last word.

Castille looked at the dog as if he wanted to clip him round the ear. "Well, I'll tell you then, you gobby little shit. Firstly, there aren't a hundred men on those two forts. The one on the mainland has fourteen volunteers and one officer manning it with only one working artillery gun between them. The island, although it's got all its guns, has only thirty men and one idiot commander on it, who, by the way, is the bastard who started all this crap. Secondly, we've got a man on the mainland who'll be helping us out and keeping the locals away."

The artisan, whose name was Modesto, stepped into the discussion, rubbing a fore finger around his nose and finely crafted facial hair. He finally felt in need of airing his own kind of contention to his leader's confidence. "That is all very good, Sir. I'm sure we can cope with whatever is thrown at us on the mainland or the island once we get there and I'm sure getting on the mainland will be easy enough without causing suspicion among the locals or the volunteers of the fortification, but what is troubling me Sir, and forgive me for bringing it up before you've even gone into any detail, is how the fuck are we going to get on that island without the asshole's in the navy helping us out." He smiled at Castille annoyingly as he fingered himself.

"Good point Modesto, but there really is no need to swear. Well, from the message I received last night from the agent on the mainland, we could take back our man without the English on that island even knowing about it, not at least until we're safely back across the Channel into France," Castille replied knowingly with a good dose of smarm.

"And?" enquired the artisan still fingering.

"Well, it's easy really." Everyone in the room waited for the answer. "You and I, Mon frère, are going to pretend to be English."

The artisan stopped his annoying smile and dropped his finger down, his small mouth opened and a frown formed across his smooth brow as he looked at Castille with bemusement. Everyone else seemed to do the same. The Colonel, with a grin on his face, glared at the dog. "Benno, go and tell that idiot Captain to drop anchor where we are and stop this old tub from rolling around so there's less chance of making me puke, and then come back down here. I'm going to tell you all exactly how we're going to do this."

And as the dog scampered away towards the stairs under the soft glow from the fizzing lights, the rest of the testosterone packed room moved forward a step and shuffled around slightly to get a little bit closer to the alpha male called Castille, who was still dominant as their immoveable leader, and was now the centrepiece of this animal like collection of hunters and unquestioning warriors.

Meanwhile, Cyrano Shrott was tenderly woken by the soft tickle from the dancing feet of a spider, which had stopped on his cheek whilst travelling from one part of the cell to another. Shrott hadn't been lost in the paralysis of a deep sleep or enveloped in numbness from an overwhelming fatigue so he felt the sensation of the insect crawling across his face. It was a sensation he'd felt before in other prisons which meant he wasn't startled enough to make any sudden movement or jolt upright in shock when it occurred. He merely opened his eyes and even in the blackness of the stone cell, which was only vaguely illuminated by a light source from outside, he could make out the spider's legs tapping rhythmically on his skin and an enlarged many eyed insect face looking at him as if it were saying, "What the blazes are you!" The human slowly brought his hand up and led it on the other side of his face next to the spider, whom after a couple of seconds deliberation, soothingly walked onto the open palm. Cyrano lifted it off and upon leaning up, examined it in the red, expiring embers of the fireside next to him. He turned his hand as the creature ran blindly around his finger tips with awesome agility, looking for a way out from this interruption by the oversized pink blob he was clinging too. Cyrano leant forward, rested his hand on the dusty stone floor and allowed the spider to run away into one of the prison's dark, creviced corners.

The Frenchman looked up towards the barred window, where dull shafts of foggy, orange light were creeping in through the bars from a gas fed lamp hanging steadfastly to an outside wall. He focused his eyes on the light source and tuned his ears to the only sound he could hear; the regular tinny chink of a cord flapping on a metal flagpole in the gusty, ocean fed wind. It was the sound of the seashore, of ships in harbours and stone walls with blooming flags upon them. The room was cold, the fire being almost lifeless. It gave off no heat, just small blobs of reddened light from the few shards of wooden ashes.

He looked at his watch; four in the morning. He led back down and pulled the blanket up around himself, still fully dressed with only his shoes removed and sitting neatly by the side of his thin, damp smelling mattress. He supposed he was lucky to have got a mattress and a blanket to sleep with at all, especially after being in jails where if anything, he'd only had a patch of straw in the corner to curl up on and instead of spiders crawling on his face, there had been scorpions or heavy footed lizards, chasing equally heavy footed, hair raising, alien like beetles or overblown insects across the floor, and him. Still, in those sorts of places it was warmer, even at night, and he didn't need a blanket to keep him comfortable. Even if it was cold, it certainly wasn't as cold as England in early February.

At least the guards had built up the fire before they left him for the night. It had warmed him as he settled down on the slice of pungent bedding brought to him and through which he could still feel the hard stone floor. He realised from quick experience it was best to lie in one position as opposed to scraping bony corners of his body on the knobbly, granite ground. At least they had fed him reasonably well too. He'd been getting hungry by the time the doughy faced, nervous looking guard had brought him a plate of sausage and mashed potatoes with a piece of thickly sliced bread and dripping. *'A typically English meal,'* Cyrano thought. Hearty and filling, just what you need in these harsh conditions. They even supplied another mug of stewed tea and a pudding of even more stewed apples. But he realised it was asking a bit much to expect a dollop of custard with it or instead of the bland mash, a well layered, finely seasoned gratin. It was all infinitely better than a bowl of crispy bugs or a plate of mashed sheep's innards which he had received in certain Middle Eastern countries, and a decent meal also showed that Major Acres was still aware of the fact he might be wrong about his suspicions of Mr Edwin Ralph.

However, now Shrott had fully woken up, he felt he needed the toilet to relieve his stomach of the sausage, mash and boiled apples which were now bubbling up nicely inside his guts. Although there was obviously still a guard outside the door, this opportunity of going to the bog might offer up a chance to escape, but deep down he didn't want to disturb the thin coating of warmth he was under from the grey army issue blanket laid over his prone body.

He'd had a long evening of more pointless, repetitive questioning by Major Acres and in return had ramped up his levels of annoyance at the situation enough to make it look like he was an innocent man who had been stretched to near breaking point by an implausible event. From his often heated exchanges with Acres he had worked out the men from London wouldn't get here until after high tide, which was around four in the afternoon and the boat bringing them would take an hour or so to reach the island from the mainland anyway. After the initial realisation of having to possibly think of a way to escape, Shrott had come to the conclusion it would be difficult to do that from an island in the middle of a tide controlled channel where, after sailing the waters for the last few days, he knew the leftover mud was just as dangerous as the twice daily sweep of brown water. That water, on which he had sailed to observe this place, was now its best asset at keeping him imprisoned here. Even if he had been able to overcome a few dozy watchmen, which he was obviously confident of doing, and could get to either his yacht or some other kind of boat he could still easily miss the tide and get stuck in the mud a couple of miles out from shore where the coastal police would simply lay in wait for him until the tide came back in. Even if he did make it across the water in one go it wouldn't take long for the authorities to pick him up from the land side once they'd known he had escaped. He deliberated it was best to wait it out and try to continue his charade with the two bodies from the War Office. Anyway, they wouldn't interrogate him on this island for long. If they really had their suspicions about him they would want to take him back to London and really give the dirty sod a good grilling, and the best time for escape would be on that journey back to London.

Given the right opportunity and a bit of forward thinking he would probably be able to slip his minders and melt into the crowds of the train station or the bustling streets of the city and that would give him a better chance of making it to a safe house and the help of a fellow conspirator, of which he knew there were plenty in London.

One of Cyrano's main incentives for escape was that he didn't fancy getting tortured. He knew the English were pretty good at torturing people because they'd made a decent habit of it over the centuries. They weren't as good as the Russians, or the French for that matter, or the Arabs, who had found a pleasure in forming particularly good ways of inciting pain on the human body and getting people to say things they didn't really want to say. He knew the British probably wouldn't start peeling his skin off like the Afghans did but the Brits were still pretty good at making things hurt, which in Shrott's mind was always the low point of any incarceration.

But hopefully it wouldn't come to that. They still didn't know for certain if he was a French spy and might be unsure enough to let him go after a few enquiries. Once they got to the Island, it would only be a selection of token questions before they got him back to the mainland to make those further enquiries and hopefully his necessary contacts would have informed his benefactors and adjudicators who would help towards the evidence that backed up his false identity, so negating those enquiries. And if not, his fellow spies could even be putting into practice a plan to spring him once he was back in London or maybe even earlier, just in case things looked like they were going awry somewhere along the line. Either way, there was no point in making an escape attempt tonight. Especially not on the way to emptying his bubble guts and so he tried not to think of his need for taking a dump.

So Cyrano settled his head on the hammy, greasy stained pillow that had been given to him and listened to the chinking sound of the flag cord on the metal pole. He rested his eyes and quietly regenerated his body ready for a new day tomorrow. In a way he was looking forward to the London men arriving as it would inevitably lead to his leaving this shitty little island and the dislikeable attentions of the even shittier Major Acres. That man was starting to make his balls shrink. He put his hand behind his head, released a wide airy yawn and thought instead about what they might bring him for breakfast in the morning, as the chinking sound echoing in his chamber was finally interrupted by the noise of the low gurgling pop of his digesting tummy.

When the daylight finally arrived, the men across the water at Brean Down coastal defence garrison were soon up and about and cracked on with the finishing touches to building their new gun. Now, in the mid-morning fresh metal greyness which surrounded them, they were gathered around the gun emplacement and escarpments, all of them exhilarated about firing the weapon and getting their first proper practice for several months. All of them that is, except Elias Harding.

Harding's head ached from a grinding hangover caused by the laudanum and cider/whisky/gin mix from last night's high jinks. His mouth was dry and he felt a bit sick but luckily the traumatic dreams from the fitful sleep he'd had were fading away and although he remembered sporadic images and a few imposing visions from the nightmare, the supervision of finishing off the cannon build and the subsequent preparations for firing had dulled their reflection. Also, he was now more nervous about firing the gun. It had been a while since he had done it properly. Apart from being on the periphery of a firing range in Woolwich, he hadn't been in charge of an actual gun crew since his return from the Middle East over two years ago. He hoped it wouldn't bring on a turn or an unsightly episode from him in front of the men.

The chosen crew for the first practice carefully went through the procedures for loading the gun, taking their time in a nervous state of tentatively concentrated excitement. When the orders had been called out and carried through, then double checked just to make sure, the men stood back holding their breath and tensing their bodies ready for the explosion that would come. The second crew stood further away, watching, taking in the actions and trying to memorise them ready for when it was their turn. Expectation filled the cold, blank air. Grey trousers and navy blue tunics adorned the men, their round pill box hats sat above crinkled brows of anticipation. Harding took a deep breath, gave the order and Brean Down gun battery finally let one off.

There was a noise like a splat, followed by a jaw splitting cracking sound, and the whole thing nearly fell apart. Smoke belched out the side of the fixings and the bottom of the breech as the gun shuddered like a baby dragon letting out a burp. Some sparks coughed out the barrel opening, along with a cloud of soot which led the slowly floundering missile as it emerged from the muzzle like a lazy worm on a rainy day. It plopped out the end, fell to the grass on the other side of the wall and then rolled onto the rocks before ultimately slipping into the sea like runny cat shit off a rusty trowel. A bolt snapped on the mounting and the barrel, with geriatric slowness, toppled off the carriage and fell to the ground landing on Dick Pearce's foot.

Harding stood by the side of the troop, open mouthed in absolute bewilderment, as Dicky Pearce dramatically dropped to the floor and rolled around on the concrete, squealing like a scared piglet. Some of the other men stood in stunned silence not knowing what to do while the rest, including Sergeant Eves, broke into fits of uncontained laughter.

"Bless us, what a spanker!" wheezed old man Smales, before sneezing violently due to the dust.

"God's eyes," said Boulter, a bit shocked. "What a cock-up!"

"Oh shit," Elias said under his breath.

He and Barnes, the conscientious administrator, stepped over to Pearce and tried to help him. The lad stopped rolling around and sat up holding his foot, wincing and crying out in pain.

"Stop squealing boy and take your boot off," Eli snapped at the young man, annoyed that the gun hadn't worked.

"I can't, it bloody hurts!" he whined back.

"It's alright Pearce, let me take a look at it then we'll get you inside and Mr England can get you something to ease the pain," Barnes said.

Barnes tenderly took the boy's boot off and gingerly removed his rather odorous sock. When he saw the big toe already starting to swell, Barnes realised Pearce had broken it. Eli also noticed the injury. "Better get inside and wrap it up, son. We don't want you having another accident while we put this thing back together. If we can?" he said more caringly. Harding noticed the other men were still laughing and talking excitedly about the shambles they'd just witnessed. A sense of chaos and an atmosphere of unruliness began to spread through the group. Harding stood up, angered and embarrassed by the fiasco.

"Pearce!" he barked. "Get over here and help your brother into the barracks. Eves, take the second gun crew and break out some rifles and ammunition. Then get them down to the moat and give them some shooting drill," he ordered.

The men perked up and became responsive as Sergeant Eves shouted them into action, taking the hint from his Officer's sudden outburst and regaining control of the group. Barnes and Pearce's brother carried a moaning Dicky towards the mess room and Harding turned on the leftover gun crew.

"Right you lot! Let's get this bloody thing back together again and see if we can't make it fire. Then maybe we can start calling ourselves proper artillerymen," he snapped.

Although annoyed the weapon hadn't fired properly, instead just making a comical noise and falling apart, and although angry because he felt it was all his fault at not being involved and controlling enough in the overall command he had been given at this fort, the aborted firing practice had somehow calmed Eli's nerves and taken away the pressure from the situation. His hangover still harassed him, making him irate and authoritative but for some reason he felt better about firing the gun and galvanised enough to enforce his position as commander of the battery.

It had dawned on him that he felt mentally zapped over the last few days. He was drained of any enthusiasm for the role he had been given and devoid of the energy required for his life in general. Maybe it had been the constant drinking he had indulged in because of the potency of his recent episodes, possibly caused by adjusting to the new environment and the strange aura it had created. Maybe it was his indecision over silly things like talking to a woman or being sociable with the men or simply just the crap weather that had made things worse. Perhaps it was all connected. Either way, he realised the misfiring of the RML cannon had been a microcosm of the disregard and ambivalence he had shown towards the men and the day to day running of the coastal battery he was in charge of. He hadn't really cared about what was going on in the fort since he'd arrived or even given any thought to the instigation of its necessary procedures and the purposeful training he was obliged to give to the men stationed there. The imploding gun was the ultimate result of his inaction and dereliction of duty in this regard and he suddenly felt humiliated and ashamed. Elias decided it was time to wrest back his authority from the malaise that had lately clouded his judgement. His mind snapped into action and he decided to take control properly. Or try to at least.

The gun crew Harding pulled together contained the members who had been involved in the original construction the day before, including Burden and the Mule, who both enthusiastically took to the new task. It wasn't long before the weapon had been repaired and the reason for misfiring rectified. A simple exhaust hole in the gunpowder chamber hadn't been blocked resulting in loss of combustion and pressure, but luckily no real damage had been done to the mechanism of the weapon. The sheared bolt was replaced and the gun eventually reset and reloaded ready for another firing attempt. The master gunner oversaw the operation with a renewed assurance and hardnosed management and the men followed his instruction with respectful attention. They too wanted to achieve their purpose. They too wanted to make their mark in this place. When all was done they stood around the seven-ton gun with determined readiness.

In the moat, the riflemen went down on one knee, their loaded Martini Henri carbine rifles wedged into shoulders, the sights on the barrel in line to the slits of their focused, windblown eyes. They listened, waiting for the order from the distinguished sergeant next to them.

"Fire!" shouted Eves. And the row of rifles released a volley of shots into the sand bags lined up along the far side of the moat.

"Fire!" shouted Harding into the cold, still air. The weapon erupted as it should do, with a cloud of smoke and flame which spurted from its jolting muzzle, discharging the invisible shell perfectly behind it and powering the spinning missile onwards, out through the vacuous air which lay before it. Moving at an indefinable speed and force towards the open water several hundred yards away, it landed with an audible splash a few seconds after the initial explosion, not far from where Elias thought it would hopefully end up.

The master gunner didn't have a mental turn and he didn't have an unsightly episode. Instead he felt the thrill and excitement that came from being in action. He felt a twisted elation as the adrenaline oozed through his veins. The noise, the light, the tingling atmosphere, the comradeship, the stink of scorched gunpowder in his nose, all of it came flooding back to him. He no longer had the feeling of wanting to curl up in a ball and lose himself somewhere different, to escape the threat and fear of war. Without him realising it, a chimerical weight was lifted from his aching shoulders and the strung out mind within his skull. Slowly, invisibly the chimera released itself towards the ether of a drab February sky.

At the door to the guard room, Richard Pearce leant against the door frame and watched the gun firing with awe and juvenile excitement etched across his acne ridden face. He was desperate to be a part of it and feel the power of the weapon as it disgorged its dominance, covering the crew who fired it with cordite and a sensation of incomparable vigour. There was also a large degree of jealousy at not being involved because of his injury and this infantile fervour forced him to go back inside to the warmth of the kitchen and the attentions of the cook, like a spoilt child looking for the pampering of his mother. He hobbled in using the furniture as supports before flouncing down into his chair by the kitchen table and lifting his injured foot onto the seat next to him, which had been appropriately cushioned with a yellow stained, spittle encrusted, barrack bed pillow.

The cook, whose full name was Arnold Jeremiah England, looked round at the teenager sympathetically while he stood at the sink in front of the window, washing cabbage. His round stomach matched his round shaven head making him look surprisingly younger than his actual forty-eight years due to the doughy white skin wrapped around his portly frame. His over washed long johns had turned grey with age and he wore his multi stained apron as if it were his real uniform. He hadn't bothered with his dress trousers and dark blue tunic since he got here several months ago as his duties never required him to do anything mildly military. He'd been the most permanent member of the fortification during the various rounds of volunteer deployment, staying throughout to keep the place attended when there were brief periods of unmanned lockdowns in-between detachments. Along with Eves and Harding he was the only other full time enlisted soldier at Brean Down, having been stationed there after the army deemed him too old and too unfit for any further meaningful engagements. This was something he was glad of, as like Eves and Harding, he too had seen enough of war and killing. Although never a frontline soldier, being an orderly and cook during his active years still meant he got caught up in the scraps of battle and many a time his soup ladle had been replaced with a gun, forcing the normally jovial chef into the angst ridden maelstrom of violence that battle produced. He'd survived these moments wit at times bravery but mainly an uncanny sense of self preservation, an undisputable skill for any kind of warrior in the field. Arnold England was glad to be back home in Somerset after his foreign adventures to live out the last years of his service in the comfort of a simple life, hardened to the weathers of his homeland with his years of experience and a well-honed knowledge of how to stay fed. He was kind and warm hearted but with a sharp wit and shrewd brain and held the respect of others in being able to make a mean stew with the shittiest of ingredients. Everyone liked him and it was often said he'd been anointed with such a moniker as England, in an attempt to show the world that this man was the true nature and personality of the country he belonged to and thus, named after.

"I only gone an' missed out on firin' the bloody gun, the bastards," grumbled Pearce in his gooey West Country accent as he slumped in his chair.

"Don't go worryin' about that, lad. You just get on an' peel them spuds like I told you, an' make sure you take out the eyes and the sprouts too, but don't take off too much skin and leave 'em without any nutrition," chided the cook, looking out the window with a smile oblivious to the sound of gunfire outside.

Young Pearce disconsolately took up his peeler and began to insolently hack away at the potatoes, not caring how thick the peel was.

"Do you like it here, young un?" asked the cook as he gently bathed the limp cabbage leaves in the sink.

"It's alrite cook, better than bein' at home," the young man replied. "I suppose they'll ship I out now, anyway," he said with a face full of childlike dejection.

England looked at the bandage around the boy's foot. "Ah, probably they will, I'm afraid. You're not much use hobblin' around here. It's not like being posted abroad where they can't afford to send you home. There, the wounded have to hang around till they're better, or dead, whichever happens first. But here, they can kick you out and send you packing' down the road before you've had time to wipe yer arse."

"Charmin," said Pearce raising a spotty brow. "An' jus' when it were gettin' interstin' an' all." He looked sad with red droopy eyes and a tone of melancholy hung in his voice. England felt a bit sorry for him.

"Aw, don't worry Dickie lad, you won't miss much. After today, I bet a pretty penny they won't be firin' anymore guns. I'm surprised young Mr Harding let old Eves out with the rifles and I bet he ain't got much ammo to play with. It'll all be packed up by tonight. You mark my words, young un'."

Pearce looked bemused. "Why you so sure of that then, cook," he asked.

"Cause my lad, it's the cuts," began the cook, as he went back to his cabbage. "Not the meat cuts, but the army cuts. There's no money for playin' around with guns in places like Brean Down. Ammunition and gunpowder is expensive and they ain't gonna waste it."

"But we got loads in the store," butted in the boy, pointing a wet finger at the door.

"That ain't a lot really, Dick lad. It wouldn't last five minutes in a proper carve up. They gotta keep some for emergencies, so Mr Harding won't be using it all for practice. I doubt we'll get anymore shells or gunpowder this year, so that little lot will 'av to keep." The cook turned round and looked at Pearce again, this time with a serious look on his face and suddenly shook a floppy cabbage stalk at him. "I've been to forts that haven't had any ammunition for months, boy. We're lucky we even got that new gun, let alone any fuel for it. After a couple of practice rounds he'll lock it up for good." He nodded with superiority. "You mark my words, lad."

"But that's crazy," stuttered the lad, aggrieved by the knowledge. "What's the point of havin' a fort an' guns an' blokes to use 'em if no one's going to use 'em cause they ain't got no bullets!" Pearce sounded like an upset child whose toy had been taken away.

"Like I said young 'un, it's the cuts, there ain't no money. We spent all of it on goin' to war in the rest of the world, an' I been to enough of 'em to know, I can tell you. It makes sense for the people in power to send us 'ere soldiers to other places around the world and earn money off the things those people in those places own. Go to war, take the spoils and get rich off the pickins, that's what we're good at." He swapped the cabbage leaf for a paring knife and pointed this at the young man instead. "But lately the pickins ain't so good boy, and the wars get expensive, so places like these," he waved the knife around the kitchen, "places like Brean Down get left alone, forgotten about. I bet that gun only came 'ere cause they can't afford to lose it in some foreign carve-up. They'll probably nick it back when another conflict arises somewhere Godforsaken. And the powder as well." He withdrew the knife and nodded his fat head sharply at the stunned boy, then turned back to the sink as if to finish the statement.

"Wot a bunch o' bastards," moaned Pearce. "Everyone else gets to go around the world shootin' people an' all we get is blown about on this bit o' stone by the bloody wind. It ain't fair, Mr England, I tell you it ain't fair. I volunteered to get some action, not peel potatoes," and he plopped one in the bowl of water to make the point. "I might as well be at 'ome," he added with a rejected expression. The cook turned round, a colander of dripping cabbage in his hands.

"Now, now son, go steady with them spuds, and watch the skins, you're cuttin' em' a bit thick there, we'll starve if youse carry on like that," the cook said noticing the peelings as he put the colander down on the table. "Here I'll show you," and he took a peeler from the sideboard then sat down opposite the youth, being careful not to knock the young man's foot. He grabbed a soft, tired looking potato and began carefully stripping the thinnest of skins.

"Look, lad. Be soft with her, like you're taking off the clothes from a fine lady," the cook said gently as he expertly peeled. Pearce looked bewildered and even a bit scared at the man's over interest in the preparation of vegetables.

"And where is home, Dickie," asked England, resuming the conversation.

"Bridgewater," Pearce replied hypnotized by the nimble hands of the fat cook.

"And what does your father do, son."

"He labours on the farms. Me mum works in the carpet factory. I help out on the farms sometimes but there's not always enough work to go round. That's why I volunteered fer this, helps keep I out of mischief." He took up his peeler and began to imitate the cook's action. "I should 'av joined up proper, instead," he added.

Arnold placed his finished spud into the saucepan of water and took up another one. "Well, I'll be honest with you, my boy. The army ain't all it's cracked up to be anymore. It used to be a good life, I know that much. Seeing different places, just keepin' an eye on things, perhaps sortin' out a few locals now and then, it all seemed easier. Course, we had our noses bloodied by a few of 'em sometimes when we was outnumbered an' all, but in general you'd end up somewhere interestin' and spent a good deal of time just camped out in the sun or billeted near the sea for a while. As long as you weren't one of them that ended up with a bloody nose, you were alright. And even if you did get in a fight it was usually against spears or swords and there was always help on the way. But now, now you end up gettin' caught in some nasty business and left on your own to do or die. There are new weapons and ways of being killed that frighten even the old timers, like Mr Eves. And it seems the rest of the world has now got those deadly tools of war too. We aren't the powerful force of good we used to be, son. Superior strength is no longer on our side. We'll soon end up the equal of everyone else and the poor enlisted soldier will bear the brunt of it. I think in the future, my lad, there'll be a war the likes of which no one has ever seen that will change the world forever and millions of us will end up dead, whether we is in the army or not. You mark my words." He added another finely peeled potato to the bowl. Pearce meanwhile had stopped fumbling with his spud and just stared at Arnold England, fascinated.

"Blimy," gasped the boy. "You reckon."

Mr England nodded slowly and calmly took up another vegetable. "I reckon," was all he said.

There was a section of silence as the man and his young assistant concentrated on the preparations for dinner. The cook got up after a while and checked on the joint of mutton slowly roasting in the oven. The warming aroma of cooking meat filled the kitchen. When he came back to the table he was carrying another bowl full to the brim with cabbage leaves and in the other hand a bottle of dark rum.

"Might as well treat ourselves to a dram or two of rum, ay, Mr Pearce," he said smiling widely across his pudgy face. The young thin man agreed with an excited nod of his long head. Mr England reached over to the dresser and grabbed two glasses and then filled them with rum. "Go steady now young 'un. This is for medical purposes only, you understand," he said, sliding the tumbler to his kitchen aid.

"Whatever," said the wide eyed teenager as he picked up the glass and took a big gulp of rum. The hot grog seared his throat and he rasped as he shook his head slightly to ease the alcohol burn. The cook knocked back a mouthful and savoured the rich flavour of molasses on his taste buds. "Nice," he mouthed.

The youngster found enough voice to make another enquiry. "Still, bein' a proper soldier never did you no harm Mr England. You come out of it alrite in the end."

"Only, I should say, through a lot of luck and doing my best to avoid any trouble lad. I saw plenty who never made it out alive." He motioned with his head to the potatoes and they both took up the task again.

"And Mr Harding and Sergeant Eves?" continued the lad. "They come back alive."

"So they did Dickie, but they're the lucky ones. We all remembers the things we seen, some more than others. Take Mr Harding for example, he is plagued by the things he seen and the memories it can bring back. But at least we are able to remember. For many, life was taken away from them, sometimes in the cruellest of ways, and that isn't to say that all life taken away in war isn't cruel, but merely that in some places there are better ways to die." England took another swig of rum.

"Well Sergeant Eves seemed to enjoy his time in the army. He was born in the army. From the stories I 'eard there couldn't hav' bin any other job 'e could 'av done. Fightin' an' killin' was all 'e's good at. You can't tell me Mr Eves don't miss it just a little bit," suggested Pearce.

The happy cook pursed his lips together and his small bright eyes twinkled at the precocious youth. "Well, Mr Eves is a different breed to all of us, young 'un. He could have been anything he wanted to be, but in the end the only thing he ever knew was soldiering. If things were different he could have been a politician, or an explorer, or a famous artist even, he could have made a name in anything. But because his father was a soldier and he lived with soldiers from the day he was born, he ended up being one too." He waved a peeler at the boy again. "Do you know Dicky my lad, Mr Eves could have been a boxer. The greatest boxer the world has ever seen. He had the longest fist fight anyone's ever had the pleasure of watchin' in England. It's not been written down or proved in a court of law but anyone who was there knows it was the longest fight any two men could have had. And I was there, lad, I seen it with me own eyes."

Pearce stopped peeling again and stared at the cook with his mouth agape. "You reckon," he dribbled. England put his peeler down, poured himself another drink and put the bottle under the table out of sight. The young one still had half his glass left, and it was apparent he didn't really fancy anymore so the cook had another swig and started telling his story.

"You see, I knew Mr Eves long before the army decided men like me and him were no longer any use to 'em fighting on their far flung fields of battle in distant lands. So they sent us to places like Brean Down and the like to live out our twilight years. But I first met him when we were mere young 'uns, not much older than yerself, fighting in the rock and dust and snow of the Crimea. We were both in the Grenadier Guards and fought at the Battle of Inkerman and in the siege of Sevastopol back in the sixties. I was just a young orderly working in the supply trains really, keepin' the soldiers in a manner befitting their requirements. But Mr Eves was one of them proper soldiers, the likes of which that part of the world had never seen before, he and all the men he stood with. I remember seein' him in battle for the first time. Tall and strong he was, fearless, as though he knew the spears and the bullets and the swords and the bombs wouldn't hit him, they'd just bounce off and fall to the ground and he'd be free to cut a swath through the enemy whether they be hordes of heathens or rank upon rank of the prettiest

European army in their best dress. Mr Eves had guile, speed and force of nature you don't see so much in men anymore. He and his fellows would come and sit with us in the evenin', take their wittles with us around the fire and regale us with stories of the men they killed that day and the men they'd kill tomorrow." The cook said this last part dismissively like a matter of fact thrown into an informal conversation and then nonchalantly turned his attention to chopping the cabbage as he spoke.

"But for all his warmongering ways he always had a funny kind of respect for the locals and they in turn were always respectful to 'im. He'd always treat a lady right, no matter where in society she came from, and the young 'uns of this world he would treat with care, even though he was only a young 'un himself.

"Ten years later I saw him again, when we were in India, helpin' out with the uprising's over there, trying to keep the locals in order. For some reason that seemed more difficult than standin' before the ranks of ten thousand men from Russia or France. But still, they prevailed in the end, Mr Eves and his fellows; the men Britain are made of." He paused and took up some more cabbage leaves, a glassy look mellowing across his kind face as he reminisced. "My, what a place India was. You can't imagine a more beautiful country than that place, lad. One minute, lush fields with trees and flowers of every colour. The next, a dust bowl covered in shacks and mud huts. Oh, but the buildin's we created, the palaces we built from which to rule that land. And the animals we seen, tigers, snakes, elephants, a world you can only dream of boy. When they weren't tryin' to kill us the people were kind and loyal, if not a little funny in their ways and meanings. That's where I learnt to make food, using spices I'd never even heard of, let alone seen, the likes of which you'd never get in this country. Me and Mr Eves, we'd go to the local markets and bizarre to see the wonderful things they made, the trinkets and jewellery, the potions and the strange pets. Oh, what a time we had there! A time we'll never see again!

"When we got sent back home to England, we all went our separate ways, with time to spare and pockets of money to spend. Both were spent in the towns and the pubs along the coast, and that's where I ran into Mr Eves again, in the Kings Arms in Bideford, quite by chance, on a night on the lash. What a night it was too!" Mr England whooped a little and grinned at his cabbage, lost in his remembrance.

"The Kings Arms was a rough house on the waterfront. Sergeant Eves and a couple of his fellow war horses had been in there most of the afternoon when we turned up. We drank and we talked and we laughed about the old days, but we caused no ruptions and the locals didn't seem to pay us no heed. Apart from one man that is, a big man, the same size as Mr Eves he was, but a bit thicker and younger. He seemed to take unction with the tales and the stories 'e could 'ear. Especially the ones from the mouth of our revered sergeant, and for some reason, I can't even remember why, he started an argument with Mr Eves. Now, no one wanted any trouble but no matter how much we tried, this man wouldn't be ignored. 'E went on and on and no matter how many times he tried, Mr Eves would decline his offer of contest. The big bloke was bein' egged on by the other locals in the pub by then, although I suppose the beer and the rum didn't 'elp either. In the end out of sheer frustration and with a great deal of reluctance, Mr Eves took up this man's offer, and the two men stepped outside to a back alley, followed by the rest of the pub. I thought the poor old landlord's takings must have gone down by a considerable amount durin' that fight when they first left, I can tell you. How wrong I was.

"Still, there were only a handful of blokes around Mr Eves and this other fellow when they started exchangin' punches. I suppose most people thought it would be over pretty quick, one way or the other, me included, although I was confident the sergeant would see this loudmouth off, even though 'e was a biggun'. They must 'ave sparred with each other for twenty or thirty minutes, taking time to throw their punches, find the right spot and work out 'ow good each other was. And they were both good. The other bloke may 'ave let his mouth run away with 'im, but he certainly knew how to box. Gradually them punches got harder and harder, even if the ones that actually landed got fewer and fewer. But when they did land, all of us would wince as that knuckle connected with flesh and bone. You could hear the crunch down the other end of the street.

"Even so, it didn't seem to get either of 'em anywhere. So they stepped it up a notch or two and the swings got wider and fiercer. And as it went on, more people joined the throng about them. People heard about it on the street, walking along the waterfront, going into the shops or wherever they happened to be going, and then they'd come round to the back alley at the Kings Arms so they could take a look at the two big men 'avin a fight. About what they were fightin' I don't even know and nor did anyone else.

"Anyways, even the big punches didn't seem to be getting' them anywhere, anyhow. Mr Eves started gettin' a fat eye and the other bloke 'ad a nasty nose bleed and a lip the size of Steep Holm, but apart from getting' tired, nothing had seemed to do either of 'em any harm. That's when they started grapplin'; grippin' each other; pusin' to and fro, tryin' to force the other one to the ground. Like two gorillas fightin' over a tree they were. Every now and then they'd club each other with a fist over the back of the head or in the kidney's. They looked like two Greek warriors wrestlin' at the gates of Troy. At one point the other man had his hand round Eves' throat, usin' his other hand to try and gouge out his eyes. Spit and blood was everywhere. Bits of skin got in their fingernails. They started breathin' heavy, gasping for breath and spittin' out balls of gob whenever they got a chance to stand back and take a breather. A couple of times they'd stop and take long draughts of beer that the spectators would hold. Then they'd go at it again with a flurry of punches, followed by a grapple. Once or twice Mr Eves and the other man both went to the ground. Mr Eves got stamped on, would 'av broken any other man's rib cage. But he gave as good as he got by kickin' the other bloke in the kidney's a few times and then puchin' 'im in the back'o' the 'ead when 'e was winded.

"They fought each other from one end of King Street to the other and then back again. Up and down they went, like the slow trickle of grease off a roastin' goose. Sometimes they might hold each other in the same grip, ten minutes at a time, one man on top of the other, slowly trying to squeeze the fight and the life out of 'em. Other times they'd be face to face, hoppin' about in front of one another, blows raining down on one another with fists hittin' faces and knuckles like the steady beat of a humming piston engine. I ain't seen nothin' like it in all my life! Skin on skin! Bone on bone! Tis was a brawl, my son!

"More people turned up to see, there must 'av bin a hundred spectators stood around watching that fight and it had been going on for at least two hours by now, although no one noticed the time go by, we were too intrigued by this battle of willing men, neither of 'em wishing to give up, neither of 'em wishing to show any weakness or back down. It was the grit and the spit of real life, seen in all its bloodied glory down a back alley in the balls of England.

"People came and went, but the crowd still got larger. There was even a smart fella sellin' apples and pears on the side. By now a few of us were tellin' 'em to stop, sayin there was no need to go on, that it had been a fair fight and they should call it a draw. But they ignored us and just kept going, takin' chunks out of each other until we thought there'd be nothin' left.

"And then, I reckon it must of bin after two and a 'ave hours, they both suddenly stopped. The two of 'em had a bucket of cold water poured over their heads to wipe away the blood and the phlegm, and then they both drank a couple of pints of beer to settle 'emselves down again. Just as we thought they'd shake hands and walk away, they looked at each other with that look in their eyes that they knew they couldn't just walk away until the fight's been decided, till the winner's been found. And they both knew only one man would walk away. The other would be led on the ground, surely because 'e was nearly dead. With the crowd silent and holdin' their breath those two bloodied men of violence went back to it more fiercely, more determined and more bloodthirsty than they'd ever been so far that night.

"This time the punches struck home one after another. Defence made way for attack in a tired flurry of fists that pummelled faces and battered bodies. Eves would rain down several blows on the man's face, breaking his nose and splitting his eyes again. Then the other monster would come back at Eves, swinging wide, connecting with Eves' jaw, fattenin' one side of his face up like bread risin' in an oven. Their knuckles covered in each other's blood, their faces smeared with their own gore like war paint on an Indian.

Back and forth they danced, strike after bloody strike making its ghastly mark. The crowd weren't chanting anymore. Some of them couldn't even look at the carnage, even the bloodthirsty watcher's had to turn their faces away.

"Then it finally happened. After over three hours of smashin' each other to death both men barely able to stand on their feet, tired arms and legs, sometimes winging and missing wildly, the final punch was thrown. And it came from Mr Eves, thank God. It landed so square on the other fighter's jaw it knocked four of his teeth out and made a noise like a ship smashin' on the rocks in a storm. Mr Eves stepped back one or two paces. The other man swayed, his eye's rolled back into his head and he hit the stones like an old building falling down.

"Some people thought he was dead, but he wasn't. You could see him breathing through his swollen face and smashed mouth. Others didn't know whether he'd been knocked out or just collapsed through sheer exhaustion. I know Mr Eves nearly did. But he stayed on his feet, poured another bucket of water over his puffy face, drank another pint of beer and went off to have a little sit down on the waterfront and gather his thoughts. We spent the night on the landlords' cellar floor, 'e put us up for the evenin'. He said thanks to the crowd we pulled he'd never made so much money in one day.

"That was a fight, lad. They talked about it for years afterwards, although if you ask Mr Eves 'e'll tell you 'e can't really remember, but I expect he can. Men like Mr Eves don't like to gloat over the victories they've had anymore. Being humble is something you can't accuse Mr Eves of not being. In the end, that fight taught me that there are some men in this world that don't give up, son, no matter what the odds, no matter what the battle. No matter how hard it is or how far they gotta go they never give up. And as long as you're on the right side and as long as they're on your side, you should be glad there're men like them in the world. You mark my words, lad, you mark my words."

He finished speaking and examined his pile of chopped leaves. Pearce was looking at him, open mouthed in wonder.

"Bugger I," said the Young'un.

"Aye," replied Mr England, nodding his head. "Bugger I."

In the foyer of the Grand Atlantic Hotel, one of the largest and stateliest fronted buildings that paraded the newly built promenade of Weston-On-Sea, Rufus Stone sat at a table reading the Daily Telegraph and drinking a moderately well-made cup of coffee. His dress sense today was official, incorporating a dark grey woollen suit, a crisp, over starched high collared shirt and a thin, black tie. His brown leather brogues were well polished, showing off their expensive craftsmanship in their impressive, elegantly judged shine. The metal studs on the toes and heels made a sharp, authoritative clipping sound on the polished floors when he walked which gave him the air of a literally well heeled, in-control businessman.

He knew the two officials from London were booked to stay in this hotel as they would not make the last train back to London by the time they returned from Steep Holm and wouldn't want to spend the night with their prisoner in the local police cells. He had already garnered conformation of their booking from the sweet receptionist. The debonair spy had used his good looks and arrogant charm to fool the easily swayed and extremely pretty front desk girl into unknowingly offering the information. After distracting the young lady's attention by getting her to find a timetable for trains between Weston, Bristol and London, he had managed to get a look in the hotel admittance book and found a booking for two men from London, arranged by the War Office under the names of Flowers and Smith. Rufus noted the room was booked on the second floor, number 208. When the young lady returned with the timetable, smiling innocently but with a delicious hint of lusty wantonness, Stone thought that if he wasn't so busy tonight he would have asked her out to town, and in his own mind at least, would have undoubtedly ended up getting her in the sack, another victim of his rather forthright and ungracious, bird of prey tendencies.

As it was, he instead booked a room for the night, requesting one on the second floor as it would afford him a decent sea view and as it was February and the height of a quiet winter season there were plenty of rooms available, even in the best hotel in town. After checking over his room and satisfying himself that it wasn't too far from 208, he left the small leather bound satchel he had been carrying on top of the squeaky hotel bed and went back downstairs to enjoy a cup of coffee and a perusal of the paper.

At the table, after reading a report on the forthcoming Reform Act of 1884, which both he and a large section of the population of Britain mostly paid no attention too, Rufus checked his watch. It was just past twelve. The London train had already arrived at Bristol for eleven and the connecting train to Weston would have got in roughly an hour later. The regular cabs from the station should then get the two men here fairly quickly. He kept looking over his paper out of the large windows which commanded a view across the unblemished promenade. It was grey outside but dry and Stone remembered on the way to the hotel he had felt a fresh, crispy breeze cutting through the air, carrying with it a smell of wintry leaves and cold brown sea. He ruminated about the poor quality of the town compared to those of his homeland, even with its redeveloped sea front and grandiose attempts at high class colonial statement buildings. He realised it would obviously be a hugely popular seaside resort one day, but at the moment it all felt a bit shit to the arrogant young Frenchman. He would much rather be in Paris, with its architecture of historically stately exuberance and culture of naturally artistic flair, but it seemed to the spy that Weston was a long way from Paris and in his mind he realised he would be glad to be out of this peculiar English town when this little adventure was over.

Crossing his legs, he turned the page of his large newspaper and then, out of the corner of his eye, caught sight of a horse drawn tram slowly trundling along the track set into the concrete of the wide road. He watched it from over the top of his paper until it came into full view and then came to a stop opposite the hotel with a soft almost unnoticeable horse powered halt. Stone saw a small group of well-dressed ladies and gentlemen step from the tram, each carrying umbrellas and wearing expensive looking coats giving the impression they were well off city dwellers on a day trip to the seaside, ready to enjoy a spot of pompous promenading and an afternoon spent tea drinking. There was a pause as this group fanned out and then two, equally well-dressed men in thick overcoats stepped down from the tram. They were both tall and one wore a bowler hat above a serious looking face with a thin pencil like moustache under his nose. The other wore a suit hat and sported a longer, thicker military style moustache which reached down the sides of his mouth. Neither of them had any luggage. The two men looked about them, then stepped onto the road and after waiting a moment for a horse drawn cab to pass by, continued to cross. They walked through the outside piazza of the hotel, into the main doors, across the open foyer past Stones table and up to the front desk. Stone casually folded up his paper but continued to look out of the window whilst honing his bird like hearing to catch the conversation between the men and the girl with the pretty face stood prissily behind the counter.

"Oh yes, Mr Flowers and a Mr Smith," she said in her cute local accent. "Room 208, as booked, staying for just one night, I believe."

"Yes, that's right," said the thickly moustachioed man gruffly. "We're on business this evening and maybe back late. I take it there's no curfew."

"Of course not Mr Flowers," said the girl bowing her head slightly, "reception is always open at the Grand. Here are your keys, Sir, and if there's no luggage, gentlemen, I'll get the boy to take you up to your room."

"No. It's alright, we'll find it," said the pencil lipped man more kindly this time. He was slightly younger than the other man and seemed more taken with the pretty girl's manners.

"As you wish," she smiled.

Stone wondered by the man's tone if the younger War Office official wouldn't have minded taking the receptionist out tonight and possibly getting her in the sack if he too hadn't already planned to be so busy.

The two men swung away and glided up the stairs towards the second floor. Stone casually finished his coffee and stood up, putting the paper under his arm and then headed smoothly towards the staircase, flashing a crafty smile at the young lady behind the counter, which she dutifully flashed back.

On the top of the carpeted stairs at the second floor Rufus saw the two men disappear into their room down the end of the landing. He turned the opposite way to where his room was situated and once inside opened up the satchel still sat on the bed where he had left it earlier. He took out the contents as if he was unpacking his holiday clothes and arranged them on the bed. Firstly, he took out his revolver and opened the breech. After checking it was loaded he snapped it shut again and placed it on the bed. Secondly, he took out a large bottle of chloroform and a selection of white linen handkerchiefs that he placed delicately next to the gun and then finally a length of wound up twine, which he placed in line with the other contents. He was calm but there was a tingle of excitement starting to course through his body. It was edged with the requisite stab of nerves which only helped to increase his alertness and electrify his stimulated senses.

The agent looked outside the window of his austerely furnished hotel room onto the promenade below. Couples, some arm in arm, some unattached, walked slowly along the long frontage above the beach, whilst small groups of mixed day trippers and pockets of wintering holiday makers interspersed their progress with the cabs and horsed traps that rattled along the roadside. People strolled on the beach, on the seafront, along the hotel verandas to the cafes and the shops in town, all oblivious to his presence and the plans he was manipulating. He saw the slipway leading down to the beach and the handful of small rowing boats and fishing vessels moored to the sea wall, inelegantly sat in the brown, sandy mud waiting for the tide to come in. High tide would be around five and Stone knew the two men would head down to the quayside and then make the short walk to the stone jetty a little further on that allowed access to the small, chartered steam boat taking them to Steep Holm. He estimated they would do this at around four o'clock, once the tide had reached a high enough level for the boat to make ready.

From his trouser pocket he brought out a short but heavy looking, leather bound cosh that he kept with him at all times. It was discreet enough to be kept in a trouser pocket but wieldy enough to knock a man unconscious if used correctly. He stepped away from the window and stood in a corner of the room as if waiting for someone. All of a sudden, with lightning speed he brought the cosh up and down in a split second, around about head height, as if striking an imaginary opponent. When he was content with his practice he stepped over to the bed and put the gun into the bag along with all but one of the handkerchiefs. Then he opened the bottle and poured a large amount of chloroform onto the last of the handkerchiefs and then placed it with the closed bottle back inside the bag. He took several deep breaths, closed his eyes while he tensed his shoulders and sinewy back, before swiftly leaving the room without locking the door behind him as he went.

He checked the landing for any other guests and then walked slowly down the hallway towards room 208. His gentle pace hid the excitement and adrenaline flowing through his muscles. He liked these moments, the few seconds of nervous tension in the build up to an event. It was the anticipation of violence, the intention of action and the feel of apprehension in not really knowing how it would all turn out. These men were tall and strong. Would the club put one of them out of action, would they even open the door to him, would the other one put up a fight even with a gun pointed at him? Who knows? He might have to make it up as he went along. But he liked that possibility and if push came to shove, he'd just have to kill both of them in the room.

'Hopefully that won't be necessary,' he thought. *'If they act the way I think they will, the worst that could happen is they'll spend the night trussed up in a hotel wardrobe and wake up the next morning with a wickedly long lasting headache and excruciating cramp.'*

The Frenchman stood in front of the door to room 208, one hand inside the open satchel gripping the butt of his pistol. In the other hand, which was behind his back, he held the cosh. He stood casually looking up and down the hall, then using the hand with the cosh, knocked on the door sharply before putting his clubbed hand behind his back again and stood there braced, with a wide, friendly smile on his face. Through the closed door he recognised the voice of the gruff man with the long moustache answering his knock. "Who is it?" the voice said.

"It's hotel management, Sir. I've got a message for Mr Flowers. To be hand delivered, urgently," Stone replied. He heard a grumping noise and then some footsteps towards the door and he tensed himself up and watched, concentrating, as the handle turned and the door opened. Stood before him was the grouchy faced man with the army moustache, no longer wearing his coat and hat and revealing a loosened shirt and tie with trousers held up by buttoned on black braces.

"Well, let's have it then," the man snapped.

Stone looked him in the eye, his smile disappearing as he said, "I've got a message from the War Office."

Flowers frowned. He wasn't expecting what happened next and it was so quick there was nothing he could do to stop it anyway. In one lightning flash movement the agile Frenchman brought his cosh from behind his back and swiped it across the temple of the man in the doorway. There was a sickening click, like a wooden stick hitting the hollow trunk of a dead tree as the baton hit Flowers' skull. The stunned man stepped back and swayed drunkenly, blinded and confused, tiny stars bursting in his eyes, but he did not fall and was not rendered with unconsciousness straight away. He let out a little moan and Stone swung his arm again, this time bringing the club down across the tottering man's eye and the bridge of his nose. The second blow broke Flowers' nose and caused enough of a concussion to drop him to the floor with a thud. Stone stepped through the door, just as Smith also stepped out of a side room which contained the wash basin and dressing table connected to the main bedroom of room 208. His light blue shirt was undone and his face and hair were wet. Stone stood over the prone man on the floor, his gun already pulled from the satchel and now pointed threateningly at the younger man with the pencil moustache. "Don't move, don't make a sound or I'll kill you where you stand, right here, right now," said the Frenchman calmly.

Smith raised his hands without being asked, a look of shock and awe across his face as he glanced down at his colleague on the floor. Stone kicked Flowers' legs out of the way and closed the door using the same foot, all the time still holding the gun on the other man.

"Put your hands behind your back and turn around," he said in perfect English.

"Who are you," Smith blurted out shakily as he did what he was told and faced the window.

"I shouldn't worry about that, it's of no concern of yours," Stone suggested.

"Is this a robbery?" asked the pencil.

"Yes, you could say that I suppose. Get on your knees," the Frenchman said coldly.

The man did as he was told again, too far away from his opponent to be able to do anything. He hadn't been expecting anything like this when he was assigned to this job, certainly not in Weston-On-Sea. Rufus put the cosh in his pocket and reached into the bag, pulling out the cloth which he had earlier doused in chloroform and then hopped over and put it across the mouth and nose of the kneeling man. With another swift motion he hit him over the head with the pistol butt as the man began to struggle. Immediately Smith went limp and slumped to the floor.

Stone checked he was unconscious and then turned around and examined Flowers. Blood was pumping from the nostrils of his swelling, broken beak and he was starting to groan lightly whilst trying to move his head from side to side. His injured eye was starting to puff nastily and Rufus noticed spots of blood on the carpet. Putting the gun into the satchel, he pulled out the chloroform and poured a dose onto another handkerchief, then pressed it down over Flowers' nose and mouth. The man yelped a bit in his stupor and tried to move his arms but within a few seconds, as the drug took effect, he lay completely still. The French agent wiped the blood from the man's face and went to the washroom where he found a napkin, which he tore into pieces and stuffed up the nose of Flowers to try and stem the blood flow. He cleaned him up as best he could and put everything back into the satchel.

Now came the most difficult part of the job. He had to move the two sleeping men into his room to avoid the possibility of hotel staff coming into this room for any reason, perhaps to deliver a real message or the like, and finding the two unconscious men spread over the floor. He knew at least there would be no reason for hotel staff to enter his room and he felt safer knowing the Government men would be tied up in there whilst he carried on with his night's work.

He pulled Flowers up by the arms and leant him against the wall, holding him with one arm as he carefully opened the door and craned his neck around the frame to look down the landing. It was eerily quiet and there was no one else in sight. He decided to risk it. Leaving the door ajar, Stone pulled one of Flowers' arms over his shoulder and held it there as a kind of brace and then, supporting the rest of the weight of the man's body with his other arm and shoulder, stood upright and kicked the door open before stepping into the hallway. *'Make it quick, this is risky,'* he thought, as he awkwardly grabbed his bag and closed the door behind him.

The Englishman was heavy and the movement was awkward. Rufus had to huff and puff and tense up his whole body to get them into the kind of position he needed to part walk and part drag the knocked out dead weight of the bloodied man down the corridor to his own room. For a moment it was comical as the carried man slid and flopped about against the wall and doorframes of the seemingly short distance. Stone was careful not to knock into any actual doors or make too much noise for fear of disturbing the peace and bringing out a fellow patron, forcing him into some extravagant explanation of why he was carrying an unconscious man, covered in blood along a hotel landing. But he couldn't help letting out an involuntary laugh as he struggled with the human package. "Phew! You fat bastard," he puffed when he finally found some steadiness. They shuffled down the hallway, Flowers' feet dragging along the carpet and Stone using all his muscles to try and keep the other man upright and scrape him along.

It was a testament to the young spy's hidden strength and hardy stature that he was able to get the man to his room within a few seconds and more importantly unnoticed. Popping open the door, he stumbled into the room and dropped Flowers' body onto the bed. One of the plugs from his broken nostrils fell out and fresh drops of blood ran onto the bedspread. Stone rolled the man over and pushed some more paper napkin up his distended nose. He was still out cold and made no movement or sound.

Feeling hot and sweaty but desperate to get this part of the job done, Stone straightened his clothes and walked back out and down to the other room to begin the same process with the other man and his thin moustache. He noticed how much younger he was compared to Flowers, but with apparently bigger shoulders and a more toned chest. He lifted him up using a kind of fireman's lift and held him there as if Smith were a drunk being helped back to his room. At least it looked a bit more plausible because this guy didn't have blood all over his face. Again Stone shuffled awkwardly down the hallway, calling upon his last few ounces of energy to make the distance. Then, only a few feet from the door, Rufus was surprised by the sudden appearance of whom he immediately recognised as one of the well dressed women from the tram, just as she was stepping up the last few carpeted treads of the staircase.

Stone stopped dead, as did the woman when she rounded the bannister, nearly bumping into the oddly embraced duo. He stood still, holding up the limp man, his mind racing in panic, waiting for a scream; and then instinctively he smiled cheekily at the lady. Rufus noticed the woman was a lot younger than the impression he had got from the group when he saw them from across the street. She let out a winsome gasp but didn't seem overly perturbed by the sight of the two men.

"Oh, what have we here," she said in a high class accent, an elegant frown forming across her soft features. Stone tutted and shook his head while grinning all the time, partly to hide the grimace from his aching arms and partly to carry the extravagant explanation.

"I don't know," he said in his most plummy English voice. "Would you believe it, we've only been here five minutes and he's already overdone the gin. A good night's sleep is in order for this youngster," and he flashed another grin, full of teeth and aristocratic charm.

The young lady covered her mouth with a lacy handkerchief and giggled bashfully. "Oh," she goosed, "and it is only lunchtime."

Stone decided he couldn't hang around as the weight of Smith was starting to make his back crumble. "Do excuse us, madam," he said as he shuffled around the woman towards his room, but as he reached the door he turned at the last minute and said slyly to the still unmoving female, "I should watch out for this one at dinner time, my good lady," before winking at her which brought another winsome giggle from behind the lacy hanky as she held it up to her mouth. He opened the door, stepped into the room and threw the man straight onto the floor.

Popping his head out of the door to see if the woman was still stood there, all he saw was the floating bustle of her dress as she sauntered with a rustle down to her room at the other end of the landing. Stone puffed as he leant back against the now closed door, wondering how the hell he had managed to get away with it. He smiled haughtily to himself, smug at the success of this first part of the mission before looking at his watch and letting the smile fade away. It was nearly 2'o'clock.

He dragged the body of Smith across the floor to the wardrobe and then took out the cord from his satchel. He undid a long length and cut it with a penknife he pulled from his inside jacket pocket and then bound together the hands and feet of his victim. Then he manhandled, shoved, pushed and generally stuffed the man into the large empty wardrobe on one side of the room, arranging him as best he could in a sort of twisted foetal position. He made sure the door could close and then stuffed a ball of cotton in the man's mouth and tied a gag around his head before closing the wardrobe door once again.

Pulling the body and bloodied face of Flowers off the bed and onto the floor, Stone then tied his legs, feet and hands together with more of the sturdy twine, stuffed his mouth with a handkerchief and secured another gag around his whiskered face, trapping the blood soaked tache in the material. Using his feet, he pushed, kicked and rolled the large bloke half into the space beneath the metal bed frame and then from the other side pulled him completely underneath until the man was fully hidden. Flowers' body was contorted due to the angle in which he had to lie and his head lolled to one side, revealing the full extent of his broken nose and swollen eye, making his face look deformed.

Rufus Stone winced, stood up, tidied and straightened his clothes again and then walked back to room 208 where he made good the mess of sheets on the bed and tidied the loose clothes scattered on the chair. He picked up the two men's coats and then noticed the spots of blood on the carpet. There was nothing he could do about that, so he took one last look around and then noticed a small rug at the bottom of the bed which he quickly moved round to arrange over the stained area of carpet. Happy with the room, he left it for the last time, locking the door behind him.

Entering his own room again, it dawned on him that on first appearances no one would know there were two knocked out men secreted away inside. He hid the coats in the wardrobe on top of Smith and then pulled off the bedspread, which also had spots of Flowers' bloody nose juice on, and turned it over before re-setting the room. He poured another dose of chloroform onto a leftover hanky and pushed the damp rag over the face of the man in the furniture. For good measure he also poured a few drops onto the gag and then did the same to Flowers. The difficult angle of the man under the bed made Stone pour a little too much onto his gag, but he figured it wouldn't do any more harm than increase the size of his headache when he woke up, hopefully sometime tomorrow. He put everything: the chloroform, the twine, the cosh, into the satchel with the gun and pulled the neatly folded blankets down over the gaps around the bed, had one last look around the room, then walked out and locked the door.

He made his way calmly down the stairs and into the hotel foyer, with its thin red carpets and varnished furniture smelling of beeswax, where he approached the young receptionist again and began chatting easily about mundane things like the weather and the state of the burgeoning tourism industry in Weston-On-Sea. He asked for another cup of coffee and sat down in the same chair he had occupied less than an hour ago and looked out over the promenade to the beach beyond. Occasionally he glanced at the staircase and in between caught the eye of the young woman behind the counter. For half an hour they threw each other seductive, sexily clad smiles and twinkled looks. It was a shame he couldn't ask her out.

At 3'o'clock he went back to his room and checked on the two men. They were both still soundly senseless, still in exactly the same positions as when he had left them. With the amount of chloroform soaked into the gags they would remain that way for at least the next eight to ten hours, Rufus surmised, plenty of time to get the job done. He whistled shortly when he saw Flowers' face, but deep down inside his real persona, he didn't care about the man's injuries and actually enjoyed the sight of a broken nose that he had caused. After dragging the two men between the hotel rooms and bundling them away, Stone was beginning to feel tired. The adrenaline of the moment and the excitement of his actions had worn off now and a faint whiff of comedown floated over him. But he had to keep going though, even if he was feeling the fatigue from a late night, when he had traipsed around Brean Down trying to send a light box message to the steamboat waiting patiently in the Channel. He had to crouch in the freezing cold for most of the night until he saw the flashing beacon of the ship and then he'd nearly been caught by the Officer from the fort bumbling back from the village. He was glad he hadn't had to kill that man as that would have put the whole plan in jeopardy.

But however he was feeling, Stone had to stay on top of his game even more so now. He had to get back to the manor house, sabotage the telegraph line from the post office, meet the landing party and lock down the village. He suddenly felt excited again and was filled with confidence in the ultimate success of the daring plan he had helped work out. But there was also a tinge of disappointment in the likelihood that nobody outside the two forts would really know about what was happening until everyone that needed to be was at least halfway back across the channel. Everyone that is except for himself, who would have to evade the authorities and make his own way by whatever means he could, down the coast to a safe house and a boat home at some later point. That would spice the next few days up at least. *'Such a shame he wouldn't get the chance to bed the feisty Miss Danvers either,'* he thought.

He left the Grand Atlantic hotel, satchel around his shoulder and gave a nod and a wink to the pretty receptionist as he did so, knowing he would never see her again. He walked across the road to the promenade and made his way to the landing slip leading down to the beach. At the top of the slipway, two booths lined the low wall. It was here that bookings were made for the working boats that catered for fishing trips, pleasure cruises and ferry services along the Bristol Channel. He enquired as to whom was booked to take the two men to Steep Holm at high tide and he showed the identification papers he'd taken from Smiths coat before hiding him in the wardrobe. A white whiskered old man wearing a soft, plain, navy blue Captain's cap, sat inside the first booth and he studied the well-dressed young man through squinted, wrinkle covered eyes, before saying that it was he who had taken such a booking. The old sea dog didn't look at the identification card.

"The boat won't be needed today, my friend. It's been postponed until tomorrow as the two men have been delayed and won't be arriving until tomorrow. I've informed the Major at the battery on Steep Holm of this," Stone lied with an air of authority.

"That's alrite, Sir. I'll let the skipper know. He'll be able to stay in the pub all night now," the whisker's replied with a gummy smile.

"Bravo," said Stone dryly. "Maybe this will help the night along," and he passed the old man a ten pound note to lubricate the disappointment of a late cancelation. Then the suave young spy smiled pleasantly at the pensioner, turned on his heels and walked briskly down the promenade towards the town with the manner of a man who had a very busy day ahead of him.

Elias Harding walked up to the large weathered front door of the Manor House and hesitated for a moment. He studied the peeling blue paintwork and the brass fixtures which had turned green in the damp seaside atmosphere and wondered whether he should really knock on the door or just walk quietly away from the house without being noticed. But like some hypnotised insect, he had been wistfully drawn towards the house from the roadside by the faint sound of music, the tender lilting hook of a softly played violin. As he reached the door it got louder and he thought it could have been Mozart, maybe, but he knew whoever the composer could have been, it was her playing. And for a few surrendered seconds he thought she was playing for him, but he knew she couldn't have seen him from the window because he hadn't seen her. Then the music suddenly stopped as if his arrival had interrupted the flow and he felt like running away and hiding in the woods as if he were a frightened child. *'Belt up, you bungle,'* he chastised himself and impulsively gave the gothic style knocker in the middle of the door two sharp strikes and waited, as the butterflies turned cartwheels in his stomach.

She opened the door and stood before him in an elegant portrait of unprepared, natural beauty. Her long brown hair was lifted up into a hasty but perfectly set bun, the way only a woman could instinctively achieve, and long dark strands of uncaught fringe tousled sexily down her pretty face. She wore a thin green cardigan over a white blouse which revealed a soft and slender neckline. A blue skirt hugged her thin waist and then billowed out like the long petals of an unfurled flower before flowing down to almost cover her stylishly shoed feet. Elias breathed her in.

"Mr Harding," she said, surprised. The announcement hung in the air like an old sock and although they were both smiling awkwardly he could tell she was startled by his appearance at the door and was unsure which way the surprise was leaning, either towards pleasure or discomfort. A sense of disappointment and misadventure welled up inside him so he decided to bravely grab the old sock from the air and get it out of the way.

"Miss Danvers, I'm sorry to turn up unannounced," he said before hesitating again. "I was in the village and thought I'd take a chance to pay you a visit. If it's inconvenient I must surely apologise and perhaps we could arrange another time that's more suitable...only," he wavered with repression, "only...I wondered how you were getting on." He said this courteously, loading the enquiry with his sense of disappointment at being so gauche.

"No, no, don't be silly, it's lovely to see you again. I was just um...wasn't expecting any visitors today." She stopped and the initial surprise fell away from her expression to reveal one of apologetic embarrassment. "I'm so sorry. Do come in," she added quickly with a more welcoming smile across her face and she stood aside with a sweep of her small hand to beckon him in. He stepped through the door.

"I'm sorry if I seem unprepared, only I was in the middle of practising my violin," she offered, closing the door.

"Yes, I could hear it as I came down the garden. It was beautifully played. I wondered whether I should have disturbed you at all. Please, don't be sorry, I'm the one who should be apologising, turning up out of the blue like some unwanted salesman, hawking pegs." He smiled gawkily and they looked at each other with warmth.

"Well we don't get many salesmen around here, so I'm glad it was you turning up out of the blue. May I take your coat?" she asked softly.

He gave her his grey tweed coat and she hung it on a stand by the door. "Come through to the sitting room," she said and led the way through the first door within the hallway which opened into the front sitting room.

"Is your father home?" asked Eli as he followed.

"No, you've just missed him. He's out walking again." She stopped and turned in a smooth motion as if changing a dance step. "He gets bored in the house nowadays and goes walking nearly every day now." She motioned with her hand towards the soft chairs arranged around the large bay window which looked out over the front garden. Her music stand was stood near the side of the window, just out of view from anyone looking in, holding an open sheet of music. The violin she had played was laid on a small tea table next to the stand. Elias stood in the centre of the room, the window bathing him in natural light. He looked at her and saw she was smiling at him. "Where does he go," enquired Elias, feeling slightly vulnerable and on show in the open light.

"Along the beach and then the promenade or sometimes the coast path, anywhere he fancies really. He can be gone all day sometimes. He likes to think as he walks," she replied and put her hands behind her back.

"It's the best form of exercise, I believe," Elias said pointlessly. Suddenly he felt foolish again and then blurted out, "Look, Miss Danvers, I'm sorry to have arrived like this. I just thought that because it was such a pleasant few days when I stayed here, before I took up at the fort, that well...maybe it would be nice to see you and your father again. But, perhaps it was a bit presumptuous of me. I feel I really may have disturbed you…and…well….it is a bit rude of me….” his nervous twitter began to grind to a halt but thankfully the young lady threw him a lifeline.

“Really, Elias, I think we know each other well enough to be able to call each other by our first names, so please, call me Victoria. And it’s not rude of you at all. You haven’t disturbed me and it is lovely to see you again. I wasn’t sure if I ever would see you again, but I am sincerely glad I have. I too, had a very pleasant time while you stayed with us, as did my father. It felt very relaxed and natural and we both wondered how you have been getting on and how nice it would be to see you again. Please make yourself at home. Would you like a cup of tea? And it’s not just a polite gesture, I really am very thirsty after my practice and a cup of tea was just what I needed. It would be all the more worthwhile to have someone to enjoy it with, particularly if that someone is you.” Her face was full of honesty and empathy and Elias fell into her charm like a pebble onto a drift of freshly fallen snow.

“Thank you, a cup of tea would be lovely,” he melted.

“Please take a seat, I won’t be a moment,” and she floated off into the dimly lit hallway.

His nervousness subsiding, he looked around the room and absently wandered over to the music stand to peruse the open sheet of composition. It was a selection of Mozart practice pieces for violin and he felt a pang of smugness at his correct assumption when he was stood at the front door. Eli thought how nice it would be to hear her play them all, to lie back in one of the soft armchairs and be immersed in the woman’s mystique as the featherlike touch of real music poured over him. He flicked himself out of his love struck reverie and made a decision not to be so soppy in her presence. *‘Take it easy,’* his mind advised him like an on board therapist, *‘don’t go making a goose of yourself, she won’t be impressed by you turning into a blithering fop every time she opens her pretty mouth.’*

He smiled and paced slowly along the bookshelf lining one side of the room, noticing the fine selection of classics including Homer and the works of Shakespeare as well as some recent novels by Dickens and Victor Hugo. One shelf was dedicated entirely to travel writing, both home and abroad which Eli remembered was her father’s preferred reading matter. Past the bookshelf hanging on the wall was a framed photograph of Victoria when she was a child, stood between both her parents who were sat austerely, as was the fashion for portraits, but the small girl’s presence gave an unconquerable air of happiness about the image. He remembered her father telling him one night how Victoria’s mother had died when she was still a girl, probably not long after the photograph was taken, and how they had looked after one another even when the wealth was gradually lost over the years, mainly through ill-advised foreign investments and the steady rise of prices across all classes of society. After losing the servants and cutting costs, all that was left was the house and each other, hence the need to take in paying guests to supplement the few rents they still received from some of the houses in the village. "Bloody Empire never made me rich!" Elias recalled her father barking out one night at dinner. "Bloody Empire nearly killed me," he remembered replying to the outburst which made her father laugh heartily and made him realise how relaxed he had felt in their company.

"Here we are. Oh dear, you're not looking at that old photograph are you? I was such a callow young thing when I was a child," Victoria said as she breezed in with a tray, only the sound of the china pots chinking and the sweep of her dress audible as she walked.

"Oh, let me get the table," Eli said as he hopped over picking up the violin in one hand and moving the table into the space between the chairs with the other. "On the contrary, it's a very joyous portrait of you as a family. It's nice to be in a place that has a feeling of home about it, the fort can be a trifle functional at times."

"Thank you, Eli," she said as she put the tray down before replying to his comment. "I can imagine it needs a woman's touch, although I can't imagine many women who would want to stay there with all those men around, her work would be never ending." For some reason she blushed.

"Quite." Elias stood there for a moment and then examined the instrument he was still holding. "Do you get time to practice much, or do you keep getting disturbed by unwanted guests." He smiled coyly at her while she poured the tea.

"There's plenty of time to practice if I'm honest. Usually in the evenings, after dinner, but sometimes I just can't muster the enthusiasm. It's always better to have someone to play with, you know?" she said innocently.

"Yes. I haven't played since I was here, probably gone a bit rusty again." He put the violin carefully onto a nearby cushioned footstool.

"Do you take sugar? I'm afraid I can't remember."

"Yes please, just the one."

She handed him his cup and then plopped two spoonful's of sugar into her cup and sat down in one of the soft chairs by the window. He took a seat opposite her. They sat there for a few moments, taking tentative sips from their cups and both thought about how to start the next conversation.

"So how is life up at the fort?" Victoria began. Elias looked at her and smiled ruefully before gazing out of the window.

"It's..." he searched the garden for the right word. "Different," he added finally. "It's kept me busy over the two weeks. The lads are a good bunch really, but it feels like we're all starting afresh. Before I went abroad I used to take pride in knowing how to run things. But 'pride comes before a fall,' as they say." He looked at his cup sadly and then said, "Since getting back, I'd sort of forgotten what it's like to be in the army, although I'm not sure Brean Down is the best place to start remembering." Elias made a face as if he shouldn't be saying any of this and then smiled to cover himself.

"We don't give ourselves much to do, though. I don't think the weather's been too kind since I got here, it makes everything seem hard work."

Victoria rolled her eyes and snorted in agreement, keeping her reply in the quickly changed mood of platonic lightness. "Oh, it's been atrocious. The rain just seemed to keep pouring and sometimes you think it's never going to stop. We should be used to it by now but it feels like it gets worse every year. But it's alright, Elias, we don't blame the ghastly weather on you turning up," she said with a hint of mischief.

"I hope not either, or I'll have every poor blighter who's been flooded trying to blow me out of the fort."

"Like the three little pigs," she quipped.

"And the locals are the wolves," he added.

They laughed. It was easy now, relaxed and comfortable. Eli liked her and was pleased he had come. He hoped she would come out with him but even if she didn't the young soldier was glad of the fact he could have a pleasant conversation with a woman and make sense of it. He didn't feel like reality was slipping away from his grasp anymore and he could feel normal, and enjoy it.

"Talking of locals," he put his empty tea cup on the small table. Victoria motioned to the tea pot and asked if he wanted another one to which he nodded. "I met a few at the local hostelry in the village last night."

She pretended to be startled. "The public house, Mr Harding, how louche of you. I hear 'The Dolphin' is a house of debauched drunkenness," she said in a faux old lady accent and then flashed a playful grin.

He laughed at her again. "Louche indeed! If only. It was a bit quiet really. I only went out for a walk and thought I'd see where the locals went for entertainment." He decided not to mention last night's aborted attempt at seeing her.

"And how did you find it?" She put the pot down after filling his cup.

"Thank you," he said acknowledging the re-fill. "Well, I don't think the regulars took to me to be honest. If it hadn't been for Patrick, the postman, turning up I'd have probably left after the first drink. He's a good chap, Pat, but as for everyone else, I never felt welcome in there and I don't think it was just a case of my finely tuned sense of paranoia."

"The people in the village are an odd lot," she began, but it felt to Eli she was trying not to be too derogatory. "They have a peculiar way about them." She too looked out to the garden. "I often go to the village and virtually know everyone who lives there. After all I've lived here all my life and I suppose they except me as one of their own, but I know how you must have felt," she crumpled her brow in thought. "They don't trust strangers. Most of them lead reasonably secluded lives compared to people like ourselves Elias."

'People like ourselves! Yes, we are of the same kind, you and I. There is no reason for us not being together, either as lovers or, if such is life, just as friends. Our world is normal when given room to breathe, away from this place, this seclusion.'

His mind drifted into feathered visions of togetherness with this young woman at his side. As he watched her talking, her soft, tender mouth moving in rhythm to the music, he could hear Beethoven in his head.

"I'm sure they'll get used to you after you've been here a while," she continued. She leant forward and put her hand near her mouth as if telling him a personal secret. "I guess it might be more of a case of whether you'll get used to them." He couldn't help but gaze at her smooth female skin, as though beige silk had been draped over the sensuous frame of her face. "To be honest, I don't think I've ever got used to them either," she whispered, eyes twinkling in enjoyment at this covert interaction. Elias thought he fell in love.

"Perhaps we never will," he whispered back, tranquilized.

They both slowly sat back a little in their chairs, suddenly aware of the attraction they felt for one another, brought out into the open by being alone together and the subtle closeness of their being. They allowed the cold light of day to invade the intimacy and so restore a sense of inhibiting repression. Elias coughed lightly, covering his mouth. She gently ran a knuckle along her lips as if wanting to bite on something to suppress her emotion. They looked at each other intensely and there was a delectable silence.

'God's eyes!' Elias thought, *'I think she fancies me! I think she bloody fancies me!'* And as if in response they both darted their eyes from the sensuous gaze they were locked in and looked towards the window and the garden outside.

"So," he began, feeling as if the silence would make him explode and to relieve the sense of pressure he resumed with some light conversation, "How has life been here? Have you any guests?"

She made a face like he'd thrown the old sock back into the conversation and it had landed on her lap. It was a mixture of relief at feelings being tempered and composure being regained but also annoyance at remembering her everyday world. "Yes," she said under a wrinkled nose. "A Mr Stone is staying with us. He's from Edinburgh University no less, writing a thesis on nature, apparently."

"Well, well, an educated man," observed Eli.

"One might say so, although I get the impression there's more to him than a studious academic. He can be quite evasive and…" she paused for thought, "and a little disguised. But not in a good way."

"Really," Eli questioningly replied. "Bit of a dark horse is he, to use a cavalry term."

"No, not so much that," she countered herself again in an attempt at not sounding too rude about someone else. "Oh, he's very pleasant and good mannered, but it's just, you know, it must be something about naturalists," she looked outside again trying to find the right words in the wet leaves and bare shrubs, "They always seem to be examining everything. Studying the way things live, whether they are animals or humans." She pulled an expression like she had said something naughty.

Eli watched her manners and smiled, enjoying her discomfort at being discourteous to someone else. "He's out there now, probably up on the Down somewhere, examining something that doesn't want to be examined or watching some creature that doesn't want to be watched," she said rolling her eyes and then fixing them on Elias again with the faintest of seductive smiles.

"I guess the world needs to be examined sometimes," he said easily.

"Depends on who's doing the examining," she replied.

"Is he staying long?"

"No. I think he'll be leaving tomorrow. All the creatures of the Down will be left in peace then." She grinned.

"Perhaps one will bite him before he leaves," Eli offered cheekily.

"Let's hope so."

They continued to gaze at each other unaware of their simple conversation. She drank in his rough looking but elegant charm. She liked his short, cropped hair and the long sideboards falling down his thin face which led to his unfashionable but none the less roguish looking, clipped stubble. He was beautiful and natural and honest. She felt thrilled he had come to visit her, the initial awkwardness now a distant memory. He was interesting and she knew he had a story to tell about the past, the present and the future. She didn't get to meet many men in her life, not pleasant, good looking ones with attractive attributes. They were usually moneyed morons with overbearing conversation and little, if any charm and Victoria felt that no matter how nice they would come across in public, these men were always, somewhere deep down, capable of being bad. But Elias Harding was a good man, she had always felt it from the moment they first met and even more so now. Plus, he could play the piano, appreciated music, and always wore a handsome coat.

"Would you like to stay for dinner?" she asked.

He was still absorbing her elegant chic when she said the words and it took a while for him to register the invitation. His mind was filling itself with her, her beauty, her involuntary reverence. He'd noticed a strand of hair fall across her face a couple of times and the way she tucked it back behind her ear without diverting her attention from what she was doing. An imprint of her embracing personality and unknowingly mesmerising manner were secretly tattooing themselves on his way of thinking, consuming his subconscious and overcoming his desires. Her soft eyes entranced him. She was the most beautiful and breath-taking spider hiding in the dark rocks within the corner of this desperate world, and he was glad to be the fly that fell into her soft, enchanted web. He felt like a bastard in turning down the invite to dinner but the pull of the army could not be opposed.

"There is nothing more I would rather do tonight than stay for dinner with you, your father and even the evasive naturalist, Mr Stone, but alas I must remain dutiful to the course chosen for me by others, Victoria," he said theatrically. He tried to smile but couldn't hide his disappointment at having to decline the offer, but he knew he must decline for he couldn't skive from the fort tonight, questions would be asked. Major Acres might find out. She looked a little deflated.

"That's a shame, Elias. I would have liked you to play the piano again, but I understand. It is a bit short notice, perhaps another time," she replied politely.

He felt rude at his rebuttal, no matter how dramatically put, and reverted to the original cause for his visit hoping it would restore their engagement and he sat forward as close as he could to Miss Danvers.

"Yes we must, perhaps next week even, for there is a reason why I came here today, Victoria, and I sincerely hope you can accept my invitation to you in difference to my refusal of your offer to me," he blabbed, and she looked at him confused. He rubbed his hands together and looked at his shoes as his toes rubbed the carpet as if trying to grind the old sock into the ground forever. There was a sudden fear he might stutter. "Would you like to accompany me to an afternoon concert at the pavilion next week? I was just wondering, I thought you might like to come...with me that is." He stopped as if aware of a terrible mistake he might have made. "There's a local orchestra playing Mozart and Brahms and I would like nothing better than to go with you, apart from having dinner with you tonight of course, which I am most sorry I can't do and I would dearly like to make it up to you by taking you to the concert and possibly to dinner afterwards, perhaps...." He trailed off with a slight look of pleading and insecurity in his face. His head rattled with doubt, the previous feelings of confidence and enthusiasm abandoning the ship of his mind and drifting away to an island he'd only just left.

"Oh," she noised in reply and tucked a strand of hair behind her smooth ear. For some reason Elias prepared himself to receive the backhand of rejection. "I would love to go!" she beamed, her bright eyes finding him again in their magical trance. "That would be wonderful! It would be a pleasure to accompany you," she said, and her lips parted in a happy smile showing just the edges of her beautifully set teeth. She touched his hand lightly and inside Elias was overcome with emotion. Immediately his body was filled with the warming tingle of niceness and overwhelming captivation. It felt better than any dose of laudanum or hit of booze. His skin prickled with all that was good with the world.

“Well that’s fantastic, I’ll get the tickets straight away,” he blobbed woozily and they both smiled and laughed and made plans as they bathed in one another’s presence.

When they said goodbye a short time later, the two people gazed at each other with the doughy resonance that moonstruck lovers in the prime of youthful enrapture often portray. Elias wanted to laugh and kiss her on the lips but instead he just stood there grinning clumsily with his hands behind his back and rocking on his toes in small metrical movements. They said goodbye quietly and parted with a final look of momentous but kind hearted probity.

He got the tickets to the concert that day, luckily hailing a cab on the edge of the village to take him to and from town. As he walked back to the fortress across the dreary late afternoon gloom of the Down, Elias didn’t think about the chores required at the battery over the coming hours and days. All he thought about was the wonderful woman he had met and the joy of being with her again in a few days’ time. He felt his heart jumping and wondered if it was love.

Oh what a Charlie he was, this young man bounding along, full of the joys of a love struck moon bear. The world was before him, around him, behind him and within him. He felt there was nothing in this world, past or present that could stop him in the heartfelt pursuit of his glorious future. He pondered on the possibility that this was the first time in his life he felt truly happy and hopeful.

How twisted, this world can be.

The next day, Eleanor Penfold, a middle aged chambermaid at the Grand Atlantic Hotel, unlocked the door to room 216 and immediately noticed the bed hadn’t been slept in but the top cover had been left at a rather untidy angle. Whilst she reset the bedcover, surmising that the patron of this room was probably still out on the razz somewhere, she noticed a shiny brown brogue poking out from underneath the bedframe. When she looked beneath, Eleanor let out a horrific scream which alerted the hotel management and most of the other guests in the hotel.

Major Flowers of the War Office and formerly of the 3rd Dragoon guards, Berkshire regiment, was dead. During the previous day he had stopped breathing. The swelling from his badly broken hooter and the plugs of congealed blood and tissue wedged in his nostrils blocked the airways from his nose and the chloroform soaked gag in his mouth restricted his breathing along his windpipe. His unconscious body woke itself up when the lack of oxygen reached a critical point and caused alarm in his senses, overriding the drug. But his tied hands meant he couldn’t free himself and his life melted away through suffocation as he wriggled and quaked frantically under the restricted space of the bed.

When the manager and bell boy eventually pulled out his ever stiffening and grossly contorted body they heard a muffled scream from inside the wardrobe. When they opened it, another man fell out onto the floor, tied and bound and screaming in agony from behind a gagged and frothing mouth. He had cramp like you couldn't imagine.

8. The Night.

Gordy watched the fire dance through zombie like eyes, still unable to move his dulled and flaccid body. It felt like his whole being was one, long, dead leg received from a swarm of schoolyard bullies. His mind however, was uncontrollably active within this numbed carcass and although he couldn't feel himself properly, only some basic, non-specific nervous reactions to outside influences like cold piss and hot wind, he could see the events unfolding within the spectrum of the flames and subconsciously experience everything that was being shown. His ears could hear the voices of the people as they spoke, sometimes from the images visualized in the fire, sometimes from the mouth of the figure, still sat darkly behind the flames. He could smell the sea as it appeared in each act and taste the rain as it fell from the leaden sky. Time was incoherent. There was no world outside anymore, just the superimposed one transmitted from the centre of this room and the accompanying lights, visions and fleeting shadows that swooped around the walls. He could not move to touch any substance or picture, whether real or merely represented, but he could fully comprehend and wholly sense the story as it was revealed with each passing moment.

Then Gordy sensed the atmosphere change again. It had always held an aura of disquiet, even in the moments of dampened joy, but now it darkened still further and reached a new depth of malice. Although he couldn't physically feel anything, apart from what was happening in his mind, Gordy's subconscious was filled with a sense of fear and all-consuming trepidation. The words that accompanied the scenes bore into his mind, growing deeper and more threatening, while the room seemed to blacken as the lights from the conflagration in front of him died, creating an almost dusk like quality to the surroundings. The whole bunker was then swathed in a bleak vision, full of heavy, storm filled clouds which tumbled across an enveloping night sky cast above a foreboding and dark chocolate coloured sea.

They rowed long and hard, deep and wide. Six men at a time worked the oars as the occupants took their turns in pulling the simple, open craft across the cold, choppy water. Their shoulders stung, their muscles ached and their tensile bodies strained rhythmically as if they were a machine digging pointless holes in a vast expanse of sticky, wet mud. Their comrades, who laid low in the bowels of the lifeboat, absorbed the sudden jolts and swooning pitches caused by the active waves as they ploughed through the estuary. Hidden by the shadows of the sea, which waved like the gently swaying fingers of an ebbing darkness reaching out to the covering hand of a blackened sky, the crew took a wide berth from the end of the Down, staying far enough away from the possibility of being caught by the sweeping net of a watchman's squinted and prying eyes.

Then, not far from the shoreline, they turned the boat parallel to the beach and followed their French noses toward the hulking mass of dark land that lay ahead, until they reached the secluded sands of a seaweed strewn beach which met the rocky base of the towering hillside. It was here they found another French nose, waiting for them patiently, mingled with the seaweed and the creeping shadows of the cliff. He was one of their own. His name was Phillippe Roumieu, otherwise known as Mr Rufus Stone, supposed academic and watcher of birds and nature.

Earlier in the night, further out in the solitude of the open estuary, this boat had been lowered into the heaving sea from the deck of 'The Small Fish' using a steam powered lifting crane. Another boat of the same size, but different by the fact it had a small mast rising from the centre, had also been lowered onto the surface and was similarly filled with a cargo of twenty or so men who hunkered down into the large frame of the wooden vessel and hugged their cloth wrapped rifles against their dark bodies to avoid the cold splash of watery spray which fell all around them. There were no lights on the mother ship as it moved biliously on the swell and the men who boarded the two smaller boats were silent as they clambered inside and prepared their individual space for the uncomfortable journey ahead. The only sound was the chugging thump of the crane and the smack of wood on metal and then water onto wood.

Castille made no gesture as he watched the boats move off once they were ready and rowed away by their respective crews in different directions. One went towards the far off mainland, while the other headed for the closer, solitary mass of Steep Holm Island. Once the boat heading for the island was in clear water the crew pulled in their oars and hoisted the tiny sail into the gust driven, easterly wind. Castille turned to the other boat stroking its way to the mainland and caught a farewell glance from the face of Benno, his second in command, sat in the back of the lonely looking craft. The Colonel smiled forlornly at his friend but knew he was too far away to see.

"Right then Captain," Castille said sharply. "Head for the Island, but remember, give it a wide berth and keep the lights out. Then turn this crappy crate around and head back, getting close enough to it so I can spend as little time as possible in that shitty rowing boat. The sea looks choppy tonight."

The Captain looked at the Colonel with a hint of worry mixed with his normal expression of disdain towards his disrespectful master. "Aye, Aye Mr Castille," he replied bitterly. "It's always choppy on this Channel, especially at night." He paused a moment and then added slyly, "But I think the sea will be the least of your problems tonight, eh."

"I don't give a shit what you think, Captain," Castille barbed back in reply, and then whilst swinging round, he gave the sailor a withering look of animosity before stepping into the cabins and heading down the steep metal stairs towards the hold where he could change his clothes and make ready for the night ahead.

In the fort on Brean Down the men were sat inside the barrack room, eating heartily. Cook England's roasted mutton with boiled potatoes and cabbage in a thick meat juice broth was going down well with the diners and there was a general feeling of relaxed wellbeing once again. Some had already eaten and were sat around talking and smoking, empty plates in front of them, whilst the rest of the volunteers savoured the last of their meals and took gulps from mugs filled with salty tasting water. The fires were roaring and the room was warm. Dicky Pearce had already moved to his bunk so he could rest his aching foot and let his food go down. His brother, Daniel, was still at the table scoffing down a plateful of seconds, especially given to him to try and build up his stringy body and sate his seemingly unending hunger. Next to him, Haines the scribbler, old Mule and Burden were sat chatting and laughing peacefully as they filled their respective pipes and cigarette papers. At the other end of the table, Eves sat eating and talking about the state of the nation with the lumpy looking Boulter, the bespectacled young administrator Robert Barnes and the older and most aged looking of all the men, Atticus Smales. George Gosfor and Stanley Pickles sat in attendance as well, using their knives to draw pictures and write easy words into the leftover gravy on their plates, giggling occasionally and wisely keeping out of the heady discussion going on beside them. Cook moved systematically to and from the kitchen, clearing plates and preparing a pot of coffee, which all had agreed would be the ideal dunking fluid for an accompanying plate of past their best, dry as sand, oat and flour pudding biscuits. In the far corner, on his bunk near the fire, Grayard Evans smoked smoothly as he read his latest book, a dog eared, worn covered copy of Herman Melville's Moby Dick. Sat in front of the fire wearing past their best, under washed long johns, whilst coughing loudly and picking his toenails, was the unsavoury character of a young man called Ezekiel Ford. He was in his early twenties, of noticeably poor health and had the constant, unenviable odour of damp onions about his person. Although new to the group, his bellicose manner and tendency to annoy, which was caused by years of living hand to mouth in various cities around the country and surviving only through his crafty guile and stubbornness, hadn't helped ingratiate his personality to the rest of the already bonded volunteers. They were not a particularly difficult society to get on with and usually accepted all sorts within their fold but for some reason Ford just hadn't really fitted in and he hadn't done himself any favours in the meantime. His more unsavoury personal hygiene habits had offended some of the members of the group and from his first arrival at the fort he had been openly critical of some of the older part time gunners. Undaunted, Ezekiel was happy to be considered the only real outcast within the fort and made no effort to change that position. Whenever watch duties were being assigned, his bodily odour and his lack of interaction with the rest of the men meant he was always considered first. Tonight, because of the buoyant mood arising from the successful firing practice earlier in the day, there was no watch assigned yet and Ford was destined to spend the night with everyone else, albeit at the other end of the room.

Evans lifted his head from the book and glared at the man playing with his feet by the fire. "Stop picking the toe cheese out of your nails, Fordy. It's putting me off my book," he said with a scowl.

"Bugger you Evans! I'm checkin' fer' foot rot," Ford retorted. "All the rains played 'avoc wit' me feet."

"I'll play havoc with you if you don't pack it in you gobby little shithole," the reader returned fiercely. On the other side of the room Dick Pearce laughed. "You tell im' Evans," he chortled.

"You can piss off too Pearce," Ezekiel Ford replied in response. "If yer not careful I'll break yer other foot as well."

Evans winked at the youngster led on his bed with bandaged toes and then grinned. "At least his feet don't smell like he's stepped in dog shit," he said, glaring at Ford.

The onion man flashed an angry look back at Evans and started to say something but was interrupted by Eves who had heard the spat from the other end of the hall. "Now, now children, settle down. All that talks putting me off my dinner, any more an' I'll 'av you all out on night duties," he chided.

Grayard smiled sarcastically at Ford and continued reading his book. Ford looked at Eves sat behind him at the other end of the room and then started putting on his boots which had been drying by the side of the hearth. "I need a piss, anyway," he spat in irritation.

He walked towards the back door with his boots undone. The laces wriggled across the floor like small, thin snakes. He grabbed his tunic as he went and pulled it on by the time he reached the exit. Scruffily, he walked down the small corridor between the washroom and Eves bunk house and opened the metal outer door which led onto the rear courtyard and the latrine situated a few feet away. It was pitch black outside and a cold gust of wind blew through him as he stepped into the night air. He pulled the dark blue tunic around his neck and walked a few feet over to the small, stone built, square building attached to the main moat fortress wall with a simple overhang serving as a roof, which all together, formed the outside latrine. One wall was half lined with tiles in a basic urinal above an open drain which led through the bottom of the boundary wall and poured unhygienically out over the rocks below. At the farthest end of the fort a few yards away from the urinal was another small toilet block built into the side of the Down where further ablutions could be performed in private. The latrine was open and impersonal but it was closer to the barrack room door than the actual toilets and saved time and a further, colder walk when a quick leak was all that was needed.

Ford fumbled with the buttons of his long john's, then breathed a sigh of relief as he started to piss. He looked out across the top of the urinal walls to the dark blue mass of sea that pulsed inland under the rolling clouds of a soot black sky. It felt like rain was coming and it made him shiver.

Then he let out a noise not dissimilar to a pig squeal as the outline of a strange form appeared in the opening at the other end of the latrine wall. He fell forward in a frightened panic and sprayed some piss over his tunic and underwear before rolling along the wall to get away from the emergence, his flaccid penis hanging out of his pants like an uncooked sausage, still squirting urine in weak thinning arcs of wee as if it were rainwater spluttering from a broken fountain nozzle. Ezekiel reached the end of the splash back and was about to cry out louder when he realised what it was in the opening, as the form defined itself through the darkness. Staring at him with wild eyes, chewing laconically on a tuft of grass, was a goat. Its white and brown hide was now showing up in the gloomy light from the barrack room windows, and the interior illumination was being reflected back from the goat's weird shaped eyes making them seem a sinister orange colour. It stood perfectly still, watching Ford as he flustered and sorted out his still uncovered cock and tried to wipe the piss from his clothes. "Bastard goats!" Ford shouted angrily at the animal; but the creature stayed where it was, unperturbed by the outburst.

Finally, after checking out the scruffy human for what seemed like an age, the goat turned away from the opening of the latrine and walked casually up to the gun emplacement walls and hopped up with a skilled agility Zeke Ford could only dream of. The goat ended up stood on the top of the escarpment, outlined majestically against the night sky like a white mammalian ghost. Ford watched it move, still feeling nervous at the shock of the creature's sudden appearance but with a growing sense of stupidity at being frightened by a goat and subsequently pissing on himself. Then, after a few seconds of waiting, almost as if it were taking a moment to stare out to sea and admire the view, the animal spontaneously darted away along the ridge of the boundary wall and down to the rocks near the waterline. There, it acrobatically hopped across to the other side of the open moat and up into the far side of the Down's rocky cliff tops before running along the grassy sides until it disappeared mystically into the darkness.

Ezekiel watched it go, transfixed for a moment by the animal's graceful movement. Then he gritted his teeth angrily and tried to cover up the wee stains on his clothes before heading back inside, suddenly aware of his own sense of vulnerability and silliness coupled with a realisation of just how cold it was out in the open.

Unknown to him, if he had kept looking out to sea, without the appearance of a nosey mountain goat to distract him, he might have noticed a large rowing boat heading through the waves along the shoreline towards the bottom of the Down and the steps which led to the cliff tops not far away. If he had, he might have wondered what it was doing and why anyone would possibly be going fishing at this time of night. But he hadn't seen it, and he didn't wonder, so instead, as he went back inside the barracks, he was blissfully unaware of what was going on outside the walls of the fort. So too, was everybody else.

The fishing skiff was low in the dark water as if it were carrying too much weight on board and the sail which silently propelled the skiff was as black as the pitch night surrounding it, making the craft seem illusory. The French Legionnaires, dressed all in black with faces smeared in the noir paint of clandestine war, laid low and quiet. Only the darkened shape of one man who controlled the rudder and another who watched from the front of the boat broke the indefinable outline of the gunnels on the unknown craft as it glided like a shadowy spectre through the fluid of oiliness. Before them, the island approached fast, huge now, as the rocks that jutted from its watery base sucked the wooden boat towards their mineral teeth like the waiting mouth of a hideous river monster. As the wind and choppy sea pushed the boat on, a figure pulled in the sail and the rudder man forcefully pushed the tiller to one side, bringing the craft alongside the rocks and slowing its progress enough so the skiff could bump into the land mass without smashing itself to pieces on the sharp rocks. An oar was extended to buffer the impact, arms reached out with a grappling bar. The men braced themselves to land.

There was a dull thud as the side of the boat hit the first of the rocks and for a moment it felt like the hull had given way. The swirling waters rocked the vessel violently for a few seconds as it clattered against the rocky outcrop but then, as the grappling bar found a hold and arms reached out to grab the boulders, the boat settled against the jagged shore and came to a bobbing and disconcerted rest. The occupants clambered out one by one onto the slippery rocks, rifles slung tightly across their backs as gripping hands clung to the island, desperate to gain enough of a hold to heave themselves out of the rolling boat and away from the water's edge. They climbed across the treacherous stones towards the rock face leading up to the bramble covered clifftops. Soft and silent, dark and invisible, the figures moved secretly among the rocks like insects across a garden wall.

The boat load of commandos had headed for the quietest part of the island, a landing area in a blind spot, away from the barrack walls and gun emplacements of the Gun Battery above. They had approached in a wide arc after being dropped off by the steamer two of three miles out to sea, undercover of a heavily clouded night sky. The boat had used sail to cut discreetly along the channel towards what was the only possible place to make a covert landing. With no lights on that side of the island and without a clear sky and moon to illuminate the sea, the small boat had been virtually invisible and gone in completely unnoticed by the only set of eyes anywhere near that part of the island. Those eyes belonged to a guard keeping watch from the only gun emplacement overlooking that part of the estuary facing the Welsh coastline. He could have seen the boat as it came around but he would have probably thought it was just a fishing boat on a night sailing and even then he wouldn't have seen it tuck in and head for the back of the island as, at that close distance, his eye line would have been obscured by the contour of the rising ground he was part of. As it was, he wasn't even looking in that direction anyway. He had spent the whole time watching the oncoming lights from a small steam ship as it approached noisily from the other side of the atoll.

The 'Corrine Marin' had covered up her moniker using wooden buffers slung over the side of the boat and she chugged slowly towards Steep Holms jetty with all her deck lights blazing and a series of triumphant bursts soaring from her steam whistle. A Union Jack had been hoisted up on the rear flagpole to complete the disguise and Castille had hailed the island sending a semaphore message to the men stood on the jetty who were wondering what the hell this boat was doing turning up here at this time of night. The small steam ship was still too big to land on the islands short jetty and so weighed anchor approximately 50 yards out to sea. Castille stood on the deck with the artisan called Modesto alongside him. They were dressed in brown and grey tweed suits covered with buttoned up heavy overcoats. The Colonel wore a checked, thick brimmed trilby hat while the artisan had greased back his hair. Castille held a loud hailer to his mouth and so began the ambitious ruse.

"Major Acres! Is there a Major Acres about! My name is Flowers! From the War Office!" shouted Castille in his best and perfectly acceptable, cut glass English.

From the main building, Acres walked down to the jetty and testily grabbed hold of a loud hailer from one of the other soldiers. "Well about time, Sir!" he called rudely. "We've been waiting for you!"

"Apologies Major. We were delayed on land. Have we permission to row over?" Castille bellowed.

"Permission granted!"

Castille looked at his accomplice and grinned widely. "Ready for this Modesto," he said chirpily.

"Not really," replied the artisan with laconic uncertainty as the two men made their way clumsily over the rope ladder, down the side of the ship, and into the rowing boat bobbing awkwardly on the water below.

Two of Castilles men, dressed in ships boiler suits and wrapped in navy pea coats and woollen hats pulled the oars as Castille and Modesto sat at either end of the tiny boat looking intently at the men stood on the jetty. The Colonel felt confident and excited at the performance he was about to give whilst Modesto looked serious, trying to hide his anxiousness about the whole experience with a look of stern discipline. They both knew whether or not they would get away with this would depend on the reaction of Acres the moment they met face to face. They had the forged identification papers with the names given to them by the agent on Brean Down in the message they'd received the previous night and the English accents and city gent clothing they had were as good as any actors might wear, but it would all hinge on that one key moment when they first met the islanders. Castille hoped the landing party were in place just in case it all went pear shaped straight away.

'Don't kill anyone. Whatever you do, don't kill anyone.'

The words he had told his men before they set off rattled around inside Colonel Castille's head as he approached the island's low, harbour wall.

Harding watched through his binoculars from the window of his quarters as the rowing boat reached the jetty and took a bite from his cold, gravy covered potato as he did. "Must be those chaps from the War office turned up at last," he said to himself. He smiled as he watched the two wobbly figures disembark from the tiny boat as it pitched on the vomit inducing swell and inched up his binoculars onto the sniping frame of Acres waiting impatiently on the wall. "Rather them, than me," he mused with a mouthful of gravy and potato, and then got up and went to the sideboard to fix himself another glass of gin.

"Major Acres, good to meet you. My name is Flowers." Castille extended an open hand towards the Major and the two men shook hands.

Acres looked the tall Frenchman up and down and narrowed his bird like eyes upon the man. "I was expecting you to turn up on the normal ferry service from Weston-On-Sea," was all he said with a hint of annoyance.

"Yes, well, that was the plan, but our train was delayed at Bristol so we had to charter this steamer from Avonmouth instead. Bit of a cock up all round really. Still, we're here now." Castille replied in the old school Eton English he'd mastered whilst interned at a British prison camp in India. "By the way, this is Mr Smith," and he presented the artisan who was stood stiffly beside him.

"Major." Modesto nodded, taking the line that the least said, the better.

"Mr Smith," replied Acres equally stiffly.

"So anyway, Major Acres, shall we see the prisoner?" Castille said, flashing Acres a cheesy grin. The Battery Commander looked even smaller in comparison to the two French hoaxers and he gave them another up and down look with just the beginnings of an alternative scowl across his face.

"This way," he sniped. "Lieutenant Pontefract will sign you in at the office. Then I'll take you to see our Mr Ralph or whoever the hell he is." And Acres led the two men up to the main building whilst the two men in the row boat stayed where they were, keeping their heads down and trying not to catch anyone's eye. The few guards on the walls of the reception house and in the courtyard beyond, murmured to one another and looked on with intrigue.

The main gun emplacements and barracks at Steep Holm were on top on the Island where the best firing coverage across the estuary could be found. But at the foot of the steep cliff face on the English side, above a sharp slope of shingle, there was also a terrace of small buildings adjoining the jetty and landing slip which led into the sea from a short stretch of pebbly beach. These buildings contained the reception area, main stores and some offices, one of which now served as the confinement area which held Edwin Ralph. Inside the reception, Pontefract examined the false papers offered to him without so much as a second look and booked the men into the fort. "Welcome to Steep Holm, Sirs. Glad you could make it, we don't get many visitors to the island, not important ones, anyway," he gushed with a wide, gay smile.

"Give it a rest, Pontefract," Acres snapped from behind. "This way please, gentlemen." He turned and walked briskly away with the two Frenchmen quickly following behind him.

Castille sensed the Major's testy demeanour and encouraged by their success at getting onto the island unchallenged, began to charm him while they walked along the stony corridors with a series of plaudits at apprehending the possible agent provocateur.

"If this is the man we think it is Mr Acres, you will have done the country a great service by catching him," he cooed.

"Really," replied Acres showing a little interest. "So, you've been after a particular person for some time, I take it."

"Oh yes, Major. That's why we came down straight away. We've had a suspicion that an agent has been working in these parts and gathering classified information for the last few months. Isn't that right Mr Smith?" the Colonel said, looking over at his partner with a mischievous grin.

The artisan threw a glance at Castille that was full of daggers. "Yes, several months now," he stuttered in reply using his best but slightly stodgy English voice.

Acres stopped dead in the corridor and swept round to face the two men. They almost overshot him by a step and Modesto nearly bumped into his leader trying to avoid the rigid Major. "Is that right," said the hawk faced Battery Officer, eyeing the other men with a wrongly angled suspicion. "And you think, Mr Ralph could be your man," he oiled.

Castille sidled up to the smaller man and dripped some creeping acclamation over him. He was enjoying his part in the theatre being performed and was stimulated by the apparent success it was having.

Something inside and the growing realisation that Acres was a bit of a ding dong, made him feel they were going to get away with this. "From your description, I believe this is just the man we've been looking for. And my superiors at the War Office will be most impressed by your catching him for us," he oozed confidently.

Acres relaxed a little and a small smile crept onto his upturned mouth. "So they bloody should be, Mr Flowers!" he said outrageously. "Being in charge of a place like Steep Holm Battery takes experienced discipline. Not many would know the difference between a suspicious character and a genuine member of the public. It takes a fine attention to detail and a knowing eye."

It was all Castille could do to stop himself from laughing at the absurd irony that Acres had just presented but he swallowed down his derision and remained composed. Modesto stood, eyebrows upturned, stunned into a continuation of his astonished silence.

"Well, you'll certainly be remembered for this," Castille quipped slyly.

"So I should be Mr Flowers, so I should. This way," said Acres and he marched off down the corridor smiling. Castille stood and looked at Modesto with a crazed grin on his face, his eyebrows almost lifting off his face at the credulity of the Major.

It wasn't until Flowers walked into the cell room and actually saw Mr Ralph that something else was aroused in the back of Major Acres' mind. Up until that moment he had been taken in by the Frenchmen pretending to be Government officials. There had been no reason not to. They had seemed perfectly genuine and plausible even if one of them had been over bearing and the other a little quiet. But when he led them into the room and Edwin Ralph had stood up from his chair and caught sight of the incoming Mr Flowers for the first time, Acres noticed the miniscule expression of Mr Ralphs' face as he was instantaneously caught off guard. Acres got the distinct feeling that the two men had met before and knew each other. It was an intuitive and instinctual sensation that ignited a spark of indecision in his mind and set to work the simmering paranoia that was a symptom of his suppressed, schizophrenic tendencies.

Castille and Shrott did indeed know each other. They had met several times in the process of their clandestine operations and had even socialised together after being involved with the same missions. The world of French espionage was relatively small and the same faces would often be part of the various different events. The two men weren't expecting to bump into one another here, and were surprised as each other when they first saw one another. They both thought they covered their recognition of the other man well enough but neither appreciated the true extent of Major Acres' insect like sensitivity. He made no show of his sudden concern and instead began to battle with the other facet of his personality that was the growing inflammation of indecision. Regardless, the pantomime continued unabated.

Once Shrott had realised what was going on, he played along with the deception, even taking the heavy handed approach that Castille began to portray as the French Colonel's own confidence in the subterfuge grew even further. He began shouting at the prisoner, accusing him of being a traitorous spy and putting the lives of thousands of men in great danger. At one point he even pretended to strike Shrott and the imprisoned agent cowered back from the interrogator's raised hand in mock fear. Modesto tried to act cool as the other two men played out the scene before Acres, but the artisan couldn't help wondering if the façade would push the whole fraud overboard.

On the contrary, the over dramatization was good enough to make Acres doubt his fears about the two men knowing one another and merely increased his uncertainty over whether something dodgy was actually going on. The raised temperature of the questioning made him think it was genuine and he pushed his fears to the back of his mind. In the end he felt like he just wanted them gone and the Island routines could return to normality. There was a sense of relief when Castille put the handcuffs on Shrott and led him by the arm down the corridor towards the outside doors.

"I'll be recommending you for a commendation, Major Acres," said Castille as the four men walked briskly.

"Thank you Mr Flowers. Much appreciated," Acres puffed, hiding the mental instability still going on in his head. "You'll speak to Admiral Pickering on my behalf then," he asked.

"Yes, I'll pass on your name, don't you worry," blustered Castille as he sped up towards the door, Shrott skating along next to him.

"Really," replied Acres, his mind starting to race, thinking of a ruse to try and confirm his suspicion. He was unable to control a need to confront his indecision and so take some kind of resulting action.

"Ah Mr Flowers..." Pontefract raised a finger to the men as they approached the door. "Could you just...."

"Not now Pontefract!" interrupted Acres, the strain of nervous energy showing in his voice. He wanted these men gone but there was a desire to satisfy his uncertainties about the whole situation and his superciliousness took over. Castille and Shrott reached the closed heavy metal door leading out to the courtyard and stopped suddenly. Acres and Modesto came to a halt behind them. Modesto got the impression something was wrong but stayed silent. The other two Frenchmen were busy thinking of the finishing point in this racy escapade, which was the steamer waiting out at sea.

"I just need you to sign the prisoner out, Mr Flowers, ah...before you go," Pontefract stammered quickly before he could be interrupted again.

"Admiral Pickering doesn't work at the War office," said Acres in a matter of fact way, his disturbed arrogance taking control and deciding to show its hand.

There was silence. Castille looked at his three compatriots and then switched his fix to Pontefract stood behind a small counter near the closed door.

"I'm sorry Lieutenant, what did you say?" he asked calmly, craning his ear forward in a dismissive manner.

"You need to sign the prisoner out," repeated Pontefract with an innocent smile, pushing forward an open ledger book with a pen laid on top of it.

"Of course," Castille replied, taking the pen and signing the book.

Acres remained silent but looked at the tall man as he wrote, watching as he signed the false name. It seemed natural enough without any hesitation in the writing as there may have been from someone who was nervous.

"Admiral Pickering isn't part of the War Office," the Major said again, this time with more emphasis. Modesto stood back a little, unnoticed by the others, preparing himself for the consequences. Pontefract continued to grin inanely.

Castille didn't look up from the ledger. "No, I don't believe he does, does he? To be honest I don't know who's in charge of what in that place these days." He turned and looked Acres in the eye. "But don't worry Major, when I get back to London with this spy, I'll make sure everyone knows it's down to you." He glared intently without smiling at the small Commander. An awkward feeling and a rising sense of danger filled the hallway.

The feeling wasn't sensed by Pontefract though and he innocently opened the metal door allowing the wind to blow noisily into the space of the stony corridor. "We really must be going Major Acres," Castille said through the wind. "We have a train to catch." He turned away from the birdman Commander as Pontefract stood to the side allowing them to leave.

"All the best, gentlemen. Safe journey," said the Lieutenant gaily, as the agent and his prisoner stepped through the door.

"What about the yacht, Major Flowers," Acres called after them. The tides of suspicion ebbed and flowed over him like the waters of the channel, but strangely, he didn't know what to do.

"We haven't time for that, Major, not tonight. We'll pick it up as soon as possible. I'll send someone down," Castille called out without looking back as he strode with Shrott onto the courtyard. Modesto skipped after them and caught up with his leader and his retrieved prey as they headed with determination down to the jetty.

Acres put his fist to his mouth and bit a finger as Pontefract checked the ledger on the counter. "Aren't you going to say goodbye, Mr Acres?" the young man asked his Officer nonchalantly whilst still looking down at the book. Acres stepped into the doorway, hesitating, his mind tumbling over itself in the turmoil of insecurity, not knowing whether he should or could interfere with what was or was not happening. Surely they weren't all spies on a mission to take back one of their own. That would be madness. What if he made a fuss and he was wrong about them? About everything!

"Oh sugar!" Pontefract exclaimed as he suddenly noticed something in the pages of the book. "I say!" he called out, grabbing the ledger and pushing past Acres before running through the door to the courtyard outside.

Away from the Island, on the headland across the sea, shadows moved through the darkness like ghosts drifting through the dreams of the sleeping. They too were soft and silent, dark and invisible. The stygian forms moved without disturbing the nature around them. They hid in the ground, melted into the bushes, unseen, unknown and unwanted. They spread like a handful of released seeds scattered in the swirling winds, ready and waiting. Unseen, unknown and unwanted, they crept ever forward under the inky veil of night in a sinister game of sleeping lions.

Below the ghosts, perched on the rocks just above the sea, lights from the windows of the fort and the flickering oil lamps on the outside walls were the only illumination on the enveloping darkness. They betrayed a place of warmth and protection to the watching shadows. Further away, floating on the void of sea, other tiny pinpricks of light could also be seen. These different constellations disclosed nothing of the estuary or beyond to the waiting phantoms but might as well have been the distant starlight from an unknown entity in the space of an inconsequential universe.

And so the shadows of night waited. The air was suffused with damp, already coating everything it touched with an ultra-fine layer of misted moisture, whilst the stench of the sea filled their nostrils in an irksome stink of crab claws and seaweed.

Behind one of those windows which betrayed a place of warmth, the shadows saw an old man sneeze.

"AAATTCHHOO!" exploded the old man, his whole body being thrown backwards and forwards by the violence of his sneeze as it was shockingly released from his unprepared face. "Bless us! That nearly blew me 'ead off!" Smales cried as he recovered from the shock, his eyes bulging and red.

"Bless you Smales! That nearly blew my 'ead off too!" barked Jimmy Burden, laughing at the suddenness of the old man's outburst. Everyone else laughed too.

"Ere Atty, old man, why don't you give us a song, instead of givin' us all a heart attack with your bloody cow nosed sneezin'," suggested Mule from the other side of the table as he rolled yet another fag.

"Aye, give us a tune Mr Smales," Dicky Pearce called out from his bed.

"Only if you give us a jig, young 'un," added Gosfor to a chorus of more laughs.

"Go on Atticus, get yer squeezebox out and sing us a song, we could do with some entertainment tonight. It'll warm the damp air and brighten the chill in our souls," said Haines. A few of the volunteers looked over at the Sergeant eagerly. Sometimes a song went with a drink, just to keep the men's spirits up and help while away the evenings during these dark and gloomy nights. Eves stood up with his pipe still in his mouth and the room went a little quiet.

"Go on then Mr Smales, sing a song or two if it pleases you. Thou might have a shit stoppin' sneeze but yer voice is pleasant enough for a lullaby. And get the grog out lads, you deserve a free night," the big Sergeant said, creasing his large eyes up with a bushy smile.

"I'll get the cider!" cried Lumpy and he jumped up faster than he'd moved since he got to the fort and headed to a small cabinet in the corner near the kitchen. He lifted out a large clay demi john full of the local scrumpy cider, bought from a farm a few miles down the coast and drunk when the fort's rum and water grog got a bit over groggy. He pulled out the bloated and discoloured damp brown cork and sniffed the aroma which was released from the pungent old juice. "Phew, she's startin' to turn, lads," he winced.

"I'll leave you all to it, gentlemen, just in case you ask me to dance along. Besides, that stuff gives me the shits," Eves said still smiling. He turned around and began walking towards his own room in a puff of grey pipe smoke but turned on his heels half way along and called out to the men as he continued to walk backwards, "Not too many mind lads, and not too late, we're still supposed to be soldiers, after all," he said with a hint of warning as he disappeared into the corridor.

"Pass I my squeezebox then," grinned the old man through missing and crooked teeth. The instrument was passed down the line of volunteers until it reached Smales and after getting comfortable on one of the stools by the fire he gently pushed and pulled on the bellows of the little, battered looking accordion before starting to squeeze out a simple, scratchy sounding tune. Boulter and Mule poured the cider into everyone's cups and handed them around. Smales stopped playing and downed his in one, then let out a chesty wheeze. "What dew wanna' ear then, boys," he croaked.

"Hares on the Mountains!" piped up the Pearce brothers gleefully.

"Aye, give us a jig!" the other men called out in unison.

So old man Smales began singing and playing the accordion whilst sitting in front of the fire, bathed in the cosy light from the overhead oil lamps and the men took long draughts of cider as they listened. His old and cracked voice sounded vulnerably sweet and tuneful accompanied by the reedy notes which floated out from the breathing music box.

'If all those young men were as hares on the mountains,
Then all those pretty maidens will get guns, go a-hunting,
With ri fol de dee, cal al de day, ri fol idee,'

'If all those young men were as rushes a-growing,
Then all those pretty maidens will get scythes, go a-mowing
With ri fol de dee, cal al de day, ri fol idee,'

As the verses repeated, some of the volunteers joined in whilst the wiry Daniel Pearce danced a grinning jig with the leathery Mule as a partner. Gosfor and Burden clapped along merrily. More cider was poured out from the clay jar and drunk thirstily by everyone. The men smiled and their eyes twinkled through the smoke as the old man's fragile and lilting voice sang around the joyful barrack room atmosphere. Pickles laughed along and thought he heard his name called out by someone.

Behind another one of those windows from the illuminated fort, Arnold England stood in the gloomy light of the kitchen, listening to the sound of song from next door as he washed up, yet again. He was alone and content in the therapeutic qualities that the repetition of this nightly chore afforded him. He could think about life, the universe and everything, his place within it and the meaning of existence. Or he could just think about naked women and getting drunk. Either way, it was a simple hour or two with usually no interruptions, as the rest of the men whiled away the evenings in the barrack room, smoking and talking, drinking tea or tots of grog or even singing and dancing along to another night of Atticus's local drinking songs, as it was on this night. He knew Eves would've already retired to his bunk to get some privacy while the other volunteers sat and led around the main hall listening to the music. The kitchen man could hear the drone from the accordion and the faint croon of the old man's song in the other room interrupted by the odd rattle of wind on the window pane in front of him. The only light in the kitchen came from a large oil lamp strategically placed on the cooker hob affording the washer upper a more relaxing tone of light.

The cook thought about the sly drop of full strength rum that he would enjoy after his chores were finished, instead of the watered down grog and rancid cider that the other men were drinking, and then looked out of the window into the lonely night. In the patches of blackness defining themselves as undergrowth on the dark slopes of the Down, which eternally rose away towards the clouded night sky, he suddenly thought he saw something move.

"What the blazes was that," he muttered to himself, mildly surprised. The cook screwed his eyes up and peered into the murk outside the window trying to focus on the area of suspected movement. There it was again. A gentle shake in the outline of the manky formations that he knew were just the brambles and ferns growing on the rise, but in the darkness were shapes of indistinguishable shadowy masses. He stopped moving his hands in the lukewarm, soapy water. There it was again, something moving. It was bigger than an animal making the bushes move. *'Was it a person?'* he thought.

"What the hell is that? I'm sure I saw something or somebody out there," he said aloud to no one but himself. England leant right up to the glass to try and block out any distraction to his peripheral vision from the room light behind and squinted to concentrate his focus. There was stillness. *'Perhaps it's my mind playing tricks on me,'* his mind counselled.

Cook suddenly spun round in fright, the distinct tingling sensation across his body that someone was behind him, sitting in the chair at the table. He flapped in shock, his wet hands grabbing the edge of the sideboard, the sharp stab of fear in his heart as he expected to see someone there. But all he saw were the shadows in the room and the wavering flickers of light from the oil lamp. His stabbing fear turned in an instant to a feeling of icy coldness that was suddenly all around him, immersing his large frame into a chilly grip. He glimpsed to one side of the cave-like kitchen and thought he noticed the door to the guardroom slowly closing but upon proper inspection realised it was already shut and the movement was just an oppressive, stationary shadow on the wall, flickering slightly in the lamplight. The singing and the floating buzz of music coming from the next room took on a distorted and wavelike effect. He held a breath and his eyes widened as he gradually looked around the room. There was nothing there and, almost as quickly as it had arrived, the extreme coldness he felt faded away. He let the withheld breath inside his lungs out through his dry mouth and the tightness in his chest immediately receded. Cook turned back round and looked through the window into the blackness outside.

He saw another movement, straight ahead. This time it was a definite disturbance in the mingled outline of shadows. There was something out there.

"Pickles!" he shouted. "Go and fetch Mr Eves, I think we got some reprobates and high jinkers outside!"

No one responded.

"Pickles!" Cook called out again

Stanley Pickles heard his name but because of the music he was listening to couldn't catch the rest of the words coming from behind the kitchen door. When he heard his name a second time he finally went over and opened the door, craning his long neck around the frame. He saw cook wiping his hands on a tea towel, an angry look on his round face. Getting a fright had made him testy.

"What's up, Mr England?" the lanky young man asked cautiously.

"Go and get Mr Eves, young 'un. Somebody's outside. I'm gonna 'av a look an' see who it is," the cook said, huffing as he headed through the guardroom to the main gate with the tea towel still in his hands.

He angrily pulled open the unlocked iron railings that barred the main entrance to the fort and strode across the moat bridge into the wide grassy space before the start of the gentle rise up the slope. He stood still, staring menacingly towards the area where he saw the movement, the wind tenderly billowing around his legs and lifting up his apron like a balloon.

"Who's there, yer buggers? You can't fanny about up 'ere! This is army land!" he called out, into the darkness.

Twenty yards away, further up the slope in the gorse and bramble thickets where cook was staring towards, the young French Legionnaire knelt perfectly still with his Lebel bolt action rifle close to his chest. He held his breath, hoping to be silent, only the sound of his own thumping heart in his ribcage and the blood rushing around his cold head hammering inside his ears. He could see the fat man's mouth moving but couldn't understand what he was saying. "Come out! I seen you! I'll give you a bloody good hidin' if you don't show yerself!" the mouth shouted.

England paced up the slope looking about the undergrowth but aimed steadily for the area he was convinced something had been messing about in. As he wandered from the nearest and brightest light source that was the dull outside wall, oil burning lamp, it became increasingly difficult to make out anything in the thick mass of tangled bramble either side of him. Within a few yards he was encased in complete darkness. He reached the area he was aiming for and threw a nervous glance back towards the gates of the fort. No one was there. He looked into the growth.

"What the hell's that?" he grumbled audibly.

The ice man didn't flinch. The damp penetrated his black woollen jumper and his camouflaged face stared straight ahead. The cold made his fingers fizz.

The cook bent forwards to peer into the thorny mess of hedge like covering growing along the edge of the road. The hand with the tea towel dropped to his side.

"Who the blo…."

There was a shocking sound, like a heavy piece of metal hitting a pile of china plates, sharp and startling. Then a sudden, deathly silence once again. Cook wrapped both hands around his throat and stood upright, making a squeaking, gurgling noise. The pupils of his eyes almost rolled into his open eyelids and he wobbled back a few steps, quick, whistling gasps coming from his nose and mouth. Blood filled the tea towel still in his hand, now clamped together with the other one under his chin, and blood began to trickle through his fingers. He turned in the direction of the fort and staggered like a zombie down the hill, still holding his neck, mouth open, facial expression aghast like a pained apparition arisen from the dead. Somewhere in the distance, far away, was the faint sound of popping.

The bushes either side of him remained still. Halfway down the slight descent of grass, just as he reached the ring of light from the wall lamp, cook's big round body swerved ninety degrees and he pitched over onto his back, his pudgy, red stained hands falling away from the wound in his throat as he hit the ground. The red soaked tea towel fell from his fingers. The blood soaked through his clothes and oozed onto the front of his apron. The gurgling noise stopped. The last breathy gasps fell silent.

England was dead.

No one inside the fort heard the gunshot above the continuous sound of song and dance.

"I say!" called the smooth but unusually objective sounding voice of Pontefract as he entered the courtyard on Steep Holm Island. Castille stopped dead. It had been stony quiet as the three Frenchmen walked briskly towards the rowing boat but when the words rang out behind Castille, they had caught him like a well-aimed fish hook. He froze where he stood and immediately regretted it.

"I say! Mr Flowers, hang on a moment!" Pontefract repeated in his public school accent as he caught up with the three men. Castille turned round as Ponty daintily stepped up to him, holding the log book in his hand.

"Um, I'm awfully sorry Mr Flowers but I forgot to take your identification number for the Battery's log." The words tumbled out nervously. "It's just for the paperwork, you understand. I just need to see your papers again. The number should be written along the top. Sorry to be a nuisance," he squeaked.

Castille darted his eyes quickly around the small open courtyard area, assessing the situation as he did so. He noted Acres, now stood a few paces behind Pontefract, looking on with a frown upon his face but remaining quiet. There were four other Artillery men stood within the courtyard and along the parapet of the main walls. The two men on the walls were armed while only one of the two men in the courtyard held a rifle. Neither of the Officer's had a weapon. Castille hid his sudden nervousness with a feigned look of annoyance.

"If you must young man," the fake Major retorted. "But hurry up. We've got a train to catch." He looked at the artisan, stood rigidly beside him, and then threw a signalling glance towards the men behind, stood up in the boat, which still bobbed nauseously alongside the brief jetty. He prayed the other commandos were in position around the fort and then took out his false papers from the inside pocket of his overcoat.

"Oh, well done sir. I am sorry about this," Ponty stuttered, smiling anxiously like an untrained counter clerk in a high street bank as he took the purple coloured document from the visitor. He couldn't write properly holding the log book, i.d card and his pencil so he flapped around for a second or two then clumsily got down on one knee and leant the book on his raised thigh so he could write down the number written along the top of the false document. When he finished, he got up and handed the card back to Castille.

"Um..." Pontefract started to say something then stopped as if he was thinking about it for a moment before continuing anyway. "I say, Mr Flowers, it might be an idea to get your document renewed. It looks to be out of date."

Castille gave the young Officer a look as if the boy had just defecated in front of him and then switched his eyes to the pass and saw that the date stamped on the front was six months out of date. Modesto had been the one who had filled out the false documents only a few hours ago and must have put the wrong date on the stamp by mistake. Castille turned his head and glared at the artisan sourly. Behind the now stretched façade of his pretence he wanted to stab the suave looking commando there and then. Modesto looked away awkwardly.

"Oh yes, so it is. It must have been a cock up in the administration department. I'll sort it out when I get back. Well spotted young man, very good of you," Castille said, pursing his lips with an extra clip, loaded onto his already well clipped English public school accent, before adding quickly, "Anyway, we must get on." He went to turn round again with the still handcuffed Edwin Ralph at his side but before he could walk away towards the boat he was interrupted once more by the sound of a different, much harsher sounding voice than that of Pontefract's.

"Hang on there!" Acres called out sharply.

The three Frenchmen stopped again but stayed facing the waiting boat as Castille and Modesto's hands surreptitiously reached into their deep coat pockets and wrapped fingers around the butts of their respective pistols. The Major walked forward and stood by his Lieutenant as the three spies turned around again to face him, their faces unsmiling and serious.

"Did you say that pass was out of date, Lieutenant," Acres spat casually as he fixed the men in front of him with preying eyes. His inaction had finally been confronted by an arrogant anger. He was revived with a new found sense of determination at revealing the truth behind this situation, wherever it lay.

"Seems to be sir," Pontefract stuttered quietly. There was a tense silence.

"I better take a look at that, Mr Flowers," Acres ordered confidently.

Castille narrowed his eyes at the annoying, birdlike official before him. "I haven't got time for this, Mr Acres. We have got to get that boat and then a train to London. I don't want to miss it. I have to get this suspect back to the war office for a proper interrogation. You are delaying important Government business," he said with a slap of frustration and anger in his voice, spoken through gritted teeth and tensed jaw.

"If I could just take a look at your papers, Mr Flowers, I'm sure you can then be on your way," continued Acres, a hint of a satisfied smile on his lips.

Castille thought about protesting further but decided against it opting instead to moodily hand over the papers to Acres whilst staring at him with a steely fix and waiting to see how the situation might develop. He flashed a quick look at the other men around the courtyard as an escape plan formed in his brain. However, there was still a belief in his mind that they could get away with it.

"This is indeed out of date," said Acres perusing the document. "I must have missed that earlier," he added this bitterly and held the Frenchman's glare with one of his own. He was now convinced something was wrong. "I'm afraid I will have to send a telegram to double check this," he said, the anal attention to detail and his suspicious, mildly psychotic streak finally taking control of his decisions.

"That won't be necessary, Mr Acres," Castille replied, more calmly now. His hand firmly gripped the gun inside his coat.

"I'm afraid it will, Major," said Acres, accentuating the word Major as he turned on his heels and stepped towards the office door.

"That really won't be necessary, Major," Castille said forcefully and he pulled out the pistol from his overcoat. "`A `Present!" he shouted in perfect French.

"It won't take a......." Acres began but trailed off as he stopped walking and recognised the foreign words. Pontefract turned his head and then froze as he saw the pistol emerge from Castilles's coat.

Behind the two armed Englishmen who were stood on the parapet, two shadowy legionnaires emerged from the darkness, rifles held out before them. From the bushes either side of the courtyard four more commandos stepped out of the black shadows and held their rifles on the other soldiers in the open ground, including Acres and Pontefract. Modesto had also pulled his pistol by now and the two men in the boat had drawn their rifles from under a blanket and held them up to their shoulders. The Battery guard near the wall in the courtyard raised his rifle up to his hip and pointed it at Castille, while one of the guards on the wall was quick enough to raise his gun up to his eye and point it down towards the men who had emerged from the bushes around the courtyard. He waved it between the dark figures, nervously. The commandos had refrained from killing the two guards as soon as they had moved because of the direct words from their Colonel at the start of the night. The stand-off was complete.

"Like I said Mr Acres, that won't be necessary. Tell your men to put down their guns," Castille said, breaking the silence. Acres turned round slowly, eyes wide, face distorted with incredulity. "You French bastards," he snarled. "How dare you!"

Pontefract, still holding the log book and pencil in his hand, looked between the two speaking men, an expression of petrified surprise on his boyish face. The wind blew through the courtyard but the collection of soldiers could not hear or feel it, such was the pressing tension upon them all.

"Tell your men to put their guns down Major Acres and no one will get hurt. I want you all to surrender to my men and stand against the wall with your hands above your heads," Castille asked with measured force.

"Bullshit Mr Flowers or whoever the hell you are; I'll do no such thing!" Acres barked angrily back in reply, staring wild eyed at the Frenchman.

"Don't be a hero Major. At the moment I have men all over this island rounding up the rest of your garrison. If you do as you're told no one will get hurt. If you piss about, someone's going to get shot."

"The only person who will get shot is you, you French scum, if you don't give this madness up!" Acres' face shook.

"This madness is beyond your control, Major."

"Parsons!" Acres shouted, twisting his head slightly towards the guard near the wall who was still pointing his gun at Castille, without taking his eyes off the French commander as he did. "Keep that gun on him, whatever happens, or I'll shoot you myself," he ordered the stunned looking soldier. Parsons stared intently at Castille with saucer shaped eyes and kept his gun level with him. There was fear mixed with panic and a strange, wild determination in his face. No one told him this would ever happen in his usually mundane life and he wasn't sure if he was really prepared for it. He didn't know what else to do but follow orders.

"Please Major, don't do this. No one needs to get hurt," said Castille with a tone of pleading in his voice. One of the commando's fingers tightened around his trigger as the charged atmosphere sparkled and pricked his nerves.

"You can't come to my island and threaten me and my men you French bastard," Acres snapped fiercely, pointing a rude finger at Castille. Everyone flinched.

The Colonel's pistol was steady as a rock though, his manner calm and controlled. "Stop calling me a bastard, Major," he said coolly.

"You bastard……"

Crack! Crack! Crack! Castille's pistol jolted once in automatic response to the sound of the other shots. Every French rifle went off as well, hitting targets with trained reaction. The rifles aimed at the Battery guards holding guns went off. Rifles from the sides and in the boat went off. A bullet hit Acres in the forehead. His face jerked back and his eyes stared at the enveloping night sky before his body collapsed to the floor like a dropped suit. Parsons was hit in the face and chest and although he pulled his trigger reactively at the gunfire, his safety catch was still on and the gun made no connection as his body fell back against the stone wall. Up on the parapet the young artillery man with his gun trained nervously on the legionnaires dropped his rifle before he could pull the trigger as a French bullet tore into the side of his head. He fell forward hitting the wall, before tumbling over like a sack of potatoes falling from an open cart, his body landing unceremoniously on the gravel of the courtyard with a dull thud. The other man on the rampart was hit in the back and slumped to the floor while the soldier stood in the courtyard stood still, as if unharmed. The sound of gunfire ebbed away. There was quiet. Even the wind seemed to stop.

In the following stunned silence, the blue tunic wearing young soldier who had not moved, now gracefully and quietly pirouetted where he was standing like a ballet dancer improvising to fill a pause in the music before he fell elegantly to the ground clutching his chest, where only a few seconds ago a bullet had unknowingly entered his heart.

"Oh my God," Pontefract gasped. "No!" he screamed.

His cry filled the air and he whirled around like a lost cat, dropping the note book to the ground. Panic stricken, he turned to run back towards the main building, the sound of gunshots still ringing in his ears. As he did so, the artisan's pistol rang out. The bullet hit the young Officer in the back and forcefully made its way out of his stomach. Pontefract threw his arms out in front of his toppling body as all feeling in his lithe frame gave way and the young man fell to the ground stretched out, reaching for the stone wall as if it were some sort of refuge. His face hit the gritty stones of the gravelly courtyard and he died staring across at the crumpled body of his also expired Major.

'Don't kill anyone, whatever you do, don't kill anyone.'

The words echoed softly through the back of Castille's head as he mournfully looked upon the unintended devastation within the courtyard.

"Oh shit," he whispered.

From the window of his quarters within the walls of Brean Down fort, Harding watched the disturbing events unfolding near the jetty of Steep Holm Island through his gently shaking binoculars. The ghastly theatre was lit up by the gaslights in the courtyard, which acted like spotlights on the unfortunate actors in the harrowing scene played out on an otherwise darkened stage. He saw it all clearly and emotionally like a terrible accident observed by a witness who was powerless to stop it happening. As it occurred through the viewfinders of his eyeglass, a hand gripped the window sill and fingernails gouged into the wood with despair and helplessness. He wanted to call out but was transfixed by the murderous event and could only bite his lip as the flashes of gunfire silently erupted from afar, causing the bodies to fall like upended toy figures. He was shocked, appalled and frightened by the unthinkable happening. The Master Gunner wondered what the hell was going on. In the background he heard the faint, wilting sound of singing.

Pickles leant on the half open iron gates at the entrance to the fort, gawping at the prone body led a few feet away on the thin grass. He could see the growing red patch on the chest area beginning to spread slowly over the ground. "Mr England," he said, soft and unsurely.

The lanky youngster stumbled over to the body, unable to look around; he focused solely on the figure led down. He knelt beside Cook and stared in disbelief at the open eyes and mouth of the dead man's face. Through his terror, Pickles sensed footsteps behind him and swivelled round his long head.

Stood behind him was Zanzibar Eves, flashing watchful glances between the undergrowth ahead and the blood soaked body on the grass. The sergeant had his dark blue artillery tunic on with the brass buttons done up to his chest and a thick grey scarf around his neck. In one hand he held an old looking, well used cricket bat, his weapon of choice when dealing with unwelcome visitors and unruly volunteers. Pickles started whimpering.

"Cook's…Cook's dead," he began to whine serenely.

"Calm down lad," Eves said in a reassuring tone whilst still carefully observing the bushes all around. "What happened son?"

"I....come…out…and 'e was…dead," Pickles sang in a high pitched whisper as his throat dried out with shock.

Eves' thoughts were racing manically behind his expectant blue eyes. He didn't know what had happened but whatever it was he couldn't believe the scene before him was really true. He knew his friend was dead from a gunshot wound to the neck but couldn't comprehend how or why or by whom. As he looked into the darkness, Eves had a feeling that whoever killed Arnold was still out there. He could hear the relaxing sound of the sea as it washed against the rocks and hear and feel the wind as it brushed around the headland but above it all was the siren like whimpers of young Stanley Pickles crouched at his feet. He looked down and realised the lad was going into shock. "Come on son, help me get Cook back inside," and with the soothing words he gently put a hand on the boy's shoulder.

Before either of them could move, Eves' attention was grabbed by the sight of a shadowy figure emerging from the undergrowth onto the road up ahead. The distant human form was barely visible in the faltering, dull glow from the fortresses outside oil lamps. Eves fixed the object with steady eyes and said quietly to Pickles, "Get you inside lad, now."

Pickles caught sight of the ghostly figure on the road. "But……but what about cook," he faltered.

"We'll sort 'im out in a minute, Stanley. Get inside now," Eves said more firmly.

In his distorted state, Pickles was affected by the sergeant's use of his first name more than anything else and he slowly lifted up his long body, stepping backwards as he did so, towards the bridge and the main gates, still unable to take his eyes off the dead body of Mr Arnold England.

"Monsieur, Monsieur!" The voice of Arturo Ben Arfa called out through the black night to the man stood in the pool of light in front of the fort. "We are sorry, Monsieur. This is a terrible accident."

Eves heard the words and mentally acknowledged the figure was French. His instinct told him the man was not alone. "Not bloody likely son! You stay where you are! And tell your friends to stay where they are too!" he bellowed in reply. He began to step backwards, still fixing the figure in the distance with a hard glare, occasionally switching hasty glances to the brambles either side.

"I need to speak to the officer in charge!" Arturo called out. "I have a proposition."

"We'll see about that!" replied Eves as he crossed the bridge, still walking backwards. When he reached the gate Eves dissolved into the shadows which fell across the entrance way and pushed one of the heavy inner wooden doors securing the fort up against the iron railings that fronted them. Lumpy Boulter and James Burden were stood near the door to the guardroom, immobile and dumbfounded while Pickles was leaning against the wall a few feet away with his head in his hands.

"What the bloody 'ells 'appened," said Boulter.

"Arnold's dead," Eves replied, his voice noticeably startled by the words he'd said. "He's been shot. I don't know what's going on, but someone out there has got a gun. And he's French. I can't begin to think what's happening, but whatever it is, break out the rifles Burden and give one to each man. Pickles, pull yourself together lad, and go and get Mr Harding."

While he said all of this, Eves never took his eyes from the Down stretching away from the fort into the darkness beyond and the road leading through it, on which the distant figure was now stood.

Pickles didn't respond to the request he had been given but stayed leant against the wall with his head still in his hands.

"Boulter! Go and get Mr Harding!" Eves snapped.

"It's alright sergeant, I'm here," said a composed voice from the shadows of the yard. Elias emerged wearing his navy blue dock coat, underneath which he wore his pistol belt with his combat sword attached to it, hanging at an angle alongside his thigh. The collars of his coat were turned up to cover his neck from the damp chill of the night.

Everyone stared at him with baited breath waiting for the officer to speak.

"Go on Burden, do as the sergeant says. Give a rifle to every man and share out the ammunition equally. Tell them to unblock the firing loops in all the walls and get Mule and Barnes to keep an eye on the far side of the fort, over by the latrines," he ordered the wily builder unemotionally. He looked across at Pickles now slumped against the wall. The boy's hands had fallen forlornly in front of him, his face staring blankly at the wall opposite. "Boulter, get Pickles inside and get him a drink."

The two instructed men stood dumbly looking at the officer for a second without responding, apprehension etched across their faces.

"Boulter, Burden! Snap to it!" Elias barked. "We could be under attack at any minute and we could all end up like Cook. So pull yourselves together, now!"

"Right oh, Sir," they replied quickly in unison. Burden scurried off towards the armoury housed in one of the magazine rooms near the vacant gun emplacement closest to the toilets, whilst Lumpy grabbed hold of Pickles' tunic and pulled him into the guardroom towards the kitchen.

Harding stepped next to Eves. They both stood in the shadows of the doorway looking out upon the Down with worried eyes. They saw the solitary figure begin to walk towards them. Neither of them spoke or moved.

Ben Arfa walked down the rough military road and stopped just on the edge of the pool of light emitted from the fort. He stood with his hands outstretched as if he were Jesus addressing the disciples on the Mount of Olives. His thick French accent had an entreating tone.

"Please Monsieur, we are sorry about your friend, we did not mean to shoot anyone. We do not want anyone to get hurt. Please, you must believe me, it was an accident."

Harding stepped half out of the doorway into the light. Only one side of his head was illuminated, the rest remained in shadow.

"What the hell's going on? Who the hell are you and what do you want?"

"Are you Mr Harding, Sir? Are you the officer in charge?"

"What's it got to do with you," Elias bit back. "Why did you kill my cook?"

"Please Mr Harding, that was an accident, no one was supposed to get hurt," pleaded Arturo.

"Tell that to the cook, you bastard."

There was silence and Harding noticed the Frenchman's attention drawn to the fortress walls. From two of the firing loops, Martini Henri rifles pointed out towards the legionnaire. "You assholes!" screeched a voice from inside the barracks.

"Calm down! Hold your fire. That's an order!" shouted Elias. Arturo stepped back a little into the darkness.

"Please Mr Harding, you are surrounded. All we want is your co-operation and no one else will get hurt. We are scattered all around. You cannot see us but we can see you. There doesn't have to be anymore shooting. We just want you to surrender. There are more of us than you," Arturo said in a lilting English accent.

"Surrender, like the men on Steep Holm did, before you shot them in cold blood. No bloody chance, you French shits," spat Eli. "You keep your distance or we'll open fire. I think we are in a lot better position than you are. Now piss off before one of my men accidentally shoots you!"

Elias sunk back into the shadows of the gateway and closed the other heavy wooden door as he did so. Ben Arfa stepped backwards, hands still open palmed in front of him until he too was consumed by the darkness. The Frenchman turned and trotted along the side of the road, crouching down by the undergrowth of brambles beside him as he went. When he reached the place he had originally emerged from, he ducked back into the cover behind a couple of short stubby thorn trees. Another legionnaire by the name of Laszlo was hunkered down in the damp, waiting for him. He handed back the small commander's rifle. Ben Arfa watched the walls of the fort.

"Tell the men to keep them pinned down. If anyone steps outside, shoot them. Pass word to the men on the hill to keep them out of the courtyard as well. As long as they're stuck behind those walls there's not a lot they can do."

Ben Arfa opened the bolt of his rifle and clipped it shut again, loading the weapon from the attached magazine. "This Mr Harding isn't going to give up the fort now, not after that fiasco on the island. He knows what happened. I think they're going to put up a fight. If any of them try to escape tell the men to shoot to kill if they have too, otherwise we'll wait to see what Castille wants to do," he said quietly.

"What about the man who shot the cook, do you want me to bring him to you," asked Laszlo.

"No. It doesn't matter now. The idea of no one getting hurt went down the pan when the idiots on that island lost control. Now it's us who are going to face the shit."

Laszlo nodded in agreement and silently slithered away through the bushes to pass the word onto the rest of the men hidden across the hill amid the darkness.

Behind the gates of the fort, Eli leant back against the stonework and breathed deeply. Eves looked at the younger man but remained silent, their faces vaguely lit up by the light from the barrack rooms.

"What happened to England?" asked Harding, his eyes on the gravel around his feet.

"I don't know. Pickles told me Cook said there was someone outside messing around. By the time I got out there he was on the ground, dead. He'd been shot in the throat as far as I could tell." The sergeant's gingery whiskers moved as he scowled.

"God's eyes, they shot Acres and Pontefract, Eves! I saw them. They killed them in cold blood," the words fell from Eli's mouth as he looked into his sergeant's face with disbelief. "There was some sort of stand-off and they just shot everyone, the men on the wall, the officers, all of them. They shot poor old Ponty in the back as he was running away, the bastards. I was only watching because I noticed that little steamer turn up at the island and wondered what was going on." Eli realised he was starting to ramble and tried to compose himself. Eves remained silent but took a look through an eyehole in the large gateway door to check out on the open ground beyond. He looked again on the dead body of his friend on the grass.

"Any movement," Elias asked.

"All quiet," the sergeant replied softly, thinking of his friend.

"I don't know what they've done with the others on the island but they've shot the Officers, which means they won't think twice about shooting all of us as well. This isn't an invasion. There'd be ships all over the channel. They're obviously here for whoever Acres had imprisoned, trying to get him back and keeping us quiet so we don't raise the alarm. Well they're not going to bloody well shoot me in the back, not without a fight," ranted Eli in a strangely over excited but measured way. He swallowed and bent his head round to look through the doorway towards the kitchen. It seemed empty but he could hear the sound of loud talking and the scuffling noise of furniture being moved in the main barrack hall. He turned back towards Eves and took out a cigarette from his metal pocket case, offering one to Eves. The sergeant shook his head and studied Harding as he lit the fag.

"Well Eves?" asked Eli exhaling smoke. "What do you suggest? What are we going to do?"

Eves breathed out his nose heavily and checked through the eye hole again, then fixed the officer in charge with saddened eyes.

"It's difficult to say Mr Harding. If that Frenchie's telling the truth it looks like we're trapped on the end of this bit o'rock. If they done what you say they have on Steep Holm, then they must have got what they came for. It might pay to sit it out, Mr Harding."

"Sit it out Eves," replied Eli, standing up off the wall in dismay. "I didn't think I'd hear that from you," he said belligerently.

"Maybe a few years ago you wouldn't have, Sir. But it seems to me there's not a lot we can do here. I agree, it ain't no invasion, otherwise they'd have attacked us by now and be done with it. So, as far as I can tell if they get what they want they'll disappear into the night and it'll be up to someone else to deal with the consequences."

"Leave it up to someone else, Eves!" Eli said, startled. "Bullshit. We're not bending over to get our asses rammed that easily. I won't let it happen. I haven't come through the shit in a whole new part of the world just to come back home and get my arse kicked again. We've got to get out and raise the alarm." His face became animated and he sucked on his cigarette sharply, quickly blowing the smoke back out as he waited for his sergeant's response.

"If they attack then we'll fight 'em off, if we can, considerin' what we got to defend ourselves with 'ere; a bunch of old men and kids. But I don't want to be responsible for the death of them there volunteers, or meself for that matter, especially with no good reason. There are only fourteen of us, Mr Harding, and apart from me and you, no one's ever been in a fire fight and that makes all of this too one sided in my view," argued Eves.

"I don't care how many of them or us there is Mr Eves, but if they're plan is to subdue us and keep us quiet then at some point they're going to attack and at least capture us. After what I saw on that island I'm more inclined to believe they're going to kill us. Just take a look outside at Mr England and tell me otherwise. We can't let them get away with that." Eli clenched his fist angrily and then took a log thick drag from his cigarette.

Eves looked through the door to the blood stained body of cook and thought about his friend. They had spent many years of their lives together as fellow soldiers, both in times of great danger and deadly threat as well as days full of enjoyment in places of wonder and intrigue. There was also the day to day mundane existence of army life that their banter and camaraderie helped ease and the laughter filled experiences during their times at home. He remembered the sense of loyalty and togetherness that being in the army brought to those within it and for some reason the memory of Bideford came back to Zanzibar. He turned back and connected with the blazing eyes of his officer. "Perhaps you're right," he replied solemnly.

"Damn right Eves. Someone's got to get back to the village and raise the alarm," Harding said with determination.

Eves gave him a serious look which turned into a concerned frown. "That maybe harder than it sounds, Master Harding. They got the whole Down covered most probably. You'd be lucky to get a rabbit through that lot."

"We've got to try." Eli paused. "It's only fair I go; I can't ask one of the lads to do it. If we create a diversion I might be able to sneak through. You lot will be alright in the fort. If you keep the walls covered they'll never get in. If you can hold out here until we get some help from the town, maybe then the French will give up the ghost and do a runner. I could at least send a telegram informing the navy and they could steam a ship out to meet them." Eli tossed his cigarette butt to the floor. Sergeant Eves studied the fiery young man before replying. He could see the determination in his face and the need for action in his agitated movement and wondered if the young man had been drinking.

"You should stay here Mr Harding. You'll be needed if things come to a head. We should talk to the men," he said thoughtfully.

"You're right sergeant. They need to know what's going on."

They both walked into the narrow guardroom and through the empty kitchen to emerge inside the now agitated atmosphere of the barrack room. Gosfor and Daniel Pearce we're stood by firing holes pointing their rifles into the wall as Haines crouched between them peeking over the top of the window sill. At the far end of the room Evans was leaning back against the wall loading a rifle, occasionally grabbing quick glimpses out of the window. Burden was counting out bullets from an open box and handing them to Ford who dished them out to the other men as they stood around talking in fast words about what was going on and their disbelief that England was lying dead outside on the cold, wet ground.

"Put the lights out and cover the fires!" growled Eves. "Keep out of sight, the bastards can see you through the windows like your 'avin a barn dance. You'll get yer 'eads blown off in a minute, and stop yer gossiping."

The men scurried to the sides of the room as old man Smales hobbled over to extinguish the lights and put blinds over the fireplaces. Suddenly the room became hushed and was thrown into gloom, lit only by the oil lamps shining glumly through from the outside walls.

"What about the outside lights Mr Eves, should I turn off the oil," asked Smales.

"No, leave them be. We'll need to see them coming."

"Bloody hell, it's an invasion!" cried Dicky Pearce from his bed.

"I told you it's not an invasion. It's a drill gone wrong, a practice set up by that shit, Acres," Haines snapped back, his normally soft voice taught with panic.

"A practice my arse! They're firing real bullets. If this is a practice I'm not bloody impressed, someone could get hurt," whined Smales.

"They shot Cook you idiot! Don't you understand? England's dead!" Pickles shouted out in anger. He was sat on a bunk pushed against the wall underneath the crooked print of Queen Victoria. Lumpy Boulter laid a hand on his shoulder to calm him down and took a swig from the tumbler of rum he was holding.

"Alright lads, settle down," Harding said, trying to reassure the stretched incomprehension of the men in the room. "Sergeant, check on the men outside." Eves carefully walked away through the door to the corridor by his room and Harding casually took his pistol from his belt and checked it was loaded.

"This isn't a practice, men, and I don't think it's an invasion, otherwise we'd see the whole French navy out there. But whoever's outside they're here to keep us quiet and maybe even capture us. They've killed Major Acres, Lieutenant Pontefract and several of the men on the island, so as far as I'm concerned we could be next." There was an audible gasp from everyone. "We can safely say they've captured the Battery on Steep Holm, which means we're on our own. It's got something to do with a prisoner Acres has had, but apart from that I don't know why this is happening to us, but I do know that for them to get away with this they have to take us over and deal with us in some way and I'm not going to let them take this fort without a fight."

He stopped and looked about the faces of his men watching for signs of discontent. They were silent, eyes full of fear. Harding put the pistol back in its holster. "I believe we're all in great danger and that we have to protect ourselves. We also can't let these frogs get away with the murder they've committed." The fire returned to Eli's eyes.

"Damn right, Sir. England was a good cook," snarled Gosfor, full of cockney menace and local Somerset cider.

"Don't be daft, we should give up. They said no one would get hurt if we all give up," bleated Aldous Haines in return.

"Bollocks," spat Burden still counting out the rounds.

"Giving up isn't an option," Eli said respectively. He was considerate of the fear these men must be feeling now. It was a fear he felt too.

Eves stepped back into the shadow filled main room holding a rifle. He swayed back from the window and screwed a bayonet into the top of the barrel. He was wearing his brown leather webbing belt with ammunition pouches and a holster with a pistol inside.

"Mule and Barnes are covering the far wall. They got a clear view on that side of the hill and will start shootin' if any of 'em comes that way," he said commandingly. "Get your webbing pouches on boy's. You might need a bayonet before the nights out."

"You're jokin' int you," said Dicky Pearce from his bed, as the other men reached for their pouches and nervously began to put them on while exchanging desperate glances. Harding saw the trepidation and insecurity on their faces as they moved.

"I know you can't believe what's happening here men, nor do I. But it is happening and we have to deal with it. If you stick together and stay alert you might get through this without getting hurt. Eves and I will help you all we can, but you have to be strong and you have to be tough. Do you understand? We can get through this," Eli said assuredly.

"How?" came the stark, solitary reply from within the darkened room. It came from Pickles, now stood up, a rifle in his hand and a pouch of ammo over his bony shoulder. "I ain't never done nothin' like this before," he added shakily.

After a short, thought filled silence, Harding spoke again. "It's alright Pickles, you're going to be alright," he reassured him. "Somebody has to raise the alarm, get help. We need some support from the village, the town, anywhere. If they see the outside world is aware of them, even if it's just some armed police, they may just leave us alone and make their escape."

"Send a few flares up; it might make Lavernock or the town think something odd is going on. Anyway, won't someone hear the shooting," suggested Boulter.

"I doubt it Lumpy," said Eves. "They'll probably think we're doing manoeuvres, or that its practice flares. They might not turn up until the morning, even if they did think it were dodgy."

"Acres let everybody know we would be doing a night fire practice; they might not respond at all. We have to get to the village to raise the alarm now," warned Eli. Everyone looked at each other uncomfortably.

"That's why I'm going to make a break for it, while you hold down the fort." Elias added. It suddenly occurred to Eli that his plan sounded like he was trying to run out on the men. The men cast each other more worried looks. Gosfor looked incongruous.

"No chance Mr Harding, you can't do a runner on us now, we need you here," the Londoner protested.

"I'm not going to ask anyone else to do it, Gosfor. The French could be all over the peninsular, hiding. It's going to be difficult and dangerous with a high percentage of failure, so I should go," argued the officer. He and Eves exchanged knowing glances and Eves raised his eyebrows to the Master Gunner in an 'I told you so' manner.

"I'll go," said a voice from the corner of the room. Evans stepped away from the wall, gun in hand, his unshaven stubble mingling with his dark eyes and everyone's head turned in his direction. "I can climb over the wall by No.1-gun placement. That side of the Down is grassy and open, no one's hiding there. If they are, Mule and Barnes can see them and keep them busy. I can move along the rocks near the bottom, then cross the grass up to the top so I can go over the Down and into Uphill. I'll use the ridges and hillocks to hide in. I know this place like the back of my hand, they won't even see me." He stood and waited for the response, hard faced and moody.

"I'll go too," piped up Ezekiel Ford, sat on his chair near the covered fire.

"Not with me you won't," Evans spat back.

"Don't worry Evans I don't want to hang around with you. Someone should try and get to Lanes farm and use one of his horses to get to town over the fields. It'll be a lot quicker than running." Ford's mind had been secretly mulling over the prospect that staying in the fort was going to be a bad idea. This was a good chance to escape.

"I'll go as well," Pickles said loudly, stepping forward.

"Hang on a minute Stanley, we're getting a bit thin on the ground 'ere now," butted in Burden, getting concerned.

"Maybe, but the way I see it, the more of us runnin' around out there keepin' them occupied the less chance they got of attacking this place. They 'aven't got long if they wanna get away before the tide goes out, if they chase us they'll lose time, if they don't we'll get through." The lanky youth stood even taller as his confidence grew and the vision of cook's dead face faded with the thought of revenge.

"You got a point there, big lad," agreed Grayard Evans.

"I can't ask you to do this, lads. It's too dangerous," Eli tried to argue but was interrupted.

"Sir, with all due respect, I don't think you know your way across the Down like I do. Or Fordy and Pickles for that matter," Evans said. "If they do attack, you'd be a lot more use and save a lot more lives being here than falling off a cliff out there. Let me and the others try to get the help. We'll be alright."

"You got to admit he's right, Sir," said Eves. "You're needed here and there's a better chance of raising the alarm with three of them going different ways." Some of the men nodded while others stood staring, faces full of shock.

"But I…can't expect…." Eli's words began to fail him. The show of bravery from the small group of volunteers had staggered him and confused his previously stoic resolve. This bunch of jaded humanity, this flock of beaten lives, enslaved and tethered by the spirit sapping yoke of unrewarding work and unfulfilled hope had suddenly arisen before him like worthy comrades of undeterred hope. None of these men had ever seen action and he knew they were all scared but the situation had galvanised their souls. Pride swelled within his affections for this group of apparent no-hopers and he felt uncomfortably humble. The obscure thought entered his mind that they were invincible and that none of them could possibly get hurt. They seemed so confident suddenly. He didn't know they'd all had a gutful of cider and that some of them were on the verge of being drunk. Perhaps it was the alcohol that had given both he, and them, the balls to fight. Or perhaps not, perhaps the situation had sobered everyone up and this was genuine fearlessness.

"Mr Harding, I can't believe this is actually happening to us but if it is, I think we'd stand a better chance with less of them attacking us, even if we are three men down," Boulter said responsively.

Eli thought about the idea and bit his lip, rubbing his fingers into the palm of his hands as if it would help his jilted decision making. He knew it was a good plan, helping to split up the attacking force, dissecting the enemy. It was one of the first tactics you learnt at training, although he could see on the faces of a select few that they didn't like the idea of losing nearly a quarter of the defenders.

"This is madness," squealed Haines as if on cue.

"Shut it, Scribbler!" bawled Gosfor.

"Maybe we should just talk to them, Mr Harding," croaked Smales from the corner. "This could be some sort of mistake; they might just let us be."

"Talking didn't do Acres any good. I'm not taking that risk," replied Eli darkly.

"Maybe we should organise that diversion, Mr Harding, so the lads can get going, and get the men in position," suggested Eves. The sergeant knew the diversion and escape might be the forts best chance of success but was growing concerned that the fort wasn't yet even prepared for an attack.

"Yes, you're right," Harding said finally as he visibly emboldened and sprang into relevant action. "Smales, Danny," he ordered, "Get over to my quarters and man the office and parlour windows and firing loops. Lock the hatch over the landing slipway and keep an eye on it so they don't get in that way. Richard get over to that firing loop and cover the open ground with Gosfor and Haines in here. How many rounds has each man got, Burden?" he asked.

Burden looked a little worried. "We only got one case of four hundred and a few packs of loose. There's about thirty per man."

"That'll have to do then lads, don't waste them," Eli said looking at the men in turn. "Eves get the three runners ready on the far wall, and Boulter," he said pointing to the fat man, "You and Burden come with me."

"What we doin'," Lumpy enquired swapping concerned looks with the part time builder nearby.

Eli looked around the room and then pointed to the corner of the barracks near the map hanging on the wall. "We're going to blow that bloody ship up," he said, smiling triumphantly.

Inside the walls of the rooms and above those rooms on the parapets around the gun emplacements of Steep Holm Island, the remaining French soldiers, who had positioned themselves strategically at various points, rounded up the other inhabitants. The volunteers were not aware of what had happened in the courtyard and were easily subdued at the point of a foreign rifle. Everyone had heard the staccato gunfire outside but the legionnaires remained calm and did not begin firing randomly at their other prisoners.

Unknown to most people, the spending cuts at the War Office had hit Steep Holm too. There were only twenty-four men working on the island at the time, less than half its normal deployment, and six of them were now dead. Castille had the rest divided into three groups and locked inside three different rooms within the fortress walls. Their hands and feet were bound and tied to their necks and they were all threatened with death if they tried to escape. The doors to these prisons were locked and barricaded with furniture and double stacked piles of heavy ammunition boxes. The volunteers had no Sergeant Eves among them, no resourceful or willing characters ready to endanger their lives for the sake of seemingly pointless heroism. They went like sheep to a pen, herded by fierce wolves.

Before they left, the commandos destroyed the telegraph machine and threw the rocket flares into the brown sea. They sank all the boats on the island, including Edwin Ralph's yacht and used their fishing skiff and the rowing boat to take everyone back to the steamer. The animal like pack had captured the unprepared island with relative ease, apart from a few unfortunate deaths, and left with the prey they were seeking unharmed.

When Castille got back to the ship he told the Captain to head for the peninsular of Brean Down and weigh anchor just off shore so they could pick up Ben Arfa and his men after they'd overcome the fort there. They had two hours before the tide would turn and make it difficult for 'The Small Fish' to reach deep water in the channel and make their escape back to France. As the steamer set off, making the wide turn for the headland, Castille looked anxiously towards the blackened rocks, rimmed with white spittle from the churning tides merging around them. He saw the dim lights of the fortress perched above, and whilst praying to a God he never believed in, hoped that no one there would end up dead tonight.

Elias, Boulter and Burden crouched on their haunches hiding in the shadow of the wall outside the door to Eli's quarters. The two volunteer gunners had put on their black dress trousers to mingle in more easily with the darkness around the gun emplacements. Harding had removed his sword to make movement easier and now looked into the pensive faces of the other two men while he whispered his instructions.

"Right boys, I'll creep round the wall to the magazine room, unlock the door and get a couple of shells and some powder. When I'm done you two come round and without making a song and dance about it load and prime the weapon. Boulter you load and Burden, you powder and prime it. I'll set the elevation and fix the firing pin. Hopefully, in the dark they won't see what we're doing until the gun goes off and then they'll probably start shooting, so we'll have to play it by ear after that. Until then keep it slow and steady, Eves and the others are going to fire into the bushes to keep their attention but the less fuss we make the better, until she goes pop, of course," he smiled without realising it.

Harding had the strangest sensation that he was beginning to enjoy what was happening. He couldn't quite believe it because after what he had seen happen on the island he realised that they were all in great danger. But the anger, disbelief and fear from earlier had faded. Even with the death of Mr England there was a feeling that this wasn't as bad as it seemed and that it was all too bizarre an event for anyone else to get hurt. There was a sense inside his mind that this couldn't be real. 'French soldiers on British soil attacking this shitty fort! Someone's having a laugh!' his brain rattled. It all felt like a game.

But people had been killed. He'd seen it and they could be next, so reality couldn't be denied. Perhaps, he realised, after what he'd experienced in Afghanistan, the prospect of some real action and endangerment, which without doubt this was, could be the only thing that made him feel really alive and responsive. He hoped this wasn't the case but he knew it happened to a lot of men who had seen conflict. There was no denying he was excited and enthused by these events. He gave the other two men a confident nod and began creeping along the parapet.

On the other side of the fort, crouched behind the chest high wall, Eves waited with Evans, Ford and Pickles. They too had changed into dark dress trousers and had smeared their faces with charcoal dust from the fire to camouflage their, cold, white skin. They had rifles slung across their backs and the pockets of their tunics held a handful of bullets. After the bravado of earlier, their expressions betrayed apprehension and fear, apart from Evans whose stony jaw merely tensed with steeled preparation. Eves whispered instinctively.

"Get ready lads, when Mr Harding fires the first shell and the boys in the barracks start firing make your way over. We'll keep them pinned down from here." He nodded to Barnes and Mule who raised their rifles over the wall and aimed towards the bushes on the slope. They couldn't see where the French were but once they started firing back they might be able to see the smoke from their barrels. Everyone waited.

Eli reached the heavy door to the magazine room and carefully unlocked it while still crouched down. He opened it a few inches and slithered inside the abyss. He felt his way along the covered walls, blind in the pitch darkness like a mole in the depths of the underworld until he came to the main room and the shell boxes in the corner. Cautiously he picked out a shell and headed back to the door holding it in both hands, concentrating on not scuffing his clothes and gun belt against any surfaces. He then carefully placed it near the slightly ajar door. He went back and did the same with another shell and then returned to the dank hole to get a barrel of gunpowder and some primers, by which time Boulter and Burden were waiting outside trying to hide themselves in the darkened angles and undefined cover of the new gun, still covered with its green tarpaulin.

Suddenly shots rang out from the walls of the main hall, the kitchen and the officer's quarters. One, then two more followed by a series of single shots in between short pauses of measured regularity, which seemed to make the gunfire snap loudly through the damp air. Barnes and Mule joined in and the bushes up on the hill across the moat made little twitches as the bullets hit. Eves raised his elegant eyebrows at Evans and twitched his moustache. "Wait for it," he said.

Boulter and Burden hastily took the ammunition over to the forts original, uncovered gun and began the process of loading and priming it, desperate not to make their actions any more noticeable than they possibly could be, considering the amount of movement loading a large piece of artillery required. Boulter cleaned out the barrel using a plunging rod, pushed in the cartridge of gunpowder and rammed it home, making the awkward motions as gentle as possible to avoid noise and disturbance. He moved like a cleaning lady trying to mop a floor in the middle of the night without waking the house up. Burden primed the chamber and flinched nervously every time a shot rang out from the barrack room walls. Stray shots from returning fire clattered into the stones of the courtyard but the three artillery men realised they hadn't been noticed yet and were emboldened enough to work faster.

Harding crept round to the elevation controls and using his eye, knowledge, the lights from the deck of the steamship and a bit of luck he set the trajectory, hoping to land the shell somewhere near the target. After his comment in the hall about blowing the ship up, he now realised that the destruction of their escape vessel might force the French to even more desperate measures, so he decided to send a warning shot and hope the distraction would be enough to aid the escape of the runners from the fort. He could see the lights on the ship move and heard the faint sound of her engine. She was moving.

"Ready Sir," hissed Burden as Boulter got on the floor and crept along the wall. Eli had set the lanyard connected to the firing pin and the two men traversed the gun around on its carriage a few inches in line with the lights out to sea.

"Watch out boys, here she blows," whispered Harding, and he pulled the lanyard.

KA BOOM! That was the sound she made, big and loud! The end of the gun erupted and there was a blinding flash as the explosion lit up the darkness around the three men. The sound of thunder ripped the air apart and the seven-inch calibre, rifled, muzzle loading cannon jerked angrily.

"Let's get another one off," Eli said excitedly as he looked out to sea and saw a great splash of cascading water only a few yards from the bow of the ship. He fancied blowing the whole thing up, just for the sight of it.

On the other side of the fort Eves heard the cannon explode and gave Evans a staunch look. "Go," he spat.

The three young men climbed up onto the parapet, near where the goat had earlier stood to admire the view, and keeping low to the wall, rolled over onto the grass and slid down towards the rocks a few feet below, out of sight from any Frenchmen hidden in the bushes on top of the Down. Ford and Pickles followed behind Evans, as he swiftly hopped over the sodden rocks, bracing his body with an outstretched hand and hugging the lower edge of the promontory as the sea icily licked and splashed the waterline below their feet. They crossed the gap near the end of the moat and angled their way upwards towards the grass covered rock face near the bottom of the rising hill. Shots continued to ring out from the fortress walls and returning fire rattled in the void between. The firers inside the walls flinched and hid their faces as bullets ricocheted against the stonework. The silence of the night was shattered by the sound of staccato cracks and pings of bullet brass on dusted mineral.

Around the artillerymen loading the cannon in the courtyard, bullets suddenly started to whizz between them. French rounds dinged off the walls and thudded into the grass lined tops. Some hit the gun and rebounded into the gravel and the concrete plinth. The exploding gun had lit up their position and the French legionnaires on the hillside had directed their fire towards the flashback.

"Bollocks!" shouted Burden as he tried to prime the gun again.

"Get in cover!" called out Harding and he ducked his head down while moving round the barrel side of the gun to try and better cover his body. "Move!" he shouted to Boulter, who was still trying to drop the next shell down the muzzle.

"But I've nearly done…." Lumpy began, but was cut short as a stray bullet caught him in the eye. His head became quite still apart from the nape of his neck which fell open with a splatter of blood as the bullet exited and lodged in the wall below, slowed considerably by its journey and change of course through Lumpy's wide head. Silently, Boulter swayed back an inch and hung there for a moment as the shell he had been holding slid down the barrel of the cannon and hit the cartridge below with a soft thud. Then with slow inevitability, his large, round frame tipped over to one side and he crashed to the ground against the parapet wall.

Burden scampered along the courtyard to the cover of the officer's quarters and sat back, pushing his body against the stonework as the bullets clattered all around the gun emplacement. He began staring with a terrified face at the body of Boulter. Elias covered his own head with his arms and tucked his frame into the carriage of the gun, underneath the thick barrel and out of the open air beyond. He glanced at the one open eye and the neat red wound where the other should have been in the face of the man on the floor and immediately felt utterly ashamed and powerless. He slunk back into the shelter of the carriage and wrapped his arms around his knees like a child who had just been told off. Closing his eyes, Eli's mind cast him back to the dustbowl of Maiwand and the time he curled into a ball by the carriage of another gun as the shells exploded venomously around him in a previous battle. Here, in a different time and place there were only rifle rounds tearing up the epoch but in his mind they were as deadly and destructive as a body shredding bomb. He hid away from them, wrapped in his self-contained ball of ignorance, his mind induced with a traumatic confusion.

Meanwhile, the three runners had climbed up and now led belly down on the grass above the rocks, hidden by a soft ridge which undulated along the contour of the Down. Before them was a stretch of open ground twenty to thirty yards away from the edge of the brambles and tufts of undergrowth near the summit of the hillside where the French were hiding. They would have to run, at a crouch, along the side of this open ground to reach the top of the rocks on the next section and then use the dips and wave like hillocks and rock strewn outcrops further on to go their separate ways and make their various escapes.

Eves could just see them hugging the ridge waiting for their chance. The sergeant motioned to Mule a couple of feet away and pointed towards the edge of the bushes. Mule nodded and the two riflemen aimed and laid down a blanket of fire across the bushes. As one fired, the other would load and the regular fizzing sound of bullets rushing through the foliage drifted down to the three hiding runners.

Evans made a run for it first. Head down, back arched, he strode like a bolting ostrich along the ridge. Shots fired out from the line of bushes and whizzed above his craned neck. Ten yards, twenty. He reached the protection of a patch of rock jutting out from the hillside and hid, panting in the wet wind, inside the safety of a crevice.

Ford swallowed hard and took a chance, bounding at speed after his comrade. He was smaller than Evans and his shadowy form glided along the edge of ground barely breaking the surface. More shots rang out and two tufts of grass upturned as bullets carved divots in the moist covering near his fast moving feet. This time dark outlines of human heads and chests connected to arms and the slender black barrels of guns raised themselves up out of the sinister bushes to get a better aim at the escaping runners. Pickles didn't notice them, concentrating instead on the running line as he saw Ford make the safety of the overhang. He went to go but a bullet whizzed across his path as the French attackers saw where the runners had come from and the tall youth halted and threw his long body to the ground once again.

Mule and Eves aimed for the shadows popping out of the bushes. In the protrusion of rock Evans pulled the rifle off his back and aimed across the open ground towards the shooters. One of them ducked as the covering fire rustled the bushes and cut the air around him. The other shadow fired at the crevice and Evans ducked back. Pickles whimpered and sprang up to make another run but the bushes shook in the darkness as he did and another bullet whizzed towards him. Down he went again, unharmed but increasingly panic filled as he realised he was stuck.

Mule saw a puff of smoke billowing lightly from the dark mass of undergrowth as Pickles hit the ground. "I'll shoot that oily French tick in the bloody head," he said bitterly. His gun coughed and the low calibre bullet rifled through the air quietly towards the smoke. It hit the oily tick in the head and the shadow died almost instantly. For a split second the round gored its way through his bloody mind before messily spitting outward through his temple. Silent and unknowing the end was controlled like an unwanted animal being culled.

"Gotcha!" Mule hooped, grinning widely. Evans and Eves fired at the other raised form in the bush and it slunk back into the mass under the whistling barrage. Ford beckoned frantically to Pickles and the young lad went for it, loping awkwardly along the ridge as shots rang out from everywhere until he safely reached the others.

"Right, let's get out of 'ere while the goings good," Ezekiel puffed furtively as he watched the bushes. Evans nodded and the three runners bolted away from the jut of stone towards the top of the hill using the fall and rise of the slope as cover.

Behind the wall, Eves stopped firing and checked his ammunition. Unlike the volunteers, the wily sergeant always kept his pouches full. It was a habit garnered from years of frontline action reducing the possibility of getting caught short in a fire fight. He also kept a stash in his bunk room, just in case of emergencies, and the thought entered his mind as a bullet flew overhead that he never expected to end up in an emergency situation here on Brean Down. He still had two full pouches on his belt. So he sidled along the wall, keeping his head down, towards the kneeling figure of Robert Barnes, the admin expert and reluctant warrior.

"How many rounds you got left, Barnes," he asked.

"Not many, Mr Eves, ten at the most."

"Have these, son. I'll get some more." Eves dropped a handful by the young man's knee and then went over to Mule, who was picking targets with more care than the youngster.

"Take these, Mule. I'm gonna check on the boys inside," the sergeant said and dropped some bullets into Mule's open hand.

"Right oh, Sir," the leathery old workhorse rasped still buzzing from the feeling of his first kill. It was a sensation he never thought he would have, or even wanted, but it had transformed him into a fighting man with a thirst for blood.

Zanzibar stayed low to the floor and went through the half open door into the gloomy corridor of the barrack rooms. He stood upright in the hallway and arched his back, which had started to ache from the constant crouching, and rubbed the lower part as he moved. He went into his sparsely furnished room and pulled open the cupboard by the bed, thrusting a hand inside to the box of cartridges at the back. After refilling his pouches, he strode into the main room and stood with his back against the wall as he looked around. Pearce was sat on his bed, a rifle muzzle through a firing loop in the wall as he loaded another cartridge into the breech of his Martini Henry rifle. Further down, George Gosfor had smashed a square of glass out of the window and was shooting down towards the bushes near the main gate.

"Alright in here are you, boys?" Eves said with a low but sonorous voice. Pearce jumped in fright.

"Bloody 'ell, Sarge!" he cried. "You frightened the life out of me."

"Mr Eves! The toe rags are trying to get to the main gate!" the Londoner at the window screeched. "They're coming along the side of the road, lettin' the boys in Mr 'Ardin's room 'av it," he said, reloading and loosing off a shot as he spoke.

Eves got on all fours as two shots smashed through one of the windows and hit the plaster on the opposite wall. He put a handful of cartridges on Pearce's bed. "There's some more shells, lad," he said crawling on towards Gosfor.

"I can't see bugger all through this 'ole," Dicky replied, trying to get the best view through the two inch slit.

"Just keep 'em back, lad," Eves said. He got behind Gosfor and looked over his shoulder out of the grimy window into the pool of light outside. He could see several dark clad figures crouched beside small bits of cover shooting then moving forward a few steps as they reloaded. There was the sound of braking glass and the pool of light evaporated as a French round disintegrated the outside light source.

"They're heading for the officer's quarters and underneath the bridge. Keep pluggin' away, lads. I'll head over that way. Where's Haines?" the sergeant shouted above the gunfire. He tapped the Londoner on his shoulder and pushed a handful of bullets into his hand. Another bullet splintered the glass in Gosfor's window, showering the two men in shards and then fizzed across the room, hitting the picture of Queen Victoria and sending it to the floor where it broke.

"That'll teach 'er," Gosfor joked, putting the ammunition into his nearly empty leather pouch, his eyes wide with adrenaline and cider. "Haines is in the kitchen, unless he's done a runner!"

Eves ducked to the floor and crawled over to the kitchen door. Inside the kitchen, Haines was sheltering under the sink area as bullets thudded into the stonework around the window.

"What the hell are you doing Haines?" Eves bawled at the shivering scribbler.

"They're coming, Sergeant! They're coming!" Haines cried in terror.

Outside in the courtyard, Harding and Burden stayed hidden in their separate areas of protection from the hail of missiles bouncing off the surfaces around them. Elias tried to think of some music that would help ease his twisted mind and wrest back some control from the fear and chaos cascading like torrents of water through his terrified head. But there was no music, only the sound of bullets zipping in the air and the explosions and nerve bending screams echoing through his mind from a distant battle fought long ago yet still fresh in his memory. He was having a nasty turn.

Then from somewhere, deep in the back of this untidy mental wardrobe, Eli started counting. He murmured the numbered words as they forced themselves into his consciousness. "One, one hundred, two, one hundred, three, one hundred," he mumbled with his eyes closed. The visions of the past began to fade from his mind and slowly the chaos and fear of the present began to replace them but also subside enough for the foundations of his psyche to fasten and his senses start to regain control once more. As he counted, a new energy pulsed against the palpitations of fear within him, converting it into a feeling of excitement and anger and releasing a coiled expression of sensuous unpredictability and steely determination. He opened his eyes and stopped counting, gritted his teeth and made ready to move. But whenever Eli tried to jump from the crevice of his gun carriage, a shot would slice across his bows making him withdraw back into his hole like a mouse stalked by the paws of a waiting cat. Several times he screamed at Burden to get inside, but the figure stayed frozen in the corner, his body jolting with each shot that landed noisily about him, his shocked face gazing wide eyed at Lumpy Boulter's prone, spent body.

In the next few seconds Harding got the sense that the shower of bullets had eased slightly as though some of the shooters on the hill had moved out of range. He pulled his pistol and cocked it, the thought in his mind that it was time to make a run for the door. Tensing his body and preparing his legs for the sudden spring, he ejected forward throwing his rising frame across the front of Boulters dead carcass and lunging for the cover of the wall of his quarters. He heard shots but felt no impact until he hit the stones at the foot of the wall and immediately scurried like a flailing spider along the bottom until he got to the unmoving Burden still sat by the door. Crouching down, Eli grabbed the coat of the shocked builder and tried to pull him upright so he could drag him through the open doorway.

"Come on James, get up!" Eli shouted in the sitting man's face. He suddenly had a flashback as he remembered Gunner Williams screaming in his own face in a similar situation, years ago on a foreign battlefield under a burning sun. "Get up!" he repeated.

As he struggled to dislodge Burden, Elias noticed that the man raised a hand and pointed towards the area where Lumpy was led and began to call out incomprehensively.

"He's dead James! He's dead, there's nothing we can do, come on, we've got to get inside and help the others!" Elias shouted.

Burden continued to point and then tried to scramble upright, babbling through the sound of the gunfire. "There…there's…there's one of them!" he wailed.

Harding spun round catching sight of a black faced head rising up over the wall, a pistol in one hand as his other held on to the ladder which came up the outside wall from the landing slip below. Eli instinctively levelled his pistol and fired. The gun coughed, spurting sparks from its barrel and the shot hit the Frenchman in the mouth. He leant back and then disappeared behind the wall. Eli ran over to the ladder, pistol at the ready, and tentatively peered over. The man he shot had landed on another man at the bottom of the ladder who was pushing the dead man's body to one side trying at the same time to grab his fallen rifle from the rocks. Eli leant over the top of the wall and aimed his pistol at the struggling figure, firing twice. There was an audible groan and the man toppled over into the water. Eli caught sight of a light source coming from the hatchway over the rocks but couldn't see any more men.

"Shit, they're getting in!" he shouted and turned to Burden whilst stooping over to grab Boulters rifle which had been lying on the gravel the whole time. “Keep an eye on that ladder, Burden. Shoot anyone who comes over that wall!” he shouted, unsure whether the instruction had been understood but pushing the rifle into Burdens jelly like hands regardless. He then headed through the door to his quarters leaving the builder outside, nodding his head dumbly while gazing in a sort of stupor at the top of the ladder.

Harding stood in the dark space of his crappily furnished lounge. Inside the quarters the fireplace was cold and dead as the smell of ash and smoke permeated the obscurity. From the other internal door, he could see faint light from the hatchway room creeping along the corridor. He bolted to the doorway throwing his head quickly round the frame and then pulling it back in, just as quickly. He had seen the half open door to the room containing the hatch and the light on inside but didn’t notice the almost closed door to the office room opposite.

In a rush of blood to his head, Eli darted down the corridor to the room at the end, not thinking to check the other rooms as he went. When he reached the door he kicked it open, his pistol at the ready and in the hazy yellow glow of the candlelit room he saw a French commando helping another man up through the opening in the floor. As he came to a halt the two men looked at him in surprise and Eli shot the man stood over the hatch in the chest, destroying the man’s heart. The force of the bullet threw the commando to one side and he let go of his partner, who immediately fell back down the hatch, while the intruder Eli had shot hit the floor of the room, dead.

As the other legionnaire fell through the hatch, his chin caught the outside edge of the opening, snapping his head back and breaking his neck. He was instantly paralysed which thankfully meant he didn’t feel his legs breaking as they hit the rocks at the bottom, nearly twenty feet below. His bones splintered into dozens of knife like shards which broke through into the flesh and muscle around them and in some cases tore outwards through his skin like exploded pieces of jagged white wood. His broken neck also meant he didn’t feel his back break in four different places as his torso impacted on the concrete landing plinth which was formed between the jagged rocks. He was still alive as he lay there at rest, his body bent and snapped upon itself in unsightly and incomprehensible angles while his still seeing eyes looked up towards the hatch he had fallen through with an expression on his face similar to one of someone who had just been made redundant, which in a way he had. Harding looked down at him and felt sick.

Stepping back from the hatchway, Elias swallowed down the sick feeling with a sense of relief at still being alive. He quickly looked to the door checking for movement and then picked up the lid of the floor opening and swung it over, kicking the bar which held it down across the top into the fastenings either side before clipping them shut and thus securing the hatchway.

He heard scuffling sounds and a stifled yelp from somewhere down the corridor and stepped towards the doorway. As he did so he was suddenly confronted by the sight of another French soldier dressed in dark blue clothing, wearing a woollen cap and holding a rifle pointed his way. Harding instinctively brought his pistol up and fired towards the figure, not really knowing which part of the body he was aiming at and tensing his own body in preparation, waiting for the return shot to hit him somewhere.

He heard the rifle firing but instead the bullet embedded itself into the plaster of the wall near his stomach. Eli threw his body around the corner back inside the hatchway room and used his foot to flip the door closed. As he did this he saw the French man fold himself backwards into the office room from where he had originally emerged. Harding wondered what the fate of Smales and Pearce had been and how the commandos had got into the quarters. He was annoyed at himself for not checking earlier that the slipway was secure and for not even looking in the other rooms before confronting the intruders.

Now he felt trapped. He didn't know what to do and he flapped about for a moment in a panic, listening intently and glancing chaotically around the room as the idea entered his mind that he should just charge out firing blindly. He realised that would be foolhardy. He saw the closed lid of the hatch and then heard the crack of a rifle shot echoing through the confined corridor and another bullet embedding itself in the plaster outside just above the door, not far from his own face, showering him in dust and bits of plaster through the crack in the doorway. He leant back against the wall, put the barrel of the pistol through the gap in the door and let off a round, then darted to the hatchway, unclipped the latches and noisily kicked the bar out. It made a loud clattering sound as it skidded along the concrete floor and then Eli pulled the hatch open again, catching sight of the still living but totally unfeeling man smashed on the rocks below. Harding swooned backwards into the corner of the room grabbing the door handle as he did and giving it the slightest of tugs, allowing it to slowly open fully. He leant back against the corner of the room, pistol at the ready, hiding in the shadows, as the door creaked towards him.

There was silence for a moment. He gulped and tried to keep perfectly still. He heard another rifle shot and this time a bullet whizzed through the open door and hit the concrete wall on the far side. More silence, then light footsteps, the slow and deliberately faint steps of a man approaching the room. The wind howled ghostlike, whistling up through the hatchway but Harding couldn't hear it. All he could hear was the sound of blood coursing through his head and the feeling that his chest was rising and falling heavily as he desperately tried to control his breathing. There was a sensation of gentle shaking as if he was cold and then he saw the shadows in the room change as the figure came inside and headed straight for the open hatch. Looking down, the man caught sight of his comrade led bent and awkward upon the stone below. Harding had expected the Frenchmen to at least check behind the door and had been ready to fire when he did. Swiftly and silently he stepped to one side levelling his pistol at the head of the commando. He squeezed the trigger and breathed the words aloud, "You simple bastard."

The gunshot rang out in the tiny room echoing around the thick walls. The bullet sliced through the oblivious legionnaire's young head, fully knocking him to the ground next to the hatch. Harding instinctively stepped round the door with his gun readied and looked down the corridor. There was nothing but the soft whistle from the cold wind. He pulled the dead soldier out of the way and then closed and locked the opening in the floor before walking slowly down the corridor checking each room as he went, somehow knowing what to expect, guilty that the men he had sent into these rooms had been sent to their deaths. In the parlour he saw the old dead body of Atticus Smales, a gunshot wound in the middle of his saggy red chest and a look of ultimate surprise on his aged features as if he had been frozen in mid sneeze. The old man would sing no more. As he reached the office, slumped against the wall sitting on the floor, he saw the young dead body of Daniel Jeremiah Pearce, a look of fear and pain on his spotty, adolescent face, his abdomen gorged and gouged by the point of a French bayonet, exposing the innards of his thin and no longer hungry stomach. Danny Pearce would not dance merrily again.

Anger spurted from Eli's nerve endings like geysers of electrified energy. Remorse and shame piled up inside his senses creating a tumult of confused emotions. Crack after crack of rifle shot rebounded through the outside air like he was inside some sinister brain jangling arcade machine. He thought he needed a drink and was crazily tempted to grab the bottle of rum in the office table drawer and relieve it of its mind deadening contents. All the while he kept looking at Pearce, sat against the wall with his eyes closed and a string of dribble hanging from his wet, open mouth as if he were sleeping through a vivid and fevered nightmare.

The reality of this madness hit Eli like a sledgehammer, evaporating the previous thoughts that this was possibly an invigorating, mindless romp without consequence and in a stunted daze he headed to the drawer and the bottle inside, unable to register the sounds of gunfire erupting on the other side of the walls. As he reached the broken glass of the barred window Eli looked out and saw four or five men moving along the moat, close to the stonework underneath his window. From the other side of the main gate he thought he saw Eves' face behind the shouldered butt of a rifle, firing repeatedly from the guardhouse at the sheltered attackers below. Then there was the sight of a fizzing fuse attached to a doubled stick of dynamite lofting casually through the darkness from somewhere under the bridge, heading excitedly towards the large wooden doors of the fort's entrance.

The explosion was thorough. The sound was ear splitting, much like the boom from a seven-inch cannon firing. Even at an angle the force was enough to blow through Harding's window and push him to the ground, covering him in a shower of broken window and dusted clumps of stone. The wood and iron gateway exploded in all directions, sending huge fragments inwards and outwards surrounded by a maelstrom of timber shrapnel and metal shards. There was no fireball as such, but the millisecond of massive energy which fuelled the explosion erupted in a destructive frenzy that shook the walls either side of the breech and tore up the ground in front and around it, blowing a small crater in the footings of the doorway. But it didn't manage to destroy the bridgehead, instead swiping away most of the wooden side rails like matchsticks in a gust of wind. Stone and rock scattered through the air and rained down over the surrounding grass. As the explosion died away, there were a few seconds of calm amid the resulting disorientation and then the gunfire from the bushes started again, this time much closer to the fort and from dark forms knelt on the edges of the open approach. Under this covering fire the men in the moat and the dark forms beyond began their attack.

Eli pushed himself upwards, wiping the dust and grit from his eyes and mouth, and saw the commandos scrabbling up over the rocks towards the bridge. His pistol was still in his hand and he fired at the first forms making their way onto the level ground but only heard the hollow click of the hammer on an empty chamber. He rushed into the lounge to fetch his sword which was leant against the fireplace from when he had taken it off earlier to enable him to fire the cannon. He loaded bullets into his pistol with shaking hands as he went, passing the exit leading to the main gate and noticing the door was hanging on its hinges, smoke swirling in from the outside carnage.

When the fortress entrance doors had exploded, Eves, who had also seen the dynamite lobbed onto the bridge by the attackers a few seconds earlier, had dived theatrically onto the floor of the kitchen as the glass and dust blew in with the shockwave through an already shattered window frame. Haines had still been cowering under the sink and was protected by it from the fallout but the door to the kitchen was blown off its hinges by the blast, taking much of the force of the explosion, and a cloud of smoke and dust billowed into the room from outside.

As Eves picked himself up and shook the fallout from his large body he saw the door and part of the wall to the guard room in a heap under the also destroyed window. He could make out the piles of rubble in the forts entrance with sheared bits of wood and bent, gnarly twists of metal gate poking out from within the smouldering remnants. He grabbed Haines' quivering body and thrust a dust covered rifle into the young man's hands whilst forcing the scribbler's dumbstruck head towards the kitchen window. "Shoot them, you chicken shit bastard! Shoot them!" he screamed, pointing to the oncoming commandos.

Eves managed a quick look into the barrack room and saw Gosfor recovering his posture and loading his rifle. There was a new look of bewilderment on his drained face as he loosed an approximate shot towards the open ground outside. The sergeant took his pistol out of its holster and grabbed his cricket bat from the kitchen table and then strode out into the decimated ruins of the guard room, over the lumpen rubble where the door once stood and smoothly levelled his gun on a legionnaire who was gingerly stepping over the twisted remains of the main gate, still surrounded in smoke and dust from the explosion. The controlled jerk of Eves' hand displayed the composure of his whole body as the shot blustered into the target's cheek bone and blew the back of his head off. Firing again as he stepped forward, with calmness only the King could portray, the second shot burrowed into the chest of another attacker pushing his body over the side of the bridge into the dry moat underneath. Partly covered by the debris in front, Eves stood in an on-guard, side stance position with his pistol arm outstretched, picking out each individual target with expert aim. His fast working brain pin pointed the right victim in order of danger to his own existence. The first man with his raised gun about to fire, the second stopped and preparing to fire, a third running across the bridge, rifle at his hip, bayonet fixed only feet away from lunging through the smoke into the sergeant's aura. Luck played its part, as it always does in a battle, with bullets ricocheting off the stones at his feet and pinging off the walls behind his head. He shot other men who had wasted their own shots as they perilously made their way towards the fractured fortress while others were distracted enough by the supporting fire from the walls to not get in a clear shot and take down the defiant defender. And then his pistol ran out.

Two Frenchmen, unable to gain steady footholds, clambered over the small rubble strewn crater with bayonets attached to unloaded rifles. They had wasted their previous shots and had missed the ghostlike, swaying form of Eves who was obscured by the smoke still swirling around the protruding outlines of the breech. Unable to reload in time, they lunged for the sergeant who had holstered his pistol and gripped his bat in both hands as if at the crease in a local village cricket match. Before the point of a bayonet from the near most legionnaire could find its mark, Eves struck the muzzle away like he was hitting a six and the offending rifle, bayonet and all, flew off into the night. Reversing the follow through in a lightning fast reaction he caught the man's jaw with the tip of his bat, breaking the Frenchman's blackened face and sending him crashing to the rubble. But straight away the second assailant came at him and Eves had to swipe away the thrusting rifle tip and withdraw a few steps to reset his own balance. The Frenchman held his gun abreast, now devoid of its bayonet which had clattered to the ground, and pushed forward towards Eves who managed to just about parry the attack as if he were playing a defensive stroke from an awkward bouncer. But the big man was unable to avoid the quick swing of the rifle butt from the teeth clenched intruder. It crashed into Eves groin and winded him as the pain shouted out through his stinging ballbag. He staggered back a little as the Frenchman pulled the bolt of his rifle open and injected a round into the chamber with one smooth action. But before he could aim the barrel, an area of his forehead corked outwards as a bullet from somewhere behind found its way through his brain. Sergeant Eves jogged out of the way of the dead man's falling body and saw in the damaged doorway of his Master Gunner's quarters the raised, smoking pistol of Elias Harding.

Out of the corner of his eye, Eli caught the flash of a muzzle firing in the confused gloom outside the broken fortress entrance. At the same time, his emergency reflex rolled him back behind the door just as the bullet from the flashing muzzle smashed into the wooden frame sending fragments spinning into the hallway. Out of the dusty blackness around him, the end of a bayonet thrust its way towards his body. Eli was at the wrong angle to use his pistol and only had enough time to bring his already unsheathed sword up and parry the attack. The dark blue shadow quickly tried to stab again as he clicked the bolt of his rifle backwards and forwards but Harding brought his pistol and sword hands together and upwards at the same time, catching the barrel with the handle of his sabre. The rifle went off and Eli felt the judder through his hands and the hot discharge from the bullet across his neck but pushed the man backwards towards the guardroom wall. Angling his pistol at the man's head, it went off, blowing the attacker's neck inwards and splattering blood over Eli's face. As the shadow crumpled over the debris across the ground, Harding dropped to one knee and fired at more of the shadows trying to cross the bridge. He heard a gun discharged near his head and turned to see Haines crouched around the leftover stone of the guardroom wall, firing into the gloomy approach. Eves had already got up with his still aching balls, fetched his own rifle and was also now firing repeatedly towards the road like the ticking of a very slow and out of time clock.

In the main barracks, Gosfor was still firing out of his smashed window. His bravado and odd comical asides acted like a mask that covered the very palpable fear he was experiencing. The explosion had shit him up. He didn't understand what was happening and was frightened and confused by the sudden violent chaos he was involved in. The cider buzz had worn off. Like most of the others in this band of volunteers he could never have imagined this kind of thing actually occurring and also, like his comrades, was only participating as fully as he was because everyone else seemed to be doing the same. Mr Harding and Sergeant Eves were not men to start such a deadly fight for no reason, and besides, he had seen cook was dead, his body still out there on the ground near where he was now shooting at, killed by some French bloke who then had the gall to ask everyone to surrender. This wasn't a joke and every time a bullet hit the outside wall near his window or when bullets had smashed into the panes of glass from which he was firing, he had tucked himself behind the wall and thought about the danger those small missiles presented. The reality of the situation had truly astounded his jumbled mind. His rifle fire had become looser and more irregular with long periods of hiding behind the brick work out of the way of the window and the danger of death or injury. But his poor aim was effort enough to keep the shadows at bay in the undergrowth, even though he hadn't actually killed anyone yet.

A few yards away, Dicky Pearce was just plain shit scared but his juvenile intelligence helped him suppress the feelings of fear and dread with a misguided, schoolboy excitement of action and possible danger. Part of him thought it was a game they were all involved in like when he was younger and had stone fights with the other kids on the streets at home in Bridgwater. He was annoyed his foot was broken, as it might hinder his need to run if the time came, but in his head he didn't think that would be necessary and soon all this would be over and they would find out it was all a terrible mistake caused by some stupid outside influence.

He didn't know his brother was dead. If he had it would have changed his entire outlook on the situation he was in, and the future of his life in general, destroying his youthful innocence completely. As it was, his childlike state meant he kept firing at the dark figures when he saw them and hoped when it was over no one would think he had been a coward.

So these five men within the walls of the fort, behind the broken windows, through the tiny firing loops and along the rubble of what was left of the front gate, laid down a field of defensive fire that kept the shadows of the night at bay, for now.

Across the cove, where the chocolate brown sea had reached its highest point and was now beginning to creep its way back from the edge of the beach leaving only a damp and frothy stain, the lights of the small seaside town twinkled away sleepily. A few horse drawn hansom cabs dribbled along the prom and random pedestrians, either couples braving the cold February night on the way back from a hostelry or the odd individual making the fast paced walk home, flittered about in the gas lit gloom. It was quiet on the streets. The curtains were drawn in the houses on the sea front and in the sparsely occupied hotel rooms along the prom. Patrons were preparing themselves for bed. After all, it was winter and there wasn't much else to do in the middle of the week once night had set in.

In a top floor room of the Welbeck hotel, situated at the other end of the imposing seafront terrace that also held the statelier looking Grand Atlantic hotel, Nathanial Harris and his escort, Gloria, had retired for the night to enjoy each other's naked charms. Although, to an outsider, it would have seemed the enjoyment was loaded more on Nathanial's side than Gloria's. But she was prepared for that and took it as one of the pitfalls of the job. Nathanial had already treated Gloria to a reasonably cheap dinner at a nearby café and after a few drinks in a horrid little boozer he was now treating her to his reasonably cheap affections, which would probably go on, in short bursts, for most of the evening. The room was thinly decorated in dark mahogany with a morbidly deep shade of olive green wallpaper and dark red velveteen curtains which hung either side of the dusty sash window. Only a smouldering, orange glowing, oil lamp gave the proceedings any light in the otherwise oppressive atmosphere. The early rounds of carnal shuffling had already been completed.

"What the blazes is that," Nathanial said taking a breather and walking over to the large window fully naked. "Looks like fireworks," he said with a confused look on his thin sweaty face.

"Fireworks!" Gloria squealed and her face lit up genuinely for the first time in the night like an errant, misplaced banger. She jumped out of bed and hopped over to the window, her breasts bouncing elegantly in the seedy but strangely romantic light. "I love fireworks," she said simply.

"Looks like they've just let off a big one, although it didn't go up very high," Nathan commented.

They both stood there in the dark, young and stark naked. She was beautiful and nubile, he decidedly not so beautiful and a bit stringy and mole ridden. They looked into the blackness across the bay. Every few moments a small flash of light would appear on the tip of the Down, followed shortly after by a rapid succession of a few more. Sometimes it seemed like there was a small fire in the oily blackness, somewhere near the point, but then it would disappear suddenly in the twinkling of the other lights. To the naked viewers in the window it was no more impressive than the gaslights flickering on the end of the pier further around the bay.

"Not much of a show, is it?" Gloria complained with a hint of dissatisfaction.

"Probably just some bounders, messing about after too much cider," Nathanial suggested and he turned to his female companion and lustily looked her up and down. He stealthily stood back a step, the already used pigskin condom inelegantly displayed on his lazily drooping lobber. *'No point getting another one,'* he surmised, *'These things are expensive.'* His arousal was instantaneous as he examined the sensuously formed curve of Gloria's back and bottom, running a finger along it to gain the full tangible sensation. He bent her over in the full openness of the window and slipped her his meagre length.

Gloria made the required responses relevant to the payment she had yet to receive, but generally she just stared out of the window waiting to experience the odd big firework, which sadly never came, unlike Nathanial, who thankfully for Gloria, did, and a lot quicker than usual, too.

When Elias had fired the one and only cannon shot at the small ship manoeuvring in the still plentiful waters just off shore from the tip of Brean

Down, it had splashed into the murky channel just off her bow and sent the Captain and his crew into a concerned panic. Everyone on board had waited for another shot to head in the ships direction but none came. However, Castille, now convinced the attempt to capture Brean Fort had gone even more shit shaped than his supposed death free kidnap attempt on Steep Holm, decided to lower one of the boats and take fifteen men over to sort things out.

As the row boat splashed into the water and the soldiers clambered aboard with their loaded rifles, pistols and long knives at the ready, the captain leaned over the side to give his opinion to Castille and warn him of the impending danger.

"You better get a move on Colonel," he called infuriatingly to the boat as the men inside used the oars to push the craft into the turbulent water. "The tides turned! You've got an hour before I turn this ship about and get out of this crappy shithole. If you're not back, I'll leave you here to sink in the mud!" he shouted as the lifeboats oars struck a beat on the surface of the sea.

"Get fucked Captain!" the Colonel shouted back. "You move that boat before I get back, he'll cut your balls off!" and he pointed a sharp finger at Modesto who was stood near the cabin, looking moodily at the Captain whilst picking the dirt from his fingernails with a penknife.

"You stupid fools," muttered the dispirited ship's master as he pulled away from the edge of the deck and headed into the cabin so he could begin preparations for 'The Small fish' to make way immediately and get as far out to sea as fast as possible when the time came, before she and all aboard her ended up grounded in the stinking mud of the Bristol Channel.

Up on the hill, before Benno's squad had attacked the main gate, before Castille had seen the situation on Brean Down slip into more chaos and before Nathanial had even got Gloria's knickers off back in town, the three runners had made their escape.

Running, running like you've never run before, wishing you could run faster, faster than you'd ever run before, wishing that you had more energy, your heart pounding, your chest thumping, panic and fear running through you as fast and as hard as you are physically running through the fields under your feet. Desperate to make it, desperate to escape, to find safety and refuge in a place that even you're not sure of yet. That's how Grayard Evans ran now, running for his life, being chased by men who wanted to kill him.

He had stopped ducking and diving by now, stopped using the small mounds and thorn trees and bushes to mask his direction and confuse his predators. He had given up hiding in the long grass as his chasers searched, watching the outlines of the landscape and waiting for a sign of movement so they could resume their pursuit. Now Evans was just running along the shorn grass along the spine of the Down, as fast as his body could throw him, running for his life. He had been sprinting solidly for about five or six minutes now. It felt like his brain was going to explode out of his head and his lungs would burst from the front of his chest, but fear and determination kept his legs pumping over the uneven ground.

Evans the escapee had maybe spent the last hour, he wasn't exactly sure of timescales anymore, darting between folds of scraggy, bush covered, undulating hilltops like a rabbit eluding a set of vicious dogs. After leaving the jut of rock with his two accomplices, the French had shown themselves in the deviant forms of crouched and sneaking shadows which moved through the undergrowth towards them. Ford had already slunk away down the side of the hill towards the rocks that reached the rough stone steps that led to Lanes' farm. His final uncaring words to his two comrades as he disappeared had been, "All the best, lads, I'm buggerin' off." And so he did.

Pickles volunteered to keep the pursuers at bay for as long as he could with some shadow bound pot shots while Evans made a run for it through the undergrowth strewn ridges along the top of the Down. For a while, Evans hid and then darted to the next mound of cover, hearing as he did so the sporadic rifle fire from Pickles and noticed in between movements that the dark forms were held back from following him too quickly. Crawling through the wet grass in the dip of a shallow rise he could also make out the staccato sounds of far off gunfire from the defenders of the fort and the louder airburst boom from the dynamite explosion of the front gates. He wondered what the blazes was going on down there and imagined what would happen if the fort had been taken over.

As he sprinted down an incline towards a patch of stubby trees and scrub, into which he would bolt like a scared rabbit, he quickly glanced behind him and caught sight of two shadowy outlines heading methodically his way in pursuit. Ducking into the cover and lying on his back flat to the ground, Evans took deep lung filling breaths to try and calm his racing pulse. He didn't know if they had caught Stanley, Ford or anyone else but he decided he wasn't going to let them catch him too. At a low crouch, he moved swiftly through the darkness to the next patch of fern and brambles, covering twenty yards as he did. Peeking through the tangles of foliage, he just made out the dark figures bobbing and bounding against the outline of the hill. Evans darted away again, wet and hot and scared for his life under the oppressive blackness of the cold night sky.

In the end, he stopped trying to hide. Every time he did, it felt as though the stalkers were just getting closer and that eventually they'd prod and sweep at the patch of bushes he was hiding in with their bayonets and skewer his body like a rabbit on the end of a hunter's spear. So when he reached the top of another rise and could see across the rest of the Down, with the clifftop path at the end and the few lights of the village on the other side of the bay in the distance, he thought about going for it. Then he heard the piercing crack of two shots behind him and the whizz of bullets as they cut through the air and he suddenly broke into a fast, demented, heart splitting run like the bunny heading for the hole of his burrow.

If he could get to the bridge crossing the inlet, before they caught up to him he'd be in the village and surely, he hoped, they wouldn't follow him there. When he reached the flatter part of the path with the undergrowth on either side, the cliff edge rock formations of Fiddlers Point only a few feet away, he stopped near the diversion which dropped down the slope into the marshes and the line of the inlet below. It was the same path that Harding had taken on his drunken way home from the pub the night before.

Grayo looked behind him and saw the two figures less than a hundred yards away, jogging steadily along. He bent down, hidden by the bushes on the side of the track and then scooted along the path heading diagonally down the side of the hill in an awkward stooping gallop. He tried to regain some breath. He could hear the rasp in his throat as he turned his head occasionally to check on his pursuers. His rifle was still slung across his back and he wondered if it was worth hiding in the brambles and ambushing them as they came down the path. If he wasn't seen, he might be able to shoot one of them and club the other one to death before they had time to realise what was happening.

But it was only a few feet away, the start of the marsh. A quick sprint along there and halfway down he'd be over the inlet bridge and across the beach, up the slipway to the village and eventual safety. *'Just keep going,'* he thought. His brain was aching, his temples throbbing, but he knew he still had one burst of speed left in him, one mighty thrust of energy which would get him to the village and the chance of help. Suddenly the flat part of the marsh was before him and he could see the curve along the edge of the bay. He saw the steep, jagged rocks along the end of the Down that fell into the pebbly cove to one side. He took in the thick waters of the receding channel as it bubbled along the rim of the marshland and the stony path that lead across the marsh before becoming the muddy banks of the inlet. And without hesitation, Grayo impulsively rose up like an unfurling black flower and broke into an almighty sprint.

Twenty yards in, he could see the lights of the village bouncing in front of his eyes. Looking behind briefly he glimpsed the flashing light of Lanes' farm slightly obscured by dark shapes of trees in the distance, and then in the foreground in front of that light the two fiendish shapes emerging from the end of the path, also breaking into a sprint. The rifle on Grayo's back clattered and battered across his shoulders and he feared it might slow him up, so as he ran, he pulled off the sling and threw the weapon into the marshes alongside the pathway, pressing an imaginary accelerator somewhere inside his pulsing body as he ran. And he flew like a bastard over the muddied stones towards the village.

On one side of him the marshy fields floated away into the distant darkness. On the other side a vast expanse of water, with the seafront of the town twinkling behind in the void of black. He could see the inlet forming next to the swift movement of his machine like feet and, up ahead, the bridge rapidly approaching. His legs pounded the dirt and his heart fluttered inside his chest under its beating strain like a small bird was flapping madly, insanely, trapped within his ribcage. He could sense the men behind him and thought he heard them throw their rifles away too. Then he could hear the pounding beat of their boots on the stone track as they began to catch him up. Legs and arms flashing furiously, the three men ran like the wind.

One of the commandos who was faster than the other, was gaining on Grayo and with every step towards the inlet bridge, he could almost feel the man's breath upon his neck, arms stretching towards his tunic ready to pull him back. In a split second decision he wasn't even sure he'd made, Evans skidded to a halt, tensing his body as he did so and turning himself about suddenly, fist clenched in a hammer ball of force. The Frenchman was caught by surprise with the sudden change of movement and direction from his prey. He didn't have time to swerve out of the way as Grayo's fist smashed into his face. The impact lifted the pursuer off his feet and sent his head snapping backwards, breaking his jaw and neck. It also broke Grayo's wrist and most of his knuckles and the pain shot up his arm like his hand had been set on fire and then chopped off. He tried to scream out but there was no breath in his lungs and no moisture in his throat. He glanced down at the Frenchman led on his back upon the wet path, choking noises coming from his open mouth, his eyes wide open, staring into the night.

Evans began to run again as he looked along the path and saw the other Frenchman approaching, sprinting madly like a shadowy spectre floating demonically through the air. The pain in Evans' arm was intense and he could feel the bruised sting in his toes from where they had been crushed into the front of his boots when he'd come to such a shocking halt. He ignored the sensation and ran towards the bridge. He put his feet on the slimy green wood of the rickety walkway and steadied himself so as not to fall into the muddy water below. He looked across and saw the ghostly hunter sprinting along the path still twenty or so yards away. There was a brief sense of realisation in Evans' mind that he might just make it. Then, as he jogged carefully across the slippery gangplank, he saw the figure behind angle his run towards the edge of the inlet and launch his body into the air like a flying bat from a jungle tree. The man, legs and arms before him as if he were doing the long jump, catapulted his tall frame across the six-foot-wide inlet and landed with a juddering splat on the marshy grass covering the other side of the bank. As Evans scrabbled to the end of the gangway and broke into a painful run, he saw the commando also scrabble up the bank and break into a monstrous chase, smartly angled in his direction.

Grayo hit the shingly sand of the beach, his broken wrist and hand swinging in front of him and then he felt the impact of another human being, as it dived athletically through the air and rugby tackled him to the firm but always shifting ground. Before he knew it, the attacker was on top of him, a knife pointing down to his face from the daggered grip of the man's hand. Grayo had just enough time to shift his head out of the way but the blade came down and bored into the flesh and bone of his shoulder, piercing all the way through up to the hilt. Grayo cried out in agony and groped his other arm about on the pebbly sand to fight the pain. The assailant struggled momentarily as he tried to pull the knife out to strike once more, and in that moment Grayo's hand fell upon a fist sized pebble and he brought it up with as much force as he could under the weight of the searing pain arching across his shoulder blades. The rock crashed into the attacking man's face and threw him off the wriggling body of Grayo. The two men rose groggily to their feet and came together again in a twisted embrace of combat, Evans striking the other man's face with his rock and the other man forcing the blade of his knife into Grayo's kidney as they met. But the momentum was with the volunteer artilleryman when the two men connected and he fell over on top of the commando as they collapsed to the ground, the knife being withdrawn and falling to the shingle as the man became concussed by the hard rock dashed across his temple. Grayo breathed in and the pain now scorching his lower back swarmed upwards into his chest as he knelt over his opponent like a bully on the torso of his latest school yard victim. In a frenzy of survivalist energy, he raised the pebble and smashed it into the Frenchman's face again, and again, and again, until the features of the man's head disappeared into an amorphous mass of hideous open red wounds and his body became stilled as the bloody bubbles of his final breath popped over the sand.

Grayo got off the dead man and crawled over the beach on his knees. His breath was failing him and sounded hoarse and grasping within the confines of his tight throat. There was difficulty getting air into his lungs and he felt the warm sensation of blood over his back. The pain throbbed through his whole body. His eyesight was blurring but he could just make out the slipway and the first in the terrace of village houses. He didn't want to die. *'Keep going son, you'll be alright,'* his brain told him, *'you'll be alright!'*

He collapsed in the middle of the road which ran along the row of tiny fishing cottages. A solitary gas fuelled street lamp illuminated the gloom with a hazy white glow which seemed to drift over the fallen man. Grayo rolled over onto his back and reached out a shaking arm to the quiet, curtain drawn houses in the blurry streetscape. Nothing moved, no one saw. He dropped his arm down onto the cobbled road and led there spitting blood as he struggled for breath, wanting to close his eyes and fall asleep.

Then, there came the sound of horse's hooves and a man's voice through the surging white noise inside his head. He tried to open his eyes and focus on what was happening. Through the pain filled haze and confusion, he saw over him the face of a man he didn't recognise, whispering something he could not understand. He felt his head being lifted from the ground and tried to say something but was finally overcome by the all-consuming blackness of unconscious relief.

The man holding Grayo in his arms was Rufus Stone. As he cradled the wounded artilleryman with one hand, the fingers of his other crept into the pocket of his overcoat and reached for the handle of his knife. But before he could remove it and slyly slit the throat and permanently silence Grayo, another man called out with a croaky voice from the edge of the road near the houses.

"What in God's name happened here!" cried Pat as he emerged from the shadows and raced across the road to the two men. Stones' hand came away from his coat and he looked up to the oncoming old man and then flashed a worried glance up and down the street.

"He's injured. I don't know how, I've just found him," Stone replied, faking agitated concern.

"Bloody 'ell!" exclaimed Patrick. "E's from the fort. Looks like e's bin stabbed!" The old man crouched down next to the prone body of Grayo and looked at the slowly heaving chest of the bloodied young man. "E needs a doctor," he said in a shocked whisper.

Stone looked at the old man and then spied the houses over the postman's shoulder. Nothing moved. His mind ticked like the workings of a steady clock and he decided he would have to kill him too and dispose of both bodies without anyone noticing, and quickly. *'Tricky,'* he thought calmly.

"I was on me way to the post office," started Patrick, looking down at the injured soldier. Grayo made a groaning sound but didn't wake up. "We better get some 'elp," he said looking into the hardened eyes of Stone whose hand was once again reaching towards his coat pocket. Suddenly, Pat looked down the street towards the shops further on and then his attention was caught by the sight of a lonely figure standing outside the church up on the side of the hill, vaguely illuminated by the streetlights underneath.

"Bloody 'ell, it's Morris," he said excitedly and he got up as Stone quickly turned his head in the direction of the old man's gaze.

"Morris!" shouted Patrick. "We need help, come 'ere!" he called up the hill.

Stone panicked, dropped Grayo's head to the cobbles and stood up, keeping an eye on the houses as he rose, speeding up the clockwork of his brain and trying to think of what to do next. Whoever was up on the hill was a witness and in a minute someone would come out of the houses over the road.

"We need to get him to the Manor House," he said urgently. "I'm a medical student and I have some bandages and equipment in my bag at the house. I'm staying there with the Danvers'. Help me get him into the carriage and I can treat him. We must get him inside," Stone urged the old man.

Patrick looked at the young, well-dressed man and acknowledged the sleepy looking pony attached to a small open carriage near the low wall and recognised it as Lord Danvers'.

"Help me get him in the seat, there's not enough room for both of us so we'll have to walk alongside and make sure he doesn't slip off, but it won't take long to get to the house. I can help him there," Stone said in an authoritative manner.

Patrick nodded his head rapidly. "Yes, yes of course," he replied anxiously. The two men picked up the groaning body of Grayard Evans and placed him as carefully as they could into the cart, laying him across the bench as the blood from his wounds seeped into his already sodden clothing and began to stain the chequered blanket which covered the wooden seat. Stone clicked the pony onwards in the direction of the Manor House as Patrick held onto the body of the stab victim and kept it steady in the seat. Neither of them had seen the dead man lying on the beach near the slipway and made no mention of the faint sound of pops and cracks in the distance. As they walked past the side of the hill, Pat looked up at the impassive figure of Morris in the graveyard of the church. "Bloody Morris, you bastard!" the old man quivered. "It's a good job you're a doctor and you were 'ere, ay Sir," he added, as he looked at Stone with unwary innocence.

"Yes, it is," replied Phillipe Roumiere softly as he led the pony on and regularly checked up and down the houses which lined the darkened, solitary street. All of them were silent and unmoving.

Up on the hill, Morris watched as the caravan passed by below. His unfeeling eyes switched to the insect sized black form of the dead man on the beach. He turned and walked back to the church stopping for a moment to swivel his head and look into the indefinable horizon across the bay, over the back of the Down towards the end near the sea. He was expressionless as he listened to the muted sounds of gunfire in the distance. In his soul he knew it was no practice happening in that place of threat that held the nest of omen's born from the mouth of an Iron Beast. He didn't know what was going on out there, but he knew it was the business of another world, not the one he existed in.

The gargoyles stood guard as Morris stepped through the threshold of the small stone built religious building and walked over to the cold granite anterior. On top of the simple altar a lone candle burned in a discoloured brass holder, throwing elongated shadows around the intimate church which caused the light to flicker and dance across the hollow face of its only attendant. Beside the candle was a sepia tinged photograph mounted on a cheap frame. It was a picture of a man posing on a crate wearing a peaked fishing cap and a thick white jumper. He was young and sombre looking with a serious face, as if he wanted to make an important impression and the photograph he was posing for would be his only ever portrait, seen by the eyes of an austere and insensitive world for all time to come. The brother of the man in the picture pinched out the flame of the candle and the church was thrown into darkness. He slowly turned round and walked funereally over to the first row of thin utilitarian pews and sat down. Next to him was a half drunk bottle of whiskey. Gently taking hold of it, he copiously drank from the neck, swallowing several glassfuls in one go. Morris looked longingly with an overwhelming sadness and despair in his eyes at the picture on the altar, as the sea thrown wind sang its mournful chorus through the open door and cracked walls of the exposed little church on the vulnerable hillside.

"There's a storm comin brother," he whispered.

When Ezekiel Ford had buggered off, he had also managed to get himself truly buggered at the same time. Whilst heading towards the stone steps leading down to the farmland he had seen two figures with guns loitering around the lower reaches and realised the French were covering the easy access to the open farmland. He decided to take a wide berth and use the steeper cliff edge and rocks to try and make his way down to the beach and escape that way instead. But he soon realised he didn't have a clue which way would be the best way down. Confused in the pitch darkness and frightened by the now realistic possibility of getting caught he began to wish he'd stayed in the fort. As he edged away from the grass slopes and clung to the rocks that formed the cliffs and outcrops of the seaward edge of the Down, every time he looked behind him, he thought he saw the distant forms of shadows raised against the outline of the hillsides; following him, pursuing him towards the sheer rock face. Even though it was bitterly cold on the exposed cliffs, his skin prickled with nervous sweat and his heart thumped wildly in his tightened chest as he gradually became trapped on the ever more precarious escarpments.

Then his foot slipped on a wet rock. He felt his body swaying into the open air and he desperately clutched at the now vertical stone wall, his fingers finding a tenuous clinch on the smallest of crevices, the nails crunching as they bit into the cliff, despairingly trying to hold on for dear life. His foot flailed in the windy expanse as the other scraped frantically on the porous edge of rock, hopelessly trying to find a foothold. A wave of panic and fear washed over his body and he stupidly threw his head from one side to the other, wanting to cry out in despair but his mouth was too dry from the impending thought of certain death and the buffeting wind which sailed over his useless body.

Ezekiel looked down at the black sea below him and gripped by terror suddenly looked straight upwards. As if by magic, perched on the tiniest of ledges above the crag onto which he tentatively held, was a goat. It was the same one which had interrupted his piss earlier in the night and it looked at Ford with exactly the same expression in its mad, sinister goat eyes. The hanging human didn't recognise it as the same animal in his panicked state, just blindly hugged the cliff and scrabbled insanely with his dangling boots. The goat baa'd. Ford's nails finally snapped under his weight, causing his fingers to slip from the fine crack and he fell silently into the wind.

He still didn't scream as he began to plummet downwards. He just stared madly at the goat above him who stared madly back. The goat watched as the human fell consciously through the air all the way down the rock face until he smashed himself to death on the crevices below and slowly slipped into the black water like a gently melting ice cream on a hot summer's day, gradually consumed by an oncoming tide. The goat casually looked behind him and hopped aerobically back up onto the rocks before scampering uncaringly away into the tenebrous night.

Inside the fallen walls of the fortress, Harding peeled away from the rubble of the main gate and hopped back towards the courtyard so he could check on James Burden. His sword was sheathed and his pistol had been replaced by a breech loading Martini-Henry rifle. He rounded the corner and saw the grizzled and slightly fried looking volunteer still watching the ladder on the other side of the wall.

"Alright, Jim, all quiet here?" Eli asked inconsiderately. The bullets were no longer whizzing around their heads. The sharp shooters on the hill had moved down the slope to concentrate on the defenders along the main wall but Burden kept looking at the top of the ladder in the relative peace of the night filled courtyard, then after a few seconds he turned slowly to his officer.

"No one's come over the ladder, Mr Harding," Burden said almost in a whisper. He turned his head towards the black sea and pointed a finger at the lights of the ship. "But there's a rowing boat heading our way from that ship," he said more strongly.

Harding tried to focus his adrenaline fuelled eyes through the oily smudge beyond and stepped closer to the wall. He saw the breaking lines of the oars as the row boat full of men moved through the water, approaching the peninsular edge just inland from the fort, and his mouth dropped open. "Oh bollocks," he breathed. "Shoot them, Burden!" he shouted above the gusts of wind mingling with the sounds of gunfire from the main entrance. He turned sharply to the volunteer, a look of shock on his face. "Shoot at them!" he shouted again stiffly.

Still in a daze and with a movement like a brainwashed robot, Burden knelt behind the wall near the dead body of his comrade, Lumpy Boulter, and carefully aimed his rifle at the shadowy boat. He began firing shots in a methodical, almost trancelike action.

Eli ran back to Eves, keeping his head low and led next to the sergeant as bullets dusted amongst the rubble in front of his face.

"There's more of them coming, Eves," he said, breathing hard. Eves looked at his Officer without emotion.

"We're running out of bullets, Mr Harding," he replied drily.

"I know that Eves, I bloody know that," Eli snapped, his voice breaking with a sense of panic and desperation. Zanzibar reloaded his rifle and coolly shot at one of the figures crouching in the shadows of the moat without answering the Master Gunner's comment.

"I'll try and sink them with the RML," Eli piped up after thinking for a second or two. "If they land and attack in force we might have to fall back to the magazine room. Save some ammo for then, Eves. If the bastards get this far we'll pummel 'em with the cannons till the whole place is in bits!" he added with a burst of renewed energy, his eyes spinning with crazed adrenaline. The sergeant nodded, the corners of his mouth turned down in resignation, and he reloaded his gun while Harding once again peeled away from the breech in the wall and returned to the courtyard. "If they get this far, we'll all be dead," Eves mumbled.

James Burden was by far the best rifleman in the rag tag group of volunteers at the fort. It was something he had taken great pride in during his time on deployment and was always quick to remind the others of it when in conversation. 'You couldn't hit a barn door with a brick' or 'Leave the shootin' to me,' he'd say after downing a big glass of rum or two in the canteen. There was a natural grace to his firing and an instinctual smoothness when lining up the eyesight on a target resulting in an efficient and more often than not successful action. Even thrown into this present unbelievable and frankly absurd event, which had certainly affected his normally pragmatic and confident mind, creating a man now in a stupefied state of shock, his shooting was still of a high quality. His first shot had sliced into the head of one of the rowers, causing him to slump forward and disable the rower in front, whilst the second shot had narrowly passed between Castille and the Legionnaire next to him. The boatmen started to return fire and Burden had to duck his head as the bullets rained in on him. Eli reached the old cannon that he and the two men had used earlier, which Boulter had managed to reload before he was killed, and started to work the handles that turned the traversing wheels of the carriage just to the side of Burdens crouching form. The angle was tight as the boat, although disturbed by the pot shots from the fort, continued on its journey and started to disappear out of view behind the edge of the outer walls; making for an area of landfall further down the peninsular. But Harding could still see the craft down the barrel of the cannon just inches from the far corner of the fortress wall.

"Get out of the way, Burden!" he screamed. The volunteer scrabbled away like a stunned mouse towards the door of the quarters just as Eli pulled the lanyard connected to the still live firing pin.

There was a deafening crump and a blinding flash as the cannon jumped in the air while Eli jogged away from the momentum, his head down and back bent away from the gun. There was a whoosh as the shell screeched past the corner of the wall and span towards the boat of reinforcements. The men inside saw what was happening and had just enough time to duck down into the hull waiting for the shell to destroy them. But the warhead drove into the sea a few feet to the side and exploded under the surface. The mountain of erupting water swamped the boat and threw its whole frame, crew and all, into the air before rocking it violently from side to side as it splashed down to the churning waters, still intact. As the downpour subsided and the row boat settled, the occupants realised they were drenched in stinking seawater but still miraculously alive and afloat. The rowers splashed their oars, minus two which had been flung into the outer waves, and pulled a series of drastic strokes which carried the still swaying boat through the boiling brown water and on to a group of rocks at the base of the promontory.

Harding stood upright and saw the boat disappear behind the wall, out of range, out of sight, and his head dropped down in a moment of exhausted despair. Weighed down by the heavy night air that suddenly flowed all around and surrounded him, he was consumed by an overwhelming feeling of hopelessness and desolation that was as black as the sky above and as infinitely dark and impending as the certain death he suddenly felt was upon them all.

Herbert Lanes had heard the din of gunfire coming from the fort no more than a mile away from his farm and had even gone outside to look in the direction of the scattered noise and swear loudly at the hillside which loomed above. He had been warned by Harding that there would probably be firing practice at some point over the next few days, quite possibly at night, and had grumbled in disgruntled recognition at the time, but this constant, annoying background racket was starting to make him angry. For a while he had contemplated going over there and making a fuss but Alma had managed to calm him down enough keep him at home.

When he had been outside he hadn't noticed the darkened forms hiding in the shadows of a nearby bush, watching for the moment the big farmer might make a move outside the boundary of his farm. If he had seen them, Herbert lanes would have gone potty, just for the sake of it.

As it was, he went back inside and moaned to his wife who told him to settle down by the fire and drink some cider and explained that the firing wouldn't keep going on all night as it never did on the very few times it had happened before. Herbert did settle down by the fire and he did drink some cider but all the while he stared at the open curtains of the window and mumbled audibly as his wife darned the holes in his massive woollen socks.

The trouble was, one of those dark forms hiding in the bushes had seen the farmer's wife when she'd come out to bring her husband back in and had become a little too distracted by the appearance of a woman. After all, he hadn't seen a woman for a few weeks now, since being stuck on that boat in Cherbourg for a fortnight and after the long journey back from Egypt following their previous mission. In fact, the last time Alexandre Barguss has been with a woman was when he had boned that prostitute back in Cairo. He watched the farmhouse from the bushes near the lane leading to the steps up the Down and licked his cold, dry lips.

"She looked nice," he said, as the distant sound of popping rifles floated in the air.

"Don't even go there," whispered his companion, Gerard, fully aware of his fellow Legionnaire's over active libido. The wind rustled in the bushes and the odd hardened gust blew the stunted trees over a bit more on their already crooked slant.

"I wouldn't mind another look at her before we get off this dump," added Alexandre.

"Shut up, you shit," grumped Gerard, cold and miserable in the damp undergrowth. He pulled his black woolly hat down around his ears and hugged his knees. "We're just supposed to watch the farmhouse, make sure no one leaves. Hopefully we'll get sent for and be back on the boat before long."

"Ha," snorted Barguss. "You'll be lucky. From the sounds of it, things aren't going to plan up there. From the sounds of it, it's gone to shit in fact. I reckon if it carries on, that gorilla in the farmhouse is going to blow his top and make a fuss, fetch the police or something. I say we should tie them both up and head back up there to find out what's going on. Benno might piss off without us."

They looked at each other with unsure faces. It wasn't supposed to be like this. There wasn't supposed to be any shooting. Something had gone wrong and they we're both getting cold in these bushes.

"Just wait, Alex. Give it another half hour. That shitty fort will give up soon, surely, and then things will quieten down. We can all leave as planned then," Gerard said hopefully. But in his mind he wasn't sure that would happen either.

They sat in silence for ten more minutes, Barguss smoking a fag under the cover of his dark green coat while Gerard continued to watch the farmhouse. The pop of gunfire, this time much nearer, not far from the top of the hillside directly above them caused the two men to all of a sudden worry excitedly. They were hearing the sound of Stanley Pickles covering Grayo's escape.

"Jesus, it's getting nearer," said Alex, throwing an agitated look towards the hillside and then the farmhouse.

Suddenly, the front door to the neat looking frontage of the house burst open and a beam of light was thrown into the yard. Herbert Lanes stood in the pool of light.

"You bloody bastards!" he boomed at the hill. "That's it! I'm comin' up there to give you bastards a kickin', you noisy buggers! This has gone on long enuff!" and he stomped inside leaving the door open. The two Frenchmen sprang out of their dampened foliage and trotted across the muddied yard towards the cascade of light, opening and closing the bolts of their Lebel mark II rifle's in a coordinated action as they galloped forward. Before they reached the open door, Lanes filled the entrance with his overpowering character, speaking loudly to his wife who was still within the confines of the house trying to talk her husband into calmness.

"They've gone too far this time, Alma!" he barked, throwing on a thick, black jacket as he emerged into the illuminated door frame. "I'll give the bastards...What the…" he trailed off as he saw the two Frenchmen stood before him in the gloomy farmyard, their guns raised to shoulders aiming the barrels at his large face.

"Halt!" called Gerard coming to a stop in the thin mud near the door. "Don't move! Or we'll blow your God damn head off!" he ordered.

Herbert stopped in an instantaneous moment of shock and disorientation at being confronted by the unexpected show of directed weaponry. "Who the bloody hell are you," he said in surprise.

"Get back in the house, Monsieur. We will shoot you, if you don't do as we tell you," replied Gerard in English soaked with an awful accent. Barguss thrust the point of his gun at the big farmer in a show of control. The other gunman did the same. Herbert hesitated for a fragile second and then moved backwards, his coat still half round his huge shoulder in a moment of disrepair.

"Who the hell are you?" growled the big man as he reversed into the house. "If you're from the fort I'll bloody…"

"Shut up! English shit!" shouted Barguss, in a state of adrenaline pumped excitement. "Get over there!" he snapped as the men entered the open plan house and he beckoned the point of his rifle towards the fireplace in the corner of the large space. Alma stood frozen in fear by the kitchen table. Gerard kicked the door shut when Lanes came to a halt by the mantelpiece above the flaming fire.

"Check upstairs!" Gerard motioned to his comrade still stood motionless in the lounge space as Alma whimpered slightly in the corner. Alex skipped towards the staircase in the corner of the room and the other commando waved his gun between the two prisoners "If you move, you're dead!" snarled the Legionnaire.

"You bloody shitfaced bastards!" shouted Lanes. "What you bugger's playin' at. I'm gonna complain!" he spat in a spurt of defiance, still unsure of what the hell was going on and who was barging their way into his house.

"Be quiet, farmer man!" Alex snorted as he ran up the staircase on the opposite wall, his rifle aimed in front like a searching lawman from the Wild West. Alma and Gerard swapped anguished expressions, both fearful of the sudden predicament. Lanes stared angrily at the intruder stood a few feet away, who seemed suddenly panicked by the intensity of the situation.

“You bastard,” grumped Lanes quietly. His large body bristled with anger and excitement, tensed like a coiled spring, wound up by the distaste he felt at being ordered about by strangers, with or without guns, on his farm, in his house! Unable to control the venom that overcame any fear or concern at the situation, he unconsciously released the grip.

“NO!” shrieked Alma, as her husband lunged towards the barrel of his opponent’s rifle. Herbert caught Gerard as he waved the weapon between the two householders, knocking the barrel into the centre of the room. A shot rang out but Lanes was already upon the intruder casting a strained fist across the unsuspecting jaw of the Frenchman. The gun fired innocently into the skirting boards and the impact from the punch sent Gerard wheeling backwards onto the window sill as the rifle clattered to the floorboards. With the Frenchman falling away and Lanes following after him, the duo clattered to the floor with Herbert in a frenzy of attack. While the Frenchman wondered what had happened in the preceding seconds, Herbert Lanes crouched over the man and struck his victim time after time with a succession of destructive and unrecoverable blows across the face of the intruder with the stony knuckles of his massive hands. After seven or eight strikes the man on his back stopped trying to put his arms in the way and became motionless. Lanes halted the onslaught, his arm held aloft ready to punch again as he looked down at the already bloodied face below him. His other hand held on to the handle of his small flick knife which he had pulled out in a flash and was now embedded in the dead commando’s chest.

Just as the sudden violence decimated, Barguss stood at the top of the stairs. “NO!” he called out in defiance as he descended the staircase and loosed off a shot at the hulk of Lanes now rising from the bloodied body of his comrade. “NO!” he repeated as the bullet pulsed from his gun and entered the stomach of the brave but foolhardy farmer, momentarily stopping his lurch towards the descending soldier. Barguss stopped on the penultimate stair and pulled back the bolt of his rifle and reloaded as the wounded Lanes clutched his stomach but came on, fuelled by his own angry defiance. The bang and resulting discharge of the following shot flashed through the room, blinding everyone, and this time Herbert was pushed backwards by the force of the bullet hitting him in the chest and he fell to one side, eventually crashing to the floor and pulling the armchair over as he landed. Alma screamed and stretched forward as if to save her husband from the sacrifice and Barguss stepped down onto the wooden floor of the large room as if by accident. And then straight away, the two remaining survivors of the house visibly shrivelled back as the reality of the undeniable finality within the death filled lounge sunk into their distended and distraught demeanours.

Alma stared at her husband in shock and disbelief. He was led on his back with two large red circles in the middle of his torso, the gently flickering flames of the fire highlighting his face in a warm orange glow. His hand gripped the arm of the upturned chair as a last few heavy breaths were expelled from his thick lips before he finally let go and his eyes closed as his arm fell to the floor with one final movement.

She looked at the man stood near him with a face of stunned fear. “Why?” she whispered.

Barguss stepped towards her, gun pointed to the floor, an expression on his face somewhere between remorse and psychotic confusion. “It wasn’t my fault. He should have done as he was told,” the Frenchman breathed, as he slowly approached Alma across the room. She began to wither back around the kitchen table, suddenly even more afraid of the other man as he came towards her, but for a different reason than before when he had just been an intruder in the house with her husband still alive.

“I’m sorry,” he whispered, leaning the rifle against the kitchen dresser which was adorned with a selection of delicately painted crockery depicting scenes of rural life. “None of this is my fault, I didn’t start this,” he continued, breathing the words out as he slid through the kitchen like a snake after a mouse. “You’re very pretty, miss,” he hissed. “I am truly sorry,” he pleaded creepily and smoothly pulled out a six-inch knife from a sheath on his belt.

“Get away from me,” Alma quivered as she backed herself against the sink, her hands clutching at the worktops, blindly hoping to grasp a utensil which she could use as a weapon. The intruder’s eyes were glazed over in a fit of insensible urge. His hand stretched towards the farmer’s wife, fingers curled, ready to grab as his other hand hovered in the air, knife at the ready. Alma gripped a plate drying on the sink area and smashed it over the head of her attacker just as he made a grasp at her throat. The impact of the plate did nothing to stop the possessed actions of Barguss and he leant over the young woman’s struggling body, bringing the knife up to her soft cheek, absorbing her weakening blows as she tried to wriggle free from his clutches.

“Calm down, miss,” he slithered over her. “Calm down or I’ll cut your pretty face,” he breathed nastily and then forcefully pulled Alma off the Belfast sink and turned round with her whole body up close to his own, arms and legs waving from beneath his menacing grasp, and then pushed her angrily onto the kitchen table.

“Stop struggling!” he shouted. “This is his fault, not mine,” he spat glancing quickly at the dead body near the softly wavering fire. “He should have done as he was told!”

Snarling with bared, foam flecked teeth and with a wild, glassy look in his eyes, Barguss lifted Alma’s head up by the neck and smashed it down on the table, once, then twice, nicking her cheek with the point of his knife. He forced her legs apart with his thighs and pushed his groin against hers with a demented animal desire. Using his knife hand to hold her head down, he freed his other hand to fumble down between her skirts. She cried out in fear and loathing and tried to grab his exploring hand, kicking furiously with her legs, her mind whirling in a sea of panic. She closed her eyes to his dark squirming face and felt the blade of his knife against her throat. She could smell coffee and tobacco on his breath as she struggled beneath his forceful body. As her offender tried to put his hand up her skirt Barguss drank in the aroma of hay and carbolic soap from Alma's tear stained cheek. From the wooden dresser to the side of the table, the red painted motif of a shire horse pulling a plough across the decorated plates looked down icily on the grotesque scene below.

Then, there was a loud crack which broke through the fetid sounds of Barguss's heavy breathing over Alma's frightened gasps of anguish and she felt the warm sensation of thick fluid across her face. Immediately his desperate body went limp like a portion of old salad leaves and his heavy head landed on Alma's stilted chest. She opened her eyes as the knife at her throat fell to the side of the table and the room was abruptly filled with quiet.

Alma felt her face and looked at her fingertips. The wetness was dark red and still warm. She thought it was her own blood then realised her attacker wasn't moving at all and in a state of sudden relief and still bubbling panic she pushed the body of the man off her own and he slid noisily to the floor with a thump. She sprang up and turned round pushing herself back against the sink once again and looked across the room. Stood in the open front door, slowly lowering a shaking rifle was the long, lanky figure of a terrified Stanley Pickles, his permanently tousled bed hair matted with damp. "I'm sorry Miss," was all he said.

When he had covered the escape of his comrade, Grayard Evans, and once the shadows he had momentarily kept at bay returned fire with increasingly accurate aim, the young lad, Pickles, had made his own escape down the stone steps towards the farmhouse. He had seen the two Legionnaires guarding the house and had hidden in the bracken out of sight wondering what the hell he was going to do, his lengthy body paralysed by the waterfall of fear which was now pouring through it. When he saw the two men skip across the courtyard, Stanley realised he had to do something and he cautiously approached the dimly lit farmhouse. He was too late to save Herbert Lanes but had caught the attempted rapist in his actions and had prayed his shot was good enough. It had been.

Now Alma looked at Stanley with wide, confused eyes. "What's happening?" she said in breaths. "Why?"

The lad gazed back in bewilderment. "I don't know, Mrs Lanes. I just don't know. We're under attack," he said in the voice of a dazed and timid child. Stan had never killed anyone before and even the justification of this kill wasn't enough to sooth his shock at the action.

The young woman looked away and saw the body of her husband led in front of the fireplace. Her head dropped to one side and she let out a small whimper as the tears welled up in her eyes once again and began to roll down her cheek, leaving trails through the smears of blood still on her face. "Oh

Herbert," she whispered through her soft crying as she staggered over to her dead husband.

She knelt down beside his body and lifted his big stone-like head onto her dress covered lap, stroking his thick short hair as she looked down onto his peaceful face. "You bloody buggers," she sobbed quietly.

Pickles thought about taking a horse from Lanes' farm and heading for town but knew he wasn't any good with horses and that he certainly didn't know how to ride one, which he realised he should have thought about at some earlier point in the night. Besides, the scene inside the farmhouse had sent his mind somewhere more over the edge than it already had been anyway. The horror of cook's death, the desolation and inducement of fear from his fellow volunteer's predicament, the fact he had just killed a man all mixed with the overwhelming sadness he felt for Mrs Lanes as he watched her stroke the head of her murdered husband, all this had tipped him into a world of lonely depression and defeatism. He thought about staying with her and trying to comfort her but knew he wouldn't be any good at that either and could only think about being with the other blokes from the fort. *'Were they still alive,'* he thought over and over again. "I'll go and get help," he said softly to the weeping young farmer's widow and he left the lonely farmhouse and headed back to the Down.

He crept along the path running parallel to the farm fields at the bottom of the hillside, watching furtively at the open ground on one side and the undergrowth lining the foot of the hill on the other, desperate not to see any movement that would betray the oncoming shadows of the night and their ultimate haunting of his fragile senses. Pickles didn't have a clue what he would do when he got near the village but the idea revolved in his mind that maybe it was the only real refuge in this abandoned world. He hoped Grayo had got away and was summoning help at this very moment and that at some point he would run into him and a load of armed coppers on their way to save the fort and the rest of his friends before anyone else had to die.

The gunfire crackled in the distance as the wind whistled along the path. The cloudy night sky seemed overly stifling and the tall youth hugged the side of the bushes hoping there were no more French commandos out this far from the fort.

He stopped for a second, noticing a lull in the dull pops of gunfire that floated from the sea around the head of the skulking landmass above. For a fleeting instant all he could hear was the sound of the wind blowing through the grass and his own deeply stressed breathing. "Maybe it's all over" he said for a moment. "Maybe it's stopped".

In a split second he was on the floor, a black form over his face and body, lying across his arms and immobile rifle. He felt the stinging sensation as a blade was shafted into his ribcage and the air was sucked from his body. Before he could co-ordinate the event in his mind the blade was pushed in again and a wave of pain flowed through his dangly limbs. Pickles tried to scream but the shadow's hand was already over his mouth and the blade went in again, twisted this time and was then left there to burn sensationally. Stanley hadn't even had time to move before the stealthy attack was over, just wonder in shocked terror at the suddenness of his own end which came as the burning sensation peaked across his body and the blackness swallowed everything before his eyes.

The commando pushed himself off the stilled, long frame of Pickles and looked slyly about before standing up and wiping the blood from his knife on the dead youth's navy blue coat. He slunk silently backwards and withdrew his shadowy form like a disappearing ghost, back into the cover of the bushes from whence he had so devastatingly come.

Phillipe Roumiere was getting worried now. The plan he had imagined for the return of his incarcerated associate from the island was now hitting some obstacles and it was obvious the over run of the mainland fort was not going smoothly. From merely keeping an eye on the locals in the village and then waiting until the right time to do a runner he was now having to work out how to deal with an injured artilleryman and what would end up as three, maybe four, inquisitive villagers. His relatively calm exterior was hiding an increasingly agitated persona.

It would take about ten minutes to reach the Manor House, he had reckoned, when they first pushed the injured body of Evans on to the carriage. They had reached the end of the main drag through the village undisturbed, and were travelling along the darkened street leading to the town and the Manor House. They were covered over head by the blackened canopy of trees that blanked out the night sky and hung across the damp roadway. Through the wood they could see the lights of the house not far away. The young Frenchman's brain was flickering like a candle whipped by draughts, trying to formulate a system for explaining away the circumstances of this injured man whilst at the same time keeping everyone calm enough to delay alerting anyone else. The explanations he thought of raced to and fro but none of them seemed plausible to the extent of not involving the police as soon as possible. In the end, the realisation dawned on him that he would have to reveal his true nature at some point and then probably keep everyone imprisoned at the house and if the need arose, just to make things easier, kill one or even all of them. As his mind ticked over, they kept walking and he managed to ignore the ramblings of postman Pat.

"He do look in a bad way, Mr…sorry I didn't catch yer name," Pat rattled nervously as he held onto the unconscious body led on the carriage. There was no answer but the old man carried on regardless, the words helping to control the concern in his own worried mind.

"What a to do this is, eh Sir? I can't imagine what's bloody happened? The poor lads bin stabbed bad an'ee. I ain't never seen nothin' like it, I can tell you! Perhaps there bin a fight at the fort, or somethin' of that manner. Or, or maybe they got trouble up there. I 'ear stories about them Revolutionaries comin' up wiv plots to take over the country, it might be somethin' to do wiv' that. Whatever it is, we better get the police as soon as we can," Pat wittered on.

Roumiere caught the last part and snapped back. "We've got to get this lad inside and do what we can for him before we start worrying about the police," he retorted whilst flashing a look at the old man. The small pony clopped on unconcerned, as did Pat.

"Maybe I should head back to the post office and send a telegram, get the police sent over from town," Pat suggested with an animated expression.

"No!" barked Stone and then tempered his response, trying to keep control of the situation. He thought of the cut telegraph wires from the post office, severed by his own hand shortly before finding the injured body of Evans in the road. "I mean, not yet. We have to get to the house first and then we can decide how to deal with it. I need your help to get this poor young man inside the Manor House, his life may depend on it."

"Yes, yes, course your right Mr…what was yer name, sir?" Pat asked again. There was no reply from the young man as they finally turned into the driveway of the large house and headed on towards the backdoor.

The two men gently slid Grayo from the seat of the open carriage and between them carried his heavy body through the main door, into the conservatory and straight on to the kitchen table. The smashing of a decorative fruit bowl on the stone floor brought Miss Danvers and her father rushing in from the sitting room.

"What the blazes is going on here!" stormed Lord Danvers, stopping suddenly as he saw the bloodied body spread on the large wooden table.

"Oh my god," gasped Victoria, a delicate hand covering her mouth in shock. There was a moment of stunned silence.

"We found 'im on the road near the beach, Miss," started Pat in thick worried tones. "Ee's bin stabbed! Your guest 'ere said he could help 'im, said 'e was a doctor,"

Rufus Stone looked around nervously trying to gauge the atmosphere of the room and prepare his response. Victoria looked at him questioningly through her look of initial shock.

"I found him led in the street. He's badly injured. I thought I could help him better if we got back here," he said hesitantly.

Miss Danvers stepped over to Grayo's body and looked at his face, reaching a hand towards the huge blood stain across his clothing. "Stabbed," she whispered.

"Stabbed!" her startled father called out, his bristly moustache twitching. "We should get the police. Who has done this? Patrick, you should get to the telegram office, get someone out here," he suddenly demanded.

Rufus Stone was galvanised into some sort of action. "Wait, we need to help him first," he said firmly and leant over the prone body and started undoing the man's tunic. "We need some bandages and hot water, quickly Miss Danvers!"

"But you're not a doctor," she replied stepping back a little and swapping uneasy glances between Stone, her father and the injured man. Grayo let out a groan when Stone pulled apart the coat and shirt revealing a blood covered torso.

"I know something about the human body Miss Danvers. If we can stem the bleeding, he might be saved. But I need your help, please," he said, pulling his face into a picture of pleading.

"Who is he?" Victoria said, still alarmed.

"Ee's from the fort, Miss Danvers. There's some trouble gone on out there. We were warned there'd be a firin' practice. Somethin' must 'av gone wrong. I should get back to the village and see what's going on," Patrick said looking around the room in a fluster.

"Yes, get the bloody peelers out here, Pat. I should use the horse and cart and head into town, fetch the doctor," Lord Danvers said using his silver topped cane to limp towards the back door.

Stone's mind raced between his pretend personality and the truth of his insidious agenda. "Wait!" he shouted, realising he was losing grip on the situation. "Whoever stabbed this man is still out there, it may be dangerous. We should stay here," he ordered as the edgy atmosphere rose.

"Where has he been stabbed?" Victoria said looking suspiciously at Stone.

"Don't worry about us, Mr Stone, we'll be alright," her father said ignoring his daughter's question. "If there's been trouble up at the fort then we should get some help. You do what you can here, Patrick and I will sort it out," Mr Danvers blustered pompously, turning towards the door.

The French spy stepped back in a panic, "No!" he barked. "Please, I beg you. You must not leave the house."

The two old men stopped by the door to the outer conservatory and swapped confused looks as Victoria gently rolled Grayo over on his side and saw the flap of dark red skin denoting the entrance of the knife in his kidneys.

"Now, now, Mr Stone," began Lord Danvers.

"Please…" Stone started to say in desperation as he reached into the inside pocket of his coat.

Suddenly, Grayo woke up with an anguished look across his face, eyes staring madly into the face of Victoria who was still holding him. He threw an arm up and grabbed her shoulder as he pulled his head up off the table. Miss Danvers saw his wound ooze a stream of blood down his back and over the table.

“Help us,” Evans gargled into the pretty woman’s flustered and fearful expression. “The fort’s being attacked, get someone, they’re going to kill everyone. Get help!” the words tumbled from his spittle flecked lips and he gritted his teeth between exclamations. “Help them!” he urged before his wounded and wracked body fell back down to the table, exhausted.

Victoria held him in her hands, her face taught with shock and anxiety. She looked at her father and realised his attention was on Rufus Stone stood next to the table holding a revolver, pointed at the two old men by the door.

“What…” she let out a gasp as she acknowledged the weapon and then looked into the face of Stone, his eyes flashing around the faces in the room, his lips curled back into his mouth. There was a high sensation of nervous tension within the gauzy light of the oil lit kitchen.

“Don’t move, any of you,” he said with excited agitation.

“You blighter, Stone!” snorted Lord Danvers. “How dare you!”

“Shut up!” shouted Stone. “Get away from the door, both of you.” His French accent burst back into his voice as he spoke.

“Ee’s a bloody revolutionary,” choked Pat in disbelief.

Roumiere looked at Miss Danvers who was still holding the body of Grayo as the injured man started to moan lightly and try to roll from side to side.

“You bastard,” she whispered to the gunman as he fixed her with hard but desperate eyes.

“Move over with the others, or I’ll shoot one of them,” he said to her.

She slowly leant back, her eyes always on him and the gun. Grayo’s arms began to flail from one side to the other as the pain in his body animated his limbs like a strange marionette.

“What are you going to do to us,” demanded Lord Danvers, pushing his chest out in an act of defiance against their protagonist.

“Shut up,” Roumiere responded trying to calm his touchiness and think of something other than just shooting them all now. Victoria gently let go of Grayo and stepped back against the sideboard on which the half eaten walnut cake she had made the day before was sat on top of a florally decorated cake stand.

Then unexpectedly, Grayo’s head shot into the air and he let out a strangled cry, frightening the life out of everyone else in the stretched atmosphere of the room. At the same time his arms flew out to the man next to him by the table and wrapped themselves around Roumiere’s waist clasping his pistol arm against his stomach and causing the pair to sway disarmingly. In an act of spontaneity Patrick shot forward and tried to push the standing Roumiere over on to the floor but the French spy managed to remain upright and wriggle his gun hand free from the octopus like arms of Grayo whilst pulling the trigger at the same time. The gun recoiled and Patrick was sent crashing backwards to the floor as the shot hit him in the chest. Grayo's flailing arms caught the gun hand again and the injured artillery volunteer let out a primal scream as the gun went off for a second time in the tangle of limbs. A small portion of his back popped outward through a torn hole in his already ripped coat and Victoria was splashed across her neck and face with a spurt of blood.

Whilst the tussle was going on, Lord Danvers struck out with his cane at the writhing forms while Victoria's fingers had already wrapped themselves around the handle of the large bread knife which she had been using to cut cake with during the day. Ignoring the blood on her face and without a second thought for her own safety, she danced around the table with such speed and determined fierceness that before a third gunshot had finished ringing out she reached the disabled figure of Phillipe Roumiere and plunged the knife upwards into his uncovered throat so hard that the tip severed his spinal cord and poked out the back of his neck, killing him almost instantly. She pulled the blade out and there was a moment of stillness. His eyes rolled back and he melted to the floor like a drained balloon.

Victoria writhed back in disgust at the traumatic horror of the scene on the kitchen floor. The tangled heap of two dead bodies beside the table, the outstretched arms of the now dead Grayard Evans hanging down towards those other victims and the shocked, frightened face of her father as he fell back against the welsh dresser in trembling astonishment. The knife dropped from Victoria's small hands and they quickly sprang to her ghostly pale face to cover her quivering mouth as the appalling events which had unfolded so suddenly just a few moments ago came to bear on her distressed and already sickened mind. Through the chaos of these strained images and her brain's contorted attempts at reasoning with the unbelievable truth of what had happened, her mind suddenly thought of Elias. She screamed.

And then the shadows of the night crept over the wall of the fort. Three of them got over, unseen, not far from the place where the impish goat had left the scene of the latrine earlier in the night. No one realised the fort had been infiltrated until Barnes felt a bullet cut into his back, bursting one of his lungs and destroying his stomach. Another bullet hit him in the neck straight afterwards before he'd even dropped his gun, but as it clattered to the floor breaking the sublime drone of the sweeping wind and the intermittent crack of rifle fire, he was already dead. Mule was reloading his rifle when he saw Barnes slump forward. Shots clattered into the wrong side of the wall he was hiding behind and he scrabbled straight for the door of the barracks.

He loosed off his freshly loaded round towards the ill-defined shapes that were the intruders dropping into the courtyard before managing to bundle himself inside the building and pull the door closed behind him, pushing the bars into the locks to secure the heavy metal door as he moved. He breathed heavily for a moment as his tingling, nerve racked body tried to settle down, his back leaning against the door. He scrambled round on his hands and feet like a rattled lizard and looked up at the locked bars.

"They've got in," he said in a whisper. "They've got in!" he called out louder this time. He remained sat down but pushed himself along the flagstone floor, crablike, past the sergeant's room. "They've got in!" he shouted again out as he turned around, got up and stumbled into the main hall.

Pearce looked round at him in surprise.

"They've got over the wall!" Mule shouted with genuine fear etched across his leathery face. "They've broken into the fort!"

Burden was the next one to die. After the failed attempt at blowing up the reinforcements on the boat, Burden had seen the intruders drop over the wall near the toilet block and had started firing at them whilst desperately shouting at Eli "The bastards are in!"

Elias was still in a state of shock after firing the seven-pound gun to no avail, trying to come to terms with the imminent arrival of more attackers, confused about what he should do next and fearful that the situation he had orchestrated was now out of his control completely. His ears rang with the sound of the artillery weapon he'd just fired and he couldn't hear properly. For a few precious seconds he was unresponsive to anything.

It was a stick of dynamite that done poor James Burden, part time builder and user of women. It flew over the roof of the barracks and came fizzing out of the black night air landing a few feet away from where Burden was kneeling by the officer's quarter's wall. To Elias's horror, he watched as instead of diving for cover behind the nearby gun carriage, Burden over ambitiously lunged towards the fizzing stick in a vain attempt at throwing the dynamite back towards the intruders before it exploded. Eli dived for cover. The fuse was too short and as James threw his arm forward and released the stick, the explosive detonated.

It blew off his arm, shoulder and a large section of his torso, along with most of his head. Parts of his body landed as far afield as the main gate and across the courtyard to the door of the magazine room while a circle of blood and human innards were splashed over the nearby walls of Eli's quarters and the barrack room. The rest of his remains fell to the floor in a gory heap as a symbol of the ultimate in bodily destruction. As his mangled body led on the gravel, one good eye still connected to what was left of his head looked frantically at the stones on the courtyard for a few seconds wondering what the hell it was seeing because the part of his brain that analysed vision was now sliding down the outside wall of Elias Harding's house.

At exactly the same time as James Burden was destroyed, the French blew up the back door of the barrack room. It happened just as Gosfor was stood in the corridor by the washroom, nervously standing guard as Mule helped Pearce hobble towards the kitchen. The explosion sent the heavy metal door flying down the hall way in front of a cloud of dust and smoke and it hit Gosfor frontally with the impact of a wrecking ball. It took his surprised body along with its bent metal flatness through the air into the barrack room and came to rest across his smashed skeleton and pulped face. Amazingly the Londoner was still alive, but as the dust settled, two French commandos came through the smoking debris, and as one of them knelt down and aimed his gun into the room, the other bayoneted the crushed man in the sternum as he struggled to breathe and push the door from his wrecked body.

During this time, Eves had felt the explosion from the first stick of dynamite behind him and covered his head from the flying bits of Burden's decimated body. Simultaneously, out of the corner of his eye, he also saw the explosion within the barrack room. It was a moment of chaos in battle that he had experienced before in his years of violent engagement but was still always unprepared for. His ears filled with the tumult of thunderous sounds from impacting atoms while all his eyes could see was dust and billowing clouds of volatile destruction. Once again it was as if time stood still and reality was paused as the degradation and ultimate death of life was cataclysmically released. He saw Haines in the leftovers of the kitchen firing towards the two commandos moving in the main hall, their guns raised in preparation for encounter. Eves saw Mule, his arm around the limping frame of the Pearce boy as they stumbled out of the other door into the courtyard, and as his battle instinct took over and he looked over to the bridge head, he saw the shadowy figures charge from the moat and roadside undergrowth towards the rubble strewn nest he was led in.

Zanzibar shot one of the shadows as it flew from the darkness. Reloading he saw another toss something alight through the void in the direction of the breech and so fired again. As he rose up and automatically withdrew, loading his rifle from an almost empty pouch, he screamed at Haines knelt near the exposed kitchen sink, "Run Haines! Run! Get to the magazine!"

Then, in a millisecond of cosmic like movement and deafening sound, as if it was the beginning, or perhaps the ending of a new world, Eves felt himself floating, suspended in mid-air, surrounded by a sudden instance of silence and consummate dark while the air was sucked from the atmosphere in a vacuum of blank unknowingness. It was almost blissful for a moment, even heavenly. Then there was a hot and stinging pain, the sensation of being thrown against a block of cold hard concrete, dizziness, breathlessness, confusion, all tossed together in a renewed world of real feeling. And suddenly, that real world was sucked back into the spatial vacuum and the chaos and terror which entwined it resumed once more. All Eves could hear now was the sound of rushing water and howling wind. Disorientating, terrifying white noise connected to juddering and hazy images. Eves saw Haines crawling across the courtyard and noticed two men hunkered down near the concrete of the empty gun emplacements. He saw a charging figure dressed in dark blue with a blackened angry face bearing down on him with a bayoneted rifle. The automatic reaction, an unthinking reaction from a life constantly peppered with the threat of possible death, made his hands raise the rifle which was still miraculously within his grasp and pull the trigger, sending the oncoming phantom of death tumbling to the ground next to him. The sergeant tried to shake off his disorder.

Harding, in a posture of genuflection, had emptied his pistol at the attacking shadows both from the area of the latrines and those emerging from the bridge. He saw eves blown off his feet and his body thrown onto the gravel and saw the big man was vulnerable. As he fired his pistol he covered the retreat of Mule and Pearce, now sat against the outer wall of the fort, and watched as Haines made it to the cover of the new gun only a few feet away, still shrouded in its green tarpaulin. The scribbler was crouched down firing then reloading and firing his rifle maniacally in a panic of survival, not really able to hit anything organic but at least laying down the threat.

It all looked thoroughly hopeless in Eli's hot and stinging eyes as he reloaded his pistol. His mind was scattered like a deck of cards thrown in the air and he felt scared of the impending doom that pervaded his psyche and clawed at his senses. The feeling of anger, frustration and fear at the probability of such a stupid and pitiless end for the people he had been given responsibility for cascaded over his emotions. But bizarrely, considering the surroundings, mixed with these feelings was the still apparent belief that this was all a dream, some crazed hallucination that would fade away and be replaced by the sober reality of a brand new morning and another regular day of peaceful drudgery and mental rebalancing.

Still, faced with this paradox of reasoning, Elias shot his gun at the shadows of the night until it was empty once again. In his mind's eye they looked like ravens waiting to swoop down from a distended and leafless tree, yet all the while he was unable to really comprehend who they were or why they had come. But within these fractured faculties, Harding could comprehend the disordered hulk of his sergeant trying to crawl his concussed way out of the open ground he found himself in, and beyond that groping figure, looming out from behind the smouldering broken wall of the fort, came the recognisable form of the dark skinned Frenchman who had walked down the road earlier in the night and asked for their submission before all this anarchy had broken out. Benno had entered the ring and Elias Harding was overcome with an uncontrollable, delirious fury.

The swarthy, bulldog faced foreigner stepped over the rocks lying haphazardly across the breech and stood at the edge of the courtyard between the two buildings with his gun held up to his hip. Eves dragged his body across the stone covered ground looking only towards the refuge of the outer wall near the magazine room. The gunfire fell away leaving a stinted, hollow silence.

“You bloody French snot! God damn you to hell!” cried Harding as he rose upright off his bent knee and drew his sword with his right hand in one elegant motion. Oh the arrogant pride, the stupidity, the misplaced honour that flowed through him as he bounced along the ground past the snaking body of Eves and brought his sword arm back ready to swipe at his victim in attack, just as Benno fired his rifle.

Eli felt the searing pain in his side, which immediately felt wet and the heat then dissipated to a degree that turned the damp area into a patch of slightly warm numbness. Unhindered, he struck out with the momentum from his spring loaded sword arm and caught the stock of Benno’s rifle with his blade as the Frenchman parried the blow but was knocked sideways in surprise. Straight away, Eli swiped with the return stroke and his opponent tried to step back and defend himself with the barrel of his gun. There was a loud tap as the two metals connected. Eli swung again, this time even harder and the smaller sized Frenchman shrunk away as his gun took the full force of the blow. TAP! Eli thought the noise sounded familiar but his deranged brain didn’t care for trying to remember where he had heard it before. TAP! TAP! TAP! The tinny sound of metal upon metal came with each angry strike and as it rang out in the black silence the bulldog was knocked back bit by steely bit.

Harding’s eyes burned with hatred and his teeth ground together in a red misted snarl. His arms swung with venomous energy and Benno, sensing the force and determination in this attack tried to push forward using his rifle to hold the next thrust. It was a moment of misjudgement on the Frenchman’s part as Eli, with a deft downward change of angle brought the sword blade pitching into the collarbone of his opponent. The knife edge dug into the thick tunic material of his coat and gouged a cleft into Benno’s shoulder, cracking the bone with its force and causing him to drop his rifle. Eli pulled the sabre away and immediately sliced across the chest of the commando using the tip to open up a nasty debilitating wound several inches long. Benno’s face took on a pained expression and with the return stroke Eli lacerated the stunned Frenchman’s left thigh making the man’s leg buckle from the scorching pain. Before the victim even had time to raise his arms in defence the swordsman hacked his steel down onto the neck and upper chest of the bulldog with such strength the sabre embedded itself into his bony chest plate and stayed there. With a spine tingling scream Benno crumpled to the floor and Elias began awkwardly falling over him, only the pitch of his tumble allowing the blade to come away from its atrocious wound as the smaller man came to rest on the ground, blood spurting from his mouth, his eyes wide with the terror of such a horrendous ending. Elias steadied his own fall and ended up stooped over the dying man watching the commando’s body twitching as trauma and blood loss took its course. He fell to his knees next to the man, sword still in his hand as he witnessed the life ooze from the face of his hewed enemy. It was shocking and despicable as the final breaths bubbled from his broken windpipe and injured chest. Harding felt sickened and disconsolate. The last thing he believed now was that what he had done could in any way be either proud or honourable. He switched his eyes away and noticed his overcoat led on the ground like a dark dead animal, cast away when he'd manned the cannon as easily as he'd cast away the life of the man at his knees. His mind wondered if this was all just another flashback, a symptom of his battle scarred and trauma ravaged thoughts, and that if he could imagine a piece of music from his happier past, all of this would go away and peace and normality would be restored. But no music came. There was only silence.

The world around him stopped as he was suddenly overcome with a wave of muted shock and strangely, even with Sergeant Eves and Gunner Haines across the yard, a feeling of being completely alone and invisible to the rest of the world. There was a sensation of being consumed in a black hole which was growing from behind the pupils of his eyes. The darkness devoured everything around him so heavily and quickly that it felt like a cloak of blackened iron was thrown over him. He couldn't feel the pain in his side which was now dulled by the regular pulse of his chemically strained body, he didn't even notice the growing disc of red blood across his waist as it merged with the dark blue weave of his sodden, broadcloth battle tunic. But somewhere deep inside of him, in a place only he knew about, the insatiable violence continued to simmer unhindered, ready to strike again if need be.

Through the oily gloom of darkness, on the other side of the courtyard, Mule and Dickie Pearce crouched on the concrete slab that should have held a gun and carriage but instead was frighteningly exposed and empty, breathing heavily into the still, cold night air. Their backs were against the parapet of the outer edge of the fort and they looked into the black openness before them unable to see as far as the place where Harding had brought down Benno, which was only yards away, let alone beyond the wall to the outside world on the opposite side of the courtyard. All they could make out was that across from them, hiding near the corner walls of the barracks, were the two men who had blown out the door to the main building and killed Gosfor in the barrack room. A shot rang out and a bullet pinged off the stonework beside them. Pearce flinched and shook with fear.

"They're like black ghosts creepin' up on us, Dickie," Mule said with a crazed laugh. "All in black, all in black, I'll lay you on yer back, and smite your bastardry into the ground, you unholy devils!" he sang in a rhyming tone as he raised his rifle at the shifting shadows moving through the smoke which oozed from the open doorway. He pulled the trigger. There was a horrid click.

"No bloody bullets, boy! Sod's law we run out'o'bullets," he grinned disarmingly. "I'll 'av to meet 'em half way, my boy," Mule continued with a throwaway tone and reached down to lift an empty rifle with a bayonet attached to the barrel onto Pearce's outstretched lap. "If they get to you son, stick 'em with this," he smiled, small clumps of foam gathering on the corners of his mouth. "If not, remember this lad: there's no better place to die on earth than 'ere." He gave Dickie a final sorrowful look behind the crumpled smile. "Remember that son," he added.

Mules black greasy hair was stuck to his head in oily clumps by sweat from a mixture of exertion and nervous energy. He'd lost his pill box cap when they'd made their escape from the barrack room and his tunic was half undone and open at the neck revealing his toughened, hairy chest. He nodded to the boy one last time then looked away into the dark with wide, shocking eyes.

"No Mule," Dickie began to plead like a child left at the roadside by his mother. The older man didn't look back.

"Come on you buggers!" the workhorse screamed as he jumped up and danced towards the black ghosts.

Mule ducked and weaved across the open ground like a frantic boxer. The first figure stood by the wall of the bunk house fired off a shot which missed the constantly moving on-comer. Immediately after, the second figure dropped to one knee and fired his weapon. This time the aim was good and the bullet gored into Mules thigh. For a second his leg bent under the force but the wound merely galvanised his attack and he practically lunged forward the last few steps in the direction of the first crouching figure, his rifle outstretched with the bayonet jutting forwards. The crouching shadow was desperately trying to reload his weapon, but with a look of panic in his face, the bullet jammed inside the breech. The leathery English workman thrust his body onwards and the point of his bayonet entered the man's cheek, pushing itself all the way through the soft tissue and out the back of his head. The man made no noise but crumpled backwards as Mule fell on top of him in a state of victorious shock. The other figure had by now reloaded and, swinging the gun about at close range, fired a round which hit Mule in the side of his head sending an arc of spurting blood up through the air from the top of his sweaty hair, and he toppled over onto the man he had just killed in the final suicidal act of his dogged and determined life.

From somewhere close to him, Dickie Pearce wasn't sure where, another shot broke through the sound of rushing wind and sent the standing black form who had killed Mule, falling to the floor where he moved once as if trying to get up before becoming completely still. In a distressed condition, Pearce craned his neck to the side and saw the kneeling figure of Gunner Haines, a rifle at his shoulder, the barrel softly smoking in the darkness.

"All in black, all in black, I'll lay you on your back," Pearce heard him whisper down the sight of his gun as if he were singing the pensive lullaby to his final cartridge as he sent it on its vengeful way.

Meanwhile, over by the magazine room door, partly hidden by the sleeping cannon, Eves had also fired his last shot. He sat on his haunches with his back against the low outer wall looking into the murky gloom. His wavy ginger hair blew upright in the stiff breeze and his once elegant whiskery moustache just swayed in the wind like sea anemone dancing in the swell of an invisible current. The explosion had knocked the wind out of him. His tunic was damp with sweat and cold. He felt tired and blown about. Mule's sacrificial attack had filled him with a sense of doom.

Pumping the final spent cartridge from his gun, he tried focusing in the area where the commandos who had been firing at him over the last few minutes, were hiding. They were somewhere in the rubble, secreted in the shadows cast from what was left of the main entrance and the thoroughfare to the courtyard. He became aware of Haines crawling on his belly along the edge of the low wall towards where he was sitting, but didn't look at him directly. Haines slid behind the resting cannon still covered in its green tarpaulin and sat down next to Eves. There was an eerie silence tarnished only by the noise of the wind whistling through the courtyard.

"Have they gone Mr Eves?" panted Haines. "Is it over?" he asked in a desperate plea.

"No scribbler," replied Eves calmly. "They haven't gone. They're still out there. But I think they've run out of bullets, just like we have," he said almost questioningly.

"How do you know that?" whispered Haines, shaking.

"Because nobodies shooting at us anymore," Eves replied ruefully. His eye fell on Harding who was knelt by the hacked body of Benno, near the door to his quarters. They caught each other's gaze. For a few moments they stayed there looking at each other in recognition of the horror and futility of what they and everyone had just been involved in. Each could not see the other's expression in the lightless gloom but they intuitively sensed in each other an understanding of their place in the world at this particular moment in time. The last few hours, or was it just minutes, one couldn't tell in the stilted time frame of violence, had been an undeniable confirmation of everything they had lived for since they had grown from boys to men and that innocence of childhood had been replaced by the realities of the true world and the war which seemed to constantly consume it. The vicious truth was that this world of theirs was one they had chosen to live in and that the enthralling experiences they had craved from their disparate youth was the reason for this life in a society of hostility and war. In that moment they both knew the conflict, whether it was here and now or somewhere else, sometime in the future, wouldn't truly be over until their lives were truly over.

Then the moment was gone, abruptly torn away by separate distractions to both men's sensitised alertness. In front of both men, the two commandos emerged from the shadows of rubble and gingerly stepped over the debris to make their way onto the courtyard, empty rifles still held before them. At the same time the young Officer was alerted from his stupor as he noticed behind him another commando climbing up the ladder on the outer wall with a pistol in his hand, held aloft while he used the other hand to pull him upwards over the rusty rungs. The intruder loosed off a shot towards Eli as he emerged, but the nimble Master Gunner swerved his body to one side and launched himself back into the open doorway of his quarters, just as another shot was fired towards him which miraculously also narrowly missed. As the two shadows from the entrance crept along the open ground towards the magazine room, the figure on the ladder jumped onto the wall and swiftly ran along the top as if heading for the still sitting figures of Eves and Haines. His gun was pointing at the scribbler.

Harding catapulted himself out of the doorway with his sword in hand and bolted like an energized gazelle parallel to the man running along the wall. Before the man could jump up to the next level of balustrade on one side of the gun emplacement and fire a clear shot at Haines, Eli lunged forward through the air and rugby tackled the running man around his waist. A desperate shot fired in the air as he wrapped his arms around the man's legs, buried his shoulder into his thigh and pushed forwards sending both men hurtling over the edge of the wall, down the slope of grass behind, before they finally tumbled onto the rocks near the edge of the boiling brown sea.

When Haines saw the other two figures approaching slowly over the courtyard he grabbed the sergeant's tunic, anguish and childlike disbelief smeared across his dewy face.

"Why is this happening, Mr Eves? Why is this happening to us!" he wailed abysmally, inches from the sergeants rock hard, hair covered face. The big man pushed Haines back against the wall and fixed him with wide, desperate eyes.

"It's just the luck of the draw, lad! Just the luck of the draw," Eves pleaded in an almost exhausted pitch, before resigning to grip his rifle in both hands and lift himself slowly upright until, with his knees slightly bent in readiness for another fray, the sergeant wearily turned round and carried himself forward, dancing into battle once again. Haines withered backwards into the cavernous shadow of the half open magazine room door, terror bleached across his face.

Eves met the two Frenchmen in the middle of the parade ground not far from the dread filled form of Richard Pearce, skulking against the wall as if trying to bury himself in the damp stonework like a frightened insect. The French commandos stood before Eves in ready to strike poses. One was huge, virtually the same size as Zanzibar, with wild eyes and broken teeth holding a bayoneted rifle in his big hands. The other was merely well built with a long dagger in one hand. The broken toothed goliath grinned and jabbed his weapon towards the defensively primed sergeant. Knowing his weapon was empty and bayonet free Eves deftly dropped the butt of his gun and grabbed the barrel, holding it like a club, and swung it sideways in one fluid motion, knocking the barrel end of the Frenchman's rifle to one side.

The frog lost his grin. At the same time the other, well-built man went to lunge forward and use his dagger on Eves. Then suddenly, out of the shadows, unnoticed by anyone, the young Dicky Pearce, fuelled by fear and a sudden rush of support for his sergeant, hopped forward like a springing toad and thrust the bayonet of his rifle into the soft stomach of the second lunging attacker.

The shock made the man drop his knife and he staggered backwards releasing his body from the impalement of the bayonet. He dropped to one knee and held his side, groaning. Eves and the other man clashed again in a sword like stick fight using rifles. Pearce awkwardly dived forward again as if he was falling in a hole and thrust out with his bayonet as the pain in his foot became apparent through the adrenaline rush. This time it entered the man's chest near his armpit and the force pushed the kneeling man backwards onto his side. He let out an agonized cry as Dickie pulled his rifle out, and then rolled from one side to another in pain as the young boy scuffled away towards the safety of the wall, swiftly overwhelmed by a sense of horror and vulnerability. He could only watch aghast as the two monster men fought without really noticing the other man's death.

Eves swung his rifle towards the head of the massive Frenchman. With speed and agility for such a big man the commando hopped backwards avoiding the stroke, before instantly dancing forwards and aiming the butt of his rifle towards Eves, whose previous swing had sent him off balance. The stock glanced off Zanzibar's jaw and he felt several of his teeth break as his head jerked sideways. Grinning again, the commando went to thrust his bayonet into Eve's stomach but the Englishman was able to parry the lunge with his own weapon and dislodge the spike attached to the barrel. But it wasn't quick enough to stop the grinning Frenchman re-swing his butt and knock Eve's rifle from his wet hands. Realising his bayonet was gone, the invader slipped his hand down the breech of his gun and also held it like a club, dancing to and fro like an agitated gorilla and swinging it behind his head before letting forth with a huge batting swing aimed once again for Eve's face.

The now weapon free sergeant held up an arm to defend himself and the butt crashed onto his forearm with such strength it broke the bones inside his flesh. He growled with pain as an intense stinging burn shot through his battered limb but ignoring the discomfort and through gritted, angry teeth Eves lunged towards the slightly swaying Frenchman and dived for his throat with both hands. Unable to raise his gun again in defence of the sudden attack, the commando dropped his rifle and instinctively brought his own hands up towards the neck of the embracing Zanzibar.

They pushed and pulled at each other in a dance of fighting creatures, stoically gripping their opponent like the entwined horns of contesting bulls. Eves had fought many men hand to hand in his lifetime most of whom were no match for his power and sheer ferocity. There had been a few who offered spirited resistance; the deformed monolith he drunkenly fought in a Padstow bar and the street fighting boxer he fought for a bet on the streets of London town, who seemed to absorb his punches until the moment Zanzibar pummelled him into submission before biting his ear off and throwing his beaten body into the river to be rescued by a passing boat. Then, of course, there was the longest fight he'd ever had with the hard man of Bideford all those years ago. But tonight, in this lonely overpowered outpost on the edge of the world, this Frenchman seemed like he might be one of the few.

With a broken arm and a smashed jaw sapping his energy, Eves knew he had to finish this dual quickly. So as they danced to and fro, gripping opposing skin and tunics, spitting in each other's faces, he sharply pulled his head back and snapped it forward, head butting the gnarly commando full on the bridge of his nose. The force of the head attack and the weight of Eves sent both men crashing to the ground with Eves on top. Without using his broken arm, he forced himself upwards with his good one and wrapped his fingers around the throat of the stunned Frenchman, growling with anger and pain as he pushed down on the windpipe of the man beneath his heavy body. He pushed down rhythmically as if trying to remove a stubborn stain from a shirt and using strength and steady momentum began to crush the man's throat. The wild eyes of the hard faced commando bulged and his mouth opened silently revealing the range of broken teeth beneath his bloody and even more miss-shaped nose. He tried to punch Eves but his position on the floor and the height of Eves' head meant his ever weakening punches had no effect. Instead he grabbed at Eves' free but broken arm, inflicting shots of fresh pain up the sergeant's limb which the Englishman ignored, as the life was gradually being crushed out of his opponent.

To the side of the two men, neither of whom knew which, a shot rang out in the rushing wind of darkness. All of a sudden, Eves' jaw was ripped away in a shocking splash of blood, taken by the impact of a speeding bullet. He fell forward, his chest landing on the face of his almost expired victim. Castille was stood to the side, near the body of the bayoneted Frenchman led a few yards away. The Colonel's arm was raised holding a freshly fired pistol. The broken toothed commando frantically tried to push the atrociously injured Eves off his oxygen starved body and managed to roll the flaccid and semi-conscious sergeant to one side. As he did so Castille loosed off another shot. This one entered the side of Eves' gingery head near his ear. His last movement was to thrust his hand skyward as if clutching at the black clouds overhead before death hastily consumed him. The King was dead.

Young Richard Pearce, who had been in a state of stupefied shock during the dual and hadn't noticed the approaching enemy Colonel step out of the shadows of the main wall near the latrines, let out an involuntary scream as he saw his revered sergeant die. He gripped his rifle and sprang upright, running at Castille, his bayonet pointed at the man in his long dark coat, screeching maniacally like a possessed warrior releasing his final, deathly scream. Castille coolly swung his pistol arm around and fired two shots into the chest of the oncoming Pearce and instantly halted the young assailant. The thin youth's lanky body flipped up and his legs momentarily dangled in mid-air before he landed with a crunch on his back, the screaming face suddenly silenced as he too looked towards the darkened sky and allowed death to finally consume him as well.

Zanzibar Eves fought his last battle and died in the fort on the end of Brean Down on the 6th February 1884. He was 52. For everyone who ever knew him, but would never see him again, his name was Zanzibar. For what reason they would never see him again they would never know, although many speculated. What his real name was and the actual truth behind his upbringing they would never truly find out. But importantly, the legend of the man still remained in the mess houses and bar rooms across the Empire he helped to build.

His real name was Archibald and he was born in Aston, Birmingham. His mother was a washer woman in a leather factory on the banks of the Grand Union canal and her husband, his father, was a soldier in the British Army.

As if in response to the death of Archibald, in the church near the village of Uphill, Morris rose from his pew in a drunken stupor and lopped towards the back of the darkened tumbledown house of religion. The bottle of whiskey was empty on the flagstone floor and as he staggered through the benches he noticed, from behind his drunken haze, the distant sound of gunfire had stopped. He gripped the rope hanging down from the high bell tower and hung on to it for a moment, supporting his weight with the thick cord as he spun slowly in a daze, listening to the growing cries of swooping zephyrs that rushed from the burgeoning gales outside. Staring through the gloom at the picture of his brother beside the orange glow from the wick of the nearly extinguished candle sat on top of the alter, he stopped spinning and began to ring the single church bell. The sound bellowed against the walls of the little building and echoed over the graveyard before being lifted by the gusts of wind and carried away out to sea. Morris wasn't ringing the bell in commemoration of the dead Sergeant Eves. He was ringing it to alert his long dead brother that a storm was coming, and to give him a signal of which way to walk home should his spirit finally find his way back to shore.

Castille walked over to the dead English sergeant and looked into the large, hideously damaged face still staring skyward. He raised his eyes upward and also stared into the blackness. The gentle patter of rain drops began to splash across his face and he felt the stinging howl of a strengthening wind on his cold cheeks. His eyes moved around the desolation of the courtyard taking in the broken walls of the fort, the large empty spaces and the bodies of the dead along the boundary. It seemed silent and still, broken only by the faint tolling of a far off bell. There was the strong smell of acrid smoke and sulphurous cordite in the air. Walking over to the prone body of his dead friend Benno, he noticed the gashed, grisly wounds and wondered how his end must have felt. The horrified look on the small man's bull dog face sent a chill down Castille's spine. He noticed movement in the rubble near the entrance and acknowledged the other members of his reinforcement team checking the rooms inside the fort and examining the bodies of their dead comrades scattered around the perimeter. A wet looking Legionnaire came up to him.

"Everyone's dead," he said to the Colonel. Castille nodded but offered no reply. "The weather's getting shittier," the soldier continued. "I think a storm is coming."

There was a pause as Castille looked over towards the magazine room and the two artillery guns nearby. He still said nothing.

"The tide Colonel, it's going out. We need to leave. Now," urged the soldier. Castille gave the man a fierce stare and then looked at his dead friend.

"Get everyone on the boat, we'll have to leave the dead here," he said bitterly and then pointed a finger at the big guns. "Blow them up before you leave," he said, giving Benno one last look.

The rain was falling steadily now and the wind blew inward off the sea with an angry temper pushing the sheets of rain against the headland with a twisted annoyance. The commando nodded belligerently at his commander and went over to the gun used earlier, its muzzle pointing forlornly out to sea. Castille took one last look around and climbed over the wall onto the ladder leading down to the slipway where the rest of the Legionnaires were now boarding the rowboat, the ever decreasing water knocking the craft against the growing formation of rocks.

The grizzled soldier took a stick of dynamite from his damp canvas shoulder bag and took a box of matches from his inside pocket. Luckily they were still dry, protected from the rain by his thick black, donkey jacket. He lit one and shielded it from the sharp rain and gusts of wind and brought the small flame into contact with the fuse under the sparse cover of the RML cannon. He paused with the fizzing stick in his hand, waiting for the fuse to burn down a little before he stuffed it into the cradle where the gun joined the carriage.

Then, he thought he saw something move nearby, and his view shot towards the magazine room door. Startled, he focused through the squally rain at the shadowy recess. Nothing moved, just stillness. Was that a figure of a man he had seen or just the wind on the half open door? The soldier couldn't see properly. He looked at the rapidly diminishing fuse and fixed the doorway again before pushing the dynamite into the gun carriage and withdrawing into the officer's quarters. He covered his ears and closed his eyes just as the ensuing explosion lit up the night and the shockwave blew through the open door sending in a ball of room filling dust and smoke and causing the tiniest of vibrations around the fortress walls against which the Frenchman momentarily leant.

As the explosion receded, the soldier recovered his senses and looked around the depressing sitting room with its cold fireplace and threadbare furniture now fused with a floating cloud of white and grey particles, and thought to himself what a miserable place this would have been to be deployed at. For a second he almost felt sorry for the Officer stationed on this barren piece of wind scorched, rain soaked rock. He craned his neck around the door and stared into the carnage of the destroyed gun, the rain steaming on the hot twists of energised metal and the smoke billowing through the force of wind in ribbons of grey as it rose from the splintered carriage. The barrel of the RML had been blown off the mounting towards a part of the outer wall now shattered by the explosion. It teetered on the edge for a moment, muzzle end facing the sea. In the distance was the eerie sound of a bell clanging repetitively, one slow chime after another. As the bell rang out through the stormy gusts of rising wind the barrel of the cannon rocked slightly and then tipped over the precipice, tumbling end over end until it clattered noisily onto the jagged rocks below. The iron casing didn't shatter, it just led nestling in the large stones whilst being licked by the ebbing tide of the grey estuary. The soldier thought about the other gun shrouded in its coat of green material and reached into his bag again, but found it was empty.

"Everybody's dead anyway," he said to himself with a shrug as he hastily strode over to the wall and climbed down the ladder. There was urgency in his movements as he headed towards the waiting rowboat which was now being pushed into the bubbling shallow water of the sharply receding channel. In the distance the bell continued to ring.

The explosion woke Elias up. So did the rain, which now fell fat and heavy on his exposed eyeballs. He looked around groggily, wondering what was happening. A few feet away, the body of the man he had tackled on the wall was angled against a large rock jutting out from the water's edge, Eli's broken sword sticking out of the man's chest like a gruesome headstone marking the fall of a dead warrior. Harding's head hurt and he felt his forehead, wincing as he fingered a small, bloody gash on his hairline. He remembered rolling down the grass towards the rocks, over and over with the Frenchman like a pair of tumbling dice, and the short fight as they grappled for Eli's sword across the treacherous rocks on the tip of the weather battered headland. Somehow Elias had managed to grab the handle of his sabre from the ground first and swung out at his opponent but the blade had broken as his missed swipe had glanced against the wet limestone. As the commando swerved to avoid the attack he lost his footing, and Eli plunged the broken sword into the fallen soldier's chest killing him instantly. But in stepping back, Elias had slipped on the rocks and gashed his head against a boulder sending a stream of incandescent stars across his eyes. As he crawled to the safety of the wet grass the concussion kicked in and he led unconscious for a while in the pouring rain.

Now the night came rushing back into his brain and the stars dissipated away while the events of the fortress attack flashed across his distorted mind. He got up and staggered through the tempest which threw itself with a growing anger upon the coastline, up the jagged rocky headland back towards the walls of the fortress. On the way he looked behind and saw a twinkling light in the bleak darkness of sky and water. It was a ship. And Eli knew it was the small ship which had brought the enemy to this unsuspecting place and had wreaked such terrible havoc. Unfocused, groggy and bewildered he clambered up the sopping grass and stood on top of the surrounding enclosure wall, and looked over the desolation and destruction that was the small coastal fort of Brean Down.

Elias made out the dead body of Sergeant Eves and the straggly arms and legs of the young boy, Pearce, nearby. He noticed the smouldering wreck of the seven-ton gun and the mangled remains of James Burden near the decimated entrance. Other bodies led in the dark corners by the barracks and the officer's quarters, Lumpy, Mule, Barnes, the enemy. Angrily, he looked out to sea and saw the outline of a row boat heading through the increasingly choppy waves towards the bobbing light of the little steamship.

He jumped down and pulled the rain leaden tarpaulin off the Iron Beast. Looking down the thick metal barrel he could see the tiny ship with the rowing boat suddenly crashing up against its side in the growing storm. Elias menacingly strode two paces, pulled open the door to the underground magazine store and jumped down the steps into the gloom. As he inched down the pitch black corridor he tripped over something large and wriggling which sent him crashing against the wooden slats protecting the wall at the end of the walkway.

"What the hell!" he shouted more in fear than surprise, scrabbling around to face the obstruction.

"Don't kill me!" screamed the wriggling shadow. Harding recognised the sound of Haines' frightened squeal.

"Scribbler!" he called out, his eyes acclimatising to the darkness. "You're alive, you bastard," he said with a tone of relief and fearful excitement.

"Mr Hardin'? Is that you, sir," Haines whispered in reply.

"Yes scribbler, yes, it's me."

"Everybody's dead."

There was a moment of silence in the dark space. The two men looked towards the sound of each other's breathing. It was too dark to make out a face or even the shape of the other person's body. Underground, in the darkness, away from the weather outside and the bodies of the dead scattered around the fort, everything seemed peaceful. Harding felt light headed. He could feel the pain in his side and across the top of his skull. The loss of blood and the adrenaline fuelled exertions during the night were now making him feel weak and a wave of tiredness crept over him. Eli heard Haines shivering with cold and fright.

"I know everybody is dead, Haines," Eli said finally with quiet reverence. He shifted uncomfortably as the pain in his waist throbbed. "But we're not," he grimaced.

"Have they gone?" asked the scribbler, his voice shaking.

"Yes, they've gone."

"Thank God," breathed the shadow.

Harding stared into the murky gloom. His head was swimming and he thought he might be sick. Swallowing hard, he turned his head in the direction of the other quivering man.

"You've got to help me stop them getting away," he said, puffing between words.

"It's too late, Mr Hardin'."

"We can sink them, Haines, using the Iron Beast."

The scribbler looked into the dark quizzically. "The Iron Beast?" he said. "What do you mean?"

Eli leant forward, not realising how close he was to the other man. Haines could feel the officer's breath on his face.

"It's the new gun. The Iron beast," Eli said again thoughtfully. The scribbler felt even more nervous than before.

"Why the Iron Beast, Mr Harding?" asked Haines quietly.

"Because we're all beasts, Scribbler, we just don't always look like it. Everything we create comes from that beast which lives inside us. We can't help it." His voice became subdued. "It seems whatever we do is touched by anger, formed for an eventual violence and a want for mutual destruction and we create the objects with which to do it. Like that god awful creation out there, Haines." His eyes bored into the dark, right into the unseeing eyes of the other man. "Only this one's made of iron. We're beasts made from flesh and blood and bone and guts while that gun out there is a beast made of iron and steel and gunpowder and explosive." Elias gulped back the bilious sensation in his stomach and a renewed but delirious and crazed energy flowed through his tired body, empowering him. "And if you help me, Haines, we can load that iron beast with shell and powder and blow those bloody beasts on that ship that came to destroy us to hell and back and drown the rest in the raging torrents of that infernal channel." The words began to spit from the agitated Officer's mouth like pellets from a shotgun. "Those bastards have come here and killed everybody in this fort, all your friends, the sergeant, the cook, those poor young brother's, Mule, Pickles, Burden and everybody else that tried to make it through life on this windy rock, everyone except us. So, it's down to us, Haines, to take revenge on those vile beasts that destroyed those innocent lives, I believe, for no good reason." Harding paused and knelt beside the Scribbler whilst fiercely grabbing the other man's coat. "As far as I can see, no one else is coming to save us from the horrors we've witnessed and the only way we'll ever live with ourselves after tonight is if we blow that bloody ship out of the water!" The final words erupted from his mouth as he stood upright in the murk of the dark, fetid corridor, the scribbler's tunic gripped in his tensed fingers, the energy and the violence coursing through his tingling body, masking the pain and making the frightened volunteer in his grip cower from the vehemence of his Master Gunner's anger.

Eli pulled Haines down the small hallway as if he were a headmaster dragging a naughty schoolboy and the two men entered the larger black void that was the main store. In the subterranean hole of the ammunition room the men were as blind as moles but Harding could see clearly everything he had to do. The mission was obvious and the means by which to achieve it were laid out before him in the stifling black of this claustrophobic space. But in Eli's twisted mind-set they were magically illuminated like treasure lit up in a secret cave. "Get one of those shells," he ordered pointing in the pitch dark at the wooden shell boxes in the corner. Haines blindly stepped over and using only his sense of touch, tentatively picked up one of the torpedo shaped Palliser shells. Harding, as if there was a light on in the room that only he could comprehend, picked up a cartridge, some wadding and a bag of gunpowder. "Come on Mr Scribbler," he said turning towards the way out, "let's make this one for the lads, eh."

And with those final words the two men, one determined and seemingly possessed, the other frightened and unsure, headed for the creation that was the Iron Beast.

Neither man spoke as they loaded the cannon. Blown by the lifting winds in the moonless night and soaked by the driving rain they worked quickly and expertly like methodical craftsmen priming their skills on some precise and strangely contoured machine. Harding was sweating profusely in the sharp cold of the night and his eyes were wide with excitement and desire. He winced occasionally as he moved but remained adamant in his point, muttering to himself privately as he calculated the necessary projections for aiming. Without noticing the fact, little calculation was required on his part as the gun was weirdly, almost perfectly set for the right trajectory. But he made the minor adjustments regardless, consumed by the robotic process he was engaged in. He switched his eye line from the aiming mechanism to the dot of light. "About 800 yards, well within range" he muttered to himself several times.

Aldous Haines' back was slightly crooked in everything he did and the look of shock and fear remained on his hollow white face. His body continued to shiver in the damp chilled air, but even with him, through these apparent discomforts, there was a presence of focused meaning. Every now and then they would both look feverishly out onto the black sea and check the position of the ship and its lonely pinpoint of identifying light. It did not move much, perhaps from the two artillerymen's perspective only an inch or two within the dark void, but for those on board, several feet at a time on the growing swell of the massive estuary.

Unknown to the men behind the small parapet, busy in their work, the 'Small Fish' had already filled itself with those men who thought they would be leaving this place and the last ferrying rowboat had been cast away to the sea, unneeded and unwanted by a Captain and a Colonel who knew time was of the essence. The engine's growled in the bowels of the ship but outside, the sound was dulled against the growing roar of the wind. Above the rise and fall of the chopping waves the steamer made way towards the open sea and the last lifeboat disappeared sombrely into the grasping night.

Finally, after only a minute or so since they began, and what was actually a supremely professional action for the two gunners to achieve on a procedure that would normally require at least three men, the gun was loaded. Harding and Haines moved around the weapon checking their work like dancers around an ancient idol in a deadly pagan sacrificial rite. Satisfied that it was ready, the bomber's stood behind the Iron Beast and looked out to sea. Neither man gave the other a final glance as they focused on the distant point of light. Their thoughts were unclouded by emotion or regret, the final mission still clear in minds yet to reel from the impact of the past few hours. There was nothing to say, no words needed to fill the space, only an undaunted desire to fulfil an action and make one last stand against the shadows of the night.

Harding pulled the lanyard and there was a cacophonous sound like the sky had fallen in. The two men expectantly stepped back and turned away, closing their eyes to the sudden tumult. Surrounded in a ball of angry, fire drenched, blinding light and catapulted with a starburst of impulsive energy, the shell exploded from the gun faster than the eye could comprehend. As it invisibly rifled through the night air its velocity dropped a little as the propulsion was spent, but it only fell in the slightest of arcs still driven by the force of nature and power of ignited gunpowder.

The two men behind the walls of the fortress watched as the shell torpedoed the side of the boat, just above the water line, near the back where the engine room was housed. As it impacted and burrowed into the metal hull with a God like force, the warhead exploded ripping a six-foot-wide hole in the side of the rusted ship, some of which was below the waterline. There was a second smaller explosion as the gas and oil fuels ignited and the steam boiler erupted. Within seconds there was a horrid sound of tearing metal and cracking bulkheads as if huge metal beams were being folded in half by a grotesque giant. The ship rocked from side to side and then tipped towards the side with the hole and as the men on board screamed with terror, the 'Marin Corinne' began to fill with water.

The wind howled down the channel in response to the men at war engaged in their angry conflict upon the land, which they had now brought to bear on the sea as well. The elements showed their distemper, and the wind blew stronger still as the sea boiled and churned with rage under the momentum of its own withdrawing force. In reply, the rain fell harder than ever before in a union of compelling nature. The ship rapidly drank in the swirling brown fluid and inhaled the breaking blasts of air. Her old steel frame split in half under the pressure and as the men on board were crushed and torn by the fractured vessel some were spilled into the sea and tossed away into the bubbling torrents.

Other men tried to swim away, but were sucked back into the chaos of the sinking boat. A few managed to grab hold onto bits of wreckage and still floating rowboats, pushing themselves desperately away from the turbulent shipwreck. But the rancid sea, chopping and twisting around them in the wind and rain, caused their loose holds to slip and they were sucked under the surface to drown as they tried to keep afloat in the cold estuary.

Some stronger swimmers, including the artisan, Olivier Modesto, managed to get away and head for the distant rocks of the shore, a sense of relief at being within reach of safety and escaping a watery death. But as their feet touched the soggy, moisture filled mud of the channel bed, their legs were swallowed up by the glutinous, sandy glue and the waters of the receding tide washed over their heads, forcing many backwards to drown in the mud, and they too were consumed by the suffocating estuary.

The remaining men bobbed desperately in the angry waters, holding their clutching hands out towards the black hulks of land in the shadowed distance, until they were dragged away into the open sea by the power of the draining tide, lost forever in the limitless abyss of the deep, dark ocean. Two of those men were Jean Baptiste Castille and Cyrano Shrott.

Haines and Harding gazed upon this scene in a transcendental state. They were transfixed by the horror of what they could see but without the feelings of guilt or regret. It was almost abstract to them, as if they were watching it from a different place, from a higher plain, detached from the reality of a world they had no control over. They knew they had caused the demise of so many lives but for a few moments there was no understanding of the implications this might have on their souls. It seemed to them that this ending was inevitable, unavoidable and an ultimate result from the actions of those who they had only just destroyed.

They watched the ship sink below the waves and then spent some minutes mesmerized by the lolling bodies of the small figures anchored in the mud, swaying gently by the gradual ebb of the dissolving tide. The storm seemed to abate and the rain became a soft drizzle whilst the howling wind was replaced by a stiff breeze. Haines stopped shaking.

"Do you believe in ghosts?" asked Harding without averting his gaze.

The scribbler didn't move. "Not really, Sir," he replied absently.

"You will now," said Eli.

Elias Harding felt the brightness and energy suddenly drain from his body. His eyes lost their wide excitement and the pupils shrank while his legs turned to jelly. His head became light again and he felt faint. Then he tipped backwards on his heels and fell to the courtyard on his back.

Haines felt his commander falling and turned to try and catch him, but was too late. He quickly knelt beside his Master Gunner and lifted his head from the stony ground with one hand, resting the other upon the stricken man's damp tunic. It felt sticky. He looked down and realised the cloth was saturated with not only rain, but also congealed blood.

"Oh my God, Mr Harding, you've been hurt," he cried, staring into Eli's tired and drowsy looking face. The sturdy look of meaning and resolution was gone. It had disappeared from both men's demeanour. The gaunt look of fear crept across Haines features and once again he began to shake.

"It's my fault everybody's dead, Scribbler. I killed all those men. If I had just surrendered everyone might have lived. My pride, arrogance and stupid fears destroyed them, like it's destroyed me," Eli said in strained breaths, his chest tightening from the pain of his wounds. His eyes widened abruptly, then closed before flapping open lazily again. He coughed a little.

"Just when I thought I'd got through. Maybe even found a future with someone," he spluttered half laughingly and then coughed with rasping heaves, a thin trickle of blood running from his nose. He screwed up his eyes. "Men like me don't deserve love or remembrance. Violence and fear control me now as it did then. The scars of the past condemn our future, Haines." Eli's eyes closed and his head dropped to one side.

Haines brought the injured man's head up facing it to the sky. "It wasn't your fault Mr Harding, this is no one's fault but those men who came here with evil in their souls," he pleaded, gently shaking the officer to try and bring a measure of life back into his weary body. Eli seemed to respond and looked into Haines's anxious face.

"I hope no one will know of what I have done," Eli breathed, opening his eyes. "What all these beasts of men have done to each other. Good must prevail, Haines, don't you think? We cannot let the legacy of hatred overwhelm the righteous, the beauty, and the goodness in the souls of people."

The scribbler started rocking as a sense of grief and vulnerability took hold of him. He began to cry and mutter and hold on tighter to Eli's body, pushing his diminutive frame closer to the dying man, hoping to gain some degree of comfort from his fading presence. "Don't go Mr Hardin'! Please don't die! Don't leave me here," he cried. "It wasn't your fault, it's no one's fault but the hand of death and the ghosts that hide in the shadows of the blackened holes that grow in all our hearts." Tears rolled down Haines's face, but his weeping was not just through sadness. Moreover, it was the trauma caused by the horrors he had seen on this night. The fear of the demons he could, and always would, see in every shadow.

Eli looked with languid eyes at the broken man holding him and smiled slightly. "It's alright Scribbler, don't cry. It'll be alright. There's no need for Mr Harding now. You can call me Eli," he whispered hazily. "The sun will come up soon. It's warm in the sun and the light will chase the shadows away. I'll remember this place in the sunshine I once saw it in and so should you. This is the greenest Down I ever did see."

As he looked up into the darkness of the expansive sky, his eyes closed one last time. His body, now devoid of any pain or sensation, created in his dying mind the belief that there was a space of pure light somewhere within the darkness all around. Inside his head he could hear an orchestra playing and a chorus singing. Was it the last movement of Beethoven's ninth or something else? He couldn't quite be sure. For a brief moment he thought he was in a concert hall somewhere, the violins calling out to him and the girl with the beautiful hair, enraptured by the music which cascaded around them. As the growing light crept into the edges of the opaque blackness before his eyes, the orchestra played on. And as he died, Elias was smiling, glad that he could hear the music once again.

9. Secrets and Lies

The two men stepped down from the hansom cab and walked across the driveway towards the Manor house door. The leading figure was tall, wore a large grey overcoat done up to the neck and sported a brown bowler hat on his head. His sharp shoes crunched on the concrete drive with each purposeful stride he took and the second man had to shuffle along to try and keep up with him. He in turn was older and had a loose brown moustache and saggy skinned eyes. He too wore a bowler hat, but his was a pigeon grey colour and looked a touch weathered and a bit too big for his head, which was in keeping with the black overcoat and brown scarf he wore. The second man spoke as they approached the porch.

"Do you think this'll work?" he asked discreetly from beneath the scarf. The front man stayed purposeful.

"Why not, it's all perfectly plausible," he said straight faced. A tone in his voice suggested a sense of irony in his answer. "Plus, Danvers used to work in the Foreign office, didn't he? His sense of duty should prevail."

"But these people aren't stupid," questioned the man behind. His saggy eyes flashed a look of insecurity at the other man's back.

"I never said they were. But gossip and rumours are the only proof they'll have to the contrary," he replied as his sharp shoes tapped up the steps leading to the flaking front door. "Besides, looks like they could do with the cash," he added sardonically as he knocked with purpose on the door.

Lord Danvers opened the door and stood before the two visitors, leaning rigidly on one side of his body against a thick metal handled walking stick.

"You must be the men from the War office," the Lord of the manor snapped stiffly. He looked tired and half-finished but his unshaven chin, topped by the bristly grey moustache he always wore gave the old man a spiky and direct aspect.

"Yes lord Danvers," said the front man respectfully. "My name is Osbourne, and this is Mr Cameron," he added flapping a gloved hand at his associate.

"Good. Inspector Frampton said someone would be along to explain whatever the bloody hell's going on here. You'd better come in," Danvers barked standing back to allow the two men in. Mr Cameron closed the door behind him. "You can hang your coats up yourselves," the Lord yapped abruptly waving a finger at the coat stand by the staircase, "There are no servants in this house sirs, they're long gone. You have to look after yourself in this part of the world I'm afraid gentlemen. At least you were quick getting here," he pulled up his chin and looked at the two men pointedly, his whiskers twitching with accusation.

Osbourne and Cameron gave each other an uneasy glance as they took off their coats and hung them up. "Yes, luckily we were in the area when we got the call from the local police. In a case like this, they have to inform us immediately so we can take control of the situation," Osbourne creamed. There were no spaces left for his bowler hat so he held on to it awkwardly. Danvers ignored him and turned around, limping hastily down the hallway, his brashness hiding a nervous frailty caused by the previous night's heinous events.

"This way, gentlemen, we're in the sitting room," he said as the other men followed him down the hall, fiddling with their hats.

They entered the sitting room where Victoria was sat in one of the soft chairs looking solemnly out of the window. It was the same chair she had sat in when she talked to Elias the day before. Her hair was picked up casually in a loose bun and the dull light from the window made her look ghostly. She turned without smiling to the two men when they entered.

"Victoria," said her father, "This is Mr Osbourne and Mr Cameron, from the War Office."

She merely gave a small nod to the men without saying anything and then turned sadly back to the window. The two officials felt edgy, unsure what to say to the woman. They knew what she had been through last night. Danvers broke the silence.

"Would you like some apple cake and tea? The cake is homemade by the culinary hand of my fair daughter. Just one of her many talents," he said proudly. The two men, aware of the lack of servants, didn't want to disturb the lady in the window.

"Um, no thank you, Lord Danvers, we've already eaten," Osbourne replied delicately.

"Mr Danvers will do, young man," corrected the bristly Lord. "Suit yourself with the cake. So what's happening then? Have we declared war on France or have they declared war on us?"

The other two men looked at each other awkwardly. Victoria sat passive and emotionless, staring out the window with distant eyes, as if oblivious to the conversation going on around her. Osbourne coughed lightly.

"Um no, no one has declared war yet, Mr Danvers." He noted a chair beside the bookcase. "Do you mind if I sit?" he asked.

"Of course, go ahead. Excuse me if I stand, it takes away the ache in my leg," and he swayed from one leg to the other as if to accentuate the point. Osbourne sat down while Cameron remained standing, examining the room. His seated superior fiddled with his hat absently as he continued to speak.

"Along with your terrifying ordeal, I take it Inspector Frampton made you aware of the terrible incidents that took place on Brean Down and the island of Steep Holm last night."

"Of course," blustered Danvers, "The blighters tried to imprison us. If it wasn't for my daughter and that last act of bravery from Artilleryman Evans, we'd all be locked in the cellar with a bullet in the back of our heads," he said, tapping the floor with his stick to make the point.

Cameron raised an uncomfortable smile. "Yes, quite. You've both been very brave and a credit to the nation. You stopped a very dangerous man."

"How many were killed?" Victoria's soft voice suddenly interrupted the masculine guff, its quiet directness cutting the room dead. Osbourne waited a moment to re-gather his purpose and replied placidly.

"We lost six men on the island and everyone in the garrison on Brean Down," he felt the young woman tense up as he said the last part and he paused waiting for her to say something or to turn round, but she remained motionless. He carried on. "There was the postman as you know and a Mr Herbert Lanes from the farm near the fort. We believe all the insurgents were killed. If it wasn't for the bravery of those men at Brean Down, they may well have got away with it."

"So no one was left alive," Victoria said without turning.

"No, Miss Danvers. There were no survivors from the fort," Osbourne lied, raising his eyes in an apologetic way.

"What about the rest of the invasion?" the old Lord unexpectedly burst out.

"It wasn't an invasion Mr Danvers," broke in Cameron. "Apparently it was an attempt by a renegade force of Legionnaire's to recapture one of their men who had been apprehended on Steep Holm."

"Renegades!" stuffed the Lord.

"Yes, we're not sure what they were planning but it didn't seem to work and got out of hand. The French authorities claim to have no knowledge of it and are suggesting it was organised by a rogue Colonel and his men. From what we can gather it seems this may have been the case." Mr Cameron smiled clumsily and tried to brighten his saggy eyelids but he just looked a bit oafish and looked out the window instead.

"Is that right," offered a suspicious Mr Danvers. Osbourne took over the lead to try and regain the purpose.

"None of this has, of course, been released to the public yet. This whole incident has huge political and sovereignty repercussions. If the events became common knowledge we would undoubtedly have to debate the merits of a war with France, the public and much of the Government would demand it," the official said smoothly.

"So they bloody well should," interrupted Danvers. "We can't expect to have our shores trespassed and our soldiers and innocent civilians killed without the perpetrators dealt with in the harshest possible way," he spiked, fixing the two men with narrowed, beady eyes.

"Indeed that is true Mr Danvers and in many ways I agree with you but the basic fact of the matter is, it would be impossible for us to engage in a war or even a political stand-off with a country like France at this moment in time, both legally and financially. We just couldn't afford it."

"Afford it!" piped the old man. "No country can afford any war they have. We've never been able to afford a war. But sometimes you just have to make do. We cannot allow this attack on our sovereignty to fester without calling for the strictest punishment on the instigators of those crimes which undoubtedly fall at the feet of the French Government. I don't give a monkeys about renegade Colonels or whatever tosh they come up with, they should still be made to pay for what happened here and given a bloody good hiding!" The Lord realised he was getting wound up and visibly eased back a little.

"Reparations will be made on the French Government I can assure you of that. They have already agreed that this was an odious crime and anyone involved with the insurgency will be found out and brought to bear the consequences. They will be handed to us and dealt with accordingly. As a result, or perhaps even a consequence of this abhorrent occurrence, the Government has garnered valuable information which will be used against the French Authorities, improving our position in the table of negotiation regarding a wide range of subjects without the need for further conflict. We are already in a position of power through the brave actions of the men at the fort, and yourselves of course, that we would never have achieved after even many years of the vilest bloodshed and warfare. But this must be kept out of the public eye for it is something the country must bear without the knowledge of its own people, for that will bring only more chaos and further destruction. As human beings with the responsibilities of governance and control we are obliged, as people of the right class and fortitude, to undertake this difficult and seemingly unbecoming course. We beg you to help us in that course." Osbourne stopped speaking and looked at the Danvers in turn.

"What are you suggesting Mr Osbourne, if I may be so blunt," replied Lord Danvers.

The official took a deep breath and kept his eye on the old man. "We're calling on you and your daughter to make a great sacrifice. We appeal to your sense of duty to help secure the safety and wellbeing of your country, both financially and in the name of peace by keeping this unfortunate affair secret. You must not talk to anyone else about it, ever. Considering the circumstances, I know it is asking a lot but it is something I have been asked to do by the Prime Minister and his inner cabinet. Something he knows people of your stature will understand and abide with, not only now but for all time. A war with France is unwinnable, Mr Danvers. It would merely become a terrible conflict of attrition that could last for years and bring both countries to their knees. It is the kind of war that could continue unabated purely through the anger and insatiable desire for revenge from its own people, something the Government is tasked to protect her people from."

"But this cannot go unanswered," began the old man angrily.

"It won't," interjected Osbourne briskly. His face took on an official expression as if he were behind a desk in an office somewhere within the corridors of power. "As a member of Her Majesties Government in the past you will be aware of the tough decisions made by our superiors. We need stability in the world and once again we need your help to achieve this."

"You need us to keep quiet," interrupted Danvers.

"Yes," Osbourne began and then hesitated. "We need secrecy, secrecy for which you will always be remembered. Your status as a revered member of the Queens Government, both in reputation and financially, will be greatly enhanced and rewarded. We will not forget the sacrifices you make in your countries hour of need."

"And what about the Queen, what does she say about all of this," Danvers asked almost standing to attention stiffly when he mentioned the monarch.

"Sometimes the Government is tasked to protect the country from not only its people but the passions of her Queen as well," Cameron added sagely. There was silence as Lord Danvers took in the revelations and his anger began to re-boil. Before he could let fly his daughter spoke.

"What about the men who died in all of this, Mr Osbourne," Victoria asked sadly whilst still staring out of the window searching the garden for her own answers to her own questions.

Osbourne lifted his chin. "To those of us who know of their sacrifice we will always be in awe of the duties they performed and their deaths must be seen in the light that the secrecy of those deaths will surely save the lives of tens of thousands of our armed forces."

"Secrets and lies, Mr Osbourne, that's what you ask of us and those men, secrets and lies," she answered still staring out of the window.

"The job of protecting this country often involves secrets and lies Miss Danvers and though it is painful to be a party to those lies they are a necessary evil in the process and security of our modern society," Osbourne prickled in reply.

"This modern society, I suggest, sucks the very life out of itself and crushes all the hope and prospect of prosperity in a vice of its own creation, and I believe one day it will destroy itself totally and we will be powerless to stop it. If secrets and lies are the price of honour, Mr Osbourne, then all hope is lost." She diverted her gaze from outside the window and looked at her lap with damp, tear filled eyes. Her father and the two men sensed her sorrow.

"How will you ever explain what has happened here," her father asked.

Cameron perused the bookshelf and continued to allow his associate to do the talking again. Osbourne looked at his fiddled hat, breathed in deeply, gathering air like it was bullshit fuel, and then fixed the Danvers' in turn as he released the guff.

"In tomorrow's papers," he began, "you'll read about a French steamship carrying a small detachment of marines during a training exercise in the English Channel. The story will describe how the ship was blown off course in the storm after developing engine trouble. The boat ended up in the Bristol Channel and tried to seek refuge from the difficult conditions near the island of Steep Holm." The War office man waited briefly for any response. On receiving none, he carried on, encouraged. "The story will inform the public that the ship's engine room exploded during the storm, destroying the boat and casting all those on board into the estuary where, due to the fierce waves and turbulent tide, all souls were lost. Boats are collecting the dead as we speak, the ones they can find at least, and many may be washed ashore over the coming days." His face took on a slightly pained expression. "It's quite strange," he continued, "When the boats went out this morning, a thick sea mist descended over the bay hampering the collection of the dead. Some bodies may not be found for several days." He gulped and grimaced before adding in a dreadful and sorry manner, "Others may never be found at all."

Cameron glassily looked at the carpet with a sad dog face. "Lost on the tides, missing forever in the murky depths," he said dolefully.

Victoria looked round at the two men, aghast. Her father's whiskers bristled angrily.

"What about the men on the fort," Victoria snapped. "They weren't killed by some accident," she added with a scowl, her voice full of disdain and her wet eyes shining with anger. Osbourne and Cameron both looked at her directly. The sitting man continued.

"The paper will tell that the reason the ship exploded was…because…" he stammered as he prepared himself for the reaction to what he was going to say. "Because…. it was fired upon by a group of men in the fort who were suffering from a fit of madness, brought on by the delusional effects associated with the symptoms of lead poisoning." There was a pause as the officials waited and Victoria and her father took in the information.

"How preposterous, I've never heard such rot!" Lord Danvers blustered. Victoria's mouth dropped open and she frowned. Osbourne continued hastily.

"Food often goes off in these places and the men don't always know it. They often eat fresh goods that are contaminated with lead used in the ammunition. They also use tinned goods that are cheap and tainted, often from abroad where they are still canned in lead. It's an unfortunate reality but something that still happens in the service of our armed forces, especially overseas. The effects take several weeks to build up but the end result, before they finally succumb to death, is delusion and madness. The report will state that the worst effected were made even worse after drinking too much of the local cider. They fired on the ship thinking they were under attack and then killed the others at the fort when they tried to intervene. The deluded died shortly afterwards from the poisoning and by murdering each other in confusion." He suddenly looked sheepish, realising the idiocy of the words he had just said and immediately stopped fiddling with his bowler hat.

"Ludicrous!" stormed old man Danvers. "What about the men on the island? Are you going to say they all died of food poisoning?"

Osbourne shuffled in his seat trying to remain purposeful. "They were killed while trying to help those on the shipwreck," he said.

"What about those men who didn't die Mr Osbourne, the ones on Steep Holm? Inspector Frampton said most of them were imprisoned. Stories will surely come out," the lady in the window asked in a barbed manner.

"The importance of secrecy has been stressed upon the survivors and as employees of the armed forces they have a duty to remain quiet. Fortunately, loose talk in the taverns will be seen as just that, drunken stories by the over imaginative," Cameron replied, in a vain attempt to deflect criticism from his manager. It didn't work.

"Food poisoning, what an outrage!" blew the Lord. "How can you expect us to remain quiet about such an extraordinary event as that which happened here last night? It should be our duty to tell the world about the crimes committed here, not cover it up with a load of bloody tosh!" The Lord struck his stick against the fireplace in rage. The sharp noise startled Victoria and she turned to her father and looked at him fearfully. The old man saw his daughter's tired, sorrowful face and he turned away towards the chimney breast, head down shamefully, screwing his eyes into the empty fire grate. He gripped the edge of the mantelpiece, rubbing his displeasure into the marble. Osbourne stood up unnoticed and stepped forward.

"After you fetched the police last night, they went up to the Down and saw the devastation. Following the protocols of such events they contacted the War office immediately. We were aware of a problem due to the officer stationed on Steep Holm and his belief that spies were at work here so we were already on route. The police were told to wait until we got here and not to tell anyone, which they dutifully did. As part of the necessary course of action to avoid the implications I have already intimated, and which you are surely aware of, it was already decided to distribute this fabrication. But, we need your support. I must reiterate that if this reality were to ever get out, the results for our country would be very grave. The French will pay for this, but it must not cost any more English lives. The loss of those men who bravely defended our shores for whatever reason and the sacrifice you must make in what I ask will not be in vain." Osbourne opened his arms to show he had nothing left to give or to hide, his purpose finally revealed in all its affronted discourtesy and there was silence as the father and daughter came to terms with reality.

"What about poor Mr Gill and Herbert Lanes, how will you explain their deaths?" asked Lord Danvers, still fixing the fireplace with angry eyes. Osbourne said nothing but glanced at his assistance quickly. The older man shuffled forward and awkwardly took over the reins of bullshit. "Um, Mr Gill was an old man and he had no surviving kin. It will be said he died of a heart attack last night in his home. As for Mr Lanes, well," he stuttered for a second and licked his drying lips. "Um, well, I'm afraid he met with an unfortunate agricultural accident. His wife will of course be well looked after." He trailed off and there was a quiet, dusty pause.

"I see," breathed Victoria presently, defeated by the horrors of the previous night and the crushing weight from the forces of officialdom. She turned her face away and gazed outside once more. Her mind was filled with thoughts of Elias and she was swamped by an overwhelming feeling of sadness, sucking her of any willpower.

"I'm sorry for my father Mr Osbourne. Pride is clouding his judgement at the moment." She gathered what little strength she had left. "You can rest assured we will keep your secrets; I'm sure no one would believe us anyway. We must remain proud in the conduct of our lives, whatever direction they may be asked to go in. We know the consequences of this event and our duty to the future lives of our fighting men will aid us in our secrecy."

Cameron's eyes sagged downward. Osbourne nodded respectively and tried to raise a purposeful smile but no one cared. "Thank you. We'll see ourselves out," he said and turned to the door.

"Pride comes before a fall," whispered Victoria.

"I'm sorry," Osbourne said, turning his head back.

"It doesn't matter. Just something someone once said."

She remained looking out of the window with her hands crossed tenderly on her thin lap. Strands of long hair fell elegantly down the back of her neck and her shoulders quivered momentarily in the overcast light coming through the window. In the reflection of the glass, Osbourne saw a tear roll down her cheek and fall softly on her long slender fingers. His stiff upper lip crumbled just a little and Cameron's hang dog expression hung up a bit more. They were moved by her silent solemnity.

The two men left the house and walked slowly in the direction of the hansom cab still waiting patiently on the driveway. Their thoughtful steps crunched the gravel as finger-rubbed bowler hats were adjusted on their heads while they walked.

"I wonder if those men from Steep Holm will appreciate being sent to the Sudan," one of them said.

"Probably not," replied the other. "But at least over there, whilst getting chased all over the desert by the Mardi, no one's going to be listening to their tall stories."

"I suppose not," admitted Mr C nonchalantly, opening the little side door to the cab. "What about that Haines fellow?" he asked as they got in.

"As far as I'm concerned he's mad as a balloon. A decent spell in the asylum will sort him out," answered Mr O carelessly.

"I suppose it will. Although he says he'd like to go back to the fort when he's better," stated Mr C and he tapped on the roof of the taxi. The cabby pulled the horse and carriage out of the driveway and started on the time consuming journey along the winding road which led to the end of Brean Down.

"Who knows, maybe one day he will," answered the other man finally.

The scribbler wrote his last letter at the table in the guardroom, by the shabby, flickering light of a single stubby candle. He took the letter and went into the kitchen, leaving the unfolded sheets of paper neatly on the wooden table along with the dwindling candle and its holder encased with the gnarled dripping shapes of yellowing, molten wax. Then he walked out into the black night, a rifle in one hand and a tied bundle of, dog eared, previously written letters in the other. The sea was black. The sky was black. He murmured serenely as he stepped, "All is black, all is black. I'll lay you on your back, and smite your bastardry..."

Walking towards the magazine room across the courtyard his footsteps were almost silent on the stony ground due to the calico cloth shoes he was wearing, normally required for entering the ammunition store. When he reached the heavy metal door he gently leant his rifle against the outer wall and unlocked the door using the key he had stolen just before lights out. He stared into the black hole for a moment then calmly picked up the rifle again, pointing it in front of him as he began to walk down the steps into the darkness. His eyes couldn't see anything in the oily depths but he knew how many steps there were to the floor, how many paces down the small corridor to take, how far away the walls were, and where the turn was to bring himself into the entrance of the main store. It was etched in his mind from that night he had been there with Elias Harding and the thousands of nights he had been there since. He could not see his hand in front of his face if he had lifted it to his eyes but his mind was as focused as surely as it ever had been in his whole life, apart perhaps from that same night years ago. The scribbler could see clearly, just as Elias Harding had all those years ago. He could see the gunpowder barrels on the floor, the boxes of Palliser shells neatly stacked in the corner and the detonators and cartridges wrapped in foil placed inside their wooden trays.

He looked back towards the entrance one last time. No light came through from the darkness outside to penetrate the inner blackness of this explosive tomb. It was cold and damp, but even though he only had on his thin cotton shirt and trousers and his dark blue battle tunic was undone, for some reason he felt truly warm inside for the first time on this headland since he'd arrived to man the guns over twenty years ago. Haines returned his gaze to the pitch black, oppressive blindness of the ammunition filled space.

The voices had stopped. The white noise of thoughts and visions that constantly flashed through his head had fallen silent and calmed to a blanket of contented stillness. Now he peacefully thought about how everything that had happened must have led to this moment and that at last there was an answer to the chaos which so suddenly tore him apart. *'The only answer there could have been',* he thought, the words rebounding around his twisted mind, *'an answer to all the secrets and lies and all the sinister degradation that has pervaded my stilted existence for as long as I can remember.'*

He dropped the bundle of letters into the middle of the pitch black room and raised the rifle to his shoulder, cocking the trigger as he did so. Pointing the barrel to the nearest tub of gunpowder which he instinctively knew was there, he breathed one last time and whispered gently into the breech of the gun.

'All is black, all is black. I'll lay you on your back and smite your bastardry into this blackened land.'

The scribbler pulled the trigger and his life ended in a split second of all-consuming heavenly light that blew his body apart and set free his tormented soul. His being merged with the exposed inner rock face of the Down and he ultimately became at one with the land on which he had lived upon for so long. He lived and eventually died within a place that had tortured his thoughts and tainted most of that life for so long because of one tumultuous event.

On the table in the kitchen, in front of the dying embers of the exhausted candle was his final letter.

February 1901

To everyone,

The world is full of secrets. Some are great and need to be honoured by those who are privy to such secrets, while others are small and inconsequential to the wider world but none the less can change and destroy the individual life on whom they are concerned. I have a secret I can no longer endure alone. I have not the strength of mind or the fortitude of character to conceal it any further. It has weakened me every day and I am tired!

Everyone else is dead. All those who were part of this ghastly event are gone and only I remain, solely entrusted with the so called honour of keeping confidence with the greater powers and remaining privy to what I know. They think I am mad. But they are wrong. I am torn apart by this secrecy, distraught by this unfathomable knowledge, haunted by it daily now. My once righteous soul has been ripped to tattered shreds by the weight and sharpness of the burden I must carry. I cannot contain myself any longer. I must tell someone!

If I do not relieve my dispirited senses of this truth, I feel I will die. Perhaps it would be best if I did, after all, everyone else is dead.

Let me tell you a story about this place.

And so it continued for eleven more pages, detailing the events of that night in all its demented glory. It was the final testament of the only surviving witness to a terrible battle of immense magnitude, if only for the men who died in it and the people it left behind.

But no-one noticed the letter during the panic which ensued after the explosion. The other members of the fort were so shockingly woken by the tremendous explosion outside, they ran around like headless chickens and scrabbled about in dishevelled grogginess trying to fathom out the disturbance, until they were given the appropriate orders by their Commanding Officer. They all missed the hand written document on the kitchen table. In the end, scribbler's letter was found by that Commanding Officer, a 2nd Lieutenant Howard Coles, who was the latest Master Gunner to be in charge of the fort at Brean Down and the only one within this latest deployment, apart from Haines, who knew of its secret past.

As he read the letter alone while the barrack room volunteers dealt with the aftermath of the explosion, he realised it was Haines who had obliterated the magazine room and in doing so, himself at the same time. He knew why the quiet and withdrawn artilleryman had done it. When he finished reading the letter he stared at the melted remains of the dead candle on the wooden table and thought for a while. He felt pity for the author of this letter and a respect for both he and the men involved. Then he turned and bent down over the fireplace hearth and gently placed the sheaths of note paper over the still glowing embers of the half burnt coals and pieces of ashen wood. He watched dutifully as the letter caught alight and burned into grey and black curls of feather like ash which melted into the hot debris of the fireplace or drifted gracefully on the eerily whistling draught which blew eternally up the soot covered, blackened chimney.

Aldous Haines never told anyone about what happened that night seventeen years ago, not even his wife. She didn't know what turned him into a withdrawn and unemotional shell of a man but after his brief spell in the asylum and spending most of his time afterwards on deployment at the fort she hardly saw her husband anyway, and in the end didn't care about him. Not that she ever did. After a few years fleecing him of the mysterious government pension Aldous received after his stay in the asylum and which continued for several years afterwards, she eventually ran off with the milkman, who had been boning her, along with several other ladies on his round, ever since she'd married poor old Aldous. When she told him and returned all the letters he had written to her while deployed at the fort, it had merely added to the mental stresses he was already suffering but in no way outweighed the main reason for his insular behaviour.

They thought he was mad. He had certainly behaved that way after the battle on the Down and his witnessing of such brutal death. Every shadow was now a demon; every night was a visage of horrors to his broken mind. But his stay at the asylum really did calm his manner, almost to the point of soporific withdrawal and his medical practitioners were unable to find reason for his continued certification. When a member of the War Office came to see him, Haines was lucid enough to secretly ask the official to be allowed to go back to Brean Down and become a permanent volunteer at the fort in return for his continued silence. The event was past; the secret had been kept. The odd rumour had gone no further than the pub it was revealed in and no one would care anyway. The official agreed and scribbler went back to the place where he'd lost his mind in the vain hope that maybe it would be the only place he could find it again. He never did. But being on the Down again helped keep the madness away for some reason, at least on the outside. He didn't shake so much in the shadows or howl and cry in the night from the dreams. Haines became a loner and sometimes a little dysfunctional, especially when his wife left him, but he didn't act weird enough to warrant anyone asking for a reason why. And he never told a soul about that night. His silence was not because of a misplaced honour to the authorities or a fear of what might happen if he broke his silence but because his mind was smashed by the disastrous events which unfolded in those few terrible hours and the shame he felt for his conduct in the part he played during those hours. He was also constantly haunted by, and so in turn ultimately lived by, his recollection of the words spoken from the man he held in his arms at the end,

'I hope no one will know of what I have done.'

10. The Shadows of Night.

"And so it came to pass that a land was made in this brutal forge. Formed from the passions of a higher being, it was born to endure the trials of hard yet sometimes joyous life and terrible, but always ultimate death. Just as this land was shaped, so too were men, carved from those same passions with all the anger and violence that nature can hold. And on this land, men will ultimately perish, like sacrificial lambs torn asunder by lions let loose upon the Garden of Eden, leaving only ghosts to mark their ghastly ending."

It was the figure who spoke these words. They accompanied the final visions that crackled and split before beginning to break up like interference on an old television screen within the swaying flames of the hypnotic but slowly fading fire. The words echoed and drifted around the concrete room like the bands of black smoke which now spiralled above the diminishing combustion. Its ending image was that of a burning letter turning to ash within the transfigured flames of a different fireplace in another time. Finally, the presentation fizzed and flashed into a thousand tiny sparks which shone brightly for a moment before they morphed to become the real and gently glowing embers of the actual fire in the middle of the darkened concrete room.

At first, Gordy thought the words poured outwards from the vision which formed in the magical flames. But then his eyes were drawn to the distant figure still sat in the corner and he clearly saw the man's murky face move shadily as the closing statement of his long story came from his gaunt, mobile mouth. When the mysterious man finished talking his dark eyes looked away fleetingly and Gordy felt a tingling across his body before suddenly realising he could wriggle his toes freely. Tempered senses of feeling and movement started creeping through his body like the slow rise of a new day sun which gradually and systematically melts a crisp winter frost. He began to unfurl his cramped and twisted fingers before managing to unclench his cemented back and lift his heavy, aching head by a mere centimetre or two. His still drowsy and reddened zombie like eyes drilled into the man opposite.

The figure didn't move but the shadows around his changeling presence lifted and crept uncannily into the dark corners of the room. Meanwhile, his features seemed to settle into the same thin and hollow face he'd started with, framed by long strands of greasy hair that clamped themselves to his head like streaks of greasy oil dripping from beneath his strangely shaped dark blue hat. It was a face that had manifested itself within the images of the flames throughout the distended night. With increasing awareness, Gordy noticed the man's navy tunic mottled with large patches of dark purple and his grey cotton trousers obscured by areas of ingrained charcoal streaks amid smears of discoloured burgundy bloodstains. A new wave of sensation flowed over Gordy's body as the realisation dawned on his muddled and over worked brain. "You're Haines aren't you," he rasped. "You're the Scribbler! You're a fucking ghost!"

As the words tumbled from his numbed mouth, Gordy dribbled and began to fidget all over trying to manipulate some more mobility around his prickling muscles. He kept watching the figure while he tried to force his body to move and managed to flop over a semi-paralysed arm to one side and push a deadened leg outwards like the sluggish movements of a severely disabled person who had fallen to the floor. He let out a stifled moan as he gazed over the dying embers of the fire and saw the Scribbler lean forward and fix him back with an evil look, a snarl forming across his sinister blue mouth.

"I am not a ghost," he growled, his pallid face darkening with anger. "I am the voice of the dead, come to tell their story and burden the living with these shadows of the night, shadows that take the living and hide the dead, shadows that wait in every corner of this wretched land until they creep upon the innocent and take them down below." The figure slowly rose up and cast ominous silhouettes behind him that seemed to dance and flicker around the gloomy walls once again. "For years I've travelled through time, before and after that terrible night, tracing the course of its twisted journey from the minds of the men who created it to the minds of the men who buried it. In the dark corners of rooms, I waited and saw, heard the talk of those who planned, those who were unwittingly involved and those who followed in the aftermath of this momentous event that wasted so many innocent lives."

With each sentence the figure's voice grew louder and more antagonistic until it bellowed with malice. He moved with slow, teasing menace around the fireplace which immediately began to inflate once more, throwing sparks into the hostile atmosphere and erupting fierce orange flames from the newly excited embers.

"I flew through time!" Haines shouted, "Across windswept lands and raging seas from now and then, from here and there. Into the realms of space and beyond I went, over the decades, through the years. But always I came back, back to this place, the place of my life and my explosive death!" He waved an arm around animatedly as if showing his passionate loyalty to the rock from which he could not escape. His face burned with a fury that had shown itself before during his telling of the story but now had a whole new aspect of malignant intent. His slow, heavy steps circled the heightened range of the pumping, angry fire. "All the killing, all the violent waste of so many innocent lives, all the lies and the hateful pride that pervaded it, I saw it all!" The snarling figure was only feet away now, his yellow teeth bared within his shaking, malevolent features, his mouth dripping with strings of outraged spit and the hateful energy of a frightening and demented spirit. "I saw it all!" he screamed. "I saw it all and told no one!" Gordy recoiled from the figure in horror as the flames rose up behind the evil spectre in a curtain of fire.

"I'm more than a ghost!" screeched Haines. "I'm the shadow that moves on a dimly lit hallway or the fleeting glimpse of an unknown and demonic presence, your fears and dread manifest in the unsure. And I'm also the voice. The voice of fourteen dead men killed in this place by demons, only to be hidden from knowledge by secrets and lies and shame, and I tell you boy! I'll range this land forever to remind the world of this dreadful truth!" the figure bellowed and his face began to distort and change colour more terribly than before. As the disfigurement took control, Gordy screamed as the man's head began to melt into a goo gore of molten skin and bloody tissue.

Suddenly Haines was stood over him. But now, surrounded by flames, the mysterious, haunted figure had turned into the hideous incarnation of a deformed and fire ravaged man. His flailed skin was charred and burnt with odious red globules of flesh which dripped from behind the scorched mask of his frame. It looked like his body had been torn off in great lumps, burnt on a barbecue and then thrown back together again, like some grisly human jigsaw. His clothing was black and had melted into the papery shreds of his leftover, flaking skin. Beneath the slivered flesh and cooked muscle lay bare bones, blackened in places by intense heat and on his disfigured face the sockets of his skull could be seen and the yellowing eyeballs were sat within burnt holes, wide and rolling, as fiercely unpredictable as they had ever been all night long. He was an unholy sight to behold, a figure of ghoulish proportions.

Behind him the fire had risen into a blanket of raging conflagration and the flames rose further as Haines lifted his arms maniacally like deadly shrouding wings. Burnt, bony, charred flesh hands clenched as he raged over the terrified Gordy, whose blood had frozen like the raspberry slush puppies from a seafront vending machine in town. Filled with this menacing terror, the young man attempted to kick out and force the ghastly monster away back towards the fire, his mind racing with thoughts of an impending and horrible death.

After what seemed like an eternity in a night trapped within a body of numbness and paralysation, Gordy felt the relieving force of movement and sensation in his legs as he tried to kick out. Suddenly a wave of energy, fused from the terror before him, seemed to burst from his heart and it forcefully let fly through his cramped body. He was able to push himself into the wall, away from the hideous creature towering over him, and his legs began to kick violently back and forth. His strained throat let out an anguished scream and he heard it through the rustling crackle of the seething inferno that seemed to fill the room and cling like burning oil to the breezeblock walls. Gordy could feel the heat and was horrified by the thought of being consumed by the flames, much as Haines had been when he'd blown up the magazine room and become this forceful spectre which now loomed above him. As the hysteria swept over his brain, Gordy kicked his legs out again like a startled pony and with each kick more stunted movement came back to his panicking body.

All the while Haines screamed a piercing, gurgling sound which bounced around the room and joined with the crackling growl of the fire which felt like it was engulfing the gun emplacement. Fuelled by terror, Gordy was able to kick himself away from the gory apparition and with an almighty effort scrabble upright and head for the doorway. In one desperate movement, he jumped through the opening, out of the concrete room and into the adjoining enclosure which led to the exit and his hopeful escape onto the freedom of the Down. As he jumped he weirdly grabbed his rucksack from the floor and jolted away without looking behind him, too terrified of what he might see. He felt the intense heat on his back and noticed his bag was alight and saw flames behind his shoulder. There was the feeling that Haines and the cacophonous fire were right behind him and only seconds from catching him in their grip, engulfing and killing him in the hideous way it had the Gunner all those years ago. The viewing platform space he stumbled into was lit up by the huge fire now burning all over the inner room he had been trapped in for so long and he instinctively skidded towards the opening on the right hand side, through which he had entered this nightmare all those hours ago.

Then he halted abruptly and let out another terror filled animal like cry. There, in the doorway, lit behind by the eerie white light of a full moon was the horrific sight of what remained of James Burden, volunteer gunner, once of Brean Down fort.

Burdens severely damaged body stood stock still in the doorway which led to the pathway of escape. Gordy was shocked by the atrocious sight of the dead man's injuries in their full dehumanised glory. The open wounds of his half exposed chest, the torso, blood red and bony in its fleshy messiness and on top of his opened neck and one good shoulder was half his head, the single good eye still looking around confusedly. Gordy screamed again, this time with full effect, and put his head down closing his eyes, the fear of entrapment and death at the hands of paranormal demons forcing him into a blind and insensible panic. Running through the ghost before him, he felt a spine tingling shock of electric before he bounded out of the opening and on to a windless and still, but shadow-filled Brean Down, eerily bathed in moonlight from a clear night sky.

He opened his eyes but looked straight ahead and sprinted up the thin pathway towards the gentler slopes leading away from the headland. His heart was thumping and the sudden quietness allowed him to hear the rush of blood around his head while his legs moved across the uneven ground. He turned around briefly, afraid of what was behind him and noticed the landscape cast in the spectral glow of the moon and caught sight of the fort in the distance as if highlighted by the cosmic entity. Burden was still in the entrance of the gun emplacement, turning round and round in confusion and fire raked from the open walls near the front and set ablaze the inky night. Gordy ran on up the hill. He realised the storm was gone and that he was in the open but he didn't look behind again, not wanting to disturb the feeling of relief that he might have got away and escaped the walking dead.

Then up ahead, just as the slim path faded into the soft grass of the middle contours of the Down, Gordy saw another figure. In fear, he slowed down to a stagger, coming to a stop a few feet away from the moonlit shape. His mouth dropped open and his heavy breathing gagged a few times as he almost fell backwards onto the ground. In a clearing near to a patch of bracken, stood the image of Arnold England, the cook, illuminated in the darkness, his fat round body shaking as he laughed, holding a half-eaten mutton chop in his hand. As the ghostly spectre threw back his head in a hearty chortle, Gordy noticed the large open wound in his neck and the dark bloodstains across his white apron.

"It's alrite boy, don't go yet, it's time for dinner," cook said and let out a chuckle, which trailed off into a bubbling gurgle as the wound in his throat affected the ghostly laugh.

Gordy's head shook, his eyes widened aghast at the vision and he started to mew like a cat as he changed direction and darted away up the slope, his body tense with fresh horror and disbelief. As he stumbled upwards he felt an ache through the heart racing fear as his muscles reacted from the paralysis he'd suffered for so long, but fright and the need to flee pushed him on.

Then, not far from cook, there was the strange, blue tinged shape of Stanley Pickles emerging from the undergrowth, long and thin with tangled, messy hair, his frightened face almost pleading with Gordy as he ran past, the bloody wound of a stabbed kidney showing up through his ill-fitting and dishevelled clothing. The ungainly spirit said nothing as Gordy choked back more fright and awkwardly moved off in another direction, shock slowing his tortuous escape. And then there was Arturo Ben Arfa, the Legionnaire coming through the silvery night as Gordy stumbled on, the shocking wounds from Harding's sword viciously gaping across the dead Frenchman's chest and neck. To one side Gordy saw Sergeant Zanzibar Eves looming out of the darkness. His chin hung down over his throat in a bloody mess and the bullet wound on his head flapped open as his muscular frame loped down the rise towards Gordy, knees bent as if dancing into battle once again. Gordy jogged to one side to avoid meeting the apparition and scrabbled away again. His eyes frantically darted up and down the landscape and he let out little involuntary groans from his parched and sour tasting mouth. Further on, there was Mule and Lumpy Boulter, sad faces staring at Gordy as he ran past.

Sat on the ground near some twisted thorn trees, the two Pearce brothers laughed as they pushed fingers into each other's bullet and bayonet wounds.

Finally, as he stumbled upwards onto a grassy mound, Gordy nearly bumped into the standing ghost of Elias Harding. The frightened young man pulled up sharply and nearly fell backwards but froze for a moment as he acknowledged the unearthly presence now stood, Gordy suddenly realised, in the same spot he had seen the Master Gunner sat upon at the start of the story just revealed to him, still looking thoughtfully out to sea from his favourite vantage point on the Down. He was dressed in his bloodied battle tunic, the top most buttons of which were undone just as they had been in the scenes played out in the fire, and his arms hung tiredly down by his sides as he stood, a look of dejection about his other worldly being. His sword scabbard was empty, as was his holster which hung loosely on his leather belt and shoulder strap. His skin was pallid and deathly white in the silvery moon but also, regardless of the moonlight, it seemed as if his body had been drained of all its blood. The thin, drawn skinned figure was plaintively staring out towards the island of Steep Holm. The ghostly apparition slowly turned his head to Gordy and looked at him sadly.

"Be careful lad. Pride comes before a fall," the ghost said softly in a melancholic, invisible voice that floated away into the wind. "Don't tell anyone I did all this," he added in a whisper whilst waving a hand out towards what had now become dozens of ghostly forms scattered loosely across the Down and swaying mesmerizingly in the glistening ripples of the moon soaked estuary mud. He gave a rueful smile before finally turning his face away again and looking out to sea.

They were all there. The men from the fort, the French commandos, Pat the postman, Rufus Stone, the drowned and the missing, ghosts of the dead, the dead from a forgotten battle in the most unlikely of places. All the characters from the crazed story relayed to him in the concrete room by the mysterious figure and his mesmeric fire. A mystery revealed in all its terrible reality and brutal abandonment told about the people who once frequented this hulk of land. The people from a secret past and their part in a story within the history hewed into the landscape all around, both known and unknown, unable to rest and brought to life again on this weird night. And they were all here now, disappearing and re-emerging within the blink of an eye.

Gordy's mind was shattered. It was fragmented like the broken pieces of a glass bottle. All sense of normality had disintegrated as he staggered around without cohesion or sense of direction. He didn't know if what he was seeing was real or just a confused flashback to the story embedded in his head. Then Gordy noticed the spectres nearest to him seemed to be coming towards him all at once. Every one of them was illuminated by the silvery blue light of the moon overhead yet Gordy could see, even in a strange way feel, the phantoms emanate their own ghostly aura of light into the silent wind as they closed in around him.

So Gordy didn't stop. He kept running up the slope, stumbling and scared, vulnerable, desperately alone. The apparitions were all around him now, reaching out to touch him, laughing, screaming and crying all at once. He swung his arms to try and beat them away but he could not touch them. They were intangible, unearthly. He tried to think it was his imagination or part of the residues from the twisted legend played out in his head by the malicious spirit of the Scribbler, but as he swung wildly about trying to get away, he knew he could feel them, sense their presence, their reality about his being, his inner self. He called out inanely with fear.

Gordy could feel them brushing his neck and back. The hairs all over his body were electrified, stimulated by the sinister spectral forces closing in around him. It was as if all the spirits had formed into one entity, one surrounding force of overpowering fear, about to consume another innocent to feed the supernatural light and fuel the shadows down below. But then he felt himself being lifted up gently and pushed away. He didn't know what it was that propelled him, whether it was the ghostly hands of the spirits sending him on his way or the energy of fear cascading him forward, but he didn't care. So Gordy ran on, stumbling up the path, skidding on the moist grass. Above his head he caught a glimpse of a starlit, cloudless night and a clear, unbroken, black sky. The stars broke through the gloomy shroud as if showing him a way to freedom. He didn't look around him again until he reached the very top of the Down. Exhausted and unable to breath properly, his fear wracked body caused him to tumble to the ground and he quickly spun himself over, terrified the ghostly apparitions would be upon him again or stood behind him like the monsters on the darkened hallway of his childhood house.

Nothing was around him apart from grass. He threw his head from side to side checking back and forth to make sure there was nothing there. Gordy calmed himself as much as he could whilst trying to slow his frantic breathing and looked erratically down towards the sea. He saw the ghostly figures of the fort but they were farther away now, standing around the edge of the fortress and gun emplacements staring up to where he was sat. To one side he caught sight of the concrete bunker, the doorway and viewing platform still alight with flames from its burning interior and noticed the ghoulish forms of Burden and Haines stood on the skinny path outside. They did not move, just looked up at him for a moment and then turned their attention towards the sea. Gordy followed their gaze and held his breath. He saw the moon, full and bright in the sky, lighting up the fort and the estuary beyond creating thousands of tiny ripples on the water and vista of endless mud in a frightening yet gloriously radiated spectacle.

Gordy screwed up his eyes, letting out little wisps of wrought breath as he focused. In the darkened mud with the ripples of silver across it, lit up by the cosmic spotlight overhead, he thought he saw what at first seemed like larger ripples that were moving hypnotically in the channel wind. Then he realised that what he could see were the distant shapes of lighted figures swaying in the wide expanse of open mud. He looked closer and, unbelievably at this distance, was able to focus on their drowned, watery faces and slowly swinging torsos reflected in the moonlight. They couldn't move freely in the mud, not like the figures around the fort, instead they were just held there as if kneeling in the viscid mass whilst swaying gently with the sea breeze, their ghostly faces constantly looking towards the Down and the lonely fort on its rocky end. There were dozens of them scattered across the wide area of exposed channel and Gordy took back a sharp intake of breath as he absorbed the sinister sight.

Most of the swaying forms were the drowned men of the sunken steamship but in among them Gordy realised he could make out the slightly different clothing and fishing attire of the dead fishermen from the village, victims of the storm which claimed the lives of Morris's brother and his crew mates. The spirits of the Legionnaires and the fishermen swayed in the wind, mouths agape, stuck in the endless mud for all eternity. Gordy suddenly felt both physically and mentally spent and strangely, his body seemed to relax by several fractions and his racing heart slowed down to a more sustainable pace as he was drawn into the fantastical scene below. As if subdued by the ghostly movement, his mind began to phase out, unable to comprehend the ghastly meaning of loss and unrest for the long since dead that their resurgent spirits were now showing in the view out in the channel.

He had spent the last half hour shitting himself about what was happening, afraid of the horrors of the unknown and the dangers it might inflict upon him, but now, sat here, seemingly above and away from the phantoms and out of harms reach, he watched the spectres reveal themselves from their coastal tomb and was possessed by a feeling of sadness and regret for their tormented souls. It was a strange feeling that may have been a reaction to the adrenaline rush of panic a few moments ago but there was also a subconscious knowledge that he felt a strange connection to the spirits plight, a connection that came from being told their story and allowed in to their secret world no matter how terrifying it had seemed to be at the time. The slowly moving, calmly swaying, illuminated dead entranced him and he stared in fascination and awe upon them. The gentle wind made a sound like singing as the remnants of the drowned danced in the mud. He thought he could hear a bell toll.

For a while the shadows of the night watched patiently from their watery grave as if waiting for something to happen, just as Gordy gazed down on them waiting for something else to happen to him, but nothing did. And then, not even in the blink of an eye, the spectres simply vanished. The lighted shapes in the water, the haunting figures in the mud, the ghostly apparitions of the characters and men from the history he had been told, all were suddenly gone from the end of the Down. The distended horde of ghosts had disappeared and all that was left was the lonely remnants of the fort and the uninhabited coastline lit up in the phosphorous moonlight.

Gordy looked down towards the gun emplacement where the original story had been recounted to him, only moments ago ablaze with fire and yellow light from its windows and open front, and saw that it was dark and featureless. There was no light coming from the side window or the doorway, no raging inferno inside and no sign of movement anywhere, by anything, living or dead.

Gordon bolted upright, a new energy coursing in his muscles born from a need to get away, an unstoppable desire to flee and not be drawn back into the spectral world. It made him turn and run for the steps leading off the Down. He didn't know how long it took him to reach the top but he knew by the time he got there that his throat was painfully tight and his mouth was achingly dry. His heart pounded furiously as if it would explode any minute and the fear and excitement tingled throughout his now fully active body as he bounded down the steps towards where he hoped his crappy bicycle would still be hidden. The rucksack bounced in his hand from side to side as he jumped two sometimes three steps at a time, his brain swimming with crazed thoughts and startling imagery from his night on the Down.

"Bloody hell," he spluttered as he darted along the stony track. "What a mind blast!"

And with that he pulled his bike out from the bushes, jumped on and peddled away as fast as his quivering legs could peddle; away from the dark hulking mass of land called Brean Down.

Gordy didn't go back to the Down for quite a while after that. He was too zapped by the whole experience to brave a return. He tried to shrug it off as just a weird night caused by some off cider and a bag of dodgy weed but something told him it was more than that. He steered clear of town for a while and didn't tell anyone about what had happened to him that night. But gradually the feeling grew inside that he needed to return, that he needed to go back and walk into that concrete room just to see what was there, to see if there was any evidence left to prove that what had happened was real. Perhaps the charcoal stains of a fire in the middle of the room or the traces of occupation left by a wayward tramp. He felt the urge to go to the fort and wander round the dilapidated rooms and walk the quiet stone parapets that looked out upon the sea. Something mysterious and unconfirmed nagged in his mind and made him want to go back. But when he did, after a few weeks, he found nothing unusual there. No remnants of a fire or the tell-tale signs of someone regularly being there, just the smell of piss and damp in an old gun emplacement and the roofless walls of an abandoned fort. And although over the years he conquered his fears and began to enjoy the place for its beauty and isolation, every time he went there, he always believed he might just see something unusual that would answer all those nagging doubts.

The rain had eased slightly now. It had stopped bouncing off the bonnet and was blobbing down on the windows in a steady drizzle. The man turned to his son who was sat staring out of the rain splashed car window. The small boy's hair was still damp and he seemed inattentive, gazing fixatedly into the distance. His father looked in the same direction to see what his son was staring at, but didn't notice anything unusual.

"Whatcha lookin at," he asked casually.

"Nothin," said the boy without looking round.

Shamus was watching a man who was stood in the distance looking directly back towards the young child. He was a dark clad figure wearing a small strange cap and Shamus thought he looked like someone he had seen before. The man was stood on some large boulders near the foot of the Down and was pointing towards the sea near the end of the rocks, all the while staring back at the child in the car. The small boy didn't say anything, a strange voice in his head told him not tell his father he could see the man.

"Come on, let's get home," said his dad and then gave the hill towering stoically above them one final glance. He thought about his night on the Down and smiled as he wondered if it was just the weed and cider which had fuddled his brain all those years ago. He switched his eyes back to his son. The boy was still gazing outside silently.

'He's too young for ghost stories,' Gordy thought as he turned the key in the ignition and started the car, before swinging it smoothly out of the sodden car park and driving away from the hulking wet mass of Brean Down to begin the long, winding journey back home.

Lightning Source UK Ltd.
Milton Keynes UK
UKOW02f0812210916

283469UK00002B/95/P